THE

RENDEZVOUS

Volume 2
PLANETS SHAKEN

Lee W. Brainard

Soothkeep Press

This book is a work of fiction. Apart from several mere mentions of actual people, the characters are fictitious. Any resemblance to people living or dead is purely coincidental.

If perchance my conception of events—geopolitical, political, astronomical, or prophetic—proves to be uncannily close to what actually transpires, let it be known beforehand that I do not have access to inside information, nor do I have the ability and wherewithal to hack into computers storing classified information, nor am I a prophet who enjoys special communication from God. The scenario portrayed is just an educated guess based on various factors: biblical prophecy, geopolitical trends, historical precedent, ancient history, ancient cosmology, electric universe cosmology, and a fertile imagination.

Cover design: Bespoke Book Covers, Bedfordshire, UK
Formatting: Polgarus Studio

1

Truckee, CA ... Winnemucca, NV
Monday, June 24, 2019

Woody woke up in a daze. *Where in the world am I?* He shook his head trying to clear the fog. The screech of train brakes echoing in his ears brought him back to his painful reality. He was on the run ... headed for Montana ... had hopped the train ... had a mishap. That's why his arms and legs throbbed with pain. How long had he been sleeping? He glanced at his watch. It was 7:15 a.m. He had only been asleep for about five minutes. *No wonder I'm so groggy.*

A strange voice cried out, "Hey, pardner!"

He turned his throbbing head toward the porthole. A grimy hobo wearing a greasy oilskin coat was leaning in the opening. "I seen ya catchin' the train on the fly and knew you wuz a greenhorn. So I figured I should warn ya. We're slow'n down for Truckee. The train makes a short stop here, twenty or thirty minutes max. Not enough time to git breakfas'. Us'ally they drop a few cars an' pick up a few. Ya need to jump off b'fore we pull into town while the train is still rollin'. The bulls don't prowl every day, but too often to take a chance.

"Wait til after ya go under the highway and over the creek. Jump off a nuther third of a mile or so up the tracks when ya see the end of the industrial park on the south side. Jump out by the trees, bust through 'em, git on River Street, and walk through town. When River Street ends at the far side of the yard, find yerself a place to wait in the woods on the north side of the tracks. Anywhere over there is a good hop out."

"Thanks."

The quirky hobo ducked out. Seconds later, he stuck his head back in again. "By the way, greenhorn. Ya made a good choice. Grainers are the best way to go." Then he disappeared again. Woody shoved his pack out on the deck and climbed out himself, expecting to see the friendly tramp. But he was gone. Woody scooted his pack to the south edge of the deck near the ladder and sat on it, ready to exit as the hobo had advised.

The train slowed down to around ten miles per hour. Apartments and a small strip mall rolled into view on the other side of the train, barely noticeable in his peripheral vision. Woody's car passed under the highway and over the creek. Then the industrial park appeared. By the time his car was nearing the far side of the park, the train had slowed to maybe six miles per hour. His legs still tender, he carefully climbed onto the ladder, gingerly stepped down to the first rung, got himself turned around despite a wave of panic, picked up his pack with his left hand, and jumped. Immediately, he sensed that he was in trouble. He was leaning too far forward.

When his feet hit the ground, his ankles and legs failed to keep him upright, and his momentum carried him forward. He contorted his body to protect his face, covered his head with his hand, and slammed into the gravel on his right side. Sitting up with a groan, he examined the damage. The back of his right hand was scraped up and bleeding, and his right arm was tenderized. *Think I've had enough of this hobo stuff already.*

Shaking his head in frustration, he dug out his first aid kit and wiped his wounds on the back of his hand with an alcohol swab. He hated the smell. They brought flashbacks of bandaging up wounded buddies. When he finished dressing his hand, he stood up, slung his pack over his shoulders, and hobbled toward the narrow strip of trees that paralleled the tracks, wincing with every step.

On the other side of the trees, he stepped onto River Street and limped his way east. A mile later, both ankles stabbing with pain, he reached the end of the street, angled across a trucking company's yard, crossed the tracks, and hunkered down in the trees. He shook his head in disbelief when he checked his watch. It was 7:36 a.m. It had taken him twenty-one minutes to walk a mile. *Definitely not a Delta pace.*

Before he could get comfortably settled, the engines throttled up, and the train began to accelerate out of the yard. *So much for a rest!* he grumbled to himself. He stood back on his feet and waited. After the locomotives had passed, he positioned himself at the edge of the track and waited for his grain car. When it drew near, he started

3

jogging, tossed his pack onto the deck, grabbed the rails, and stepped up. This time the mount-up went without a hitch. He tossed his gear into the porthole and crawled after it, desperate for a nap.

***

The squealing brakes of the slowing train woke Woody. He pulled his tingling arm out from under his head and checked his watch. It was 8:52 a.m. He guessed they were in Reno. He chucked his pack out the porthole and climbed out after it. Holding onto the ladder on the south side of the porch, he poked his head out into the pleasant breeze and surveyed the situation. The Patagonia Service Center passed by, then a stretch of homes, then a business district, and then they plunged into darkness.

When his car emerged from the tunnel, he noticed three hobos on the grainers behind him scoping things out. When they passed under the interstate, all three jumped off. That was his cue. *When in Rome, do as the Romans.* He stationed himself on the ladder, clutched his pack in his right hand, and jumped, swinging the pack in front of him as he sailed through the air. This time his exit went much better. Though he still lost his balance and fell forward when he hit the ground, he managed to land on his pack, protecting his arms and hands. Only his knees got banged up a bit.

He massaged his knees for a minute, slung his pack over his shoulders, and hobbled east. For three miles he followed the three hobos as they wandered down alleys and streets, figuring they would lead him to the hobo camp or a hop-off.

They stopped twice: once at a convenient store and once to fill water jugs from a spigot on the side of a building in an alley. Woody skipped the store but filled one of his bottles. On the far side of town, where East Glendale Avenue ended, the three got on a dusty service road that paralleled the tracks. He breathed a sigh of relief, figuring that the trek would end soon. He just wanted to sit down and rest his battered body. A quarter of a mile later, the hobos left the road and disappeared in a patch of brush and small trees.

Woody joined them in the hobo jungle and looked for a shady spot. An unclaimed milk crate behind a mesquite tree offered marginal shelter from the sun. *Guess that'll have to do.* He dropped his weary backside on the crate and leaned back against the tree. His growling stomach reminded him that he needed to rustle up some chow. He looked over to the three hobos. They were starting a fire to cook some hotdogs. *Gonna figure that means that I have time to make coffee and eat a real meal.*

He placed a wooden crate off to his side for a makeshift table, set up his stove, and put on a pot of coffee. Then he dug out an MRE from his food bag and laid it on the table. While he waited for his coffee to perk, he surveyed his surroundings. There were seven men in the camp besides himself—the three that he had followed and four others. The three looked trustworthy, though two were a bit grungy. The other four seemed like hoodlums. He avoided eye contact with them, hoping to avert trouble.

His efforts failed. The ringleader sauntered towards him with his sidekicks. Woody eyed them warily. The tough guy stood in front of him with arms crossed and sneered, "Give us some of your MREs."

Woody might have shared if the guy had asked politely. But he was indignant that the punk was attempting to rob him. He looked the scuzzball in the eyes and replied, "Sorry, kid, ain't gonna happen."

The maggot cussed, pulled a knife, and said, "Listen here, old man. Give us your food bag or I'm gonna teach you a lesson."

Woody looked up and grinned. "That ain't much of a knife." The punk rushed him. In one smooth motion, Woody stood up, blocked the approaching blade outward with his left arm, and slammed his right fist into the young man's solar plexus. Then he launched an angry fist at his chin. It connected solidly. The dirtbag dropped his knife, stumbled a bit, put his hand to his mouth, and noticed that blood was streaming out of it. He stared at Woody wide-eyed, then turned and ran, his companions hard on his heels. *Gonna feel that for a while. Really ought to practice my Krav Maga a little more often.*

From a distance the clean-cut hobo from the group of three had watched the situation unfold. When it was over and Woody was alone again, enjoying a freshly poured cup of coffee, he strolled over and introduced himself. "Howdy," he said with a distinct western twang, reaching out his hand, "my name is Lobo."

Woody extended his in return, and they shared a firm shake. The guy was impressive: clean jeans and shirt, fairly new cowboy boots, bandana around the neck western style, cowboy hat, clean-shaven, and manly aftershave. He was also toting an L.L. Bean duffel bag and a Sage flyrod case. *Definitely not your typical hobo.* "I go by Caddis," Woody replied. "Care for a cup of coffee?"

"I was hoping you'd ask." The lanky cowboy retrieved a titanium mug from his pack and held it out. Woody filled it with the brown ambrosia. Then Lobo pulled up a battered bucket for a seat. They made small talk and discovered several areas of mutual interest: army life, elk hunting, fly fishing, and women.

"So where are you headed?" Woody ventured. "Looks like you're planning on doing some fly fishing." Immediately he regretted the question since it invited Lobo to ask him similar questions.

"I'm on my way to Cooke City, Montana where I work for a friend who is an outfitter. We do trout fishing trips after the snow melts in the high country, then guide during elk season—backcountry bow and rifle. This will be my fifth season. When hunting season ends, we celebrate by snowshoeing into some low-elevation lakes for a week of ice fishing. Then I hit the rails and go south to find work, either on rigs in the Gulf or on fishing boats. Whatever comes up."

Woody liked Lobo. He found himself half wishing that he had followed his own sense of adventure and wanderlust instead of settling for a career. The freedom sounded inviting. No bills. No corporate bosses. Go wherever you want whenever you want. But another part of him recoiled at the downside. No retirement. No regular showers. And good coffee would be hard to come by.

The cowboy probed him, "So what do you do for work, and why are you on the iron highway?"

The dreaded question had come. Woody didn't respond, but stared off into the distance, hoping the question would evaporate in the hot sun. The cowboy waited politely for a moment, eyeing him intently.

Woody felt Lobo's steel-blue eyes piercing him. He cleared his throat, tried to look the cowboy in the eyes, couldn't hold his gaze, looked down at the dirt, and muttered, "Got my reasons, but I'd rather not talk about it."

Lobo reached into his pocket, retrieved his iPhone, fiddled with it for a minute, then handed it to Woody. "Does this guy look familiar?"

Woody froze. His heart skipped a beat, then raced wildly. The FBI had put out a federal warrant for his arrest and was offering a hefty reward for information leading to his capture. He was a highly trained, former Special Forces operator and should be considered armed and dangerous. His thoughts ran helter-skelter circles. *He's got me dead to rights. What do I do now? Take him out? Reason with him? Run?*

While Woody fretted, a smug grin slowly broke on Lobo's face. "Nothing to worry about pard'. If I was a bounty hunter, you would already be apprehended. And if I was going to turn you in for the reward, I would have already called." He handed over his phone. "Check my call and text history. Nothing there for the past two days."

Woody pulled them up. Lobo was telling the truth. There were no communications with anyone since Friday evening. He eyed the cowboy warily as he handed him his phone back. "So what's your angle?"

"Ain't got one. Do got some advice though. Wherever you're running to, keep your head down, wear sunglasses, and stay out of towns as much as possible. Every camera in the country is looking for you. And every bounty hunter is gunning for you. Watch out for the railroad yards, too. I saw Homeland Security agents in several of the larger ones this year."

"Thanks. I'll keep that in mind."

The cowboy continued talking. "Until a few weeks ago, you were an astronomer at Caltech. My guess is that somehow you found out that the comet which the late-night radio hosts have been warning us about is not a hoax. Shortly thereafter, you were somehow outed, and now you and your associate are on the run."

Woody tried to stay calm. He wanted to trust Lobo but wasn't sure that he could. What should he do? There was no use trying to pretend that he wasn't the man in the photo. And if the cowboy was an undercover agent or an informer, his capture was pretty much a done deal. He decided to level with him. There was nothing to lose, and the potential gain was significant. "Okay. To make a long story short, the comet is real, and I'm on the run." He then divulged his story starting with the day that Ariele revealed the existence of the comet to him.

They spent the next two hours talking about the comet and the cover-up, emptying three pots of coffee in the process. It felt strange to be sitting in a hobo camp discussing matters of such magnitude with a cowboy stranger. But the more they talked, the more confident he felt that his new friend was as committed to resisting the coverup as he was.

The conversation took a stunning turn when Lobo revealed that he had his own comet story, not merely tidbits from late-night radio and the internet. "You're not the first fugitive astronomer that I've met."

Woody was incredulous. "Seriously?"

"Yep. I met an old-timer by the name of Burt Snedeker in late November 2017. We rode south together for several days and got to know each other pretty good before we parted in Jackson, Mississippi. He was headed for parts unknown deep in Atchafalaya Swamp in Louisiana."

"I knew Burt," Woody exclaimed. "He taught astronomy at the University of Wyoming for over three decades and spent a lot of time at the Wyoming Infrared Observatory on Jelm Mountain. Why was he riding the rails to disappear in Cajun country?"

"He had been contacted by Dr. Goldblum from Cornell University about joining an elite team of astronomers and aerospace engineers in a secret government project that was codenamed Minoa. When he discovered that it involved a planet-sized comet and a government cover-up, he couldn't participate in the conspiracy. His patriot streak was unwilling to throw the vast majority of America's population under the bus for the sake of prestige and his own promised quarters in the Cheyenne Mountain Complex when things got ugly. But he knew that he would be in hot water if he verbalized his *no*. When the government makes that kind of offer, refusal is not an option. So, playing along, he told Dr. Goldblum that he was definitely on board. The bigshot told him to prepare for a meeting in Washington, D.C., the next week. That night Burt loaded his backpack, stopped at the school, appropriated several high-tech sensors and some useful hardware for infrared telescopes, and skedaddled. He left a message on his phone that he had gone black-powder elk hunting with a buddy and would be back in three or four days. I bumped into him the next day."

"Must have been a miserable journey."

"It was brutally cold, but that was more the windchill than the temperature. We spent the first three days in the compressor cubby on a reefer car of beef headed south, huddled in our sleeping bags. He kept his Jon-e handwarmer going the whole time and went through dozens of hand-warmer packets. Then we caught a ride in a grainer for the rest of the trip."

"Do you have any contact with him?"

"Occasional texts in ProtonMail. Twice this spring I carried a package for him for a stretch on the Underground Mailroad."

"The Underground Mailroad? What's that?"

"Package and mail delivery for Rogue fugitives who are hiding out from the government."

"You mean there's a Rogue Underground?"

"Yes."

"How did it get started?"

"A man who goes by the handle Krake started a bulletin board and chatroom last April in Buster which he called

Rogue Underground. It's an information center on the comet and a communication center for trusted folks. Since then over five hundred members have been added, all vetted by existing members. I'm a member and so is Mr. Fitzgerald, my boss at Fitzgerald Ranch. The Underground Mailroad just kind of evolved. Members in hiding needed things like letter and package delivery, medicine and medical treatment, and some method to indirectly order things online. The other members rallied together to help them out with these needs."

"So who is this Krake? Does anyone know?"

"We think it's Burrage Krakenhavn, who was on the air for years with his *Down the Rabbit Hole* program but disappeared shortly after he divulged sensitive information on the Rogue that had been hacked by Anonymous. Rumor has it that he is in life detainment at FEMA 286. Somehow, he has access to the outside."

"I listened to him a few times, but he wasn't really on my radar." Woody changed the subject. "So what did you carry for Burt?"

"Once, I took antibiotics for him to Baton Rouge and handed them off to a man I only know as Swamp Rat. Another time, I picked up a package from Swamp Rat which was headed for a small village in the Uinta Mountains in Utah. My guess is that it contained hard-to-find components for an infrared telescope."

Woody sat silent for a moment.

Lobo probed him. "Something on your mind?"

"I was just wondering. Do you think I could be added to

the Rogue Underground? That will come in handy when I get to my destination."

The cowboy smiled. "There is always room for another fugitive. What will your handle and password be? You'll need a twelve-digit username and a twenty-digit password along with our faux group name Pandemonium Press to access the Rogue Underground room. You'll enter all three on the group login page in your own account. Once you're in the room, you can access the bulletin board with an abbreviated username and password."

Woody thought for a moment, then answered. "How about B1GcaddisFAN for my username and 1LMS1DFwritethirteen for my password? Don't forget that B1G is spelled with a 1, not an I."

"Okay. Got em'."

"I'll use Caddis and S1DF for the Rogue Runner board."

Lobo laughed. "Seeking one delightful female?"

Woody blushed.

"Now remember," Lobo added, "you have to log in to your own Buster account, then log into the Rogue Underground, then log in to the bulletin board and chatroom."

"Okay. I'll take care of that as soon as I find my way to freedom. Hey, do we still have time to get a bite to eat before the train gets here?"

"Yeah. We got about an hour."

"Sweet." Woody reached into his chow bag and pulled out a second MRE. "Prefer mac-n-cheese or beef stroganoff?"

"Definitely want the beef stroganoff."

"Glad to hear that. I wanted the mac-n-cheese."

An hour and fifteen minutes later, shortly after 2 p.m., Woody and Lobo were sitting on the deck of a grainer heading East, with most of their gear stowed inside the porthole. As they watched the desert hills roll by, Lobo explained the ins and outs of being a hobo. He covered slang terminology, yard bulls, hobo etiquette—what precious little there was, and staying out of trouble. He especially emphasized the latter. "Most of those that ride the rails are either a couple bricks short of a full load or they are rough characters with criminal records ranging from burglary to murder. You got pretty lucky today with the dirtbags that jumped you. If they had been real criminals and not merely tough-talking punks, you could be bleeding to death right now. They don't play games."

"Good to know. But how do you handle them?"

Lobo reached under his shirt and pulled out a pistol. "They see this, and they don't give me any trouble."

Woody was impressed. "Looks like a Glock. What model is it?"

"The 17."

"That'll work."

"Yep. Keeps the riffraff away. Ninety percent of those that ride the rails are not company I care to keep. Most of the time, I end up traveling alone. Even most of the nicer kind tend to be crusties—they never bathe or change their clothes. Glad I got you for company, for a while anyways."

"Likewise."

Lobo probed a little. "So what route have you got planned?"

"I'm gonna ride the Union Pacific through Ogden to Gillette. From there I plan on catching the Burlington Northern to Billings."

"You would be better off to avoid Billings. There's a heavy federal presence there because of the oil industry."

"What would you suggest?"

"Jump off at Laurel, just west of Billings. I would also suggest switching to the BN at Cheyenne. I've done both lines on the Cheyenne to Gillette stretch and prefer the BN. Your biggest hassle, however, will be going through Wells, Nevada."

"What happens there?"

"You face a rat's nest of switching stations in the area. At least two and as many as four, depending on the route you take to the switch at Cobre. You need to make sure that you get on the right line and go straight to Ogden. You don't want to go through Salt Lake City. That's another hotbed for feds. Lots of high tech and military stuff going on there."

Woody looked concerned.

Lobo offered his assistance. "Tell you what. You keep sharing your coffee and chow with me, and I'll ride with you to Laurel and show you the ropes: which lines to take, which towns are safe, where the hop-outs are. I was actually thinking about jumping off in Laurel myself and then hitchhiking to Cooke City, Montana, to catch the start of the horse packing season."

"I really appreciate that. So what do we face on this stretch?"

"The next three stops—Winnemucca, Elko, and Wells—

aren't bad. Easy hop-outs. We can stay in the porthole if we want in Elko. The yard is relatively quiet, and they rarely do a full search there. At all three stops, we'll have time to get out and stretch our legs or even go to the store—well, I can at any rate. The only thing we have to watch out for, like I said, is the rat's nest of switches at Wells."

***

As evening descended on the desert east of Winnemucca, the low-hanging sun bathed the two riders in a rosy glow. The moment seemed magical. Woody mused, *This is what I hoped it would be like.*

Using the last hour of daylight, Woody fired up his stove to make freeze-dried chili and coffee. Then, with full bellies and steaming cups of java in hand, they watched the sun drop below the horizon, a brilliant Western sunset. As darkness gathered, they turned their focus to watching the stars. Woody marveled at the rising of Jupiter and Antares in the southeast. But what impressed him the most was the unusual wave of shooting stars. There was no regular meteor shower of significance in June, yet he was counting thirty to forty per minute, many exceptionally large and bright. Perhaps it was debris from a long-period comet showing up in Earth's orbital path for the first time. That would go along with Irina's theory, which he had heard from Ariele, that there would be an increase in comet events as the world approached the time of the apocalypse.

His mind drifted back to an exhortation Jordy had given him and Jack three summers earlier. "The stage setting for the last days has picked up the pace. A sign will soon appear in the heavens which will shake the planets. When it has been revealed, you two will have to do whatever it takes to make the rendezvous here in Montana before the sky falls. God brought us together for a purpose. He has something big for us to do." At the time, Woody had thought that Jordy was off the deep end with his interest in prophecy. Now he found himself wrestling with a nagging question. Was Jordy right that the entire prophetic message of the Bible would be fulfilled literally?

Around 11 p.m., their eyes heavy, the travelers crept through the porthole and crawled into their sleeping bags. Woody didn't stay awake long after his head hit the pillow, but long enough to appreciate the fact that he might actually get a full night of sleep for the first time in days.

2

Desolation Wilderness
Sunday, June 23, 2019

The prior evening, the rookie agents who had followed Woody into the woods started to get nervous when darkness began to fall on the mountains and their assignment hadn't returned to camp. They argued the issue back and forth.

"We need to call in right away," one timidly insisted. "We'll look bad if he doesn't show, and we didn't sound the alarm early."

The other cockily retorted, "Not gonna happen! We'll look bad if we call at 8:40, a mere ten minutes after sunset, and the rabbit shows up in camp thirty minutes later. You have to remember that this Woody guy is a fishing fanatic. He'll probably fish until it's pitch black. Then he'll walk back in the dark."

"But what if he gets away?"

"Dude! You were in his camp with me. He only took his fishing gear. He left his food, stove, sleeping bag and pad, water purifier, coffee pot, even his day pack. He would have taken most of that stuff if he was going to try to run."

"So what are you suggesting we do?"

"Let's wait until an hour after dark, say ten o'clock. If he doesn't show up by then, we make the call."

"Hang it all," the faint-hearted agent bellowed. "I wish we would have watched him closer. Then we wouldn't be in this situation." He slammed his camping cup down on a rock, denting the bottom. "We could get sacked over this, you know, before we even hit the six-months mark. My dad would kill me."

"Dude. He's coming back. Trust me. You worry way too much."

At 10:06, when there was still no sign of the man they were assigned to watch, the timid agent, against the objections of the other, decided it was time to make the call.

His buddy fumed, "You're going to make us both look like fools."

"We already look like fools." Shaking with nervousness, he pulled out their satellite phone and called the Assistant Special Agent in Charge at the Los Angeles Field Station, who was the coordinator for the assignment. "Two, this is twenty-six and twenty-seven. The rabbit has eluded the hounds. Copy?"

An awful silence followed. The rookies felt like they were on the gallows waiting for the trapdoor to drop. "Eluded? ELUDED? How did the rabbit elude the hound?" An ear-splitting tirade followed which lashed them with expletives and criticism. "Which way did he go?"

"We have no idea, sir."

"No idea. Didn't you observe which direction he went when he left camp?"

"No, sir."

"Why not?"

"Because he got up extremely early and took off."

"Why weren't you up early?"

"We were up at 4 a.m. as instructed, sir."

"Well, you weren't up early enough, were you?"

"No, sir."

"You failed to execute on a simple task. What do you have to say for yourselves?"

"No excuse, sir. It won't happen again."

"You're right it won't happen again. But we don't have time now for the butt-chewing that you deserve. Get out there and start looking. Look for any sign which might indicate which way he went."

3

Desolation Wilderness
Monday, June 24, 2019

Monday morning at 5:48, when it was light enough for a landing, an Air Force MH-60G Pave Hawk Sikorsky landed and unloaded two tracking teams from Vandenburg Air Force Base, an Air Force officer who was supervising the canine teams, and the Assistant Special Agent in Charge, who was overseeing the entire operation. Over the next half hour, three more choppers landed and unloaded six more tracking teams: two from the FBI, two from the Sheriff's department, and two from Camp Pendleton. The canine officer was confident that they would track Woody down within a few hours. He couldn't have gone far. He was a middle-aged man with a slight paunch, the surrounding territory was rugged, and the presumptive theory was that he had either gotten lost or injured on his fishing venture.

At 7 a.m. three Airbus H125 helicopters arrived and began to search the area from above, focusing on the nearby streams and lakes.

Throughout the morning, the Pave Hawks continued to

ferry in men and supplies: federal agents, two dozen special operations troops, and two civilian tracking experts. By eight o'clock the command center—six folding tables under a tarp—was buzzing with activity. The Assistant Special Agent in Charge shared the space with a communications team from the Los Angeles Field Station, the officer over the canine teams, and an assortment of other command and liaison personnel.

By four o'clock that afternoon, the mood among the task force leadership had grown somber, and frustration reigned among the search teams. Despite the fact that they had eight canine teams on the ground, the dogs had failed to find the fugitive's scent outside of his immediate campsite. Nor had any of the other search teams found even a single clue that might indicate the direction he had traveled. The rabbit had vanished without a trace.

The officer in charge of the canine teams grumbled to the other officers and agents sitting with him at the lunch table. "Something doesn't add up. I think our search theory is wrong. These dogs are well-trained and experienced. They always find a scent, even when it's forty-eight hours old. Yet we searched for three miles in every direction and didn't find a single whiff. To be honest, I don't think this man went fishing. He isn't lost or injured. I think he nailed a brilliant getaway."

An agent across from him nodded in agreement. "I suspect you're right. Makes me wonder, though, what the official report is gonna say."

"Not much they can say," another chimed in. "They'll probably give it some indistinct resolution as *likely deceased* with a comment about the rugged wilderness."

4

Caltech
Monday, June 24, 2019

At 8:03 a.m. as Sally was sitting down at her desk to get the day started, Sterling barged into her office and demanded, with noticeable agitation in his voice, "Where's Woody?"

Sally shrugged her shoulders. "Well, it's long past breakfast, so I would assume that he's wetting a fly on an alpine lake somewhere in the Sierras."

He shouted in frustrated surprise, "The mountains! What in the world is he doing in the mountains?"

Sally eyed him with raised eyebrows as if he had just asked the dumbest question in the world. *Hope that look throws him off.* "Sterling," she said patronizingly, "Woody goes backpacking every summer in June. A little over a week ago he asked for this week off so he could go on his annual June trip. I said *yes*. Is there a problem with that?"

He glared at her like a drill sergeant trying to intimidate a recruit. "You know full well what the problem is."

She locked her eyes with his, giving him her best got-no-idea-what-you're-talking-about act, and refused to show either the anger or the nervousness that was twisting her insides into knots. She despised the slimeball. He was incurably insolent and conceited.

In a rage, Sterling tore into her. "Why didn't you cancel his trip on Friday before he left? You saw that he was on the Orange One list as of last Friday's afternoon report."

"Actually, I didn't get around to reading the FBI memorandum on Friday. I had a hair appointment right after lunch, followed by a conference call with Dr. Goldblum and several other members of the Research Team which lasted for over an hour. Then I left early on personal time and took in a fly-fishing demonstration at the Orvis store in Pasadena. But I plan on getting to the memorandum first thing this morning. If it's any consolation, I did call the Field Station around 7:30 p.m. on Friday, well within the four-hour window, and filed the required vacation report for Orange Two employees." *Hope that flies, or at least buys me some time.*

Sterling shook his head and walked out, indignant. Sally sensed that she hadn't fooled him. He was aware that she was playing dumb and that Friday's flurry of activities had been an intentional ploy to keep her from reading the memorandum. She could almost see the evil gears turning in his head. If he exposed her effort to aid Woody, then her downfall was assured, and his promotion would soon follow. *What a despicable ingrate!*

5

on the road in Utah
Monday, June 24, 2019

Ariele rolled over in the narrow bed and grumbled to Andrius, who was waking up in his hammock barely two feet from her face, "There's hardly room in here to move."

Andrius retorted, "You're welcome to set up a cot on top of the van and sleep outside. I'd love to have my bed back."

She huffed, surveying the cramped environs, "I can't imagine that we really need all this stuff. There's enough food in here for a month, enough camping gear for a half-dozen men, and enough electronics junk to send a spaceship to the moon. And what are you going to do with all these books? You'll never read a quarter of them." She kicked a box clogging the walkway. "Here's a whole box on stuff like going underground and traceless communications. Seriously? You are the geekiest geek I know."

"Room? You're complaining about room?" Andrius snarked. "There would have been a lot more room if Miss Coffee Snob hadn't brought along dozens of bags of coffee beans, a grinder, a tea kettle, and a French press. I mean, coffee is coffee, right? Just buy any supermarket brand of coffee and call it good! Oh, and did I mention the grocery bag full of wild-colored hair dyes? Seriously?"

The urge to giggle at the absurdity of their cramped circumstances and Andrius' comedic take on her additions to the chaos melted away Ariele's frostiness. At least she was safe, on the road, and headed for Montana, a destination that left her both excited and nervous. She knew *where* they were headed, but the *why* part was a mystery. "I'll meet up with you in Montana at the rendezvous site," Woody had whispered as he slid the napkin across the table on the evening of her flight. That implied that an intentional gathering had been planned for an end-of-the-world scenario—like the one they were in. A sense of destiny gripped her soul.

But her sunshine quickly dispersed again when she thought about the day ahead. After two long days on the road, they had only made it to Beryl, Utah, when they could have been in Two Dot, Montana, already! They still faced four more days of driving because Mr. Perfectionist had cobbled together a zigzag route that followed county roads and rural roads as much as possible—a route that tripled the length of the journey. *I'm so done with Andrius and his over-the-top ways.*

She grimaced. Maybe she was being too hard on him. She had to admit that his route minimized contact with the highway patrol and avoided the cameras which scanned the major highways. They would be in deep trouble if her face was picked up by one of them. She laughed at herself. Only three months ago she had been a staunch advocate of cameras as a tremendous asset in the war against drugs and terrorism. Now she saw their ugly side. They were a crucial tool in the creeping dystopian control over the population. Her radical change of view reminded her of a quip Irina had said to her once. "One truth bomb can change everything."

***

Ariele was tired of watching the dreary desert scenery roll by. It all looked vaguely the same. And she was tired of Andrius blathering on about things she neither understood nor cared about. *Gotta fix this before I go crazy.* She interrupted his discourse on the importance of capacitors in electrical systems and steered their conversation toward things more personal. "Tell me what it was like when you first came to America."

"Sure … um … I was raised in Kazlų Rūda, a small village near Kaunas, Lithuania. When I was nine years old, my father died in an industrial accident. A year later, my mother married an American missionary, and we moved to California, just in time for fifth grade."

"I'll bet that was rough."

"It was. I didn't know English apart from a few slang terms and cuss words. I struggled the first year and hated school. The only class I did well in was math."

"But you made it through. You figured out the English language and American culture."

"Well, I got the language down anyways."

"How did you get into welding? You're insanely smart.

Why didn't you go into some science field?"

"It was a simple matter of economics. I didn't feel like paying tens of thousands of dollars to go to school for four years so I can land a job that pays less than a skilled trade and then struggle for the next twenty years trying to pay off my school loans. So after high school, I enrolled in a welding program at Los Angeles Trade-Tech College. When I finished the one-year program, I took a position at Hi-Tech Fabrication, where I specialize in stainless and aluminum welding."

"I get that. Still, you have so much talent that is going to waste."

"Going to waste in whose eyes? Look, I admit that I was treading water in a job that was merely a stepping stone. It didn't give me any satisfaction beyond mastering a valuable skill. But I haven't found my life calling yet."

"How about an engineer or a teacher?"

"Nope. Neither of them sounds attractive to me in the least."

"Do you have any idea what you want to do with your life?"

"Not really. I just want to do something where I get to use my hands and my brains and where I have a lot of freedom to express my creativity."

"So how are you going to recognize this something when it shows up?"

"That's like asking me how I'm going to recognize cute when I see it. A guy just knows."

"So what are you going to do with your life while you're

waiting for this something to show up?"

"In case you've forgotten, right now I don't have much of a life. I'm busy helping a criminal elude the FBI and trying to bring her safe to some secret hideout in Montana. If I'm caught, I'll have even less of a life. But I guess I could strive to be the best electronics technician in whatever FEMA camp I get assigned to. And to be honest, that actually sounds like more fun than what I'm doing right now."

Ariele shot him a glare of scorn and looked out her window. But her frown quickly melted. She knew that he was right. She really had upended his life. Hopefully, things would work out for him at the hideout in Montana.

6

Monrovia, CA ... Topock, AZ
Tuesday morning, June 25, 2019

Sally's stomach was in knots, and her hands were shaking as she applied her mascara. In the middle of the job, she threw her brush down on the counter in frustration. Normally, she aced the thin, light coat that she preferred, but today she kept getting globs. She had already redone her eyelashes three times. Biting her lip and fighting back the tears, she tried to face her fears about the day in front of her. *Think positive, girl.*

She meditated on one of her favorite quotes—from Meriwether Lewis of the Lewis and Clark expedition—"As I have always held it a crime to anticipate evils, I will believe it a comfortable road until I am compelled to believe differently." But it didn't calm her. The road in front of her just wasn't comfortable. Sterling Fitzgerald—his name made her cringe—had reported her yesterday morning, and she faced an interview this afternoon with the FBI. Simmering with anger, she pictured the conceited jerk getting run over by a steamroller. But pangs of guilt forced her to think more civil thoughts, like him throwing a tantrum when he didn't get promoted after her removal.

Thirty minutes later as Sally walked out of her house, she noticed a black SUV parked across the street three houses down. Two men in suits sat in the front seat. *Hope that isn't who I think it is. Looks like the vehicles that the federal agents use when they come to the Cahill Center for seminars and inspections.*

When she headed up the street, the vehicle pulled away from the curb and followed her, staying half a block behind. She nervously eyed it in her rearview mirror. It was still trailing her after her first three turns. *Great!* she muttered. *I'm being tailed.* Originally, she had figured that she would have the entire week that Woody was supposed to be in the woods to plan her own escape. But ugly reality had t-boned that idea an hour earlier when her secretary had texted her with a heads up on the FBI meeting. Now bad had gone to worse. With the FBI on her tail, she had minutes, not hours.

I need a plan fast. She made a last-second left turn into a strip mall parking lot, wheeled around, scooted back onto the street, and raced in the opposite direction.

Back home, she turned into her driveway with a chirp of her tires and bolted for her house as if she was in a hurry—and she really was. She grabbed her ceramic travel mug, filled it with refrigerated coffee from her cold press, placed it in the microwave, and set the timer for one and a half minutes. Then she hustled into her bedroom, opened her top dresser drawer, and quickly threw a few things she might need into her purse, including her stash of cash and a business card for a local cab company. Finally, she grabbed a Percival shopping bag from her closet and placed a lightweight gym bag, a tan skirt, a light yellow blouse, and a pair of tan, strapped, high heels in the bag. She was back out the door in three minutes with her purse, the Percival bag, and her travel mug in hand.

When she headed up the street again, the SUV followed her again, though more closely than the first time. That seemed odd to her. *Don't they realize that I can see them in my rear-view mirror? Or maybe they want me to see them? Maybe they're trying to intimidate me?* She headed for Percival's clothing store, which was only a short distance off her route to work. Instead of turning on East California, she went past it and took historic Route 66. *This is happening way too fast. I'm not half ready. As Woody would say, I'm flying by the seat of my pants.*

While stopped at a red light, Sally called her office and informed her assistant that she would be about an hour late as she had to make an exchange at Percival's at One Colorado Mall.

When she arrived, she parked by the entrance closest to Percival's, clenched her teeth, and exhaled heavily. Hopefully, her ruse would throw the boys in the suits. In the mall she borrowed a cell phone, called the cab company on the card, and requested a cab to pick her up in ten minutes at the northwest doors of the mall. She handed the phone back and scurried down a side wing to a ladies' room where she took a stall. Hastily she changed into her tan outfit and shoved the baby-blue outfit she had been wearing into the Percival bag. Then she dropped her shopping bag in the trash can, covered it with a layer of crumpled paper towels, and headed for the door. Halfway there, she stopped dead in her tracks, slapped herself on the forehead for being braindead, and wheeled back around. She retrieved her phone from her purse, turned the ringer volume down to zero, and deposited it in the trash too, pushing it to the bottom. *Good thing Woody warned me about cell-phone tracking.*

As she hustled down the mall toward the northwest doors, waves of worry washed over her. Where should she go? She didn't have time to think about it. The cab pulled up just as she burst out of the mall doors. She flung open the cab door, jumped in, slammed it shut, and blurted out, "Any major car rental in San Fernando."

Thirty-seven minutes later, after enduring a crazy ride in morning traffic, the cabbie dropped her off at Enterprise Rent-A-Car on San Fernando Road. "We here, Miss. Cost $66.50."

Sally handed the Chinese gentleman three twenties and a ten, told him to keep the change, hopped out, and rushed into the office. Before the gal even greeted her, Sally requested a Taurus for three days for a drive to Seattle. After ten minutes of paperwork and some small talk where she mentioned that she planned on taking scenic routes on her way north, she dropped $445 in cash. Mentally she subtracted the fee from the remainder of her stash. *Down to $1200. It's going fast.* As she walked to the car, clutching the keys tightly in her trembling hand, she reflected on her stratagem. Hopefully, it would buy her a couple of hours and wouldn't cause her sister in Seattle any great problems.

Once she was a few blocks down the street, she pulled into a parking lot, removed the fuse cover, yanked out the fuse marked GPS, and replaced the fuse cover. *Good old Woody*, she thought, recalling his mysterious comment last Thursday while she was examining his Russian dry flies. "How do you avoid being tracked in your car if an Orwellian government wants to track you? Toss your phone in the garbage and pull the GPS fuse in your car." She marveled at him, not merely because he had the wisdom to know what to do, but because he had the foresight to give her the advice she needed.

Back on US 5, she decided to head toward Flagstaff. That would give her plenty of time to figure out her next step. She relaxed a little as she turned northeast on Highway 14 and skirted the San Gabriel Mountains. She knew this route well, so there was no pressure for navigation—Highway 14 to Palmdale, Highway 18 to Victorville, US 15 north to Barstow, then east on US 40 to Flagstaff.

Three hours later as she drove through the Mojave Desert, she was still wrestling with the situation, trying to come up with a viable plan. She figured she was running out of time. By now the authorities had almost certainly figured out that she was missing. They may have even figured out that she was not on her way to Seattle. She had to get off the highway because an APB would go out for her soon if it hadn't already. As for options, she only had two. She could take the back roads, or she could ditch the car and hitch a ride. She didn't dare do the former because she feared getting lost or running out of gas in the desert. That left ditching the car. But where? She needed to hide it where it was not likely to be found any time soon.

By the time she reached Fenner, a plan had gelled. She pictured a spot on a river-like arm of the lake that was north of Topock, AZ. Its steep bank and deep water seemed like an ideal place to ditch her car. She had stumbled upon it while exploring some years back. Could she find that spot again? She hoped so. The downside to her plan was that it was a long walk back to the highway—in the heat. But she would have to grin and bear it because she had no other plan.

***

Around 2:30 p.m., she turned north on Old US 66 toward Topock, then made a left at the first intersection she came to—it seemed to jog her memory. When she crossed a nasty-looking green slough, she knew she was on the right road. About a quarter mile later, she turned right on a gravel road that paralleled the Colorado River and followed it for four dusty miles to a landmark she recognized, a collection of ramshackle buildings and battered construction equipment. With anticipation, she turned right and drove several miles until she arrived at the meander. There the road curved to the right and paralleled the water. She followed it, slowed her pace, and watched the bank on her left. When she found her spot a quarter mile down the road, she pounded her steering wheel and squealed with delight. There was a small pullout, some brush, and a steep drop into the channel, just as she had remembered.

With her heart pounding, she parked the car with its nose over the edge of the road, rolled down the windows, opened the hatch door, grabbed her bag and purse, put the car in neutral, and attempted to push it toward the water. It wouldn't budge, no matter how hard she pushed and grunted. She turned around, placed her back against the car, dug her feet in good, and pushed until her lower back hurt and her legs burned. *Rats!* It still wouldn't budge. She pounded her fists on the back of the car in frustration and fought back tears. But while she was venting, she recalled some advice Woody had given her once. "Desperate circumstances call for desperate measures."

Buoyed with newfound resolve, yet trembling with fear, she climbed back in, left the door open, started the car, shifted it into first gear, gave it a little gas, and lurched the vehicle forward until it was entirely off the road and starting down the steep incline toward the cliff edge. Panic-stricken, she leaped out the door, smacking her shins on the way out. Flopping face first into the dirt, she quickly craned her head and watched as the Taurus—seemingly in slow motion— careened down the hill, ricocheted off a scrubby tree, rolled over the bank edge, and plunged into the murky, grey-green waters.

She got up, massaged her throbbing shins, dusted herself off, and walked to the edge. It was 2:49 p.m., and the car was sinking fast. In less than a minute, it was gone, hidden under eight feet of water so discolored that you couldn't see more than three feet deep in the best conditions. On top of that, the spot couldn't be seen from the road. With a sense of satisfaction, she retrieved her purse and gym bag and started walking back to the highway.

A half mile later, her wobbly right heel collapsed. *What a clutz! What a dumb blonde! Why didn't I wear clothes that were more appropriate for the occasion?* Frustrated, she took her shoe off, twisted the heel all the way off, and flung the stiletto angrily into the brush. Then she slipped her other shoe off and slammed its heel against the ground until its high heel popped off. Her sense of relief was dampened when she slipped her shoes back on and realized that heels without the heels are not flats. Grumpy as a cat in a bathtub, she continued her trudge down the road, wincing in pain from her burning toes and aching arches.

7

Topock, AZ ... Flagstaff, AZ
Tuesday afternoon, June 25, 2019

After an hour of misery, Sally reached the road along the river, limping from the beating her feet were taking. *Count me as the newest convert to tennis shoes.* She turned and trudged south. Five minutes later, exasperated, she removed her shoes, carried them in her hand, and started walking barefoot. Not a minute later, a white Camry raced past her from behind, then stopped quickly in front of her, raising a cloud of dust. A well-dressed man rolled down his window, smiled broadly, and asked, "Do you need a ride?"

Something inside her warned her to say *no*, but she was too tired and frustrated. "Yes, I do," she replied.

"Where are you headed?"

"Flagstaff."

"That's right on my way. I'm headed to Albuquerque for an insurance-sales conference. I can drop you off wherever you want."

"Fantastic. Thank you." *Yes! This is twenty-one flavors of sweet.* She climbed in the passenger seat, buckled up, and checked her watch. It was 3:30 in the afternoon. She could be in Flagstaff by 6:30, though she didn't know what she was going to do once she got there.

Her good Samaritan introduced himself. "I'm Calvin McClellan, by the way. My friends call me Cal. I spent twenty years in the Army as an MP. I retired a few years ago, but couldn't bear to sit around doing nothing. So I began a new career selling insurance. My region is fairly large, and I spend a lot of time on the road."

Their conversation was interrupted by his scanner. "We have a domestic problem at 587 Front Ave, Mohave Valley, unit 5 respond. Repeat, we have a 10-16 at 587 Front Ave, unit 5 respond."

She swallowed hard. *Great. Just what I need. Hitch a ride with a retired cop who has his scanner on. Hopefully, the FBI hasn't already put out a bulletin to the region to be on the lookout for me.*

Cal chatted incessantly about himself. She patiently listened while he told her the story of his life: his upbringing in small-town Arizona, his time in the Army, how he ended up in Mohave Valley, and his award-winning success in insurance sales. His garrulousness and boasting rubbed her the wrong way. *Seems like a nice guy, but he could talk the ears off a mule. And he's trying way too hard to impress me.* Nonetheless, she didn't mind letting the windbag do all the talking. The less she had to talk, the better.

Without warning, Cal jumped from regaling Sally with his success in life to asking her about herself. "So what's your story? How did you wind up in the middle of nowhere hitching a hide to Flagstaff?"

She grimaced. *Gonna need to make up a story fast.* "I was visiting a friend."

"Where's your car?"

"At home."

He looked quizzically at her.

"I took a bus out here from California."

He nodded. "I see. Why isn't your friend giving you a ride to the bus depot or wherever you are trying to go?"

"I didn't give him the opportunity. I just got out of there. I wanted nothing to do with that lowlife loser."

Cal was confused. "But you came out here to spend time with him, didn't you?"

"Yea, I did. It's a crazy story. I was on the rebound, and we met online. He sounded interesting, so I took a bus out here to visit him. We planned on driving to the Grand Canyon together. Then he was going to take me back to California."

"But things didn't work out?"

"No. I got there and found out that he had another woman living with him. All the creep said was, 'Sorry. I got the dates confused.' What a bum!"

"So why are you traveling to Flagstaff instead of going back to California?"

"I already took my vacation days, so I might as well use them."

"So what was this guy's name?"

"Fred Johnson." She was starting to get nervous. *Don't know how well or how long I can keep this charade up before it breaks down.*

"Don't recognize the name. What road does he live on?"

"I don't remember. I had it written down, but I gave it to the cab driver who picked me up at the bus station."

"Does he live on the road where I picked you up?"

"No. Somewhere in the backcountry off that road."

"How far had you walked before I picked you up?"

"I don't know. A few miles I guess, maybe more."

"Well, there are only a few homes on the roads that branch off this road, which happens to be called Upper Levee Road on this stretch." He eyed her suspiciously. "What color was his house?"

"I don't remember. It was an old, non-descript trailer house." *Think I'm digging my own grave.*

"Where did you take the cab from?"

"Kingman."

"How much was the cab fare?"

"I didn't ask. Just gave him my credit card."

"You know. It's probably none of my business, but your story just isn't adding up. Either you are a quintessential dumb blonde, or you were in a pot fog the whole time, or you are a poor liar who is doing a miserable job of covering something. So tell me. Are you a dumb blonde, a pot head, or a criminal on the run?"

She forced a bright smile and said, with a coy laugh, "Definitely a dumb blonde." That was hard to admit but true. With inexplicable obliviousness, she had watched the situation overtake her, crafted a hasty plan at the last minute, and wore stupid shoes. *Too bad this isn't a video game. I could just push the reset button and start over.*

Cal asked about her line of work. She decided to tell the truth as far as she could. *Already told too many lies to keep straight.* "I work at Caltech in astronomy in the NEO program." He gave her a knowing look. She sensed that she had made a critical mistake and expected him to call the FBI right then and there. But he didn't. That raised an inkling of hope. Maybe she was reading into his facial expressions. Maybe no APB went out for her. Maybe he didn't hear the APB. But then again, maybe he was just enjoying the cat-and-mouse game. The suspense was killing her.

Cal continued the conversation. "So you're looking for the end of the world, eh?"

"Yeah, and hoping we don't find it."

They continued chatting about astronomy until he swerved up the last exit ramp in Kingman, Arizona. When she looked nervously over to him, he informed her, "Just stopping at the truck stop to use the restroom and get a coffee. It's a regular stop of mine." He parked, motioned for her to get out, and asked, "Do you want a coffee, too?"

"Please. That would be great." *A coffee might be the only thing going right for me at the moment.*

Cal finished in the men's room, strolled into the lounge, pulled out his phone, and called the Mohave County Sheriff's Department. When the dispatcher answered, he said, "Hey, Betty, this is Cal. Can you play an APB for me, the one that went out this morning about the astronomer from California?"

"Sure, hon'."

He heard a few mouse clicks, some static, and then the

message played. "We have an APB issued by the FBI for California, Oregon, Arizona, and Nevada. BOL for a white female, five feet, eight inches tall, slender build, weight 140 pounds, hair blonde and shoulder length, age 38, by the name of Sally Evans. The suspect was last seen on security camera leaving One Colorado Mall in Pasadena, CA, wearing a tan skirt, a light yellow blouse, tan high heels, and carrying a blue gym bag. The suspect is wanted for Homeland Security violations and possible terrorist connections. Anyone having information regarding the whereabouts of this suspect, please call the FBI and ask for the Minoa Hotline."

"Thanks, Betty. Listen. I think I have the suspect traveling with me. I picked her up in the desert between Mohave Valley and Topock. We just stopped at the truck stop in Kingman. In a few minutes, we'll be back on the road and headed for Flagstaff. I'm driving my white Camry with plate number CAMSLAM. Will you call the FBI? I assume they will intercept. If they have different instructions, call me on my cell phone."

"Will do, darlin'."

Cal was just stepping away from the counter with their coffees when Sally returned from the ladies' room. He handed her one of the cups, and they walked in silence back to his car. A few minutes after six, when they were around fifty miles from Flagstaff, they passed three highway patrol cars parked on the shoulder. Immediately, all three pulled out. Two zoomed passed them and blocked both lanes in front of them. The other vehicle pulled in behind them and hit his lights. Cal feigned surprise and pulled over. One of the patrolmen from the car directly in front of them walked back and asked Cal for his license. He briefly compared Cal's face to the picture, then he asked Sally for hers. Tears welled up in her eyes as she dug out her license and handed it to him. He compared her photo to her face, stared inquisitively at her for a few seconds, then walked back to his car. When the check dragged out for more than a few minutes, Sally figured that she was in deep trouble.

Ten minutes later, a pair of black SUVs pulled up. Two men jumped out of the lead vehicle. One of them leaned Sally against Cal's car and cuffed her. The other retrieved her bag and purse. Then they walked her to their SUV, placed her in the rear driver-side seat, and buckled her seat belt.

"Where are you taking me?" Sally enquired, scared.

"You'll find out when we get there."

"I need to use the restroom."

"We'll make a brief stop in Flagstaff."

"Then what?"

"No more questions please."

Sally fretted to herself. Things were looking like a trainload of ugly. *Always a day late and a dollar short. Doesn't matter if it's men, money, or making decisions at difficult junctures.* The stirrings of regrets and fears brought Woody to mind—long her greatest regret and now her greatest fear. She hoped he was safe. With a sigh, she tried to put her negative thoughts out of her mind and engage with the situation in a constructive manner, but she fell into the careworn ruts of memory lane. For the next forty-five minutes, she relived the events that led to her present predicament. Fate had dealt her a cruel blow.

On a cold, blustery, overcast evening the previous December, she had been sitting at her kitchen window in Monrovia, watching the rain fall on the San Gabriel Mountains and indulging her blues. Nothing exciting ever happened to her—not in romance, not in her career, not in her hobbies. She had never been in a heart-palpitating relationship. She hadn't made any amazing discoveries. She hadn't written any paradigm-challenging papers. She hadn't climbed any mountains, run any marathons, or taken adventure vacations. Nothing she had ever done or experienced had given her the feeling of exhilaration. Her life was boring.

While mired in her pity party, her cell phone rang. She didn't feel like talking to anyone. When it rang for the twelfth time, she shuffled across the room, grumbled *hope this is important*, retrieved her phone from the kitchen table, and answered with a tired voice, "Hello."

"Sally?" It was Dr. Goldblum, a professor she knew from various astronomy conferences and meetings.

"Hi, Jonathan."

"In a few minutes, you are going to receive a call from Harold Cutting, the National Security Advisor. Do everything he says."

"What's going on?"

"I can't say anything now. But you'll find out soon enough." He paused, then ended the call. "Sorry to be curt, Sally, but I have to go. Time is of the essence."

Sally's mind was racing as she hung up. *What is this*

about? SETI? An asteroid? A new program in cooperation with the military?

While she was pondering the strange call, her phone rang again. She picked it up, trembling slightly. "Hello." A husky voice boomed, "Ms. Evans. This is Harold Cutting, the National Security Advisor. In thirty minutes a black Tahoe will arrive manned by two agents. They will transport you to Los Angeles International airport for your flight to Washington, D.C. Your tickets are already purchased and waiting for you at the American Airlines counter. Upon arrival at Ronald Reagan Washington National Airport, two agents will meet you at your baggage carousel and transport you to the Americana Hotel. Tomorrow morning, the same men will meet you in the lobby at 5:30 a.m. and transport you to your six o'clock meeting. Pack your bags for a minimum of three days. Do you understand your instructions?"

"Yes. But can you please tell me what this meeting is about?"

"I have no more information for you at this time except to warn you that this meeting is classified. Do not speak to anyone about this call, this trip, or this meeting. You will be permitted one phone call in the next few minutes to leave a message on your office answering machine to let your secretary know that you will be out for several days. Do not say why or where you are going. Just inform her that an emergency came up."

"Okay."

Having secured her compliance, he abruptly said, "Goodbye, Ms. Evans," and hung up.

Sally's heart was pounding. Excitement had come knocking on her door. But it left her with an uneasy feeling.

The next day, to her surprise, she was ushered to a special meeting in the Cabinet Room at the White House attended by a handful of scientists. Harold Cutting, the National Security Advisor, opened with a warning that the information they were about to hear was sensitive and must not leave the room. He was followed by Dr. Goldblum, who gave a presentation on the Rogue and the government's response. She was unsettled by the news that a planet-sized comet was on course to smash through the asteroid belt and cross paths with Mars, that Earth would be bombarded for decades with massive asteroid impacts, and that the government had code-named this threat and their response to it *Minoa*, an allusion to the extinction of the Minoan empire. She was even more unsettled when she learned that she had been appointed team leader for the Research Team, composed of the many scientists in attendance.

That evening, for the first time in her life, Sally gave some serious thought to the end of the world. She didn't have much to go on: bits and pieces of the Christian view like the flood in Noah's day and fire from heaven at the end of the world, jarring scenes from Hollywood movies, and the growing fears about things like global warming and nuclear winter. She wasn't sure if any of them fit with the present scenario. But perhaps it didn't matter. Earth getting bombarded by a wave of asteroids knocked loose from the asteroid belt was an end-of-the-world situation in its own right. With a shudder, she shifted on the couch, tucked her knees up to her chin, and drew her blanket around her tighter. The end was coming and there wasn't much that she or anyone else could do about it.

8

Flagstaff, AZ … Albuquerque, NM
Tuesday, June 25, 2019

Sally was startled out of her reflections with a hard toss to her side. She looked up. The SUV had swerved into the right lane to take an exit ramp. The junction looked familiar. They were in Flagstaff on the ramp that leads from Interstate 40 to Interstate 17. *Wonder where we're headed?* Her thoughts were interrupted by the agent in the front passenger seat saying to someone on his phone, with exasperation in his voice, "We're going as fast as we dare in heavy traffic." Someone hollered back loud enough for her to distinctly hear the reply, "I don't want to hear your excuses! I want you to be in the air in ten minutes! You will make the appointment on time!"

That answered Sally's question. They were headed for the airport. Six minutes later, at 6:46 p.m. by the clock on the dash, they pulled up to a hangar where a Gulfstream GV was waiting with engines idling. As soon as the SUV stopped, the agent in the front passenger seat jumped out, opened her door, and said flatly, "Step out of the vehicle." When she struggled to exit with her cuffed hands—it didn't help that she was exhausted and dehydrated—he grabbed her arm and pulled her out. The smothering heat, which was lingering unusually late in the day, almost overwhelmed her. The shock of the abrupt change from the air-conditioned vehicle to the simmering tarmac seemed a fitting metaphor for the shock she had experienced when forced to step out of the comfortable life of a university professor and go on the run as a wanted fugitive.

The agent, keeping a firm grasp on her arm that dug into her flesh, briskly escorted her to the aircraft. At the top of the boarding stairs, she turned and looked back, tears welling in her eyes, knowing that she was saying goodbye to her life. One of Woody's favorite sayings came to mind. "One day can change everything—for good or for bad." This was definitely for bad. Her escort yanked her around and dragged her inside. The inside of the jet was smaller than it looked from the outside, with six single seats on each side, a narrow aisle, a tiny galley, and a small restroom in the back. He guided her to the aisle seat near the door and cuffed her right arm to the armrest. Then he sat down across from her. A few minutes later, they were taxiing down the runway.

The hour and a half flight had been desperately boring. Sally had tried to engage the agent assigned to her with small talk, but he had politely refused. Since there was nothing to read, she had retreated into her own thoughts and once again replayed the past eighteen months. Nothing changed. Her poor choices looked just as ugly this time around. Discouraged, she leaned her seat back and closed her eyes.

She woke with a start when the aircraft banked to prepare for landing at Albuquerque International Airport. After a hard landing, the Gulfstream rolled toward a hangar buzzing with Homeland Security and FBI activity. Before the aircraft had come to a complete stop, the agent assigned to her unlocked her cuffs, raised her to her feet, and guided her to the door. Looking out the window, she watched the ground stop moving, the airstairs unfold, and a black SUV roll up.

The copilot opened the door, and her escort hustled her down the steps and transferred her to the waiting agents, who deposited her in the back seat. Around fifteen minutes later, the vehicle arrived at the Albuquerque Field Office. Her escorts guided her to a bare room on the sixth floor, removed her handcuffs, pointed to her chair, and departed. She took a seat and surveyed her accommodations. Light green paint on the block walls. Four security cameras, one in each corner. An analog clock. A table with three chairs, hers and two across from her. The minutes dragged by. She was miffed at the wait. *So much for hurrying up so we're not late for an appointment.*

Twenty minutes later, two agents entered the room, sat down across from her, laid their folders on the table, folded their hands, and stared at her.

Wonder if they are going to offer me a cigarette like they do in the movies?

They didn't. The door opened again. An agent pushed a cart into the room laden with electronic equipment and wheeled it up to Sally. Another followed with two rolling chairs. The second one set her up for a polygraph, with a pneumograph around her chest, a blood pressure cuff on her arm, and electrodes on her fingertips. The first one placed the Casper cap on her head and played with some switches and dials on the control unit. It was a weird, almost painful sensation when the hundred and twenty electrodes of the Cerebral Stimulation Pattern Recognition unit poked gently into her scalp at the same time.

Sally's heart began to race. She was trapped, and there was nothing she could do. The truth was going to come out.

The agents that had sat down across from her didn't waste any time with preparatory questions. They took turns peppering her with critical questions.

"Did you suspect that Mr. Lundstrom would attempt to run?"

"No." *I knew he would attempt to run.*

"Did you suspect that Miss Serrafe was going to run?"

"No." *I knew she was going to run.*

"Were you covering for either of them?"

"No." *Just being slow and sloppy with the facts.*

"Why did you fail to report that Miss Serrafe was engaged in undirected research in the Taurus sector?"

"I reported her the same day that I faced definitive evidence that she had been doing undirected research."

One of the interrogators raised his eyebrow slightly.

At least I got a rise out of him, Sally mused to herself.

"How did Ms. Serrafe hack your computer?"

"I would like to know myself."

"Why didn't you follow federal guidelines when you processed Mr. Lundstrom's request for vacation?"

"I did follow them."

"Were you aware that Mr. Lundstrom's status had been raised from Orange Two to Orange One at 1 p.m. Pacific Time on the Friday that he left on his hiking trip?"

"I was not aware. I was busy Friday afternoon and did not find out until Monday morning. My apologies for the oversight."

The agents plied her relentlessly with questions for an hour and a half: seeking details, probing her story for holes, and occasionally dropping psychological control questions. Abruptly, her interrogators gathered up their notes and stood up. "Thank you, Miss Evans," one of them said. "There will be no more questioning at this time."

She forced a smile and asked, "So did I pass the polygraph and Casper?"

"It isn't up to us to interpret the data," he replied blankly. "All we do is ask questions and gather data."

She resisted the tears that wanted to flow. Her fate was certain. The machines would reveal that she was bluffing. Most likely, even the agents knew that she was bluffing.

The two interrogators walked to the door. A dull, metallic click echoed off the walls, they exited, and the door closed behind them with a clunk. A minute later, the other two finished disconnecting their equipment and rolled their cart and chairs to the door. The exit process repeated. Once again, Sally sat alone in the silence. While it was a relief to have the interrogation behind her, the silence itself made her uneasy. She wasn't sure whether it was her friend or enemy.

She started counting the blocks in the bare walls. She

needed to do something to keep her mind busy. Otherwise, the time dragged by agonizingly slow. While she was counting the third wall on her fourth count of the room, the click of the door lock startled her, shattering her concentration. The two agents who had escorted her from the airport stood in the doorway. "Come with us," the one in front said in a firm monotone. She rose and followed them, her insides churning with apprehension. While she had no idea where they were taking her or what she faced next, she knew it wouldn't be good. Her future appeared to offer nothing but bleakness.

At the airport, they handed her off to the same agent she had flown with, and he ushered her back onto the same jet. This time she didn't try to engage him in conversation. She reclined her seat, closed her eyes, and hoped she would fall asleep.

9

Joby heard a vehicle driving up into his yard. *That's odd. Wonder who that is? Mom, maybe?* Nobody ever came to visit him. He looked out his window and did a double take. A black SUV parked next to his Toyota pickup, and three men climbed out, all wearing suits. *Law enforcement? What are they doing here?* He was almost paralyzed with fear for a moment as a flashback of his pot arrest as a teenager reverberated through his mind. Joby opened his door before the men reached his porch. The one in the lead stepped up on the porch, flashed his badge, and said, "FBI. Are you Joseph Rosenthal?"

"Yes."

"We'd like to ask you a few questions about Mr. Woodrow Lundstrom."

He looked at them like they were out of their minds, but then it dawned on him that they were asking about Woody. "Do you mean Woody Lundstrom who works at Caltech?"

"That is correct."

"Not a problem. Come on in." But he did have a problem with it. Woody and the FBI didn't seem to belong together. Had he done something questionable? Joby couldn't imagine that. So something must have happened to Woody. But what?

Joby turned and retreated into the security of his cozy home, but the agent speaking with him said, "Sir. You need to follow us." As the nervous young man turned back around, he saw a large utility van pull up and park next to the SUV. Two agents stepped out, walked to the back of the van, and held the doors open. Joby's eyes fixed on a chair with restraints that was surrounded by electrical equipment. Panic set in, and his pulse started to race.

The three escorted Joby to the van, strapped him into the chair, hooked him up to a polygraph, and placed a Casper cap on his head. He was nervous. He had read about the Cerebral Stimulation Pattern Recognition technology— theoretically, it was unbeatable.

The interrogator looked emotionlessly into his eyes. "Were you and Mr. Lundstrom friends?"

"Yeah, I guess so. More like acquaintances, though."

"How long have you known him?"

"About five years."

"How did you meet?"

"I met him the week I started working at Sierra Coffee Company. He was then, and still is, a regular customer."

"Did you ever spend time together?"

"We didn't hang together, but he came up to my place a few times to give me a hand on my house and farmstead. In return, I did some furniture restoration for him."

"What do you know about his recent camping trip?"

"Not much. Only that he was headed for the Susie Lake area. Said he was gonna do his usual early summer backpacking trip. Wanted to do some fly fishing and catch the early hatch."

"Did he say anything to you about this trip that sounded unusual or out of the ordinary?"

"Nope."

"Did anything unusual happen in the weeks prior to this trip?"

"The only thing out of the ordinary was a message that I received in my email three weeks before his trip from someone I didn't know, which I was supposed to deliver to him."

"And what did this message say?"

"Not much. Just 'time to float the Sundown River.'"

"Any idea what the message meant?"

"I assumed that it referred to an upcoming fishing trip later this summer out West."

"Any idea who sent the message?"

"I would guess that it was his Western-trip partner, who I suspect is either a close friend or a relative."

"Any idea why this particular communication came through such an unusual channel?"

"Nope."

"Had you received any similar messages in the past for Woody or anyone else?"

"Nope. Not once."

"Did you receive any similar messages since then?"

"Nope."

"Do you have any idea where Mr. Lundstrom might have gone?"

"If he isn't on the trail that he said he was going to be on, then I have no idea where he might be."

"If you were going to look for Mr. Lundstrom, where would you start?"

"Somewhere out West."

"The West is a big chunk of territory—over half a million square miles."

"Sorry. He loved the West—the whole region."

"Can you narrow things down? Did he have a favorite haunt or two?"

"If he did, he didn't tell me about it. Over the years he has mentioned Wyoming, Idaho, Montana, Colorado, Utah, the Black Hills, Nebraska, Arizona, New Mexico, and Nevada, as well as California, Oregon, and Washington. Pretty much anywhere in the western states where there were trout to be caught on a fly rod."

To the disappointment of the agents, the polygraph and Casper came up negative. Joby hadn't colluded with Mr. Lundstrom and wasn't covering up his whereabouts. His only part in the matter had been innocently delivering the unusual message that was giving the FBI fits. While they suspected that it was related to his disappearance, there wasn't any evidence or cohesive theory linking them. The note might have been entirely unrelated—merely a reference to an anticipated fishing trip.

The agent who had been questioning Joby turned the machines off and disconnected the nervous young man. "Thank you for your cooperation, Mr. Rosenthal. There will be no further questioning at this time." He handed him a business card and said, "If you hear anything relative to the whereabouts of Mr. Lundstrom, please call this hotline number immediately and ask for Task Force Minoa."

"Yes sir," he replied. But as he walked back into his house, he felt more nervous about the FBI than he did Woody. He was skeptical that Woody was involved with something that was truly criminal. *Sure wish I knew what was going on here.*

***

That night Joby lay in bed, staring at his repurposed timber rafters and processing the events of the day. Why was Woody being pursued by the federal government? Why was a special task force involved? He mulled the agent's admonition to call the FBI hotline number and ask for Task Force Minoa if he thought of anything that might be helpful to law enforcement. It didn't add up. Woody was a man of high character, not a drug dealer or a terrorist. The only clue as to why the FBI was looking for Woody was the name of the task force—Minoa. That rang a bell. He vaguely recalled hearing about it in high school. *Maybe if I researched Minoa, it might shed some light on this.*

His curiosity got the best of him. He hopped out of bed, plopped down at his laptop on the kitchen table, and googled *Minoa*. After several false leads, he discovered that the ancient civilization known as Minoa had come to a catastrophic end late in the Bronze Age and that its demise was followed by the abysmal centuries known as the Dark Ages. While archaeologists agreed that Minoa had been entirely destroyed, theories abounded on the cause of its ruin. Some favored the explosion of the Santorini volcano, some a massive earthquake, some a massive tsunami, and some the invasion of the Sea Peoples.

He crawled back under his covers and pondered what he had just read. Did the destruction of Minoa actually shed light on the present situation? His thoughts were disrupted by the memory of listening to a broadcast of the late-night talk show, *Down the Rabbit Hole,* during a drive from El Matador State Beach back to his cabin. The host had made the absurd claim that a planet-sized comet was headed for Mars, that the impending collision posed an existential threat to Earth, that NASA denied the comet's existence, and that the government was masterminding a cover-up called Minoa, which was an allusion to the destruction of the Minoan empire. He had further insisted that the true cause of Minoa's demise, according to many ancient historians, was a massive comet making a near pass of Earth. This visitation caused a raft of calamities—volcanic eruptions, earthquakes, tsunamis, and mass migrations of pillaging, seafaring nations—all of which played a part in the downfall of the Minoan empire.

As Joby contemplated these mind-bending ideas, he was jarred by another memory, the time when Woody had helped him set the ridge and rafters for his cabin. His astronomer friend had been unusually chatty that day. While talking about his upcoming fishing trip, he had mentioned that he would be accompanied by a cousin who worked for NASA. No sooner had Woody revealed this information, than he immediately clammed up. When Joby tried to pry more from him, he had jumped up and said that it was time to get back to work. He never again spoke another word about his cousin.

The young man sat up in bed, tingling with excitement. The pieces lined up. Or they seemed to at any rate. The government used the term Minoa because Earth faced an existential catastrophe from a comet even as Minoa was once destroyed by a comet. Woody's cousin, who worked at NASA, had found out about this threat and had sent the Sundown River note to warn his cousin. And Woody vanished after he received the note. This startling solution to the puzzle turned his world upside down. *Holy cow! Woody went on the run because the fake news about the comet wasn't fake news after all.*

10

Jack stared into the mirror at his reflection. He didn't mind the gray hair. It made him look distinguished. But—he shook his head in frustration—the wrinkles under and around his eyes made him look old. *Might have to try that face cream you see on the infomercials.* He splashed his face with hot water, lathered up with shaving soap, and picked up his razor. As he was finishing his neck, his phone summoned him with a riff from *The Magnificent Seven.* He wiped the worst of the shaving creme off his neck, walked to his dresser, and picked up his phone. It was an unknown caller.

"Hello."

"Hi, Jack." The voice was familiar, but it took a few seconds to make the connection. It was Samantha, the attractive divorcee from his department who had asked him out a few times but had given up because he always asked for a raincheck. She was good-looking, but not his type—too high maintenance. He probably should have just given her a straightforward *no* but didn't want to hurt her feelings. Was she making another effort? The moment felt awkward. She continued, "Don't come in today. The FBI is waiting for you here at the office. They know that your cousin has fled, and they suspect that you tipped him off. I overheard the agents talking with Hugh when I was delivering a memo from Security to the main office." She hung up immediately. Jack's sense of awkwardness turned into mild anguish. *Poor girl. That call is going to cost her more than she could possibly imagine.*

His mind raced. He had known that getting apprehended before his planned escape was a possibility, but he had figured that the odds were low. Now he was in a tight spot. His plan to flee this coming weekend under cover of a motorcycle ride with the Coronado Cavalry was no longer feasible. He had to flee now. *Time to improvise.*

He relathered the unfinished part of his neck and picked up where he had left off, coolly determined to maintain a little normalcy in his life. As he shaved, his mind ran a hundred miles per hour. Could he have done anything a little differently and changed the outcome of this situation? Probably not.

He revisited that fateful day three and a half weeks earlier when his eyes had chanced upon an unfinished top-secret memo on Dr. Fairchild's computer while updating software. As head of IT Security, he alone possessed the necessary clearances to work on computers used for programs that were regarded as beyond-top-secret. Seeing the memo was a shocker. The head of NASA had left classified information exposed to unauthorized eyes.

When his eyes had tracked across the screen, they had fallen upon the phrases *massive comet* and *national emergency*. His curiosity had been aroused, and he had found himself torn between his duty to ignore information that he was exposed to and the temptation to read more. Temptation had won.

He had read a few lines while pretending that he was looking for the cursor. Then he had surreptitiously read a paragraph out of the corner of his eye while pretending that he was picking lint off the laser mouse. His charades were an effort to throw off security if they were watching him through the security cameras—which they likely were.

The memo was an introduction to Project Minoa for someone who had just been granted Minoa clearance. A comet called RN13 that was eighty percent of the diameter of Mars was headed for a near brush with Mars. It was likely to bump numerous asteroids out of orbit when it passed through the asteroid belt, spawning multiple extinction-level events. It was regarded by the White House, NASA, and the Pentagon as the most serious threat to mankind in the history of the world. A covert national emergency had been declared.

The revelation had left him thunderstruck—*Holy Toledo! This is a bona fide Sundown River event.* His heart had pounded as wildly as it had during firefights in his SEAL days. When about forty-five seconds had elapsed since his eyes had first alighted on the memo—far too long—he had decided it was time to skedaddle. He shook a triumphant fist as if he had fixed the mouse problem, clicked the save-and-exit button on the memo, closed the other applications, and upgraded the workstation software.

Jack caught himself staring blankly in the mirror, growled at himself for drifting off, and refocused on his Adam's apple. But the normally unflappable veteran was having a hard time concentrating. His life was going full chaos, and there was nothing he could do about it. Most likely his boss and the FBI had been aware all along that he had seen the memo and had assumed that he had followed protocol. But now that Woody had disappeared under peculiar circumstances, they appeared to have connected the dots between his exposure to classified Rogue information and Woody's disappearance. So what was he going to do? *Just need to come up with a field expedient plan—fast—execute it, and whatever happens, happens.*

He rinsed his neck with water, wiped with a towel, and checked his neck in the mirror. *Done.* He walked to his closet, grabbed clothes and shoes suitable for hiking, and got dressed. He left his cell phone on the dresser. Then he grabbed his emergency go bag, added fresh water and granola bars, and headed out the back door, grabbing his Jeep keys on the way out. He was almost an hour ahead of his normal departure time. *Hopefully, they are only staking out my Taurus on the street and not my Jeep in the garage.* He pulled out of his garage, turned left—that gave him more cover—and headed down the alley. Out of the corner of his eye, he thought he saw a black SUV parked on the street a couple houses down from his. *Hope they didn't see me sneaking out the back way.*

He turned right out of the alley, opposite the direction he would normally take to work. Today he wouldn't be heading south out of Greenbelt on the Baltimore-Washington Parkway. Instead, he was going to take Interstate 495 west and south around the Washington, D.C., metro area, then head for the Blue Ridge Mountains.

Once he was on 495, he grabbed a burner phone out of his go bag and dialed his secretary. "Hi, Margaret. I won't be in this morning. I'm gonna take a hike in the woods, get some fresh air, and unwind. I'll be in after lunch."

"Okay, Jack. Gotcha covered. Did you change your number?"

"Yeah. Got tired of all the robocalls."

"Might have to try that myself. Okay, got your new number down. Drive safe."

After he hung up, Jack pulled the battery and the SIM card out of the phone and dropped them in the ashtray. *Call number one is done.* He knew his cover story wouldn't raise any suspicions with Margaret as he often took a morning off to enjoy a getaway in nature. He only hoped the call would buy him enough time to make his getaway. Once the FBI discovered that he wasn't coming in for work, they would start looking for his Jeep.

He reached into his bag for another burner, then called his friend Thomas "Buzz" Mason, the vice president of the Coronado Cavalry, a bike club in Manassas, Virginia. The club was composed of local tradesmen and businessmen who shared a distaste for Big Brother government, hence the picture of Edward Snowden that hung in their clubhouse, an old service station they had purchased and remodeled.

"Buzz here. Who's calling?"

"Shogun."

"Hey, Jack. What's up with the new number?"

"Serious trouble brewing. Big Brother is on my tail over the big rock."

Buzz teased him. "So the big rock story on the internet was true after all?"

"Sorry I doubted you. But we both know that ninety-eight percent of those stories are fables. How do you know which ones to trust?"

"Got me there."

"Listen. I need an exit strategy—fast. I'm in my Jeep, but I don't know how long I have before they'll be looking for it."

"Understood. For now, meet me at your storage shed at Zeke's place in the country. You can park your Jeep inside. I'll call you back in ten or fifteen minutes with the rest of the plan."

"Roger." He liked Buzz's way of thinking. The feds probably had no idea that Jack had a secret storage unit at the home of one of his biker friends outside of Manassas. *It'll be a long time before they find my Jeep.*

Twelve minutes later, Buzz called back. "Here's the plan. We'll meet at your storage unit, and I'll drive you to the Weddelwood Trailhead in Shenandoah National Park. From there you'll hike the Overall Run trail down to Overall Road. Somewhere between a half-dozen and a dozen bikers from the Freedom Riders club in Middleton, Virginia will meet up with you. They have a bike for you—a 2012 Road King, riding clothes if you need them, and a wig with shoulder-length black hair in a man-pony. They'll escort you to a trusted bike club in Lexington where you can hole up until the next stage of your journey. The plan is for you to travel with the Lexington club to the Sturgis rally in August."

"Sounds like a workable plan to me. Thanks."

"You're welcome, Jack. Good luck."

Jack opened up his phone, removed the SIM, flexed it back and forth until the connector started to break off, rolled his window down, and flicked the SIM out the window. It sailed into the ditch. If he got stopped, he didn't want Buzz or any of his biker associates to be implicated. Then he tucked the unusable phone into the glove box.

Twenty-five minutes later, he took the US 66 exit at Dunn Loring. As he sped up the ramp, he noticed that the dark-green Taurus which had been following him for the past five minutes also took the ramp. Worse, it stayed on his tail as he headed west. *Am I being tailed?* He decided to take an alternate route and see if the vehicle followed him. He swerved onto the Nutley Street SW exit and headed south to catch US 29. When he turned west on US 29, the Taurus was right behind him. Now he was extremely uneasy. *Only one way to know for sure.* He turned off his route, drove several blocks, and pulled into the Big Kahuna Coffee Shack.

The Taurus again followed him and parked on the edge of the lot. While Jack waited for his flat white—he didn't like milk froth with his espresso—he flipped his rearview mirror to watch the car that had been following him. It was a dark-green Ford Police Interceptor with federal plates. Nobody got out. That wasn't a good sign. The barista handed him his drink, and he pulled back out on the road. To his frustration, the Taurus followed. That was definitely a bad sign.

A few miles down the road, he noticed that there was no oncoming traffic. That was strange because the traffic in front of him was fairly heavy. He checked his rearview mirror. Police cars were halting the traffic far behind him. Two more cruisers were right on his tail. He noticed that White Post Road was blockaded. So were Cedar Spring Road and Pleasant Valley Road. *Looking uglier every minute.* A quarter mile up the road, an SUV roared out of a parking lot in front of him followed by two squad cars which slowed him down, trying to separate him from the traffic in front of him. He heard squealing tires behind him and checked his mirror. Two more cruisers and another SUV were behind him. Jack sighed. He was completely surrounded. *Looks like the game is up.*

The motorcade slowed to a crawl and turned south on Virginia 234. He followed—he didn't have a choice. It seemed surreal to see no traffic on the road but himself and federal law enforcement. They turned into the Henry Hill Visitor Center at Manassas National Battlefield Park—no tourists or employees were in sight—and guided him to the center of the parking lot. An officer pointed to where they wanted him to stop. He shut off his Jeep and placed his hands on his steering wheel. Six agents approached with guns drawn. *Looks like I'm going to be doing some prison ministry.*

11

dig site near Jensen, Utah
Wednesday, Jun 26, 2019

Kit chuckled ironically to herself as she swept away the loosened sandstone from the mastodon tusk that she and Sam were carefully exposing. *Why do things always go odd-duck crazy for me?* Their dig site was primarily a duckbill site. Yet she and Sam had uncovered a mastodon in a layer that was supposedly Cretaceous. Worse, last summer they had excavated a tyrannosaur eighteen inches above the mastodon. How was she going to report the anomalous discovery? She was already in hot water for publishing her findings of non-fossilized tyrannosaur bone fragments, many with well-preserved red blood cells. That had resulted in stern lectures from her dig sponsors, who threatened to pull her sponsorship and blacklist her from publishing opportunities if she didn't desist.

Kit, her birth name was Katrina Lundstrom, had earned a double master's degree in geology and paleontology from the University of California, Berkeley. Immediately upon graduation, she had been offered a position on this Utah dig, which was sponsored by her alma mater and the Smithsonian Institute. Now she was frustrated with the system that had given her an education and a career. *Guess I'm just a chip off the old block.* Her father, Woodrow "Woody" Lundstrom, was a jaded astronomer who had been blacklisted by a peer review system that ignored or trampled evidence that was contradictory to relativity theory. Now she herself was losing her enthusiasm because of a peer review system that ruthlessly defended the standard model of prehistoric history and refused to let discoveries take science where they would.

Her dark musings were interrupted by a booming voice speaking to her. "Excuse me, I'm looking for a Miss Katrina Lundstrom."

"That'll be me," she said, standing up and extending her hand. The man made no effort to shake her hand or in any way acknowledge her formality. Instead, he flashed his badge, identified himself as "Agent Kirkwater with the FBI," and informed her of his purpose. "We have a few questions that we would like to ask you. Follow me."

Cold and rude, she thought as he turned away. But she was more concerned about the purpose of his visit than his manner. *I wonder what in the world they want to question me about?* She doubted it was her love for "unscientific" books on young-Earth creationism and anomalous discoveries in archaeology and paleontology. And it likely wasn't her disapproval of the direction America had taken, which she had voiced on social media. America wasn't a full-blown police state yet. But totalitarianism was definitely a growing problem. *Sure wish we still had the freedom that Daddy enjoyed when he was growing up in the sixties and seventies.*

They marched her to a large van and beckoned her inside. A hard-bitten woman pointed to a chair, and Kit slumped down, trembling. Her anxiety turned into fear when they placed the Casper cap on her head and she felt dozens of probes poking into her head. Fighting back tears, she mustered her courage and challenged the agent prepping her. "Is this legal? Where are my constitutional rights? What is this all about?"

The agent replied, "The Homeland Security Act authorizes federal law enforcement to detain, search, and question any citizen who might have information pertinent to any case involving national security."

The lump in Kit's throat tightened, a mix of indignation and panic. She wasn't ignorant of the Security Act but wondered what this had to do with her.

A male agent set up a chair facing her and asked, "Where is your father, Woodrow Lundstrom, right now?"

Her heart skipped a beat, and she began to worry. "In California as far as I know, working at Caltech."

"Have you heard from him in the past two weeks?"

"No. I haven't."

"Did he say anything in recent months that would suggest that he was involved in illegal activity or associations?"

"No. Absolutely not. Not ever." *What are they driving at?*

"If he was going to flee, where would he flee to?"

"I have no idea. Probably somewhere out West. *Rest assured, if I knew for sure, I wouldn't tell you.*

"What was his attraction to the West?"

"Mountains, pine trees, and trout."

"Did he have a redoubt somewhere out West?"

"A redoubt?"

"A redoubt is a hideout where you flee to when society collapses or you are running from the law. Many preppers have them."

"If he had a redoubt, he never told me about it. And to be honest, I don't think my dad is a prepper. He isn't prepared for retirement—his 401K is pathetic—much less the end of the world. He did carry a readiness bag in his car for disasters like earthquakes, forest fires, and terrorist attacks, but the California government recommends that."

The agent questioned Kit for two hours about her father, asking about his habits, his hobbies, his friends, his travels, his topics of conversation, and the books he read. She was able to piece together from the questions that her dad was regarded as a fugitive, that he had fled California the previous weekend, and that he was wanted for activities that ran afoul of the Homeland Security Act—in short, they regarded him as a traitor. That seemed unlike her father who was a military veteran, a patriot, and a supporter of groups like the NRA, the Rocky Mountain Elk Foundation, and Trout Unlimited. Surely, this was all a mistake.

"We have no more questions at this time," the interrogator said, "regarding your father." Kit relaxed. *We're done finally.* She reached to undo the blood pressure cuff. The woman brushed her hand away. "We aren't finished yet." A different agent took the chair in front of her. She sighed.

"What do you know about Jack Lundstrom's political leanings?"

Their interest in her father's cousin surprised her. "Not much. He tended toward the conservative side of the spectrum."

"Were you aware or did you suspect that he was involved in illegal activity that was detrimental to the security of the United States?"

"No. And, to be honest, I have a difficult time believing that he would intentionally undermine the security of this country—a country that he took a bullet for."

"Do you have any idea what kind of issues or grievances he may have had that may have led to his becoming a suicide bomber?"

She gasped. Tears welled up in her eyes. The news—or rather the insinuation—was a shock to her system. He continued to question her for another half hour. By the time he was done, and she was allowed to go, she was emotionally exhausted.

She retreated to the camper trailer she shared with Sam and had a good cry. Then she made a pot of coffee and sat at the table, numb, trying to make sense of things that didn't make sense. Her father and Jack weren't criminals or traitors. If they had run afoul of the government, it was for a good cause. She was certain of that. Besides, Jack wouldn't have killed himself, much less engaged in a suicide bombing. So what was the real story? Why was her father on the run? Why was Jack being framed? Something Snowden-esque? Likely not. Whatever it was, the government was pursuing an astronomer and an employee of NASA. A secret military project? An NEO that poses a serious threat to Earth? SETI? *Smells like a conspiracy brewing.*

12

The train stopped in Wendover, WY and backed into a siding. While the train was jockeying around, unhooking and hooking cars, a pony-tailed hobo poked his head in the porthole, grinned, and climbed inside. The newcomer sported a bow tie and dress suspenders, a dress shirt that needed a wash, grimy dress pants and jacket, and black oxfords.

Lobo gave him a casual nod. "Librarian."

The quirky fellow quipped back, "Nice to see you again, Lobo," and took a seat between Woody and the cowboy.

The newcomer opened his knapsack and retrieved a carton of chocolate milk and a bag containing newspapers and paperbacks. He set the bag down, opened the carton, and took a long drink. Then he leaned his head back against the wall and sighed as if he alone were bearing the weight of the world.

Woody turned to his new neighbor. "Are you called 'Librarian' because you carry books?"

Lobo chuckled. "No. He was nicknamed after the hero

in the *Librarian*, the made-for-TV movie series about a booklover who is the only person that can save the world from the conspiracies which threaten it."

Librarian retorted, "Nobody believes me. But behind the scenes, the nefarious shadow leaders are foisting their conspiracies upon the unsuspecting public as they advance their cause of world domination. And the people have nobody to blame but themselves. If they would quit wasting their time on mindless games, television, and social media, and start reading serious books, they wouldn't be deceived, and they wouldn't be following the pied pipers."

Lobo quipped back, "I'm not denying the dangers of shallowness. People waste a lot of time on things without real value. But as far as the masses are concerned, you can't fix stupid. It's not an information issue but a prejudice issue. People believe what they want to believe. They want to follow pied pipers who tickle their ears."

Librarian was unfazed. "We have to stop the shadow government. We have to stop the pied pipers."

Lobo parried back, "Shadowy global-domination organizations and pied pipers aren't the problem. Individuals are. 'All we like sheep have gone astray, each to his own way.' Men don't need conspiracies to go astray. They go astray just fine without them. The only way to fix the problem is to fix individuals, one at a time." But Lobo didn't want this to degenerate into another hours-long debate with Librarian over conspiracies, so before the wandering windbag could respond, he changed the subject. "Where are you coming from, and where are you headed?"

"I spent the last few weeks in Omaha, Nebraska working through a temp agency. I'm headed for Wisconsin for the next few months. Then I'll head south for the winter. I'm thinking Mobile, Alabama. Maybe find some work at the docks or on a boat."

Woody expected Librarian to reciprocate and ask Lobo where he was headed. But, as the cowboy had guessed, the conspiracy panderer wasn't interested in socializing. There was critical information to assimilate and a world to save. He pulled out the *Wall Street Journal*, snapped it open to the World News section, and began reading an article entitled "Russia Massing Troops on the Belarus Border."

Woody looked over his shoulder and muttered, "World War III is starting to look like a certainty."

"It's all an Illuminati plot," Librarian snorted. "The real power brokers behind both America and Russia are pushing this nonsense so they can sell arms and weapons systems to both nations and make a fortune. China is in the mix too."

Librarian hated it when people read over his shoulder, so he, slightly peeved, offered Woody his other newspaper, the Wednesday edition of the *Casper Star-Tribune*. Woody graciously accepted it, masking the fact that he himself was peeved. The inconsiderate hobo had invaded their enclave, planted his butt between the two traveling companions, and then implied he would like silence in his study so he could concentrate on his super-hero task.

Woody unfolded the paper and stared in shock at the top headline, "NASA Security Official in Suicide Bombing," and the two accompanying photographs. *No, God! Please, no!*

The first photo showed a man sitting in a Jeep that was surrounded by law enforcement vehicles. He was holding something in his right hand and gesticulating with his left. While the license plate was obscured, Woody recognized the vehicle as Jack's by the stickers in the back window—a soldier kneeling at the cross on the bottom right corner and the Navy SEALs Trident on the bottom left.

The second photo showed a mangled Jeep that was surrounded by damaged vehicles, the scene cordoned off with yellow police tape. Fighting the lump in his throat and the tears that begged to flow, he stumbled his way through the article. It stated that a high-ranking official with NASA employed in the security division, whose identity wasn't being released until relatives were notified, was facing charges regarding classified information and had attempted to flee. When he was cornered in a park near Manassas, Virginia, he had detonated a suicide bomb rather than surrender, killing himself and two federal agents. Woody couldn't read any further. He was numb.

Lobo noticed that Woody was upset. He sat down beside him, glanced at the story, and probed. "Somebody you know?"

"My cousin," Woody groaned. He was too heavyhearted to say more. The lump in his throat felt like it was going to explode.

Lobo pulled out his iPhone, logged in to his Iridium account, and googled "NASA+ bombing." He selected a newscast clip from CVN. Judging by the file size and the download speed, he estimated that it would take about fifteen minutes to download the file. "Good thing my satellite service only costs a dollar per minute," he joked, trying to lighten the moment. But Woody could only nod.

When the download finished, Lobo handed his phone to Woody. The video showed footage, apparently shot from a helicopter, of Jack's Jeep racing down a country road, fleeing law enforcement. The commentator announced, "Authorities have prepared a trap, blocking off roads at every intersection and forcing him down roads that lead to a safe place where they can apprehend him with the least threat to the public."

Eventually, the car was forced down the access road to Henry Hill Visitor Center in Manassas National Battlefield Park. When it raced into the visitor center parking lot, it was forced to brake and skid to a stop. The only road out was blocked and vehicles ringed the entire area. There was no escape. The pursuing vehicles forced the car up against a parking barricade, and it was immediately surrounded by officers and agents with guns drawn. The film switched to a camera on the ground. As the officers and agents moved in slowly, a loudspeaker blared, "Hands up. Keep your hands up. Do not move or we will shoot."

The man in the car, shouting and gesticulating, bent over slightly and reached for something. The camera panned sideways to show a team of agents responding with a blaze of gunfire. An explosion rocked the camera. It panned back to reveal a burning chassis and mangled pieces of the vehicle skewed in various directions. Then it zoomed out to show that the surrounding vehicles had also been destroyed. The clip then cut to an interview with the FBI official who had been tasked with catching the fugitive.

But something was wrong. Parts of the account didn't sit right. There was no way under the sun that Jack had detonated a suicide bomb. Plus, the driver was shorter than Jack. Moreover, everything seemed choreographed. And how did the news team get on site quick enough to film the blockade, the gunfire, and the explosion—from a high-mount vehicle no less? The camera had peered down into Jack's Jeep over the top of an SUV. *I'm gonna get to the bottom of this.*

Lobo tried to encourage him, but he shook his head and mumbled, "Sorry, I just need some time to work through this." He leaned his head back against the headwall and closed his eyes, pain gripping his morose soul like a vise. Was Jack dead or alive? He didn't trust the news that he was dead. He was likely still alive. But where? Was he headed for a FEMA camp? Was he okay? He felt like crying, but the tears dried up before they started. *Got to stop this pity party. Can't think clearly when you're nursing your pain like it was a baby on the breast.*

The train lurched again, only this time it began to accelerate. They were finally leaving the yard. Once they were out of town, Woody dug out his stove and coffee pot, crawled out on the porch, and brewed himself a cup of mocha. As he sipped the piping hot drink, he recalled his friendship with Jack over the years.

Their first deep discussion occurred more than thirty-five years earlier at a family reunion while they were yet in high school—he a sophomore and Jack a senior. Jack had observed that he liked to slip away to a quiet place like the hayloft and read. Being a bookworm himself, his older cousin had followed him to the barn and tried to strike up a conversation with him. At first, he had been perturbed with the unwanted presence. But he had warmed up when Jack informed him that the book he was reading, *Lucifer's Hammer*, was one of his favorite apocalyptic books. Soon they were deep in conversation about the end of the world, potential apocalyptic scenarios, and other books they had read. *Alas Babylon* was another mutual favorite. They had talked until the wee hours of the morning, forging a friendship closer than the bonds of blood.

Over the following decades, they had enjoyed many conversations about natural disasters and TEOTWAWKI, the end of the world as we know it. Jack generally steered these talks towards biblical prophecy. He was particularly fascinated with the book of Revelation and its devastations from heaven—mountain-size asteroids, hundred-pound steinhagel, water-fouling poison, and forest-consuming fire. He interpreted the horrors of the biblical apocalypse literally and believed that they were right around the corner.

Woody had enjoyed their conversations, but he hadn't really been a believer himself. It didn't seem likely to him that the apocalypse might come in their lifetime. He hadn't even been greatly concerned about comets or asteroids slamming into Earth. He had been more worried about scenarios that seemed much more probable: World War Three starting in the Middle East, a worldwide epidemic, a massive EMP from the sun that crippled the world's infrastructure, or a 9.5 earthquake leveling California.

But he had been wrong, and Jack had been right. Once again, he was eating humble pie. Now a massive comet was threatening Earth, he was on the run, Jack was captured or dead, and he had no idea where Ariele was or how Sally was doing. He found himself looking at prophecy with renewed interest. If potentially world-ending signs were appearing in the heavens, then perhaps the Bible was right after all. Maybe Jack was right that Russia's expansionism would lead to the Russian invasion of Israel in Ezekiel 38 and 39. And maybe he was right that the breakdown of the Judaeo-Christian ethic in society was part of the prophesied apostasy in the last days. At any rate, he figured that it was time to give Bible prophecy a serious look.

13

Andrius and Ariele stopped at the Grizzly Bar and Grill in Roscoe, Montana, famished and road weary. While Andrius went inside to order burgers and fries, Ariele called Red to give him a heads up.

A husky voice answered, "Grubstake."

"Hi, this is …"

"Ariele."

"How did you know?"

"Woody called me a few weeks back and told me to expect you sooner or later."

"But how did you know that it was me and not some other woman?"

"Wasn't magic, hon'. Less than a dozen folks have this number, and you're the only female in the bunch." He paused, then continued, "I assume you're coming from California."

"We are."

"How can we recognize you?

"A 1972 Toyota Hilux van, faded blue and rusty, with

California plates." She turned the conversation to more important matters. "So how much did Woody tell you about the comet?"

"Not much. He said that a planet-sized comet was headed for Mars, that it will disturb a number of asteroids when it passes through the asteroid belt, that some of those asteroids will pose a serious threat to Earth, and that the government is covering the whole thing up. He also told me that you would be bringing a laptop full of technical information so we can get a better handle on the threat."

"That's pretty much the situation in a nutshell. I'll fill you in on the details after we get there. I figure we're maybe six hours away. Right now we're in Roscoe. We plan on taking back roads from here."

"Good call. So what route are you taking?"

"Let me pull out the map," Ariele replied. "I don't remember all the towns. Let's see," she said, tracing her finger on the route Andrius had marked. "We'll head up to Repelje, then over to Sourdough, then north and west on back roads to Melville, and then over to the Compound."

"That'll work just fine. When you get to Melville, call me back for directions."

"Okay."

"And make sure you drive the last two hours under cover of night. We don't want anyone to see a van with California license plates anywhere near Two Dot, much less near the Compound."

"No problem. We can handle that."

"Say, you keep saying *we*. Is there somebody with you?"

"Yes. His name's Andrius."

"Can we trust him?"

"I think so. I trust him. He risked and sacrificed a lot to bring me to Montana."

Red didn't reply. As the seconds ticked, Ariele's stomach started twisting into knots. On the brink of panic, she offered information she hoped might allay his fears. "He's a friend of Irina, the gal who discovered the comet. He talks about Bible prophecy all the time."

The awkward silence continued for a few more seconds, then Red replied hesitantly. "We weren't expecting two. Hopefully … he'll, uh … fit in here and not cause any problems."

Indignation rose in Ariele's breast in defense of her friend, but she held her tongue. Now Red grew uncomfortable with the silence, so he changed the subject. "How is Woody doing? Is he on his way too?"

"I suspect he is unless he's been captured. The last time we talked, he said he was in danger too and would have to flee. But I suspect that my disappearance made his flight a lot more difficult to pull off."

"That's—"

Ariele cut him off. "Hey. Gotta run. Andrius is returning with our dinner. I'll tell you the whole story when we get there."

"Looking forward to that. Just make sure you get here safely. And don't forget to stop in Melville and call for directions. The roads in this neck of the woods are confusing. If you try to figure it out on your own, you'll definitely get lost. We have to replace the mailman two or three times a year. Some of them have never been found."

"What?"

"Just pulling your leg. But seriously, call for directions. The roads are a maze. Many have no name. And some of the named roads are actually a network of related roads."

"Okay. I'll give you a call when we get to Melville."

***

Some six hours later, shortly after midnight, Andrius parked his van on a wide gravel shoulder on the edge of sleepy Melville, a few homes in the middle of nowhere, and Ariele called Red. He gave her detailed directions, with all of the distances in tenths of a mile. When he was finished, he enquired, "You got all that?"

"I think so."

"Read it off to me."

She rattled off the landmarks, turns, and distances.

"Good job. You got every step. Just watch carefully for the gate. It's a typical metal ranch gate—red and rusty—on a barbed wire fence. Count the miles on the odometer from where you turn off of Melville Road onto Rein Road. When you get to the gate, give me a call. It'll take me a few minutes to drive down from the house."

***

At 1:24 a.m. Ariele picked up the phone, stifled a yawn, and dialed Red. A few minutes later, headlights appeared, bouncing across the prairie toward them. Near the gate, the lights swerved away from them onto an unkempt turnaround of trampled grass and sagebrush, then came back around toward them just on the other side of the fence. A pickup rolled in front of their headlights, turned up the road away from them, and stopped.

A tall man in cowboy boots and hat hopped out of the truck and strode toward the gate. After fiddling with the lock, he walked it open and waved them through. Once the cowboy was back in his rig, Andrius followed its bobbing tail lights up the rocky road.

Shortly after they reached the treelined, they passed a large house on the right, and the taillights in front of them disappeared around a corner to the left. Seconds later, the young man yelped with fear when a gate appeared in front of them, swinging back shut, and there was no way to avoid it. He threw up his arms and covered his head. The van pushed through the barrier without harm

Ariele teased him, "What's the matter, nerd boy, never seen a bump gate before?"

He shrugged his shoulders and stared straight ahead, rattled by a wave of shame that was burning so hot he could barely concentrate. Nothing unnerved him more than a bruised ego.

A quarter mile later, Red stopped in front of a large log-cabin-style lodge, and Andrius parked his van next to Red's truck. The exhausted Californians climbed out and were greeted by the lanky cowboy. "Welcome to the Compound," he said taking Andrius' hand and pumping it vigorously. I'm Red if you haven't figured it out yet. You two grab what you need for the night, and I'll show you to your rooms." Then he turned to a younger cowboy. "Park the van in the machine shed, Blake. We'll unload it tomorrow." The cowboy jutted his chin and climbed into the van. When Red noticed Andrius looking confused, he explained. "Sooner or later, the feds will be on the lookout for California plates in the West. We don't want your hippie van sitting out in the open where satellites and drones can find it."

The young man nodded in approval. But inside he was kicking himself for not thinking of something so obvious himself.

Ariele squealed with delight when they stepped inside the front door, and she spied the great room. "Ohhh ... wow! I love the rustic decor and the split-stone fireplace!"

"Me too," Red replied, grinning at her reaction. "Make yourselves at home. You'll be the only ones here for the time being. Blake has an apartment over the barn, where he can keep his eye on the horses." He pointed down the hallway. "There's six bedrooms down there. The first room on the right belongs to Woody and Jack. You're free to pick any of the other five you please. The bathrooms are at the end of the hall—girls on the left and guys on the right. Feel free to help yourself to anything in the kitchen. The cupboards, fridge, and freezer are well stocked."

The country gentleman slipped his hat back on his head and tipped it. The tight grey curls on his temples made him look distinguished. "Much as I would love to be brought up to speed on the Rogue and the cover-up, that will have to wait until tomorrow. I need to hit the rack. See you two in the morning."

14

the Compound
Friday morning, June 28, 2019

The next morning, Ariele was awakened by a phone ringing, an unusual ring that sounded like the phones in old movies. She ignored it, hoping it would stop. It didn't. She boiled out of bed, ran over to Andrius' room, and hammered on the door. "C'mon, dude! Answer the phone! You're the one that told me that my voice can't be heard on the phone."

Andrius staggered out of his room in cotton sweatpants and a Linux sweatshirt, his hair sticking up like Beaker from the Muppets, and stumbled over to the phone, a seventies-era wall mount with an extra long cord. Ariele giggled. It always took him fifteen minutes or longer to wake up. And few things were funnier than a groggy nerd. He picked up the receiver and mumbled, "Hullo."

"Good morning. This is Betsy, Red's wife. I'm bringing over fresh blueberry muffins for you guys to enjoy with your breakfast."

"Oh, okay. Thanks."

"By the way, who am I talking to? Red said he didn't

remember the young man's name."

"Um … uh …"

Betsy's loud Jersey voice could be distinctly heard, "Don't worry about security, son. The phone lines aren't connected to the outside world. We have our own phone system here that connects the entire Compound with rotary phones from the sixties and seventies. Just pick up the phone and dial a single digit. One is our house. Two is the lodge. Three is the barn. Four is Blake's apartment. Five is the cabin on the hilltop. Six is the phone at the covered patio. Seven is the shop. Jordy and Beth will get eight when their house is done. Their boys have nine and zero set up for them, assuming they actually move here. We can combine symbols with numbers if we need to add more."

Andrius replied animatedly, "Cool. Sometimes old tech is better. My name is Andrius, Andrius Markunas. I'd love to take a look at the comm center and the old-school switches. I have an idea that might clear up the static on the line—most of it anyway." Ariele was surprised to see Andrius grinning and speaking with a clarity that he usually didn't have until he had been up for half an hour.

"Red would be tickled to death if you could do that. Well, you two get yourself decent. We'll be over in a few minutes."

Ten minutes later, they were startled by a loud rap. The front door flung open, and Betsy walked in with Red in tow. The attractive woman, dressed pretty chic for the wife of a cowboy, was carrying a tray of fresh muffins. She flashed a radiant smile at Ariele, set the tray on the table, and retrieved a cast iron fry pan from a lower cupboard. "I'm going to start some bacon and eggs," she hollered over her shoulder to Ariele who was searching the cupboards. "Plates and glasses are in the cupboard to the left of the sink, Hon', and silverware is in the drawer underneath."

Ariele glanced over at Andrius, who was standing awkwardly by himself instead of visiting with Red. *C'mon bro. It can't be that hard to start a conversation that doesn't involve differential calculus or voltage equations.* Annoyed, she struck up a conversation with him herself. "So how big is your property, Red?"

"Our spread is a little over two sections. Half is prime ranchland. The other half is forest, mountains, and hilly sagebrush scrubland."

"A section?"

"A section is a square mile of land."

"So you own two square miles of land?"

"Yep. Plenty of room to relax and roam. And we don't have to worry about neighbors or development. We have National Forest bordering on two sides, BLM land on one side, and a friendly neighbor on the south side who will never sell or subdivide."

"When did you buy the ranch?"

"In the spring of 1998 when land was still relatively inexpensive in this part of Montana."

"Did you move here right away?"

"No. First, we had a contractor from Big Timber build our home. The following year he built the barn. We moved here in the spring of 2000, right after the crash. After we moved, I continued to operate my business here in rural Montana."

"How did you get interested in cowboy stuff and ranches? Did you grow up on a ranch?"

"Almost. I grew up in Fort Stockton, Texas, in oil and ranch country, and used to spend my summers on my uncle's cattle ranch. There I learned to ride horses, fix stuff, build stuff, hunt, and fish. I also got a taste for country music. Really love Charlie Pride and Johnny Cash."

"What did your dad do?"

"He managed oil rigs for one of the big outfits."

"And what do you do for a business?"

"I'm a trader—mostly in mining stocks, petroleum stocks, and commodities. I retired in 2014 after thirty years in the business, but I still keep a few positions on."

"How did you get into that line of business?"

"I worked on oil rigs for two years after high school to save up enough to go to college, and fell in love with the petroleum industry. In school I majored in geology, petroleum, and business. One of my professors inspired me with a vision for the wealth that could be made in petroleum and mining, a wealth that could bring freedom. After graduation, I moved to New York City and took a position with Lehman Brothers where I worked with a fund that focused on mining and oil. Eventually, I started my own hedge fund. My partner bought me out when I retired."

"So why did you choose Montana?"

"I wanted to move somewhere away from big cities, high crime rates, and over-reaching government—a place where I could enjoy a simpler lifestyle. But more than that, I wanted to move somewhere where I could prepare for the world-ending scenarios that threaten mankind. When we first moved here, Montana was regarded as one of the last redoubt states, and most experts had it on their shortlist for the best states to prepare for TEOTWAWKI. But in the past few years, the Big Sky state, like other freedom-loving states, has largely caved in to the federal government on agendas that have stripped Americans of their freedom: homeschooling restrictions, firearms regulations, and the recent ban on many forms of alternative medicine."

"What happened to the folks who fled here for freedom?"

"Most of them are still here. There wasn't any place to go that offered more freedom unless you were willing to move to places like Peru or Argentina."

Ariele ventured a hint that she wasn't a right-winger. "My father used to fear that the preppers and patriots were gearing up for a civil war."

Red shook his head. "That perspective was largely fostered by the media. The truth is, real belligerents never comprised more than a tiny minority of those folks. The majority were average men and women who, despite their strong belief in the Constitution, in freedom, and in the Second Amendment, never had any designs or desires to shed American blood, not even the blood of radical-left nutcases. For them, freedom meant that such nutcases were free to disseminate their left-wing nonsense, so long as they didn't ban them from being right-wing and pro-God.

"Furthermore, most of the talk about civil war, secession, and a new revolution among the right is pure bravado.

Nobody in their right mind actually believes that a handful of men armed with AR-15s—most of them in their forties or fifties and out of shape—are a match for a company-size deployment of SWAT officers and soldiers backed up with armored vehicles, 50-caliber machine guns, M240s, infrared, drones, and even Spectre gunships."

Ariele smiled and nodded. "Reminds me of something my grandpa used to say. 'A living dog is better than a dead lion.' I think it's from the Bible."

Red grinned. "It is in the Bible. Ecclesiastes 9:4. It's one of my favorite verses. Don't take unnecessary risks."

***

After breakfast Red and Betsy gave the newcomers a tour of the Compound. Ariele whooped when they walked into the east kitchen, accessed through the pantry. "A real cookstove! And it's a Heartland! That's been at the top of my wish list for a long time."

"I love them too!" Betsy exclaimed. "You don't have to worry about power outages. And they're really handy during the winter. You always have hot water and soft butter, and the honey flows nicely."

"Wow! You're even set up for canning and butchering!"

Red laughed. "Yep. We're ready to be self-sufficient no matter what kind of doo-doo hits the fan."

When they walked into the conference room and library in the east wing, Andrius darted over to the shelves like a kid in a candy store, nodding his head with delight at the extensive selection of prepper, back-to-the-land, and

Christian titles—with a large section on Bible prophecy. When he noticed that there was a lot of empty shelf space, he was ecstatic. "Hey Spunky! Check it out. There's enough room here for all my books."

Red looked at him with raised eyebrows.

Ariele piped up, rolling her eyes. "Sir Android owns shelves upon shelves of books on nerdy subjects like math, soldering, welding, electronics, computer programming, and computer hardware. He just needs to get them out of storage somehow."

Red looked at Andrius, and the young man sheepishly confessed, "I shipped my books and magazines by freight truck to a storage unit in Casper, Wyoming, and paid a premium for the owner to load them into the shed for me. I also shipped a lot of my tools and a dozen pails of spare parts that I couldn't bear to leave behind. I just need to get down there somehow, someday, and pick them up."

Red gave him a sympathetic nod. "We'll just have to arrange a trip, then, because we'll be doing a lot of soldering and welding when we get further along in the telescope project. And while a couple of us know how to weld, none of us can do a professional job."

Andrius shot Ariele a smug look. She responded by slugging him in the shoulder. They were starting to interact with each other like brother and sister.

They followed Red down a wide stairwell between the kitchen and the great room which led to a spacious basement with plain block walls. Ariele stared in amazement at the massive Russian fireplace, constructed with beautiful red granite, that dominated the center of the basement. "Easily heats the whole building even when it's thirty degrees below zero," Red informed them.

They continued to the woman cave, where Andrius fidgeted like a redneck in a ballet class. But his pain was Ariele's glory. She loved the spacious pantry, the laundry room, and the sewing room. The latter even had a treadle machine.

The geek was impressed, however, when Red showed them the computer and communication center. Several computers were set up on a long bench and one wall was piled high with boxes of unopened equipment. "We have everything we need for a worldwide outreach on the internet. I picked most of it up over the past six months." He looked pleadingly at Andrius. "We could use some help with this project. My original plan was for Jack to set everything up. But—at least for the time being—he's out of the picture."

Andrius gave him a little side eye and said, "How do you plan on masking the traffic flow? To the best of my knowledge, you can't hide the kind of traffic you seek. It would draw the attention of the NSA."

"Yeah. I thought about that. My plan is to upload our material in small uploads, using Tor to hide its path, to a server in a country beyond the easy reach of the U.S. government—like Russia maybe."

"That should work. What's the focus of your outreach?"

"A little prepping, a lot of Bible prophecy, and updates on the comet."

"Nice. Who's Jack?"

"Woody's cousin," Red replied. "We expected him to arrive around the same time as Woody, but his arrival has been delayed."

Ariele noticed a hint of heaviness in his voice, so she didn't pursue the matter.

Neither of the newbies was impressed with the man cave on the other end of the basement. It was a room set up for outdoorsy things like reloading and fly tying. Andrius complained, "What's that horrid smell?" Ariele wrinkled up her nose in agreement. But the odor hanging in the air was perfume to Red. "Love the smell of Hoppe's gun oil. It's better than perfume. Reminds me of elk hunting."

On their way back through the kitchen, everyone grabbed another blueberry muffin. Then they headed outside where Red beckoned them to climb aboard his UTV. Neither Andrius nor Ariele had ridden in a utility vehicle before. Red gunned it when he started, eliciting a squeal of delight from Ariele and a panic-stricken reach for a grab handle by Andrius. When his terror had subsided, the crestfallen geek realized that he had dropped his muffin on the floor. Ariele smiled and handed him hers.

Red drove around to the back side of the lodge and showed them the woodshed. It featured a long overhang on the front to keep the weather out and two distinct bays: one for twelve cords of wood, and one for the chainsaws, bowsaws, mauls, and a log splitter. Several pots of flowers hung in front—petunias and geraniums. Red chuckled. "Betsy loves to come out here and split kindling. She says that gives her the right to add her own feminine touches."

Ariele smiled. *What an interesting woman. A cross between me and Irina. Classy gal with a Mother Earth News streak.*

Red showed them the rest of the Compound: the reserve wood sheds, his charming Tudor-style home with outbuildings and garden, the cozy guest cottage, Jordy and Beth's building site, the barn and pasture, the machine shed, the garden, the beehives, the orchard, and the berry patch down the road beyond the barn.

While they were heading down the road past the barn, Red noticed Ariele's interest in the horses that were prancing and trotting in the field. He probed, "Do you like horses?"

"I do," she replied, "but I've never ridden one." She continued watching for a moment, then asked, "What kind are they?"

"The small ones are mustangs—Blake loves them. The rest are draft-horse mixes, mostly Percheron. They can carry or pull heavy loads. In the winter we use them for sleigh rides."

At the far end of the horse pasture, the road turned left and headed up into the Crazy Mountains. As she soaked in the beauty of the country, Ariele marveled. *God's ways sure are amazing. He ripped my dream out of my hands, took everything from me, then brought me to a paradise like this. I need to learn to trust Him more.*

After winding up the ridge for a half mile, the road ended at a log cabin on a knoll. Ariele stared wide-eyed at the structure with its stone foundation, rough cedar shakes, and split stone chimney. "Insanely gorgeous house!" she exclaimed. "Whose is it? And what's with the huge garage, the gigantic driveway, and all the posts?"

Red smiled. "That's Blake's place. He built it himself. The garage is his workshop. He's building a telescope in there, and that's where he'll house it when it's completed." Both Ariele and Andrius stared at Red with mouths agape. He grinned and continued, "The driveway is actually a slab for his telescope. The posts are supports for a patio roof that will cover the back half of the slab and hide the shop door from prying eyes above. He'll add a fireplace, a grill, and a couple picnic tables to enhance the deception. The uncovered portion of the slab will be for observing the heavens."

"How far along is he on the telescope project?" Ariele enquired.

"Right now, he is mostly researching the design. He has a lead on a supplier for a sixty-inch mirror, but mirrors of that size can't be imported legally except by registered astronomical organizations. We're still looking for leads on where we can procure the infrared technology that we need."

Andrius, who had been pretty quiet for most of the tour, chimed in. "Infrared? Sixty-inch mirror? Sweet! That's a project I definitely want to be involved in."

Ariele teased him, "Sorry, nerd boy. You don't get to play with the cool stuff unless you do a little dirt and manure time."

He scowled at her. "You don't need my help feeding animals, cleaning chicken coops, or weeding gardens. You do need my help in electronics, welding, and soldering."

"What's the matter? Are you afraid to get a little dirt under your fingernails?"

"No. I did work for years as a welder if you haven't forgotten."

She laughed. "How could I forget? When you came home from work, you couldn't get in the shower fast enough—like the grime was poisonous. Talking to me for a minute or two before you showered was a death sentence. We need to find you a sterile job where you can wear a white lab coat and vinyl gloves."

But Andrius was in no mood for teasing. His mind was already working ninety miles an hour on how to build a sixty-inch, infrared telescope on a chassis that would not only be able to travel at five miles per hour but would also be able to raise the telescope platform five or six feet so it could gain a few degrees more clearance over the house and the trees. He also thought it would be nice if the carriage featured a heated cabin, a windshield defroster, a wireless connection with the cabin, and a dual-battery power system.

For the first time in his life, Andrius sensed a calling from God beyond the generic call to follow Jesus. He felt drawn to help with the telescope project. As he thought about the project, he was filled with wonder and began humming one of his favorite hymns, *God Moves in a Mysterious Way*. The past few weeks really had been mysterious. His life had morphed from drudgery to chaos to amazing. And though he hated to admit it, he actually liked having a sister—the sister he had never had—despite the fact that the red-headed pest loved to tease him.

Andrius was stirred from his daydreaming by Red's deep voice. "I have to run to Billings this morning and pick up a load of building materials. So we'll have to head back now. Feel free to explore all you want on your own, anywhere you want. And if you come up with ideas for improvements, feel free to speak up." The three hopped back in the UTV, and this time Andrius enjoyed the bouncing, jolting ride.

15

the Compound
Friday evening, June 28, 2019

Ariele hit the brakes hard, raising a cloud of dust, and brought the UTV to a stop next to the barn. She hopped out, brushed the dust off her jeans, and smiled. It had been a good day. After Red had dropped the newbies off at the lodge, she—bitten by the UTV bug—had wandered over to the machine shed and taught herself how to drive one. The endeavor, though, hadn't merely been for fun. Red's ranch was a big spread, and she had no interest in walking everywhere. While the learning curve had been a little rocky at first—the clutch had a different feel than her VW—she had quickly gotten the hang of it. Once she was comfortable handling the buggy at road speed, she had zipped down the road to visit Betsy. The two had spent the afternoon together, laughing and working in the garden. Now it was time for some exploring.

She bounced through the open barn door, gasped at the immensity and rustic charm of the structure, and strolled down the center. On her left were several large stalls and a few small pens, apparently unused. On her right was a carriage house holding two carriages, a wagon, and a sleigh. Next, she passed the tack room and grooming room on the left and hay storage on the right. The back half contained twelve horse stalls, with horses in four of them. When she reached the end, she stood spellbound in the rear opening, captivated by the mountains and the horses trotting in the pasture.

Keep on task chick. She returned the way she came, located the stairs on the back side of the carriage house, bounded up them two at a time, and froze at the top. *Whoaaaa! This is awesome!* The heart of the loft replicated a recreation center and restaurant from the seventies in Western decor. There were jukeboxes, pinball machines, and a soda counter with a full kitchen. What grabbed her attention the most, though, was a massive painting of John Wayne hanging above the soda fountain that watched over the room like a guardian angel. *Irina would appreciate that.* She snirkled as she thought of her classy friend with a penchant for cowboys, an attraction that had been kindled by the flood of Western movies that had invaded Ukraine after the collapse of the Soviet Union. For her, the American cowboy was the quintessential symbol of freedom and bravery.

Her eyes drifted to the right, admiring the antique restroom signs and the Victorian chairs with matching lamp tables on the back wall. But it was the non-antique sign in the middle of the wall that arrested her attention. A striking plaque with crossed arrows and the Latin phrase *De Oppresso Liber* stood sentinel over a door. She walked over and investigated. The door was unlocked. *Must not be serious about keeping snoops out.* She pushed it open, exposing a narrow hallway illuminated by a window at the far end. The walls on either side were festooned with pictures of military heroes: Washington, Patton, the 82nd Airborne at the Battle of the Bulge, the marines on Iwo Jima, SEALs in Nam, etc. Part way down the hall were two doors, one on either side. *Must be where Jordy's boys stay when they're here.*

She returned to the main room and poked around in the kitchen, impressed with how well it was set up and stocked. Whether Tex-Mex or burger-joint fare, somebody had thought of everything. While she was prowling around, checking the cupboards and drawers, she heard footsteps coming up the stairs. A tall, handsome cowboy, Stetson and all, strode into the room. Butterflies danced in her stomach. *That's a sight for sore eyes.* She walked over to the apron rack, which housed a collection of truck-stop and restaurant aprons, donned one from Junebug's Diner, and sauntered over to him. "And what can I get you tonight, Mr. Cowboy?"

Blake, who had been working all day on his cabin and telescope, replied, a little stunned, "Um … I'm not used to being waited on. I usually take care of things myself."

"Well, we have new management around here, and we're shaking things up a bit." She guided him to one of the tables, sat down across from him, and introduced herself. "I'm Ariele. I assume you're Blake, the astronomer working on the telescope?"

"You got it. And you must be the astronomer who was forced to flee after you uncovered the Rogue?"

"That's me, though I didn't really discover it. A friend did. I just illegally used the Hooker telescope for verification, then hacked into my boss's computer and stole a bunch of top-secret emails to find out what the government knew about the approaching behemoth."

Blake stared at the saucy gal, more than a little impressed, and remarked, "So the redhead not only comes with an overpowering personality, she's super intelligent and an accomplished spy too. Scare the guys away much?"

Ariele wasn't sure how to take this. Was it a compliment? Or was he being negative? Uncertain how to respond, she changed the subject. "I'm going to have a Blue Rooster. Care to join me?"

"A Blue Rooster? Never heard of it. What's that?"

"A craft lager made with an infusion of spruce and bergamot. It burns real good going down. I brought along a couple cases from California." She watched him carefully, looking for his response, hoping it was positive. *He's totally hot.*

He smiled and rejected her offer. "Sorry hon', but I'm a Christian and I don't drink. I'll take a cherry coke and ice tea mix. We call that a Ruddy around here."

Ariele frowned internally. *Guess he's a better match for a religious girl like Irina than me.* "Sure. What do you want to eat?"

"Jalapeno poppers, fries, and a cheeseburger with pepper cheese and onion. Oh, and bring ketchup, Tabasco sauce, a spoon, and an extra fry basket so I can dip my fries in hot ketchup."

Ariele back peddled mentally as she tried to get a read on the cowboy. *Scratch Irina. She hates hot foods.* She returned to the kitchen and fired up the grill and a fryer.

While she was puttering in the kitchen, Blake hollered out, "Set the timer for twenty minutes. That's about how long it takes the fryer to get up to temperature."

"I said I was going to cook your dinner," she retorted. "I didn't give you permission to tell me how to do my job." Nonetheless, she followed his advice, then returned to the table with his Ruddy in hand and slid it over to him. Determined to salvage the awkward start to a conversation, she tried again. "What's with the pinball machines?"

"Jordy's boys hate video games but love pinball. I'm not much for either. Between the horses, the cabin, and the telescope, I don't have a lot of time for playing. Just work, eat, and sleep."

"Been there, done that," she replied. "The six months I invested in Rogue research while I was working my normal job were dreadful. I didn't have a life." But she suspected that the cowboy was hiding from his inner emptiness. *He just needs a woman in his life. Then he'll find plenty of time for downtime.*

Blake didn't reply. The conversation wasn't going anywhere and awkwardness hung in the air. Ariele was perplexed. She didn't usually find it this difficult to get a conversation started. She decided to try again, this time bringing up the comet rather than making small talk. "Woody said that I should talk to you about the Rogue."

The cowboy perked up. She had his full attention now.

107

"I'm all ears. Red said you had classified information on an insanely massive comet."

"That's right. It all started when I received a mysterious package in the mail—"

Blake cut her off. "Hold on a second. Have you already filled Red and Jordy in on the details?"

"No. Red gave us the grand tour this morning—the lodge, the ranch, and the cabin—then he had to run errands in town. We didn't get a chance to talk about the Rogue. And I haven't met Jordy yet."

"I'm thinking that Red didn't bring the comet up this morning because he figured we should have everyone together when you share your story. That way you only have to tell it once, and we can all process the information at the same time."

Blake strolled over to the cradle phone on the sandwich counter and dialed 1. When Red answered, he filled him in. "I'm thinking we should have the whole crew meet at the Hallelujah Tavern for dinner tonight. Ariele wants to fill us in on the Rogue. And she volunteered to cook dinner too." He stood listening and nodding for a minute. "Perfect. That'll work just fine." He hung up and gave the frowning female a thumbs-up. "It's all set. We can expect Red and Betsy in thirty minutes or so. Jordy and Beth will be here shortly after. And don't worry about the extra mouths. I'll help you in the kitchen."

"I'm assuming you want me to hold off on dropping your order."

"10-4." Ariele looked at him blankly like he had just spoken to her in Swahili. "That's 10-Code—also known as

CB-radio talk—for *affirmative* or *I understand*, depending on the context."

"So, in plain English, you said *yes*."

Blake grinned and nodded. "Might as well fire up the second fryer," he added. "We're gonna need both." Then he started walking back toward the table.

Ariele reminded him, "You need to make one more phone call."

Now it was his turn to give her a blank look.

"We need to include Andrius in this too."

"Forgot you came with a sidekick."

"Try the lodge first, then the shop. Most likely, he is either holed up with some nerdy tome, or he is exploring the shop, as excited as a kid in a toy store."

Blake grinned and picked up the phone. There was no answer at the lodge, but when he dialed the shop, Andrius picked up after the sixth ring. "Hello?" he said, hesitantly. The conversation started slowly, but the two ended up chatting for several minutes about the tools and materials needed for the telescope project.

When Blake rejoined Ariele at the table, he was obviously impressed. "Turns out your sidekick knows quite a bit about welding. He's gonna come in pretty handy around here."

"I think so too. He really lit up when Red told us about your telescope project. When I left the lodge this morning to visit with Betsy, he was already drawing sketches in his notebook." *Hope I'm going to be needed around here as much as he is. Don't want to be relegated to kitchen duty after I share my story and emails.*

She changed the subject to get her mind off her melancholy thoughts. "Why do you call this place the Hallelujah Tavern?"

He grinned mischievously. "Jordy's boys nicknamed it that a few years ago when they were home on leave. It was their way of politely complaining that it doesn't serve liquor."

Ariele squirmed—*guess I won't be putting my beer in the fridge*—and changed the topic. "So what brought you to Montana?"

"I grew up in Wyoming, so I love the wide-open spaces of the north-central Rockies. I don't feel at home anywhere else. I spent ten years working in the oil fields in Texas, North Dakota, and Utah, following the booms and running heavy equipment and cranes. After I saved up enough, I started looking for a piece of land where I could settle down, build a log home, and assemble a big telescope. My wish list included mountains, pine trees, blue skies, elbow room, trout fishing, elk hunting, and dark skies for prime astronomy. After a little research, I settled on a rectangle in Montana whose corners, roughly speaking, were Lewiston, White Sulphur Springs, Harlowton, and Monarch. Four years ago, I moved to Harlowton, rented a hotel room, and started investigating properties.

"The first Sunday in town, I visited Jordy's church, and he invited me over for lunch. We started talking about prophecy and discovered that we had a lot in common. I told him about my hunch that the inner planets were going to be knocked out of their orbits in the last days and wreak havoc.

He was fascinated with the thought and said it clarified several passages for him. After that, I began attending his church regularly and got to know Red.

"A couple months later, I dropped in on Red for advice on a piece of land that I was thinking about. As I explained why I thought it was suitable, he stopped me mid-description and cautioned me that I was settling for less than what I really wanted. Then he told me to hop in his truck. I complied, though I wasn't sure what was going on. He showed me the knoll where I am currently building. It was perfect—exactly what I was looking for. On the spot, he offered the site to me for free with two stipulations: the property would remain under his name, and he would reimburse me for the house if I ever decided to leave. That was a deal I couldn't pass up. I became a member of the Compound that day and started building later that summer."

Their conversation flowed easily for the next twenty minutes as Blake outlined his plans for turning his infrared telescope dream into reality. Ariele found herself attracted to the soft-spoken cowboy despite the fact that he was a teetotaling Christian. *What's not to like? Masculinity, humility, and intelligence in the same male. And he's a hottie too.* While he was describing the sixty-inch mirror that he wanted to order from Germany, Jordy and Beth made their entrance. Blake stood up to greet them and introduced them to Ariele.

She promptly engaged Jordy in conversation. "Red told us that you're a pastor. But he also told us that you're moving to the Compound. Will you be making a long commute?

Jordy smiled. "I pastored the Bible Church in Harlowton for twenty-six years. But after the Anti-Discrimination Act was passed, it became evident that the legislation was being used to force churches to receive people as members who rejected the Bible's authority and morality. The church elders and I, after a few weeks of prayer and discussion, voted to fold the church, dissolve the corporation, and sell the assets. We sent the proceeds to indigenous missions in Asia and South America. Some of the members joined other churches, but most began to meet in small home meetings with a more informal structure. Because my small group is the Compound membership, moving here is a matter of practicality."

"Meeting in homes. That's an interesting concept. I'm used to thinking of churches as buildings."

"Most do. But the church is really the people. Meeting in homes was the church's practice during her humble beginning, and it is how she survives in times of persecution. With Bible-loving churches now being persecuted for disobeying laws that require disobedience to God's word, going back to the home-meeting format makes sense. It makes it more difficult for the government to control them."

She raised her eyebrows with interest. Encouraged by her interest, Jordy launched into an account of the home-church movement in China, largely initiated through the work of Watchman Nee. But he barely got started when Red and Betsy burst through the door. The flamboyant woman shouted, "Sorry we're late. We had to wait for a flock of sheep wandering down the road to let us through." As she finished her outburst, Andrius appeared on the landing behind them.

Jordy shrugged his shoulders. "I'll finish the story another time."

With the whole crew settled at the table, Ariele pulled an order book out of her apron pocket and took their orders. She was surprised that most of them asked for spicy-lime chicken strips and fries. She was even more surprised when most of them requested Ruddies. *What's up with the cherry coke and tea? Must be a western thing.* Andrius hesitated on his drink choices and uncharacteristically chose to gamble on a Ruddy. Ariele was amused. *Mr. Food Wuss is embracing his wild side.*

About fifteen minutes later, Ariele and Blake wheeled over a cart and set the platters of steaming hot chicken strips and fries on the table, Red gave thanks and the hungry crew dug in. Several chicken strips into his basket, Red nodded to Ariele and prodded her. "I didn't come all the way over here to watch you eat chicken strips dipped in Miracle Whip."

She blushed. "Sorry. Guess I'm pretty hungry. The only thing I ate since breakfast was a leftover muffin around midmorning."

Red smiled at Ariele and winked at Andrius.

She relaxed. He had only been teasing.

He turned back to her. "What can you tell us about Woody?"

"Not much. The last time I saw him, he said that I should

flee to Montana and that he would probably be joining me there soon."

"Did he say anything about his timetable or travel plans?"

"Nope. Not a word. Knowing Woody, however, he probably came up with a brilliant plan."

Red chuckled. "I suspect so too. Something that will leave his pursuers frustrated and scratching their heads. I just wish that he kept himself in better shape. I would hate to find out that he died of a heart attack on the way here." His eyes began to mist up as humor gave way to concerns, so he quit talking. "Okay, time for your story."

Ariele began, "My story starts with a package I received in the mail in November 2018 from a fellow Caltech student, Irina Kirilenko who was working in TNO research at Cornell. An enclosed letter detailed her discovery of a massive comet, her interactions with the MPC, and the government's coverup. She had also included a DVD with her research and plates on the comet. I wasn't sure what to think. I wanted to believe her, but I had a hard time believing that the government really would cover up something like that.

That evening on my return from Mount Wilson, it dawned on me as I was pondering the rumored comet that my favorite late-night program, *Down the Rabbit Hole*, which had mysteriously gone off the air, had only done so after Burrage Krakenhavn had gone on a tirade about the government covering up a massive comet that was headed for Mars. He had claimed that his report was based on intel hacked by Anonymous from universities that were involved in research on the comet. At the time I had laughed, thinking it was just another crackpot story on late-night talk radio. Now I had my doubts. Maybe the comet really was real.

I searched the *Down the Rabbit Hole* folder in my podcast program, located the program on the comet, and listened to it. After hearing the information that Krake presented from sources that were completely independent of Irina, I went numb with shock. The comet wasn't a hoax."

She then walked them through her involvement with the Rogue: sneaking time on the Hooker ... pirating Caltech's version of OrbFit ... stealing her boss's password and using it to pilfer top secret emails ... giving her research to Sally and getting turned in to the FBI ... agents staking out her apartment ... fleeing to meet Woody at the diner ... Woody advising her to escape to Montana ... fleeing the diner and collapsing exhausted in the park ... and Andrius coming to her rescue.

Blake was amazed. "Wow! That's quite the story. I have long expected that something like this was going to happen in the last days. The history of the world from the flood through the eighth century B.C. was marked by a string of planetary visitations—mostly Mars and Venus—that brought global catastrophe. Since history tends to repeat itself, it seemed safe to assume that the catastrophes at the end of the age would also involve planetary interactions. And that implied that something was going to happen in the last days that would disrupt the solar system and knock some of the planets into elliptical orbits. The most likely scenario in my estimation was a large body blasting through the inner solar system, whether the core of the planet that once orbited between Mars and Jupiter or a rogue body passing through our solar system."

Ariele laughed. "Irina tried to tell me about stuff like that on several occasions. She believed that a large comet was responsible for bringing about the calamities that ended the Bronze Age. At the time I was skeptical. I thought she had a screw loose—that she was one of those insanely brilliant people who have a strange fascination with bizarre theories. To be honest, the theory of planetary catastrophism still seems like a stretch to me. It is just so far removed from what I was taught in school—you know, billions of years of tiny incremental changes. But you can't argue with facts. A planet-sized comet is headed for the inner solar system on a trajectory that could bump the Red Planet out of its orbit. That challenges the paradigm that I was educated in."

Red laughed. "It sure does. Throws it right out the window."

"Speaking of throwing stuff," Andrius interrupted, "I don't want to throw cold water on this discussion, but aren't we operating on the assumption that the Rogue is going to cause problems? Have any of you considered the possibility that it won't knock a single asteroid out of orbit and will miss Mars entirely?"

Ariele jumped to the defense of the catastrophic perspective. "I thought about that possibility too, but if Woody's electric universe theory is true, then the Rogue could pass Mars at twice the forecasted distance and still bump it out of orbit. It doesn't have to hit it to disrupt its orbit. Ditto for the asteroids. So it is unlikely that the Rogue will manage to sneak through the asteroid belt without bumping anything into an Earth-threatening orbit, and there is zero chance that it won't bump Mars into a new orbit."

Andrius rolled his eyes. "If? If his theory is true? That's a lot of speculation based on a hypothetical theory."

"If you have a problem with speculation," Ariele indignantly replied, "then you might want to give the electric universe theory a serious look. It contains far less speculation than the Standard Model. Woody makes some strong arguments, strong enough that I'm pretty nervous about the approaching dance between the Rogue and Mars."

Jordy shook his head. Watching the two scrap was like watching siblings argue over what TV show they were going to watch. After listening to them fight for a few minutes, he chimed in, hoping to temper the conflict. "Woody is the expert on the electric universe stuff, so when he gets here— *if he gets here*—we can have him shed some light on the subject for us.

"In the meantime, whether or not Woody is right on the electric universe theory, we have the plain testimony of the Bible that the planets are going to be severely disturbed in the last days. Luke 21:25-26 says, 'There will be signs in the sun, in the moon, and in the stars, and distress here on Earth … men's hearts failing them from fear … of the things headed for Earth because the planets of the heavens will be shaken loose from their orbits.' Notice the contrast. The sun, moon, and stars are going to manifest signs. And the powers—the planets—are going to be shaken loose from their orbits, resulting in large bodies passing close enough to our planet that mankind will be terrified. This contrast is even more apparent in Matthew 24:29 where we're given the actual signs: the sun darkening, the moon turning blood red, the stars falling from their places in the heavens, and the planets being loosed from their orbits."

"But," Andrius piped up, "I read several translations, and none of them say *planets*. They all say *powers*. And none of them say *shaken loose*. They say *loosed*. Every prophecy teacher I have read or heard teaches that the powers being loosed is a reference to the atoms of the universe dissolving into nothing in one gigantic fission reaction."

Jordy smiled and calmly made his case. "I am fully aware of the translation and interpretation issues. But there are several things that you should consider.

"First of all, the events in prophetic passages are described from the perspective of the man on the street watching them unfold, not from the perspective of the theoretical insights of modern physics. The stars rolling up like a scroll, for example, are the stars rapidly moving across the visible heavens (due to a polar shift or rotational acceleration), not Einstein's flat universe rolling up and ceasing to exist. Likewise, the powers in the heavens being shaken are visible bodies that can be seen with the naked eye being moved from their orbits, not invisible atoms breaking up into smaller sub-atomic particles.

"Secondly, the prophetic language of the New Testament is largely derived from the Septuagint, the ancient Greek translation of the Old Testament. In this version, dunamai (translated *powers* in the NT and *host* in the OT) refers to visible bodies in the heavens which mankind watched and worshipped—sometimes in a broad sense for all the visible bodies, frequently in a narrower sense for the five visible planets in contrast to the sun, moon, and fixed stars. To make *powers* refer to anything other than visible bodies which the ancients worshipped is a departure from the historical-grammatical method of biblical interpretation.

"Thirdly, the *powers loosed* cannot mean the universe dissolving into nothing and ceasing to exist. This flies straight in the face of plain statements in the OT. For instance, God gave his word in Jeremiah 31:35-36 that his promises to Israel are eternal, even as the sun, moon, and stars are eternal. If the present universe is not eternal, then God's promises to Israel are not eternal. If the present universe is going to cease to exist, then Israel is going to cease to exist.

"It also flies in the face of common sense and science. The atoms breaking up into sub-atomic particles would not cause the universe to cease to exist. It would merely change it into a cloud of particles.

"Now we don't know for sure that this comet is the means that God is going to use to knock the planets around like pool balls. The Bible only tells us that the planets are going to be knocked out of their normal orbits. It doesn't tell us what mechanism God is going to use to accomplish that. It could be the Rogue. It could be a rogue planet or a brown dwarf coming from another solar system. It could be the sun or one of the gas giants going micro-nova and ejecting a large body. It could be something else that we haven't thought of. But whatever the cause, some of the planets are going to be loosed from their orbits, and the inhabitants of Earth are going to be so terrified by the planets and asteroids that are headed for Earth that men will drop dead from heart attacks and cardiac arrest. However, when we consider what an extraordinarily rare phenomenon the Rogue is—the last comparable event in history was the comet at the end of the Bronze Age—then it seems likely that the Rogue really is the harbinger of the last days."

Ariele was intrigued. "So you think that this comet is likely to result in destruction like that which ended the Minoan and Mycenaean empires, except that instead of being regional, it will be worldwide like the biblical apocalypse?"

Jordy emphatically replied, "I most certainly do."

Ariele sucked in her breath slowly while trying to wrap her brain around the concept of planetary catastrophism, then responded. "Tell me more about the ancient calamities that were caused by planets."

Blake answered, "According to ancient history, when Venus first appeared, it was a massive comet that traveled on an elliptical orbit that interfered with Mars and Earth. Eventually, it brought the Silver (or Second) Age to an end with a rain of fire that devastated the world from Scandinavia to North Africa. At the same time, it caused a polar shift which brought massive climate change around the globe. For instance, it sent Scandinavia farther north, transforming her temperate climate into sub-arctic and arctic. The majority of the inhabitants fled—becoming the Sea Peoples of ancient history—and headed for warmer climates. When they showed up in Egypt, they told their hosts that their homeland had been burned by fire from heaven, their star chart had been changed significantly, and their climate had changed from warm to cold."

Ariele probed him. "Is there any evidence of this change aside from the ancient records?"

"Absolutely. The climate change at the end of the Silver Age is corroborated by archaeological discoveries which have established that the northern climes were much milder in the past than they are now. The ancient Scandinavian forest, for instance, was temperate woodland dominated by beech and elm before it was replaced with the northern boreal forest that we see today."

"If the Scandinavian region was shifted north," Ariele observed, "then every location on the globe would have either shifted north or south too."

"You're exactly right. I believe that is why tens of thousands of so-called ice-age mammals have been found frozen in the permafrost in Siberia. The polar shift caused enormous tsunamis which buried them in muck. When the waters retreated, the muck was exposed to unusually cold arctic temperatures, and the carcasses were frozen in place. And this is why a once temperate Antarctica—demonstrated by the fossils and petrified trees found there—became covered with one to two miles of ice."

"Can you correlate this event with the Bible to help me get a handle on the timeframe that we're looking at?"

"The catastrophes at the end of the Silver Age correlate with the time of Abraham and the destruction of Sodom and Gomorrah by fire that fell from heaven."

"Is there any evidence that substantiates the claim that Antarctica passed from a temperate to an arctic climate in recent history and not geologically ancient history?"

"As a matter of fact, there is. Old maps have been found, which claim to be copies of extremely ancient maps, that accurately portray Antarctica's coastline. This tells us that the continent was ice-free at some point in recorded history. Interestingly enough, modern man was unable to map the coastline until technological advances allowed him to penetrate the ice with radar surveys in the 1950s."

"What?" Ariele cried out in astonishment. "Are you telling me that Antarctica was ice-free in early Old Testament times and that sailors mapped its coastline?"

"That's exactly what I am saying. The most well-known of these ancient maps is the Piri Ries map. Google it sometime."

She shook her head, half convinced and half skeptical. "So how did you guys learn about this stuff? I never heard a whisper about such things in any of my college courses. I've never even seen a passing mention in any book that I've read."

Jordy replied, "In college you're taught a revisionist history that reinterprets or ignores every point in history which poses a threat to evolution or corroborates biblical history. The fact is, the religion of evolution doesn't trust ancient history any more than it does the Bible. It was a huge blessing when I discovered that ancient history taken at face value corroborates the history of the Bible taken at face value. And ancient history is permeated with catastrophism that meshes with the catastrophism we see in the Bible, both Old Testament and New."

"But how did you find out about this stuff?"

"From Blake. He introduced me to ancient history and planetary catastrophism."

Ariele turned to Blake.

The cowboy grinned. "While studying Creation apologetics, I stumbled across a book called *The Mars-Earth War*, which led me to Velikovsky's books, which led me to websites like thunderbolts.info that promote electric universe theory and catastrophism."

The conversation continued for several hours, dwelling on the historicity of the Bible, revisionist history vs. ancient history, and the end of the world according to Bible prophecy. When the group finished their third round of Ruddies and jalapeno poppers, Jordy and Beth bid their friends good night. Red and Betsy followed. So did Andrius. An hour later, Blake and Ariele called it an evening.

As she slowly walked back to the lodge under the starry canopy, pondering the evening's conversation, Ariele found herself drawn by the Bible in a way that she had never felt before. It wasn't a mystical draw like a religious man feels for a religious book. It was the draw of irresistible facts—the same kind of draw that had warmed her up to electric universe theory and intelligent design. She sensed that the facts and the God of facts might make her a little religious.

That was okay. She could live with that. She just didn't want religion standing at the gate and arbitrarily deciding what was true and what wasn't. That was superstition. True religion, she instinctively sensed, was based on facts, truth, and reality. And as such, it was every bit as valid as science.

That night, as she lay awake in bed, she decided that she needed to put God at the top of her life priority list. *If the prophecies of the Tanakh and the New Testament are being fulfilled before my eyes, then I need to start reading them and find out what God is doing and what His plans are for His people, Jew and goy alike.*

16

Sally stared out the window of the small airplane, scrutinizing the hilly terrain below her, trying to figure out where they might be. The man beside her stood up, walked to the cockpit, opened the door, and spoke with the pilot, his voice barely audible over the whine of the engines. Then he returned to his seat.

Two minutes later, the craft dropped into the low-lying clouds and started to bank. After some turbulence, they dropped below the cloud cover and the runway appeared. Sally processed what she saw. *Looks pretty small. Definitely not a major airport.* The plane touched down, rolled to a stop, and sat on the tarmac. The man beside her remained seated with his cellphone glued to his ear, apparently waiting for instructions. After several agonizingly long minutes had dragged by, he pocketed his phone, unhooked Sally's handcuff from her armrest, clapped the open end on her left hand, and raised her to her feet. The co-pilot opened the door, and they descended the stairs to a waiting van with a faded Freedom Transport logo. The transfer confused her. To this point she had been under the watch of the FBI and Homeland Security. Why the change now? She thought about asking where they were taking her, but checked herself. She knew she would get a canned response that wouldn't be helpful.

Thirty-five minutes later, the van pulled up to the gate of a bleak-looking compound surrounded by a high fence and concertina wire. After checking his paperwork and ID, the machine-gun-toting guards waved the driver through, and he slowly worked his way across the broken blacktop, headed for what appeared to be a former factory. Sally rolled her eyes in disbelief. *What a dismal dump! Guess it doesn't take much remodeling to turn a worn-out plant into a FEMA camp.* He stopped at the main entrance on the side of the building, opened the rear door, motioned her out, and grumbled, "Welcome to 286." With a heavy heart, she followed him inside. He poked his head in the doorway of a small office in the main entry, nodded to the woman inside, wheeled around, and left Sally standing alone.

"Don't just stand there!" the woman barked. Sally wilted, steeled her inner woman, walked through the door, and found herself facing a robust, scowling woman who complained to no one in particular, "I've told Homeland Security a half-dozen times that it's a pain in the derriere to process new arrivals on Saturdays. I have to summon detainees during their time off and require them to open supply and the commissary, all of which costs me extra paperwork."

Glowering, she addressed Sally with frustration in her voice. "Take a seat." Sally settled into a ratty chair. The agitated female continued, "I'm Sharon Baumgardner, weekend director of FEMA 286 and a proud American. Consider yourself lucky that I'm strictly forbidden from dealing with terrorists, spies, and traitors on my own terms." She glared at the newcomer icily.

Sally winced and braced herself—*I'm not going to let this old battle-axe intimidate me*—and returned the glare. After what seemed like an eternity, Sharon looked away, picked up a clipboard with several processing forms, and slid it over to her.

Twenty minutes later, as her processing was drawing to a close, Sally was given a choice of kitchen duty, laundry duty, or boiler and back warehouse duty. Her first inclination was to choose either the kitchen or the laundry. They were more her speed. She had never worked in any kind of manual labor. In fact, she had worn high heels since high school. But on a whim—or was it inspiration—she chose the counter-intuitive option. "I'll take the boiler and back warehouse." The words seemed odd coming out of her mouth. But it was the right choice. She knew that if she was going to have any chance of getting out of this rat hole, she would have to reinvent herself. And the boiler slot was a good start. Since she would be responsible for all the pipes and radiators, the position would provide her with the opportunity to explore the entire complex.

The director approved her choice and dismissed her. "Go find Bryce Callahan and have him show you the ropes for warehouse and boiler duty. Most likely he is in the maintenance shop in the west warehouse. Turn right down the hallway, turn left at the T."

After asking several people for help, Sally found Bryce leaning over a workbench in his wire-mesh partition working on a spare controller panel for the boiler. She introduced herself. "Hi, I'm Sally Evans. I've been assigned to boiler and back warehouse duty."

"Have you been to the commissary and supply yet?"

"No. I was told to visit with you first and then go to supply."

"No problem. What kind of experience do you have with boilers?"

"None, to be honest. My closest experience is boiling water in a teapot."

"Well, that's a start. A boiler does the same thing, except that it holds the steam, builds up the pressure, and shoots the steam through pipes to heat a building." He checked his schedule. "Monday will be your first day on boiler duty. I'll walk you through your daily inspection routine for a few days and show you which dials you need to watch, how to read the digital panel, how to look for leaks, and so forth. I'll also give you two books to read. One is a trade-school introduction to steam boilers. The other is the maintenance manual for our boiler. And don't worry about breakdowns. If you find a real problem, I or somebody else will show you how to fix it. Oh, one other thing. There won't be much to observe or record for a couple months yet. The boiler doesn't fire up in the summer very often."

"Glad to hear that. Gives me a while to get up to speed."

"Yeah. You should get at least ten weeks before the boiler starts firing up every day."

Sally changed the subject. "This place is worn down and dingy."

Bryce chuckled and replied, "Just be glad that you're in a 200-series camp. Every once in a while, mistakes are made in processing, and folks that are supposed to be detained in a 200-series camp get sent to a 100-series camp."

"I have no idea what you're talking about."

"Don't you ever follow alternative news sources?"

"No. Never."

"There are three series of camps. The 300-series camps are for patriots and deucers whom the government deems a threat. These camps are run more like prisons with far tighter security and far less freedom.

"The 200-series camps are for people guilty of white-collar crime or non-violent terrorism, the so-called soft terrorism mentioned in the Homeland Security Act. Soft terrorism is really just a euphemism for security breaches that involve sensitive information on the Rogue. Because these detainees are hard-working, honest professionals, who don't really pose a violent threat, the camps give the detainees a lot of freedom.

"The 100-series camps are for drug abusers, drunkards, street people, transients, petty criminals, the perpetually unemployed, and so forth. They are far more rundown and dirty than the 200-series camps and remind me of the dystopian future portrayed in Hollywood films, except that the problem area is a small fenced-in compound rather than a large inner-city area."

Sally eyed him inquisitively. "How do you know so much about these things?"

"I read about the FEMA camps on alternative news sites before I was detained. But I learned the ugly truth about the 100-series camps through personal experience. When I was originally detained, I somehow ended up in a temporary cell of street people, petty dealers, and third-strike DUIs who were all transferred that day to a 100-series camp—I with them. Because I arrived at camp without paperwork, it took several days for the mess to get sorted out." He shook his head and laughed. "Nothing like sleeping in an open room filled with druggies going through withdrawal, drunkards suffering delirium tremens, and assorted crazies."

Sally got the creeps just thinking about it. "Yikes. That would be uncomfortable. So what's it like here?"

"It isn't too bad actually. We don't have to worry about bills or taxes. We enjoy a lot of freedom. And while the accommodations aren't worthy of a spread in a magazine, we have it pretty good. We have a library, exercise opportunities, and three television rooms—one for news, one for sports, and one for soaps and prime time. The two things I like the least are the paltry five dollars per week that they give us to spend in the commissary and the lack of privacy in the bathrooms and dorm rooms."

Sally winced at the latter. Her discomfort didn't escape Bryce's attention. "Well, enough whining about the negative stuff," he said. "Come on. I'll show you around the back warehouses. We have a couple hours until dinner."

He started in the maintenance bay, introducing her to the folks she would be working with, then showed her the boiler room, the storage rooms, the freezer, and the rest of their facilities. Two things stood out to her. The first was how small the boiler was compared to the vast complex it heated. Perhaps there was an object lesson in that. The second was how ingenious the prisoners had been in rigging up the shower rooms, the laundry room, the gym, the basketball court, and the chapel. That kind of skill could come in handy.

As they returned from the chapel, again walking past the massive pile of boxes and crates in the east warehouse waiting to be processed, he explained her job slot more fully. "Just a heads up. While opening these boxes and crates and sorting their contents is technically your secondary job, you will actually spend more time here than you will maintaining the boiler. And you will often be working alone."

She nodded in approval. She didn't mind. Opening crates and boxes sounded kind of fun to her, almost like Christmas, since most of the time she would have no idea what she was going to find.

At the T, Bryce pointed down the hallway. "Go to Supply and tell Cassie that you need a lady's maintenance package. Then come back to maintenance, and I'll issue you a toolbelt and a tool bucket with all the tools that you'll need. Once you're set up with clothing and tools, I'll show you the ropes in the warehouse—best ways to open boxes and crates, how stuff is to be sorted—so you can get a feel for the job. On Monday after we finish your boiler tour, you can go back there by yourself and start your work in earnest."

When Sally stepped into Supply, Cassie cheerfully greeted her. "You must be the new girl."

"News travels fast."

"It doesn't have far to go," the friendly gal replied.

The two shared a laugh, then started chit-chatting. After some considerable time had passed, Cassie checked her watch and raised her eyebrows in shock "We better get down to business if you need to report to maintenance before lunch." Item by item, she asked Sally for her size, hunted down the items, and stacked them on the counter: three pairs of jeans, five shirts, a pair of boots, six pairs of socks, and two pairs of leather gloves. When the whole kit was assembled, she pointed to the ladies' restroom. "You can change in there."

When the chic female emerged, looking like she had just stepped out of a clothing catalog, Cassie gushed, "Wish I still cut a figure like that in jeans."

Sally blushed, said "See you at dinner," and scurried out the door.

Ten minutes later, Sally, lugging her heavy tool bucket and belt, struggled to keep up as Bryce strode briskly down the hallway. When he stopped at the pile in the east warehouse, she dropped her tools and pleaded, "Can I leave my tool bucket here? I don't want to lug it back and forth every time I work back here."

"Absolutely," he replied, chuckling. "You're not in Los Angeles anymore. Nobody is gonna steal your stuff here."

He pointed at the pile. "Start here on this corner and work your way down both faces. We want to make more room here on the backside for the walkway to the chapel, and we want to increase the width of the passageway on that side over there for access to the docks."

A large crate about six feet away caught her eye, and she resolved to work her way through the pile toward it. Moved with anticipation, she grabbed a nearby box, then stared at the wide plastic banding. Bryce smiled, took the box from her hands, and demonstrated how to cut the bands with a Stanley knife. Then, moving among several crates, he showed her how to use the metal-band snips, the wrenches, the nut drivers, and the screwdrivers. When she seemed to have the hang of things, he handed her a two-page outline. "This tells you how the items are to be sorted and where they are to be stored."

She nodded.

"Well, training is finished. You're on your own now." He smiled and headed back to the maintenance department.

Sally's gaze returned to the pile. The concept of unmarked boxes intrigued her. Every one would be a surprise. She didn't have a lot of time, but she figured she could open a few more before quitting time. She wouldn't worry about sorting. That could wait until Monday.

***

At dinner that evening, Sally was sitting with her new friend Cassie, the two Joyces, and several other ladies when a pretty brunette walked up. Sally sprang to her feet, shouted "Irina!"

and smothered the gal with a hug. "Good to see you again!"

"You too!" the brunette replied as she returned the embrace. Then she stepped back and grabbed her friend's arm. "Too bad it's under such circumstances."

The ladies at the table looked at each other, dumbfounded.

Sally explained, "I was one of Irina's instructors at Caltech for both her Master's degree and her PhD. I also had the honor of being on her thesis committee."

The ladies scooted down and made room for Irina to join them at the table. She immediately turned to Sally and asked the question that was burning on her chest. "So how did you wind up in this place?"

"It started with the letter you sent Ariele," she replied. "She spent six months scanning the heavens twice a week on the Hooker after she received your letter, verifying your data and finding two further confirmations. I knew she was doing that, but I pretended to be oblivious. Based on her research, she wrote a paper which she gave to me, trying to convince me of the comet's existence.

I played ignorant, but I already knew about the comet because I was part of the Minoa Research Team—the team appointed by the White House to head up the investigation of the Rogue. Sterling Fitzgerald, my assistant, overheard our conversation and forced me to report Ariele to the FBI. I had intended to overlook her indiscretion, as I had already been overlooking her Hooker indiscretions, so I was hopping mad over his drum-beating and chest-thumping."

"I'll bet you were. So where is she now?"

"I wish I knew. I worry about her every day."

"Any information at all?"

"The only thing I know is that she fled from her apartment on a bicycle on Tuesday evening, June 4. She had been interrogated by FBI agents earlier that day and must have sensed that things weren't going to turn out well."

"Did she get away?"

"I don't know for certain. It looks promising. About a week ago, a couple of days prior to my arrest, she was still on the loose according to a contact in the FBI."

"I'll continue to pray for her, "Irina promised.

"Please do that."

"Do you have a job assignment yet"

"Boiler duty and back warehouse."

"Great. I'm assigned to the kitchen but have freezer duty twice a week. That's in the north warehouse near maintenance, so we'll bump into each other and have some time to catch up."

"That will be wonderful."

17

Laurel, MT ... the Compound
Monday, July 1, 2019

Monday morning at 3:30 a.m. Rocky Mountain Time, after a week on the rails, Woody hopped off the train outside Laurel, joined by his new friend Lobo. They walked together to Pelican Truck Plaza and parted company in the faint glimmer of dawn with a handshake. Both made the other promise to stay in touch. Lobo moseyed inside the truck stop to get a shower and a big Western breakfast. Woody stationed himself in the trees at the southeast corner of the truck stop, pulled out his burner, and called Red.

"Grubstake, this is Tenkara. Are we secure?"

"We are secure, Tenkara. Good to hear your voice! You had us worried. We feared that you might not make the rendezvous. What is your location?"

"Southeast corner of the Pelican Truck Plaza in Laurel, concealed in the trees."

"Hold your location. It'll take me approximately three hours to get there. When you see my old F-150 stop at the intersection east of you, step out of the trees and start walking west on the shoulder. When I drive up, toss your stuff in the back and hop in the cab. My estimated time of arrival will be around 7 a.m."

As the morning dawned brilliantly, Woody's mind wandered in good memories. He and Jack had first met Red fifteen years earlier at Dan Bailey's Fly Shop in Livingston while looking for patterns to match the hatches on the three forks of the Missouri in late June. Red had noticed them climb out of a Jeep with out-of-state plates, then watched them shop indecisively for dry-fly patterns. He had sauntered up to them and recommended several caddis and stonefly patterns that the local experts favored. While they were gathering a selection of the suggested patterns, the stranger had stretched out his hand and introduced himself. "I'm Robert Reddington, by the way. Most folks just call me Red."

Jack had smiled and gripped his hand firmly. "I'm Jack. And this" he added, nodding in his cousin's direction, "is Woody."

"Glad to meet you two," Red replied.

"So, do you do much fly fishing yourself?" Jack probed.

"No. My expertise lies more in elk hunting, though I do enjoy wetting a line a half dozen times or so every summer."

The trio struck up a conversation that eventually turned from fly fishing in Montana to Montana's rugged beauty to Montana being an ideal retreat if things ever went south. After they had talked for maybe ten minutes about hard times and prepping in general terms, Red enquired about their preparations for hard times and catastrophic scenarios, trying to feel them out. Jack answered evasively, noting that they had put some thought into the subject, but not as much as they ought to.

Over the next few minutes, Red's amiability and down-to-earth honesty disarmed Jack, much to Woody's surprise, and soon the three were openly talking about prepping. They started with scenarios they figured were the most probable, like a once-in-a-century storm, a powerful earthquake, a volcano roaring back to life, or nuclear terrorism. Soon they were talking about far more troubling scenarios like nuclear war, biological war, or the impact of a massive asteroid or comet.

They chatted for half an hour by the dry-fly bins, then moved to an outside table at the deli next door for pastries and coffee. When Woody started getting antsy about getting back to camp so they could catch the evening rise, Red had graciously encouraged the two of them to be on their way. As they stood up to go, he extended an invitation to spend some time at his place after they had finished fishing the three forks. He quickly drew a map on the back of a napkin and handed it to Jack. It was a crude map to his spread, nestled in the foothills at the base of the Crazies about twenty-four miles out of Two Dot on Sweet Grass Creek. They both smiled, and Jack said, "No way that we're gonna pass up an opportunity like that. Tell you what. I figure it'll take us three days to fish the three forks, so you can expect us to show up on the fourth."

Four days later, they had shown up as promised and spent their second week at his cabin, fishing the local streams, cooking steaks on the grill, and chatting around the campfire. It seemed like heaven. They enjoyed the isolation, the big skies, the stars, the herds of antelope and mule deer, and the coyotes yipping every evening. By the end of the week, their friendship with Red was cemented.

At the end of their stay, as they were stowing their gear in Woody's Jeep, Red had invited them to return the following summer. "Absolutely. We wouldn't miss it," Jack insisted. Woody nodded and added dryly, "Not even if the sky was falling," drawing hearty laughter from his companions.

The next summer, they had returned as planned. Near the end of their second stay, Red again extended the invitation to return. During their third visit, he had invited them to be members of his end-of-the-world survival compound. They jumped at the offer. Jack mostly for the prepping opportunity. Woody mostly for the brown trout fishing. After that, they had returned every summer.

When Jack and Woody had first started coming to the Compound, Red had not been particularly religious, though he had been raised and married in the Episcopalian church. His wife Betsy had been a little more religious, attending the Lutheran church and occasionally joining a women's Bible study. Things had changed in the spring of 2008 when Red was on a buying trip for the Compound. In a military surplus store in Columbus, Missouri, he met a fellow prepper who pointed out that the Bible is the guidebook to the apocalypse. If you don't know the prophecies of the Bible, you can't possibly have the low down on what's going on in the world. He also pointed out that the spiritual aspect of the battle going on in the world was a thousand times more important than the political aspect. Men needed to know the Light of the world if they would find their way in the growing darkness. That thought etched itself into Red's mind.

When he returned home, he began reading the Bible, starting in the Gospels as the man in the store had suggested. Within a few weeks, the light came on in his heart. A rabbi carpenter from Galilee—who was far more than a mere man—had lived and died and rose from the dead for mankind. And in this humble Galilean, the seeker will find life's true meaning and purpose.

Several weeks later, Red stumbled upon the small Bible church that Jordy Backstrom pastored, and the two of them quickly became close friends. Their wives enjoyed each other's company too, though Red's wife Betsy reminded Beth Backstrom of Lisa Douglas in the *Green Acres* television show—a cultured city woman who left a refined touch on every country thing she did. Red himself was an interesting mix, like putting Clint Eastwood and a Wall Street fund manager in a blender.

Woody's reminiscences on Red's spiritual renaissance led him to reflect on his own state. He didn't like what he saw. Jack had been reignited by Red, but he felt like he had dropped anchor in a stagnant pond. *Need to change, but I'm not sure how.*

He was startled out of his reflections by the sound of a pickup approaching. He checked his watch. It was two minutes after seven. A truck that looked like Red's faded-green F-150 stopped at the stop sign. Woody stepped out of the trees onto the road and started walking as he had been directed. The truck pulled up beside him and stopped. Red smiled and waved. The weary traveler swung his pack into the back of the truck, climbed into the cab, and found himself greeted with a familiar scent—raspberry scones. Red pulled back the lid on an insulated container sitting on the seat between them, revealing a huge breakfast burrito and two raspberry scones.

"Betsy sent those along for you," Red offered as he put the truck in gear.

"Sweet," Woody replied, reaching for a scone.

"You're not smelling too bad for a hobo."

"We took advantage of a garden hose last night to wash up and shampoo our hair."

"We?"

"Yeah. I met a seasonal worker by the name of Lobo. He labors on oil rigs and fishing boats in the winter and works for a horse packer in the summer and fall." He turned and looked directly at Red, "He also knows where Burt is."

Red's eyebrows raised up high like big shop doors. "Your missing astronomer friend from Wyoming who was accused of stealing banned infrared technology from the government?"

"Yep."

"How does he know him?"

"To make a long story short, Lobo met Burt on the rails, knows that he is hiding out in the Atchafalaya Swamp in Louisiana, and is associated with him in the Rogue Underground."

"So the rumors about a Rogue Underground are true?"

"They sure seem to be."

"Sounds promising. Louisiana is a lot closer than Russia. That would make it easier to obtain the infrared sensors and associated hardware that Blake needs for his telescope."

Red took up the delicate question that he didn't want to ask. "Have you heard anything from Jack?"

"No." Woody stalled. He didn't feel like talking about it but knew that he needed to. "I haven't heard a word from him. And the story I read in the paper last week makes me pretty nervous."

"Yeah. We saw the story on the evening news. Do you think that really was Jack?"

"Well, it was Jack's Jeep. I recognized the stickers in the back window."

"But you don't think it was Jack?"

"No … I don't … I mean … anyone can crack. But Jack—that just seems so unlike the Jack that I have known for four decades. He wouldn't blow himself up. He was no militant. He didn't read that kind of literature. Didn't hang around that kind of people. But I really don't know what to make of the situation, whether he's dead or alive. And if he is still alive, then he is destined for a FEMA camp. Maybe stuck in one already. I think I hate that thought almost as much as the thought of his death." His lower jaw started to tremble.

Red looked away, uncomfortable.

Woody regained his composure and enquired, "Did Ariele arrive safely?"

"Yes. She arrived last Thursday with a nice but dorky guy friend. He's super smart in electronics and computers, and he can weld up a storm. He's already welded the cracked brackets on my brush hog and stiffened the bucket on my tractor. But he's definitely a city kid. Never been fishing. Never been in the woods. Never even picked berries. But now that he's here, I guess he has to stay."

"What's his name?"

"Andrius Markunas."

"Never heard of him. Couldn't be a close friend of hers."

"He wasn't. Ariele had only met him once while visiting church with her friend Irina. But he must have made quite the impression on her. When she was in a bind trying to flee the FBI, she called him."

"The dork part doesn't sound like her," Woody remarked. "She must have been really desperate. But attending church with a friend makes sense." He paused. "Speaking of the safety of young ladies, I'm pretty nervous about Kit. She's likely to face suspicion and interrogation."

"Yeah. No doubt. Her father's a federal fugitive with a quarter million dollar reward on his head."

Around ten-thirty that morning, Red pulled up in front of the lodge. The whole crew came rushing out to welcome Woody. As he stepped out of the pickup, Ariele flew into his arms and gave him a crushing hug. "Glad to see that you're safe." Tears started to roll down her cheeks. "I was afraid that … I would never see you again."

A lump gathered in Woody's throat, and he fought the waves of emotion that threatened to break him down into

143

open tears. "I'm glad to see you too, Moxie. I was worried sick."

After a few hugs and an introduction to Andrius, the rejoicing bunch dragged Woody into the lodge to hear his story and indulge Betsy's raspberry scones.

That afternoon, Woody stood in the room that he and Jack had shared for over a decade, awash with a wave of nostalgia. Looking at the rack of fly rods on the wall, he knew that he was going to have a hard time wetting a fly without thinking of his cousin. He quelled the anger that simmered in his breast, reminding himself that you can't blame God for the things that wicked men do. God was probably just as mad about the situation as he was.

His eyes wandered over to the bookshelf. Jack had been a bona fide bookworm, though secretive about his prepper interest. When he had purchased titles on prepping, he had picked them up one or two at a time from scattered bookstores and had paid in cash. He didn't want to leave a trail of prepper breadcrumbs. The volumes that he finished, he deposited here at the Compound.

With the books were a row of bound notebooks filled with notes on fly fishing and prepping, many adorned with artsy sketches, all written in his fine, impeccable handwriting. He chuckled to himself. *How does a guy write so elegantly? Mine looks like scribbling.* Every summer Jack deposited one or two of his notebooks at the Compound, each one holding hundreds of entries on things like wild edible foods and wilderness skills, as well as notes on streams, fly patterns, hatch dates, and camping sites. They were a treasure trove of information.

He opened the bottom-right desk drawer and pulled out six cigar boxes. The emergency funds Jack had squirreled away were intact—fifty thousand dollars in twenties and twenty thousand in anonymous five-hundred-dollar debit cards. It was part of his retirement plan if the sky fell and his IRA became worthless.

The closet held a broad assortment of gear for camping, survival, and prepping, including a box of burner phones, most of it purchased by Jack. Woody had been lackadaisical about prepping. While he had kept go-bags in his car and at home for run-of-the-mill problems like power outages, earthquakes, and severe weather, he had been loathe to put hard-earned money into preparation for an apocalypse that he doubted would materialize in the next few centuries, much less his lifetime. Instead, he had focused on paying off Kit's school loans and building up his retirement accounts.

Woody spied the parachute bag that was sitting on his bed and remembered why he was in the room in the first place. He unzipped the bag and retrieved a small, bulky bundle. He removed two wraps of tape, then carefully unwrapped the towel he had used for padding, revealing the Swarovski crystal dove, an antique Christmas-tree ornament that Anne had received as a wedding gift from her mother. He stared in heartbroken shock. The priceless treasure lay in two pieces. The head had broken off in the middle of the neck. Carefully, he wrapped the pieces back up in the towel and placed the towel in his sock drawer. For a moment, he was tempted to slide into the morass of despondency. His life was a painful trail of broken things—broken bones, broken careers, a broken marriage, broken dreams. He resisted the gloom, sighed, and shrugged his shoulders. *Maybe it's time to let go and move on, quit nursing the old painful chapters, try to find the next chapter in my life.*

18

the Compound
Monday, July 1, 2019

In celebration of Woody's safe arrival, the Compound members gathered that evening for a cookout of wild boar ribs, fresh corn on the cob, and stuffed jalapenos. Afterward, they sat by the fireplace under the covered patio and talked about the comet and then segued into a discussion of Bible prophecy.

Jordy shared the results of his latest studies on the Russian-led invasion of Israel detailed in Ezekiel 38 and 39. "There is a crucial timing element in this passage that many miss. At the time of Russia's ill-fated invasion, Israel will be living in unwalled cities, enjoying a time of peace. Such peace is not possible while her ancient neighboring enemies—modern-day Palestine, Lebanon, Jordan, Syria, and Saudi Arabia—remain as military threats."

He turned to Psalm 83. "In this passage, these very nations are crushed by a judgment from heaven when they band together to wipe Israel off the map. This can't be a reference to the Yom Kippur War, the Six Day War, or any other war in Israel's past, for none of them involved this particular confederacy, none saw the military threat eliminated, and none involved direct judgment from heaven. This war is a prophecy waiting to be fulfilled. It is the means God uses to introduce the time of peace that Israel enjoys in Ezekiel 38 and 39."

Andrius probed, "So the war in Psalm 83 precedes the Gog and Magog invasion in Ezekiel?"

"In my understanding, the order of events will be the Psalm 83 war, followed by the destruction of the Russian juggernaut in Ezekiel 38 and 39, followed by the tribulation—the last seven years—when the revitalized Roman Empire will dominate the world."

"So the next thing we're looking for in the prophetic timetable is the Psalm 83 War."

"That's my understanding. And the Middle East is barreling down the road to that war. Interestingly enough, Israel insists that she does not want another war, but she also insists that if her neighbors start one, it will be the last war that she will ever fight with them."

The conversation turned to the nations that compose the Russian juggernaut. Jordy opined, "I suspect that the Scandinavian countries are going to join Iran, Ethiopia, Libya, and Germany in the coalition of allies with Russia."

Andrius was intrigued. "Scandinavia? Really? I haven't heard that position before. Most scholars regard Togarmah as a small region in modern Turkey."

Jordy defended his view. "Ezekiel 38:6 indicates that Togarmah is in the *uttermost parts of the north*. This is not a description of the location of Turkey—neither strictly speaking nor relative to Israel. Turkey is far south of the far north, and it is relatively close to Israel. But this description is spot on for the Scandinavian peoples who live in the far north. And it is vast ignorance to insist, as some do, that this can't be a reference to the Scandinavian peoples because they were so isolated that they had nothing to do with the Mediterranean and the Middle East. Many historians have observed that the Scandinavians exported amber and heavy-maned fiord horses from their homelands on the North Sea and the Baltic Sea to various Phoenician ports in the Mediterranean. Ezekiel himself mentions this expansive trade in 27:14 where he observes that Togarmah traded horses, chariot horses, and fiord horses in Tyre."

"So what do you do with the fact that many scholars and maps place Togarmah in Turkey?"

"They are confusing the colony with the motherland. The house of Togarmah did colonize parts of Turkey, as did their Scythian and Germanic cousins. And Turkey derived its name from the Turks who invaded from the steppes beyond the Caspian Sea, a people who were themselves descendants of Togarmah. But the original Togarmic peoples, along with the original Scythian and Germanic peoples, live in their ancient homelands to this day, far less mingled with foreign blood than the descendants of their colonizing ancestors."

"But why the confusion between the homeland and the colony?"

"Revisionist history teaches that no advanced societies

arose outside the Mediterranean and the Middle East. This requires men to insist that the colonies in Asia were the original homeland and that the northern homelands were the colonies."

"How about Turkey?" Andrius continued. "Will she be, as most prophecy teachers teach, one of the nations allied with Russia?"

Jordy continued, "I won't be surprised if Turkey herself is part of the juggernaut too. Her gene pool is flush with the bloodlines of the other invading nations like the Scythians, Gomer, and Togarmah."

Andrius queried, "You mentioned Germany as one of the invading nations. Is Gomer a reference to Germany?"

Jordy replied, "I would rather say that Gomer is a reference to the Gomerians, also known as the Cimmerians or Germans, who dwelt in their homeland in modern Germany as well as in their colony in what is now Turkey."

"So Germany and the Nordic nations," Woody interjected, "are going to align themselves with their Scythian cousins in Russia? That would be a powerful economic bloc."

Jordy nodded. "I don't see how we can escape that conclusion if we let the Bible and the facts of history give us our understanding of Ezekiel 38 and 39."

"How about the fire that falls from heaven and obliterates the Russian juggernaut?" Andrius asked. Will it be literal fire from heaven or nuclear weapons launched by either the West or Israel?"

"Literal fire from heaven. That is the precedent in the Bible. A well-known example is the fire and brimstone that fell on Sodom and Gomorrah. While the Bible only mentions the ultimate cause of that judgment, which was God himself, the secular accounts mention the secondary cause, which was the planet Venus. At the end of the Silver Age, she rained fire from Scandinavia to North Africa and caused Earth to roll on its axis, changing the location of the north and south poles. While the revisionism that reigns in the educational institutions regards this as a fable, the ancients recorded it as history.

"And Venus will return. I believe that she will be the source of the fire that falls upon the Russian juggernaut, the nation of Russia, and the rest of the nations who dwell carelessly on Earth. The morning star will herald the soon coming of the Messianic age."

When Woody and Andrius went to bed that night, their heads were reeling with new information and ideas. Andrius sensed a need to pursue a deeper understanding of Bible prophecy and not be satisfied with the common superficiality. Woody sensed that it was time to get serious about the Bible in the first place—both its Messiah and its prophecies. *If this stuff is going to happen in my lifetime, I want to be on the right side of the one who is behind it.*

19

After Irina finished putting away the dry goods from the prior day's Katahdin Foods delivery, she decided to do a little exploring instead of going straight to the deep freeze in the north warehouse. She frequently poked around in the warehouses while on freezer duty. This wasn't shirking on her part. There just wasn't that much to do. Today, she felt like nosing around in the East warehouse. Half of the main room was a jumble of crates and boxes, mostly salvage from suppliers, warehouses, and bankrupt businesses. Little by little, folks from maintenance opened the crates and boxes and sorted the contents into piles: in-house use, Salvation Army, recycle, or trash. She was curious to see what they had found. There was an unwritten rule that detainees were allowed to take what they wanted from both the unsorted and the sorted piles—a courtesy offered by those who processed the salvage. No one had bothered to ask the camp director if he was okay with the practice. Last week, she had picked up two extra-plush bath towels. Maybe she would find something she could use today. Or maybe she would run into Sally.

As she walked down the east corridor past the boiler, the laundry, and the shower rooms, she found herself thankful that the detainees had it pretty good here—way better than if they had been incarcerated in the federal prison system. They enjoyed a great deal of freedom, and they didn't have to worry about prison gangs.

When she strolled through the open overhead door into the east warehouse, she stopped and stared in wide-eyed amazement—nearly in tears. A baby grand piano sat on a crate bottom, with the crate sides and top leaning against the wall of containers. *Now that's an answer to prayer!* It reminded her of Pastor Vargas' dictum, "Before we pray, the answer's on the way." She sat down and began playing *A Mighty Fortress is Our God*, her favorite hymn since childhood. *Gorgeous tone. Definitely needs tuning though. Gonna have to ask Bryce to order a tuning kit from our supply angel.* As her fingers deftly danced on the keys, oblivious to the world, someone touched her shoulder. She nearly jumped out of her skin.

Sally laughed. "A little jumpy are ya?"

Once Irina recovered herself, her fright turning to giggles, she jubilantly remarked to her friend, "Wow! A grand piano, no less."

"Isn't that the coolest? The first time I looked at the pile, this crate caught my eye. I had hoped to work my way to it yesterday morning. But opening and sorting went slower than I anticipated. When I finally got to the crate late in the afternoon, Bryce slid it out with a forklift so I could access all four sides. Sometime today, he is going to move the piano to the chapel."

"It's a Baldwin in pristine shape. Any idea where it came from?"

"Yeah. The top of the crate and two sides were stenciled with the shipper and the receiver."

Irina examined the top. The block letter writing, though lightly faded, was easily legible. The sender was BALDWIN PIANO AND ORGAN COMPANY, LOVELAND, OH, with a date of 1988. The intended recipient was WHITE SANDS MISSILE RANGE, MAIN BASE, OFFICER'S CLUB. "I'm guessing that it was ordered at the tail end of Reagan's military expansion, but the officer's club wasn't remodeled or replaced as anticipated, so it sat in storage somewhere at White Sands. Oh well. Their loss, our gain."

Sally looked at her incredulously. "How do you know stuff like that, like military expansion and contraction?"

"Most of the prophecy teachers that I follow have an interest in the military strengths of the nations that play important roles in the last days. So I pick up a few things here and there." Irina checked her watch. "Well, I have to get back to work. I'm supposed to sort and organize the new shipment of meat that arrived yesterday morning. Four pallets worth."

Sally didn't want to part just yet. "Maybe I'll join you for a few minutes."

On the way to the freezer, Sally confided in Irina. "I need to get a few things off my chest, stuff I can't share with just anyone."

Irina smiled sweetly. "Sure. Go ahead."

"The week before my arrest, I started getting nervous that things were going to go south in a hurry. I downloaded everything in my possession on the Rogue and Project Minoa onto a thumb drive which I hid in a secluded location. It contains every relevant file and email from the time I was summoned to Washington, D.C., in December 2017 up to that point. Somehow, this information needs to get into the hands of the Rogue Underground. I also included a copy of a paper that I had hidden online earlier—"

Irina interrupted her. "Wait a minute. You were aware … the government is aware … of the Rogue Underground?"

"The government knows they exist, but they haven't been able to crack its membership or trace them to a location—not physical, not on the web."

Irina relaxed. "That's good to know. But I interrupted you. You were starting to say something about hiding a paper online."

"Yes. In March of 2018, while attending an astronomy conference at the University of Arizona, I ran into an old acquaintance, Dr. Lewellyn Ashbury, the assistant head of the astronomy department at the University of Texas in Austin. I appreciated the old curmudgeon, so I took him out for coffee. While we were swapping gripes about the state of modern astronomy, he leaned over and whispered, 'What would you say if I told you I had proof that the biblical apocalypse is on the way?' I gave him a skeptical look but didn't say anything. I didn't know what to say. I couldn't let him know that it was old news to me that this planet was headed for the apocalypse.

"He opened his attaché and slid a thick folder to me. 'This is a research paper that was given to me by a former student who was an editor at *Sci-Fi Today* until the feds shut it down. He received it a few months ago via anonymous email and forwarded a copy to me to see what I thought. Two weeks after he sent it, the *Sci-Fi Today* office was raided by the FBI, and my friend was never heard from again.' He paused for a moment, then continued. 'Everything you need to know is in here. I don't have time to do anything with it because I'm dying of cancer. I feel like death warmed over and only have a few months to live at most.' Shaking like a leaf, I picked up the folder of illegal research and slipped it into my bag. During the drive home, I thought about tossing it but didn't. The misgivings that I had started to have about the cover-up were budding into quiet defiance.

"When I got home, I discovered that the folder included the paper, a note, and the login info for an account at the University of Arizona belonging to Dr. Youngblood, a deceased professor of astronomy. The note explained that prior to his death, he had given his login info to my friend so he could posthumously publish two of the doctor's unfinished papers online. Now Lewellyn wanted me to use this login info and publish the apocalyptic paper, expanded and updated, under Dr. Youngblood's name in a masked file on his professional page.

"I set the paper aside and didn't do anything with it. I was busy at the time and not ready to commit myself against the conspiracy that I was entangled in. But that summer my indignation with the cover-up went from simmering to boiling. I could no longer repress my feelings or justify my inaction. It took me two months to rewrite the paper and expand it with material that the original author hadn't been aware of. I published it in late September.

"Ariele stumbled upon this paper while doing online research and cited it extensively in a paper she gave to me on the Rogue about a month ago. Because of the eavesdropping of a pompous colleague of mine, I was forced to report her for impermissible research. Her paper was confiscated by the FBI, and it's a safe assumption that her source paper—the Dr. Youngblood paper—was taken down too."

Irina smiled at the mileage that her article for *Sci-Fi Today* had gotten, despite the fact that the magazine had been shut down before it could be published. "So Ariele's paper didn't tell you anything you didn't already know?"

"No."

"And you were aware of the Rogue from the beginning?"

"Almost from the beginning. Less than forty-eight hours after you filed your initial report with the Minor Planet Center, the President held a high-level emergency meeting in the Cabinet Room that was attended by the Vice President, the Chief of Staff, the National Security Advisor, the Homeland Security Advisor, the director of NASA, the head of CNEOS, the head of the PDCO, and Dr. Goldblum. At this meeting, Dr. Goldblum impressed the President, who appointed him to assemble a team of twenty-four astrophysicists, astronomers, and aerospace engineers who would be responsible for Rogue research, for fleshing out a scientific-sounding cover story, and for coordinating with the federal agencies tasked with protecting the classified information. Less than a month later, I was summoned to Washington, D.C., by the National Security Advisor. It turned out that Dr. Goldblum had selected me to lead the twenty-four-member team. We spent three intense days in meetings where we were introduced to the Rogue and our mission."

"I wondered what that rascal was up to. After the discovery, he made a lot of secret trips to Washington, D.C., for NASA meetings that weren't on any NASA calendar."

"Yeah. We all did a bit of sneaking around."

"But how … when … did you get to the place where you turned on the establishment and began to go maverick in your heart?"

"I started having my doubts after a D.C. session in early March of last year. By our meeting in June, I was completely disillusioned."

"Disillusioned with what?"

"I was frustrated that the government's plans to save their own butts and the butts of a handful of powerful people while letting the majority of the population perish. They intend to take refuge in Arks, which are huge bunkers deep underground in strategic locations, and let the masses fend for themselves in Cold War-era fallout shelters and FEMA centers. They have no intention of warning the public. They intend to let them stay ignorant until some amateur astronomer notices an approaching threat, most likely an asteroid knocked out of the Main Belt when it is only days or weeks away from impact. I was outraged. Their plan is immoral."

"Did you call them out or raise an objection?"

"Asking any questions which implied that you might be having doubts about the propriety of the course was regarded as grounds for immediate removal from the team and a permanent assignment to a FEMA camp."

"So you were caught between a rock and a hard place."

"I was. But I did dare to ask, once, during a Minoa Research session what justification we should offer if the public ever called us out for hiding the knowledge of the comet from them. We were told to stick with the message. Hard decisions had to be made to preserve the human race, including the decision to keep the comet a secret. The government couldn't risk panic among the masses. When I pressed them on the problem of limited preservation facilities, their answer was similar. Hard decisions had to be made to preserve the human race. There were limited funds and resources, so it was only reasonable that there would be limited preservation slots."

"Wow. That's cold-blooded."

"No doubt. Using tax money to preserve the big shots and their friends while letting the man on the street fend for himself. It was painful trying to coexist with that kind of degraded thinking."

As they arrived at the freezer, Irina turned to Sally. "So where did you hide your thumb drive?"

"I hid it at the first hairpin corner on the Idlehour Trail about a third of a mile from the trailhead on the Mount

Wilson Toll Road. At the hairpin corner, hike NNW through the trees and look for a big oak tree with a dark rock at its base, roots growing around it. On the back side of the tree, look for a flat rock. Under it you'll find a ginger mints Altoids tin." Sally stopped and looked Irina in the eyes. "This thumb drive needs to get in the hands of people who are willing and able to disseminate the information to the public."

Irina put her arm around her. "If God wants that to happen, it will happen. Simple as that. No worries." She handed Sally a coat, hat, and gloves from one of the lockers outside the freezer and extended her an invitation. "Why don't you join me in the freezer for a while? I have to unload the pallets, shelve the boxes in the proper locations, rotate according to date, and take the pallets to the pallet pile in the west warehouse."

"Well, I hate the cold. But I can join you for a few minutes."

They walked into the freezer and examined the four pallets that straddled the center of the aisle. The first was low-grade beef, mostly shanks and extra-gnarly chuck. The second was deer meat. The last two were horsemeat.

Sally was shocked. "Horsemeat?"

Irina laughed. "It actually doesn't taste that bad. You just have to get over the shock of eating an animal that most Americans would never dream of eating. Took me a while. Eating horse is like eating the neighbor's dog."

"But I didn't think horsemeat was legal for human consumption."

"It is since the FEMA bill. A bipartisan committee argued that the legalization of horse meat for food could save the government a lot of money. Meat is expensive. Horse meat is cheap. The bill mandated that thirty percent of the horsemeat from processing plants must be earmarked for FEMA camps and prisons. The rest goes to dog food plants. You won't see it in the supermarkets."

"So where does the horse meat come from?"

"Culling the wild herds out West and repurposing old or injured horses from ranches and racing circles."

"What about the deer meat? What's the story behind that?"

"The venison comes from game farms and illegal harvests that have been confiscated by fish and game officers. We have also gotten boxes of elk, salmon, and tuna. The meat is minimally processed, bone-in, and frozen in fifty-pound boxes."

20

the Compound
Tuesday, July 2, 2019

It was a gorgeous Big Sky evening with thunderheads dominating the northern horizon and blue skies overhead when the crew gathered under the covered patio for grilled lime-cayenne trout. As they ate, the storm edged closer, punctuating their meal with lightning flashes and long rumbles of thunder. Woody took a deep breath, relishing the odor and invigoration of ozone in the air. He was back in his beloved Montana.

After they finished their dinner, they gathered around the fireplace for the first Rogue-era Compound meeting. Jordy began in his easy-going manner. "We have four items of business this evening: Ariele's new intel on the Rogue, Woody's thoughts from an electric universe perspective on the upcoming dalliance between the Rogue and Mars, Blake's update on the telescope, and Woody's idea for making contact with Kit and Sam."

He turned and nodded to Ariele. "We'll start with you. What intel on the Rogue do you have that some of us may not be familiar with?"

Ariele skewed her mouth and ran her hand through her lavender-tinted hair. "The emails that I hacked before I fled contain several interesting revelations which shed light on the behavior of NASA and the government over the past year and a half. I have summed them up in seven brief observations.

"ONE. The Rogue situation is classified Top Secret and handled under the clearance Minoa. I think this alludes to the catastrophic end of the Minoan civilization at the close of the Bronze Age and implies that the government fears a worst-case scenario.

"TWO. Contrary to the reports that NASA released to the media, the real purpose for recertifying Space Shuttle Atlantis in January 2018 was the revitalization of the Spitzer and WISE space telescopes so they could be used for cold-body research on the Rogue.

"THREE. Spectroscopy conducted by the Spitzer found that the comet is composed of iron, nickel, cobalt, and platinum-group metals, with high amounts of rare-earth elements, tungsten, and molybdenum. Due to the high percentage of heavy metals, NASA estimates that the mass of the Rogue is nearly equal to that of Mars."

Blake exclaimed, "That's nuts! A planet-sized comet that is denser than iron." He shook his head. "I still haven't psychologically adjusted to this situation. It's one thing to theorize about the planets being shaken in the last days. It's another thing to realize that the planet shaker is headed for your backyard."

"I hear ya," Woody agreed. "And the shaking is certain. With that kind of mass, the Rogue will definitely knock

Mars out of orbit, even if it passes by twice as far away as expected."

Ariele smiled at the guys and continued. "FOUR. The unusual launch window for the ESA's ExoMars mission was due to the fact that NASA usurped the mission for their own purposes. They intend to fake a failed orbit around Mars, use the Red Planet like a slingshot, send the probe towards Jupiter, pretend to take up a new Trojan mission, and land the probe on the Rogue.

"FIVE. Scientists are convinced that the comet won't develop a coma because it is a rocky body, and therefore they believe that the public won't find out about its existence. They are married to the dogma that comas only develop when frozen snowballs get too close to the sun, and the ice sublimates. But I suspect that they are in for a rude awakening. If Woody is correct that comets are stony bodies and their comas are formed by ionization through electrolysis, then the Rogue is going to explode on the scene as the largest and brightest comet the world has seen since the monster that destroyed the Minoan and Mycenaean empires around 1500 B.C.

"SIX. According to NASA's latest calculations, the Rogue will pass Mars at about 18,000 miles. This may seem like a great distance, but it is terrifyingly close. To put things in perspective, imagine that the moon was twelve times closer to Earth, which would make its diameter in our sky twelve times larger. Now picture that disc expanding another fifty percent. This gives you a rough idea of how large the Rogue would appear from the surface of Mars if it passed at 18,000 miles."

Woody shook his head in disbelief. Though a trained astronomer himself, the illustration drove home the sheer magnitude of the threat and made him shudder—a visceral uneasiness. He looked around. The others appeared unnerved too.

Ariele continued, "SEVEN. The government expects the Rogue to knock a few asteroids out of orbit on its way through the asteroid belt, and these asteroids are the only threats they anticipate for Earth. As for its effect on Mars, they foresee it giving the Red Planet a slight gravitational nudge that will warp its orbit maybe one percent max, an aberration which they expect will correct itself over the next few centuries."

Blake enquired, "So where is this comet now?"

"According to my calculations and the latest reports on the internet, it is around one hundred million miles inside Neptune."

"How long do we have until it reaches Mars?"

"Just over five years—in late August 2024."

Ariele fielded several more questions, then Jordy turned the floor over to Woody. "From an electric universe perspective, what do you think will happen when the Rogue makes its near pass of Mars?"

Woody grinned. "Before I address that point, I have a confession to make. I used to think that Blake was a little unhinged because he read Velikovsky's books and believed the ancient accounts about the planets periodically visiting Earth and bombarding it with stones, fire, and the thunderbolts of the gods. But after facing the undeniable evidence that a planet-sized comet is headed for Mars and likely to bump it out of orbit, it no longer seems ridiculous to believe that some of the planets had comet-like orbits in ancient times and periodically wrought devastation on Earth. The fact is, these near passes and visitations handily explain why ancient man worshipped and feared Mars and Venus—under different names in the different cultures."

He looked around and was pleasantly surprised to see Ariele nodding in agreement.

"Now as far as the interaction between the Rogue and Mars goes, it will be characterized by electrical manifestations. Because the two bodies have disparate electrical charges and high capacities, they will engage in electrical interaction even if they pass at a distance of 50,000 miles or greater. This exchange will be manifested in three primary ways.

"The first is plasma discharges. These are the thunderbolts that the ancients witnessed their gods (the planets) hurling against each other. The upcoming battle between the Rogue and Mars will be visible from Earth with the naked eye.

"The second is surface restructuring. The plasma discharges are, for all practical purposes, insanely large plasma cutting torches. This electrical arcing will excavate canyons and craters and fling enormous amounts of debris into space. Valles Marineris, the massive canyon on Mars, is an example of the staggering power that can be unleashed in these arcs. According to the ancients, this massive scar appeared when the goddess smote Mars with the thunderbolt of Jupiter."

Andrius shook his head—it seemed like scoffing to Woody—and interrupted, "Aren't most scientists convinced that Valles Marineris was caused by flowing water?"

"That's the prevailing view," Woody replied. "But it's based on wishful thinking, not scientific evidence. The canyon's elevation gradient and its lack of an outlet testify that it was not formed by water drainage. Furthermore, the fractal patterns, the scalloping on the walls, and the detached pitting associated with the canyon are hallmarks of electrical excavation by plasma discharge.

"On top of that, ninety percent of the Martian craters are better explained by electrical excavations than impacts because they feature ninety-degree angles, not random angles as we would expect from random impacts. They also demonstrate other electrical quirks like strings of craters, craters with central peaks, and the same ratio of large to small craters. All of these features have been replicated in the laboratory with spark-machining apparatuses, validating the electrical excavation theory."

Woody tried to make eye contact with Andrius, hoping to gauge the impact these facts were having on him, but the young man looked away. *That implies a bullseye.* He continued with his observations on the electrical interactions that could be expected. "The third thing we can expect would be mutual electromagnetic repelling which would lead to the orbital displacement of both bodies. Where their new orbits would take them is hard to tell, but the odds are pretty high that at least one of them, given time, would pose a threat to Earth."

The contrary young man interrupted again. "A threat? Isn't that a bit of an understatement? If either Mars or the Rogue made a near pass of Earth, wouldn't that be a true extinction-event scenario?"

Before Woody could reply, Jordy interjected, "No. There is zero chance that an extinction event is in man's future. Our future is not in the hands of random nature. It is in the hands of the Almighty God who controls the whole of nature for his own purposes. And the Bible clearly teaches that He has chosen to dwell with mankind on this planet forever in his eternal kingdom."

Woody nodded in agreement, then continued. "In a near pass with Mars, Earth would face a variety of dangers like plasma excavation, gravitational effects, and electromagnetic phenomena. But I'm going to direct this question to Blake since he has spent more time studying planetary catastrophe in ancient times and has a much better handle on what to expect." He nodded to the younger astronomer.

Blake obliged. "The first thing that comes to my mind is tsunamis. A near pass would create enormous swells—more like the monster waves in movies like *Deep Impact* than anything the modern world has seen. Greek historians inform us that the comet which brought the Bronze Age to a close was accompanied by a gigantic swell of the sea— known as the Deucalion flood—which not only wiped out all of the coastal villages but also many that were miles inland. Archaeology has uncovered evidence of this mega-tsunami. On several Greek islands, massive slabs of coastal basalt have been found miles inland and hundreds of feet above sea level. This implies a tsunami of monstrous size and force—hundreds of feet high.

"Last night I made some rough calculations on what we could expect if Mars made a close pass of Earth. At the same distance as the moon, its gravitational pull would be nine times greater than the moon's and would produce tidal swells nine times greater than the tides produced by the moon. At 24,000 miles, its gravitational pull would be ninety times greater than the moon's. Can you imagine the global destruction that would occur if we were walloped with tides that were ninety times more massive than our current tides?

"Besides the monster tides, the gravitational tug would also pull the crust up in large rolling land waves, causing every fault to slip, and it would heat up the mantle, setting off dozens of volcanic eruptions. The planet would be engulfed in a chaotic nightmare of mega earthquakes, titanic tsunamis, and super volcanoes which would resculpt the surface of the Earth. Mountain ranges would be collapsed and raised, islands erased and formed, valleys filled and carved, and waterways drained and created.

"Earth would also be battered by showers of stones up to boulder size and possibly choked in a cloud of red grit and dust. Worse, the Martian material could introduce perchlorate poisoning. The bottom line is, if Mars makes a close pass of Earth, it will be the worst global disaster since the comet visitation that destroyed the Mycenaean and Minoan empires and brought the Bronze Age to a close."

Ariele glanced at Andrius. He was struggling with the

jump from run-of-the-mill asteroids in the last days to planetary catastrophism. She wavered between empathy and frustration. While it did take time to process the information—her own journey hadn't broken any speed records—he was far more emotionally unreceptive to new ideas than most. *Oh well. He'll get over it. He just needs time to get over the psychological shock of having his beliefs challenged.*

Jordy directed traffic once again. "Now that we got you talking, Blake, how about an update on your telescope?"

"Andrius and I have started working on the plans for a motorized carriage with a heated cab, but our main focus right now is finishing the covered patio. We anticipate that the actual construction, once we get started, will be fairly straightforward. The difficult part will be obtaining the banned components. As you know, the Homeland Security Act forbids the possession or import of infrared sensors, super-coolants, and mirrors over twenty inches for everyone except NASA-affiliated astronomical organizations."

"Have you come up with any workable ideas?"

"Our plan for obtaining coolant is to fabricate our own system for making and storing liquid hydrogen. We are currently researching sources for an electrolyzer, compressors, heat exchangers, and storage tanks. I think we'll be able to get this equipment through stateside connections in the petroleum industry.

The sensors will be tougher. Rumors in the *Planet-X Cover-up* chatroom suggest that the black market in Russia is our best bet, though I have no idea where to start with this lead. We face a similar problem with the mirror. Alluna

Optics in Germany offers a sixty-inch ceramic option which is ideal, but ordering one directly is out of the question. My idea is to have a third party in Russia order one for us, then we retrieve it while on our infrared-sensor mission. The downside to this solution is that the mirror weighs over two thousand pounds—a logistics nightmare."

"No worries," Jordy replied. "I have a hunch my boys will have a few ideas for us when they show up later this summer."

Ariele enquired, "Home on leave?"

"No. They're getting out."

Woody spoke up, "I think I might have a lead for infrared sensors. While riding the rails, I met a cowboy named Lobo who mentioned that he had bumped into my old friend Burt Snedeker, the senior professor of astronomy at the University of Wyoming for many years. Apparently, the story about Burt getting lost in the mountains while elk hunting was fake news. In reality, he had been invited to a research position in the Minoa project, which we know is the government's cover-up of the Rogue. When he was informed that the project was Top Secret and involved covering up the existence of a comet that posed an existential threat to mankind, he wasn't interested. But he didn't admit that over the phone. Instead, he feigned interest. After he hung up, he drove to the university, 'borrowed' some valuable infrared tech, returned home, packed his bug-out bag, left a message on his phone that he was going black-powder elk hunting with a friend over the weekend, and hopped a train headed south. According to Lobo, Burt is hiding out somewhere deep in Atchafalaya Swamp in Louisiana."

"That much classified information came out over the phone?" Jordy asked.

"I suspect it was a case of loose lips," Woody replied. "Burt was very highly regarded in the astronomy world. I think someone let their guard down and overshared."

Jordy eyed Woody. "You trust this cowboy?"

"I do. He could have turned me in for a reward, and he didn't."

"Maybe he's waiting to catch a whole nest of troublemakers instead of a lone ranger."

"My gut instincts tell me that he really is a member of the Rogue Underground."

"No matter what your instincts say, we need to verify that he can be trusted before we contact him about this lead on infrared sensors. To do that, we need to connect with the Rogue Underground and find out if he is a bona fide member. The problem is, we can't join the room unless a member sets up an account for us."

Woody replied, "We can verify if Lobo really is who he says he is in ten minutes. He told me that he would set up a Rogue Underground account for me. So all we have to do is try to log in with the username and password I gave him. If we get in, then he's legit."

Jordy nodded. "Sounds like a plan. How about tonight? We can use Red's Buster account."

"Not gonna happen tonight. He told me to give him four or five days. It was going to be that long before he could get to a secure site where he could safely set me up."

Jordy continued, "Okay. We'll take care of it later. Let's move on to the last item of business, which is making contact with Woody's daughter Kit and her dig partner Sam. They are currently on a dig in Utah. Woody, you mentioned that you have an idea?"

"I do. Several years back, Jack devised an emergency contact plan for us and the girls to use in TEOTWAWKI scenarios. I found his notes on the plan in one of his notebooks this afternoon and brushed up on it. It's a simple plan that uses burner phones. But I need to initiate contact a long way away from here in case their phones are compromised."

Blake interrupted, "What kind of timetable are we looking at?"

"As soon as possible. In the next few days, preferably."

"Well, I need to make a shopping trip to Billings and Williston for materials for the telescope and a few other projects. We could leave tomorrow morning, stop in Billings, then head to Williston. You could make your contact on Thursday morning while I'm poking around in the Williston area."

"What about security? I can't afford to be noticed by a camera."

"You would have to stay in the camper. Andrius and I would ride in the truck."

"Sounds like a workable plan to me."

Blake turned to Jordy. "What do you think?"

"I'm on board with the general idea. But Thursday is July

4th. Is that going to be a good day to do your shopping in Williston?"

"July 4th will actually be a great time. Places like Bernie's Metals will still be open and will have lower than usual traffic."

Jordy and Woody glanced at each other, then nodded in approval.

Blake was excited. "Great. Since everyone appears to be on board, let's plan on leaving tomorrow morning right after breakfast."

"How about an escape plan?" Jordy interrupted. Contacting them won't be that difficult. But how are we going to get them out of there if they are under surveillance?"

Woody answered, "I don't think we'll have to risk entering the dig site or even getting close to it. Sam will figure something out. She has more experience in getting out of tight situations than the rest of us put together."

"Alright." Jordy conceded. "We'll let you and Sam worry about the girls' escape plan." He looked around. "Is there anything else we should discuss?"

Ariele spoke up. "What can we do for Irina? We are indebted to her, after all. She's the one who discovered the comet and sounded the alarm. My guess is that she is in a FEMA camp somewhere. I think we should see if we can locate her and maybe break her out."

"Break her out of a FEMA camp?" Andrius exclaimed. "That's crazy. We're not the team from Mission Impossible. We're a bunch of nobodies who are already in over our heads. I go to bed every evening expecting to be awakened in the middle of the night with dogs barking, a flashlight in my face, and soldiers surrounding my bed. Now you want me to think about going inside the barbed wire? No thanks."

The ladies nodded their heads in agreement. They didn't like the thought of their husbands getting involved in such a caper.

Woody calmed the scene down. "Let's take things one step at a time. The only thing we need to worry about right now is locating Irina. We don't even know if it's possible to locate her. The FEMA camps used for those accused of Security Act violations are secretive. The government doesn't even acknowledge their existence."

"Do you have any ideas, Woody," Jordy asked, "on how to get the ball rolling with this?"

"Possibly. I'm gonna contact Joby, my old barista, and see if he's willing to help track down Irina. He told me once that he had a private investigator friend who despised Big Brother government and wasn't averse to taking slightly shady jobs."

"Get on it," Jordy encouraged him. "But I suggest that we make Kit and Sam our primary focus until their situation is resolved." The crew voiced their agreement. "One last chance. Any further items of business that need to be addressed?"

Ariele piped up. "We absolutely need a small-batch coffee roaster in the lodge." Everyone chuckled and Woody seconded the motion.

21

Williston, ND ... dig site near Jensen, UT
Thursday, July 4, 2019

Blake arrived early at Bernie's Metals in Williston, North Dakota, but not early enough to be first. Over a dozen trucks from oil field construction companies were already waiting in line. At 7:15 a.m. the office manager drove up in an F-150 King Ranch, unlocked the gate on the chain-link fence, and waved the line through. Andrius was boyishly wide-eyed as they entered the expansive yard and drove past row upon row of neatly stacked piles of various grades and gauges of structural steel, iron, aluminum, and other metals. While the boys drove around the yard looking for steel in angle, channel, and tube that was suitable for their telescope project, Woody sat in the camper, anxiously waiting for two hours to pass so he could send a secure text to Sam. *Time never goes slower than when you desperately want it to go fast.* He needed to wait until 8:15 a.m. Mountain Time before he sent his text because he wanted Sam to be on site digging when she got it. It would be too risky to send it earlier when she might be sitting in a morning meeting or chatting with someone.

Sam was busy picking and sweeping a mastodon tusk, enjoying the cool Utah morning, when her phone made two brief vibrations in the thigh pocket of her fatigues. She was tempted to ignore the text message, but curiosity got the best of her. *Who could that possibly be?* She rarely received texts. None of her closest friends were texters. She retrieved her phone. The number was unfamiliar. But the message identified the author. "Hey Bag Lady. I want a rematch. Roadrunner. If interested, call me back on your way to your happy place." A smile crossed her face. It was Woody. And he was safe. *Kit is going to be ecstatic.* The poor girl had been worried sick since she had learned that her father was a wanted fugitive.

She chuckled at the *Bag Lady* and *Roadrunner* remark. It brought to mind one of her fondest memories, the camping trip in the Uintas four years back when she, Kit, Woody, and Jack had gotten together for five days at a picturesque lake nestled at 8500 feet. They had enjoyed campfires, fly fishing, hiking, and a gunny sack race. Because of the torrid pace that Woody had set on the trail during their hikes, she had given him the nickname Roadrunner. When it came time for the gunny sack race—they actually used woven-poly bags—the girls had insisted on slowing the guys down by putting rocks in their bags so that the race would be fair. Jack's rock had been quite heavy, and he had come in last. Woody's had been a bit lighter, and he had been in the lead most of the race, but she had nipped him at the finish line. While all four were rolling on the ground in laughter, Woody had teased her about being the fastest bag lady on the planet. The name had hung on, though more of an inside joke than a nickname.

During those days in the mountains, Sam had fallen in love. She hadn't felt such feelings since she was twenty-five when a dashing officer in the British army had swept her off her feet. She had walked away from his charms after he had given her an ultimatum that she couldn't submit to—give up her search for diamonds and gold in South America and settle down with him in England. She hadn't been ready to settle down. When the new rush of feelings had swept over her in the mountains of Utah, she had resisted in a similar manner, uncertain what she wanted. Fast forward four years, and now she was ready to settle down—half settle down at any rate. But the man she pined for was supposedly dead. She consoled herself with a dose of sour grapes. Perhaps it was better this way. It would be worse if he were alive and the feelings weren't mutual.

She dragged her swirling emotions away from the bittersweet memories and focused on the matter at hand—Woody's message. His text was clever. She could picture the FBI agents that were monitoring the transmissions in and out of the camp reading a risqué element into it that didn't belong there. What the text was trying to convey wasn't difficult to figure out. Call him back when she was on the way to her happy place meant to call him when she was on the way to her campsite—when no prying ears were around.

The text was followed by a call-back number. She recalled that she was supposed to remember something about call-back numbers. *C'mon dig deep girl … oh, yeah, the phone number code that Jack made me memorize during the Uinta camping trip.* At an evening campfire, while imparting some of his spook-craft wisdom, he had talked about scrambled call-back numbers. "If you get a message from an associate with a call-back number, you need to transpose the numbers according to an agreed-upon pattern. My favorite is to move the odd numbers to the next odd slot to the right, subtract two from all the even numbers, and reverse the first three." She smiled as she recalled his efforts to get her to memorize the pattern, quizzing her later on that evening, the next day, and their last day together. What she hadn't known at the time, but knew now, was that the call-back code was part of Jack's plan to communicate with Kit and herself if things went south.

And they had gone south. Her thoughts quickly descended into the depths of the dangers they faced, replacing the pleasant memories with uneasiness. Woody was on the lam, wanted by the feds. Jack was reportedly dead. And the FBI was keeping a close eye on Kit. *What in the world is going on?* She couldn't believe that Jack and Woody were real criminals. What had they gotten themselves tangled up in? She hoped that Woody would shed some light on what was going on when she called back.

Gotta get back to work. She memorized the call-back number in case she lost her phone, then returned to her pick and whisk broom. She would transpose the numbers later and record the number in her pocket notebook, masking it with the secret code that she developed in Africa to safeguard the information that she needed to bust the ivory smugglers and put them behind bars.

22

When her workday drew to a close, Sam carried several large fragments of the mastodon tusk that she had excavated that day to the preparation tent for cleaning and restoration. Then she returned to her camper, changed into fresh jeans and a safari shirt, quickly packed her duffel bag, and climbed into her Jeep. A smile crept across her face as she turned the ignition. She was on her way to her happy place, an untrammeled plateau that bordered the Uinta mountains and overlooked the Green River. It was the perfect place to indulge some loneliness—at least for her. There was a babbling stream, plenty of firewood, and one of those breathtaking postcard views that Utah is known for.

When she was thirty-nine miles from the dig site, and sixteen from her campsite, the cell phone tower she was looking for peeked out from behind the hill, sitting alone on the distant horizon. This stretch was one of the few in the area where she could get a signal. She could have gotten a slightly stronger signal from the hilltop about a mile back, but she felt exposed up there. She pulled onto the side of the dirt road, gawked at a couple dozen mule deer relaxing in the shade, then retrieved her phone from her purse and stepped out of her Jeep to make her call to Woody.

But something didn't seem right. She thought she heard a muffled lawnmower sound in the still mountain air and looked around. On the horizon about a mile behind her and at about 10,000 feet, she spotted a speck moving through the air. She pulled out her binoculars, found the speck, and focused. *Bunny raisins.* A drone—probably a Predator equipped for surveillance—was making broad loops. Scanning the area underneath the drone, she noticed a cloud of dust rising above the hill a mile back. Moments later, a dark van with whip antennas crested the hill and stopped. *Add rats to the raisins.*

She swung her glasses around and began glassing the hillsides as if she were scanning for more mule deer. The surveillance van looked like that one that had been parked near the dig site for the past week listening to their calls. They must have read the text she had received yesterday and become curious.

Think quick, girl … I got it. I'll call mom, let Stingray pick up the call, and feed the fed boys a line of malarkey. She chuckled to herself. *These guys may have cooler toys than the bad guys I messed with in the past. But they're not half as cunning.*

She leaned against her Jeep and called her mother. "Hi mom, this is Sam."

"Glad to hear your voice hon'. I wish you'd call more often."

"Mom, I call at least twice a month."

"So what have you been up to? I've been fighting a nasty cough."

"Sorry to hear that," Sam said. "I've been busy with the same old, same old. Digging up dinosaur bones, cleaning them, preserving them. I did have a couple weird things happen recently though."

"Oh, really?"

"Yesterday, I got a strange text from a guy who called himself Roadrunner. Sounded like he was propositioning me. Got no idea who he is or what he was talking about. Pretty odd. I'm guessing it was a wrong number."

"That is strange. But the world is full of weird people nowadays. Anyways, back to my cough—"

Sam ignored her and kept on talking. "And last week the FBI showed up at the dig site and spent hours talking to Kit. Since then a surveillance van has been parked near the site. Makes me nervous. Is there some secret shadiness in her life or family? Maybe I shouldn't be spending so much time with her?"

"I've told you a thousand times, hon'. You can't trust anyone. Anyways, back to my cough."

Sam let her mother ramble on for a few minutes about her aches and troubles, then brought the call to a close. "Hey mom, gotta run. A thunderstorm is rolling in and I want to get some cloud and lightning pics." She traded her binoculars for her camera, then began snapping shots of the angry thunderheads rolling in from the southeast.

Five minutes later the federal agents, sensing that Sam

was a dead-end and not wanting to be caught on the hilltop when the storm hit, packed up their drone and left. But the savvy adventuress decided to wait for the cover of darkness before continuing to her campsite. She wanted to make it as difficult as possible for anyone to follow her—just in case. She retreated to her Jeep, retrieved a book on Spanish galleon wrecks out of her duffel bag, curled up for some reading time, and waited for nightfall.

Two hours later, Sam continued her journey with her lights off, ecstatic at her good fortune. Not only was her trip veiled by the cloudy night, but the rain was coming down hard enough that it would likely obscure her tracks. After a long, painstakingly slow drive, she arrived at her campsite. Though lightning could still be seen flashing over the Uintas, the storm had passed, and the stars were twinkling overhead. Exhausted by her ordeal, she willed her tired body to stay functioning long enough to set up camp, then she crawled into her sleeping bag and shut her eyes.

The next morning, Sam rose early and drove to the crest of the hill where the surveillance van had been parked, arriving shortly before sunrise. With her binoculars, she scanned the roads, the ridges, and the sky for any sign of the FBI agents or their drones. When nothing turned up, she drove back down the hill to the site where she preferred to place her calls.

Once there, she picked up her phone and texted her sister Lindsey who lived in Minneapolis. She hoped that if anyone was scanning the communications going through the cell tower, looking for action that might be hers, they would associate her with the texting and not with the secure call that she was going to make at the same time.

Five minutes into her text conversation with her sister, she picked up the secure Blackphone that Jack had given her, opened up the Tor browser, started Deadbolt Call, chose the secure VOIP option, entered Woody's unscrambled burner number, and hit the call button.

Woody was startled from his morning reading by his Blackphone buzzing on the table and answered nervously, "This is Roadrunner."

"Hi Woody," Sam said. "Sorry I didn't call last night. The feds were tracking me from a hilltop about a mile away with a Stingray setup. So I gave them a red herring instead. I called my mom and told her that I had received an odd text the other day from some unknown guy and that I figured it was a wrong number."

"No worries. You made the right decision. Love your diversionary tactics too. And I'm glad to see that you called me with the VOIP option. Sounds like you paid closer attention to Jack's lectures on secure communications than I did."

"Well, you know me. Hanging on his every word."

Woody chuckled. "So how are you doing?"

"No, ladies get to ask first, even if they are two-thirds tomboy."

"Two-thirds, how about four-thirds?" Woody retorted. He heard her snicker. It was good to hear her laugh. That implied that she was bearing up well.

"So where are you?" Sam demanded.

"I'm hiding out at a secure location which I won't disclose now for security reasons."

"How did you escape? The feds are looking everywhere for you."

"The short version is a brutal hike in the mountains, a transporter who was as cold as death, a hairy ride on a freight train, and a friendly transient by the name of Lobo. I'll give you the long version when you and Kit have safely joined us at our hideout."

"So why are you on the run?"

"An associate of mine at Caltech helped expose a cover-up. A planet-sized comet is headed for a collision with Mars. Both bodies will be bumped into new orbits, creating chaos in the inner solar system and posing a threat to Earth. The government is trying to keep a lid on this. They don't want the public to erupt in panic. I'm on the run because the government knows that I know."

"Are you telling me that the comet is real after all?"

"As real as the freckles on your face."

"So hackers really did access NASA computers?"

"They sure did. And my associate at Caltech was one of them. She hacked her boss's computer."

"Wow! That's a punch in the gut! I had ignored my usual distrust of the media because every major news outlet— liberal, conservative, and independent alike—backed the White House's official narrative that the comet story is a hoax. They claimed that nobody can hack their way past the government's next-gen firewall, which NASA deployed two years ago. They further claimed that the supposed

Anonymous leaks were part of an elaborate ruse by Russian agents trying to destabilize America with a story that capitalized on our love for conspiracy theories and apocalyptic paranoia. Supposedly, the FBI had uncovered substantial evidence proving that FSB and SVR agents—pretending to be Anonymous members who had hacked into NASA computers—had released the comet story on the web."

"Yeah. I myself believed that Russian-conspiracy spin for a while. But hard evidence has convinced me that the apocalypse is on its way. And the government is convinced too, or they wouldn't be hot on my tail. They absolutely do not want the truth to get out."

"Is this why Jack was taken out?" Her voice faltered.

"I'm not sure that he was taken out. I'm still holding onto hope … but … well … I just don't know what to think." He swallowed hard.

Sam was silent for a moment. Woody thought he heard her stifle an outburst of tears. She regained her composure and continued. "The FBI showed up last week and interrogated Kit. She took it pretty hard when they told her that Jack was a terrorist and had died in a suicide bombing. And she broke into tears when they informed her that you were being sought over Homeland Security charges."

"That would be hard news to take. Finding out that your father is a federal fugitive on the lam and a favorite relative is a suicide bomber."

"They grilled her for four hours while connected to Casper. And though they appeared to be convinced that she knew nothing about either Jack's missteps or yours, yet they are still monitoring the camp with a van parked about an eighth of a mile away. I don't think they trust her. For that matter, I don't think they trust me either."

"I was afraid that Kit would feel a little heat. And it doesn't surprise me that they are keeping tabs on you too." He hesitated, started to say something, stopped, tried again, and stopped again.

"Spit it out, Woody. Man up."

"I was just thinking. Maybe it would be better if you didn't tell Kit that you talked to me. She needs to walk around in darkness and pain, unaware that I am safe. The FBI might suspect that something is up if she suddenly cheers up."

"I agree. Her ignorance will work to our advantage." She was silent for a moment, then continued. "Woody, we don't have much time. We need to act soon if Kit and I are going to get out of here and join you guys. Yesterday, I overheard the dig-site supervisor chatting with the agent in charge. The agent told him that Kit's status is likely to change in the near future from Orange Two to Orange One, which would mean that she couldn't take any vacation time and wouldn't be allowed off-site without an appointed escort."

"That doesn't leave us a very big window. Put your thinking cap on and come up with a creative escape plan that will enable you and Kit to depart at the earliest possible date without leaving a trail to follow. Call me back Sunday evening."

After she hung up, she started to sigh, then realized that she just wasn't discouraged enough to be blue. She was prepared to go on the run and live under the radar. *Glad I took Jack's advice, read up on security and secrecy, and squirreled away funds in bank accounts in the Cayman Islands.*

That evening after the sunset, she relaxed in her camp chair by a crackling fire, indulging a mug of Masala Tea and savoring the Utah magic—the fragrance of sagebrush, the yipping of coyotes, and the vast canvas of stars. She was in her happy place.

But soon her mind was grappling with the situation and weighing ideas for their escape. She laughed at herself—and felt a little guilty—because she actually relished the fact that her life was getting exciting again. She hadn't had so much fun since her dustup with elephant poachers in Kenya and her subsequent harrowing flight from the game wardens and soldiers that had been sent to track her down. It turned out that the local officials had been in cahoots with the poachers in the illegal ivory market, and when she posed a threat to their golden goose, they had pursued her with a vengeance. That had been her first experience with government officials who looked out for their own gain at the expense of the public good they pretended to promote.

Her time in the Amazon had provided its own excitement. While exploring in the South for diamonds, she had experienced several run-ins with timber and jewel smugglers who felt she was intruding on their territory. Here again, the local authorities were taking bribes and looking the other way. But the current situation with a nationwide cover-up of the comet was probably going to top them all. It was shaping up to be a grand adventure.

23

Uinta Mountains, UT
Sunday, July 7, 2019

Sam sat in her camp chair after dinner Sunday evening, indulging the chaparral fragrance in the air and laughing at two magpies that appeared to be playing hide and seek in the cedar trees. Their antics reminded her of the FBI agents. She hadn't seen any sign of them since the first evening and chuckled as she recalled how she had given them the slip.

When it was close to seven, she quickly broke camp, loaded her Jeep, and headed back to the dig site. At her usual call site, she pulled over to the side of the road, scanned the area with her binoculars, then pulled out her Blackphone, went through the steps to make a secure VOIP call, and dialed Woody's number.

He answered on the second ring. "Roadrunner."

"I have a plan for our escape."

"Fill me in."

"Kit and I will rent a houseboat on Flaming Gorge Reservoir, power it maybe ten miles up the lake, and anchor in a good fishing area. In the middle of the night, we'll slip out of the houseboat and paddle an inflatable kayak to a predetermined boat landing ten miles or so up the lake where a crew from the hideout will be waiting for us. I was thinking that the landing on the end of NF-155 would be a good choice because it is fairly remote. I figure we can make that trip in three hours."

Woody was elated. "I like it. A water escape is less likely to be anticipated than a road escape, especially if you don't tow a small boat or take along a canoe or kayak. Plus, it doesn't leave a trail that can be followed. If you left at midnight, you would arrive at the landing around 3 a.m.— assuming your estimates are correct. The team could load you and the kayak in a few minutes and be on the road by 3:15. And whoever is tracking you would be none the wiser since they would be tracking the GPS on the houseboat, which would still be anchored in a bay somewhere.

"I'll bring your plan up Tuesday at our Compound meeting. Try and lose yourself on either Wednesday or Thursday evening and call me back. We'll coordinate at that time. In the meanwhile, look into houseboat rentals right away. You may be limited as to what you can get on short notice. I think we should shoot for next weekend, so try to rent a houseboat for Friday, July 12, through Sunday, July 14."

"Okay, boss man."

"Be careful, safari queen. And watch out for Kit."

24

the Compound
Tuesday, July 9, 2019

The crew gathered for a grill-out at six in the evening. After a feast of fresh-picked corn on the cob and elk steaks with Tatonka Dust, they settled down for their Compound meeting. There was a little anxiety in the air as everybody knew that their top priorities were two rescue missions, undertakings that seemed beyond the realm of possibility for them. Nobody but Woody had any skills or experience that seemed even remotely applicable.

Jordy addressed the group, "The first thing on my list tonight is locating Irina. Last week, Woody, you suggested the possibility that your friend Joby might be able to help us in this regard. Did you come up with any good ideas on how to get the ball rolling here?"

Woody nodded to Blake, and the young man spoke up. "Woody and I have an idea that might work. I am going to contact a friend in Scotland—we are both active in the *Planet X Cover-up* chatroom—and see if she is willing to help us connect with Joby. My idea is for her to masquerade as a salesman, walk into the coffee shop, and hand him a business card. Such a visit won't likely draw any attention, even if he is being watched. On the back of the card would be a note and her contact number."

"That sounds workable to me," Jordy replied. "What do the rest of you think?"

The group enthusiastically gave the plan a green light, and Blake said that he would get right on it.

Jordy introduced the next topic. "Woody, do you have any news for us on the Kit and Sam situation?"

"I texted Sam as planned. She called back on Friday evening using her Blackphone and the secure VOIP option so the feds would have a hard time tracing the call. I informed her that she needed to come up with an escape plan and that we would coordinate with her for a pick-up if necessary. She called me back a couple days later with an excellent plan. She and Kit will rent a houseboat on Flaming Gorge Reservoir, motor maybe ten miles up the lake, and anchor in a secluded bay. Around midnight, they'll climb into an inflatable kayak and paddle their way to an isolated boat landing on FR-155 some three hours away. A team will meet them at the landing with a pickup-camper combo, load them and their kayak into the camper, and bring them here to the Compound. This should be a pretty straightforward operation, though potential glitches include inclement weather, faulty equipment, and nosy agents.

"Sam is going to call back in the next few days to find out whether or not we approve of the plan. She and I have tentatively settled on this coming weekend for their escape, and she is now trying to rent a houseboat. Once we give her the green light, she'll proceed with preparations full steam ahead. Our main job in this operation will be to send a team to meet the girls at the boat landing. I suggest we send Blake and Andrius."

"I think that's an awesome plan!" Blake exclaimed. Most of the folks chorused their agreement while Andrius sat in aloof silence, picking at his fingernails, obviously not excited that he had been volunteered for the job.

Ariele, on the other hand, was fit to be tied. "I should be allowed to go on this mission," the frustrated young lady groused. "I'm sick and tired of being stuck here with nothing to do except work in the garden, pick berries, and take care of the chickens."

"Nope," Woody and Jordy replied at the same time.

"Why not?" Blake insisted, defending the spunky sprite. "We took Woody along in the camper."

"But Woody was needed for the phone call," Jordy insisted.

"How do you know that I won't be needed?" Ariele popped off. She unleashed a tirade, touting her qualifications. "I keep myself fit with hiking, biking, and dancing. I am trained in first aid. I keep my wits about me in tough situations. And I would be a valuable asset if the ladies show up at the rendezvous site soaking wet and cold." She glared at Woody, Jordy, and Red. "The bottom line is, you need me to be part of this mission just as much as you need the two guys."

The men were taken aback, not merely by the fact that she was a feisty gal, but also because she had a point. It would be handy to have a woman on the team. And she actually was more competent than Andrius in several areas critical to the mission. After a moment of awkward silence, Jordy backtracked. "I surrender, Ariele. You are right. We do need you on the rescue team."

Yes! she cried. Then she turned to Blake, and the two of them celebrated with a fist bump across the table.

25

Vernal, UT
Wednesday, July 10, 2019

After work, Sam jumped into her Jeep and headed for Vernal. As she drove out of the dig site valley, she felt wistful, knowing that in just a few days she would be driving out of here for the last time. She was going to miss digging. It had become part of her in a way she had never anticipated, a surprising change considering that when she first started, she had regarded it as a temporary job that allowed her to work outdoors.

In Vernal she made her way to a favorite hangout, Chang Hai's Chinese restaurant in the mall, where she found a quiet table in the back, ordered Osmanthus cake and green tea, and engaged in another round of super-spook texting.

First, she wirelessly associated a headset with her phone so her hands would be free, hooked the headset behind her ear, called James, a male acquaintance from Dinosaur National Monument, and began plying him with technical questions on geological layers and dating fossils. She needed him to ramble for a while as she had a few things to do. She figured that he wouldn't mind as he was interested in her.

He had asked her out a few times, but she had always turned him down on the plea that she was too busy. If law enforcement wanted to tap this call, they were more than welcome to do so. In fact, she hoped that they would.

Next, she opened the Chrome browser on her laptop, navigated to *Bledsoe's Archaeology Site*, and started a twenty-four-minute video on the mastodon dig in Montana where an entire skull had been found with both tusks intact. She hoped the video would mask her secure VOIP texting.

Finally, she removed her Blackphone from her purse, opened her Tor browser, accessed her secure VOIP-texting app, placed the phone on the table to the left of her laptop, and one-finger typed a message to Woody's burner number.

Woody was helping lay out the rubble-trench footings for Jordy's house when his phone chirped. He figured that it was probably from Sam, and it was. "Hi, Roadrunner, Gypsy here, secure setting, secure commo. What's the status?"

He smiled—Gypsy was a fitting handle. She oozed wanderlust and adventure—and texted back. "Plan is a go. Team will wait at designated location at designated time. Will leave two hours after designated time if no-show and don't text instructions. If visibility poor, will wave red light. Rodeo's burner # for operation is 617-635-2828. Roadrunner out."

Her mission accomplished, Sam brought the conversation with James to a convenient close by asking him if he was available Monday night. She wanted to continue the conversation in person.

He was ecstatic. "Absolutely. Let's do Corky's Lounge at seven."

"Great," she replied. "See you then." After she hung up, she felt confident about her little ploy. *That should throw any agents tapping my line, especially if I call James again this weekend.* But she also felt a little conflicted. *Think I enjoy being devious a little too much.* She shrugged her shoulders—*Oh well*—drained her tea, wrapped her cake in a napkin, dropped it in her purse, and got up to leave.

26

Flaming Gorge Reservoir, UT and WY
Friday, July 12 ... Sunday, July 14, 2019

Late Friday morning, Kit was having a hard time concentrating on the mastodon jaw that she was extricating from the ground. Her mind kept wandering off in daydreams about their plans for the weekend. Earlier that week, Sam had suggested renting a houseboat on Flaming Gorge Reservoir, and she had agreed without hesitation. It sounded like a wonderful way to take her mind off the burdens that were crushing her. She did wonder, however, why they needed so much gear. More than once she had rolled her eyes at stuff that Sam had made her pack. It was a houseboating trip in the summer for crying out loud, not wilderness camping in the fall.

That afternoon, the paleontologist and her assistant quit the dig early, quickly showered, and packed the Jeep with their gear and food. After the last load had been stuffed in, Sam slapped the hood and shouted, "Let's roll!" Because Kit was on the Orange Two list, they were required to stop at the dig-site supervisor's trailer and inform her of Kit's travel plans—Flaming Gorge Reservoir for the weekend to relax on a houseboat.

Once they were on the road, Sam kept glancing in the rearview mirror, expecting company. Sure enough, about a mile down the road, a black sedan pulled out from a side road and began following them, staying about a hundred yards behind. It was still on their tail two hours later when they pulled into the marina.

Kit was shocked when Sam filled out the paperwork. On top of the regular houseboat rental fee, Sam ponied up for a damage deposit, a week-long rental-insurance policy, and a hefty hardship charge because the owners of the marina had given up their own houseboat—an older retired model—for the weekend. All told, Sam dropped $5000 for the two-night trip. At this point, Kit began to suspect that something was up because her friend was one of the most financially conservative persons she had ever met—a millionaire who clipped coupons and shopped sales. If her only goal had been a camping trip, she would have booked the houseboat well in advance and saved a pile of money.

The young lady helping them with the paperwork slapped the keys for the houseboat on the counter. The gal had been rude the whole time. Kit winced, but she tried to be understanding. *Bet she's the one who had to give up her plans for this weekend. Sam must have pressed somebody pretty hard when she called for them to give up their own houseboat on short notice. When her mind is set, she's like a bulldog who won't let go.*

Over the next forty-five minutes, the two ladies filed

their travel plan with the marina, went through orientation with the houseboat tech, and loaded their gear on the houseboat. At 6:18 p.m., Sam slowly nosed the vessel away from the dock. When they were outside the posted no-wake area, she set their cruising speed at five knots. That was the slowest speed they could go and still make their destination before sunset. She wanted to indulge in a little relaxation during this stage of their journey because there wouldn't be any in the next.

Once they were on open water, and she could see no boats following them, Kit broached her concerns with Sam. "Okay, what's going on? This kind of haste and waste is so unlike you. I know you're up to something. I want the real story!"

Sam smiled sheepishly like a kid caught in the cookie jar. "Your dad and I have arranged a little adventure. We're outfoxing the feds, meeting a couple of your dad's friends at an arranged location, and joining him at his secret hideout."

"Whaaaaat! My dad is okay! I get to see him! Seeeeeriously!" She threw her arms around Sam and hugged her tight. "Thank you! But I'm still mad at you for not telling me earlier." She stepped back and eyed her friend pensively. "So spill the rest of the story. What's really going on with my dad? Why is he in trouble with the FBI?"

Sam revealed the situation, as far as she knew it, from the comet's discovery to her father's flight. When she finished, Kit sat in stunned silence. While it was a tremendous relief to know for certain that her father wasn't a real criminal, the truth was still a heavy burden to bear. The situation wasn't merely a bump in the road. It was the end of the road. Never again would she be a carefree young woman living the dream. Her career in archaeology was over. Henceforth, she was trapped in a dystopian nightmare and forced to go into hiding. An apocalyptic scenario was unfolding in the solar system, the federal government was covering it up, the populace was blind to the day of reckoning that was looming on the horizon, and those who stumbled upon the conspiracy were regarded as terrorists who posed a threat to the peace and prosperity of the land.

During their journey, Sam kept watch for boats or houseboats that might be following them. But nothing stood out as suspicious. When they arrived at Upper Marsh Creek bay at 8:34 that evening, their intended destination, and there had been no sign of agents tailing them, her hopes rose. *Maybe we're gonna get a free pass on this one.* Her heart feeling lighter than it had for several days, she nosed the houseboat close to the north shore one-third the way up the bay in a sheltered spot and dropped anchor. "Time to set up the lawn chairs and watch the sunset," she whooped gleefully.

Ten minutes later, while watching the sun slide behind the western horizon in a majestic blaze of color, they noticed a houseboat stop and anchor about a half mile away on the opposite shore of the bay, just inside the point. The timing and proximity made Sam feel uneasy. She opened her emergency gear bag, pulled out the low-light binoculars that she had carried since Kenya, went to the rearward room, turned the lights off, closed the sheer inner curtains, pressed the curtain against the glass with her binoculars, and scoped the situation out. While several men milling around on the deck looked like normal guys on vacation, two men in suits were visible in one of the windows. *Definitely federal agents. Nobody goes camping in a suit and tie.*

She was slightly crestfallen. *Nuts. That puts the kibosh on our plans. It would be impossible to get away tonight without being seen if they aimed an infrared gizmo this way.* She motioned to Kit who was standing in the doorway watching her. "We have unwelcome company. That houseboat is the FBI following us." Kit took the news hard. Her eyes moistened and her lower lip started to quiver. Sam tried to encourage her, "Don't worry, hon'. Unless they sent their A-Team, the feds aren't gonna ruin our party. Not on my watch." *Hopefully, my soldado can keep up with my bravado.*

Sam hustled to the front room, connected her laptop to the internet through the houseboat's satellite dish, and checked the forecast on weather.com. Flaming Gorge National Recreation Area was facing the threat of strong thunderstorms on Saturday evening. The front was moving in from the Gulf of Mexico and was expected to arrive around 8 p.m. and wind down around 4 a.m. It would bring ferocious lightning, torrential rain, and high winds. The wind would start out southwesterly and switch to southerly.

This is perfect, Sam thought as she breathed a sigh of relief. The storm was going to be bad enough that the agents would likely drop their guard, and no one would be manning the infrared surveillance. Why keep such close tabs on the gals in severe weather when they were regarded as low flight risks during ideal weather?

Their journey, though, would be hazardous because of the high winds and waves. She hoped they could handle it. On the upside, they had kayaked on big water before and had even run class II rapids. On the downside, they had no experience in inflatable kayaks, much less a two-man version. At least the wind would be at their back.

Time for some more super-spook chicanery. Leaving the weather report open on her browser, she opened another tab, went to YouTube, and searched "brown trout + flaming gorge + weather." Searching through the results, she found a thirty-six-minute video on fishing for trophy browns in the reservoir when the barometer is falling. She started watching it and to her amusement actually found it interesting. The guy claimed that the lake could be insanely good fishing on the front end of stormy weather if you hit the right bays with big jigs, and one of the bays he mentioned was the very bay they were in. She left the video running. *Just what I was looking for!*

Next, she dialed the NOAA number in Riverton, Wyoming, with her iPhone and listened to the recorded weather report. *Hopefully, Stingray will pick this up.*

While the recorded weather report was playing, she texted her hapless date. "Can't wait till Monday night. I'll be sitting in a happy place with a good man. Tomorrow evening doing some serious brown trout fishing during the storm. Just read that they go crazy when the barometer is falling." She smiled and grimaced at the same time. *I'm so bad. But this ought to be good fodder for the Stingray operators.*

After the Riverton, Wyoming, NOAA call had played

twice, she hung up and called the NOAA number in Salt Lake City to catch the Utah weather report.

Finally, she picked up her Blackphone to send a text to Blake, then decided not to turn it on and use it. The FBI would certainly pick up the text with their Stingray and deduce that it originated with her, even if they had trouble decrypting it. Instead, she went back to her laptop which was still playing the fishing video, opened her Tor browser, and opened Deadbolt Call. Next, she chose the Tower Select option, selected the weakest suitable signal, then chose the secure VOIP text option, and sent a brief message to Blake. "Friday night weather not favorable. Saturday night favorable. Be there early." *Hopefully, the FBI won't notice this encrypted message. If they do, hopefully, they won't suspect that it is mine.*

Blake texted back with his Blackphone, using language he had learned from Woody. "Friday night no-go. Saturday night go. Be there early. Copy that."

***

The next day, the girls played the houseboat vacation game—lounging in the sun, swimming, and fishing off the boat. Several times, a boat of supposed fisherman from the agents' houseboat trolled past their boat, closer than necessary if their only purpose was pretending to be fishing. Sam mused to herself. *Are they actually doing their job or checking out the ladies?*

Saturday evening, they noticed the storm brewing on the southern horizon a few minutes before seven. Sam checked the weather report again. The forecast was essentially the same. At 8:15 the towering cumulus clouds were upon them, and the wind picked up. At 8:25 a furious downpour lashed the houseboat, and darkness fell upon the lake. By 8:40 the visibility had become so poor that Sam couldn't see the lights on the houseboat that the agents were using. *Thank God for that.* After a quick discussion, the girls decided to leave early. They didn't know how long they would enjoy the cover of the gale and wanted to take advantage of the opportunity. They also wanted to give themselves extra time because their journey was going to be rougher than they had anticipated.

In the rear room, they inflated the kayak, lashed down waterproof gear bags which held extra clothes and vital gear, stuffed water bottles into their holders, and connected lanyards to their paddles. Then they donned wool long johns, poly shirts and pants, breathable rain gear, wool hats and socks, and fingerless kayaker's gloves, hoping to ward off the chill as much as possible. Sam also placed a wrist compass on her left arm. *Probably going to need that.*

They were nearly ready. There was nothing left to do but execute their misdirection plan. They spread fishing gear, deck chairs, opened sodas, towels, coffee cups, a thermos, and a waterproof radio on the leeward deck, trying to make it look like they had been fishing in the storm and gotten washed overboard. Sam tossed an ugly boonie hat upon the waves. Kit followed with her REI ball cap, a floating can holder, and a plastic cooler. They figured that more stuff would wash off the deck. The more flotsam the better. Sam surveyed their effort. *Hopefully, they'll waste a bunch of time waiting for a dive team to show up, and then waste a bunch more on a search.*

At 9:30, Sam picked up the front end of the kayak, Kit took up the rear, and they awkwardly lugged the craft out the doorway and onto the rolling and pitching deck, barely able to stand in the driving wind. They dropped their little ark into the heaving water off the back edge of the deck. With Kit holding their craft tight, Sam crawled over the knee rail and into the front seat. Then, while Sam gripped the knee rail and held the kayak against the rocking deck, Kit gingerly crept into the rear. Together, pulling hand-over-hand on the knee rail, they tugged the kayak forward until they were clear of the houseboat. Then they began to paddle as hard as they could, glad that the wind was at their back.

From the outset, they were tossed and pummeled by the waves. Not a hundred feet from the houseboat, the kayak nearly folded in half when the ends were lifted up on crests and the middle was left hanging over a trough. When they dropped in a terrifying V-buckle, taking on a lot of water, Sam hollered, "Quarter right!" and they frantically angled their diminutive craft to the waves. With sullen hearts, they faced the painful realization that they would have to tack back and forth the entire way, greatly extending the miles and the time to their pick-up point. Their sorrows increased when they left the cover of the bay because the wind was blowing more than forty miles per hour on the open water, and the whitecaps were nearly three feet high.

About ten minutes out, an exceptionally monstrous wave caught them while they were turned sideways in a trough, rolled them over, and trapped them upside down. Kit swallowed water, got confused by the inky blackness, and began to panic. They attempted the procedure for righting a kayak. But the vessel rolled just enough for them to grab a breath, and an onrushing swell flopped them back under. They tried a second time, and again they failed. Apparently, the dynamics of righting an inflatable kayak were different than those of righting a rigid kayak. Or maybe their technique was less than textbook. Or maybe it was simply the rough water.

Sam was beginning to worry. Their recovery was taking way too long, and they were cold and tired. If they couldn't get it right this time, they were probably toast. With a do-or-die burst of energy, Sam strained, extended her paddle as far as she could, and pushed with her hip. The kayak started to roll, hesitated, then righted. But there was neither time nor energy to celebrate. Sam shouted "Quarter!" as a swell lifted them, and they resumed paddling with what little energy they could muster. They didn't bother trying to bale the kayak. It would just fill with water again.

Over the next four and a half hours, they rolled over five more times, and each time they righted themselves with great difficulty—never on their first effort. Kit swallowed water every time, which caused her to throw up, leaving an acrid taste in her mouth. Soaking wet, numb to the bone, shivering, and exhausted to the point of delirium, she began to daydream about a fireplace, a Hudson Bay blanket, and a steaming mug of hot chocolate with marshmallows.

When it seemed like they had been paddling for a lifetime, Sam checked her watch. It was 2:08 a.m. She groaned. She had no idea how far they had gone or how far they had left to go. The only thing she did know was that she didn't have much gas left in the tank. Her weariness and chill were beyond anything she had ever experienced before. She was getting foggy, and a strange sensation of warmth was beckoning her to surrender.

Kit was barely paddling. Her arms were clumsily going through the motions. She interrupted the half-numb wanderings of her mind and mumbled a faint prayer. *God ... Sorry I don't pray much ... Please get us out of this jam. Help our strength to hold out. Help us to find the landing. And please let the guys be there waiting for us.*

The rescue team, however, had been waiting at the pick-up point long before Kit had whispered her desperate prayer. They had arrived at 12:35 a.m.—early as requested—and parked with the rear of the truck about forty feet from the river. At 2:10 a.m. Blake suddenly donned his raincoat, opened his door, and stepped out in the rain. As he reached for his military-style flashlight in the door pocket, he noticed Andrius staring at him blankly from the safety of the truck. The cowboy explained, "I just sense that God wants me to get out and let my little light shine." His companion shook his head at him as if he had lost his marbles. Blake didn't respond. He just flashed a smile and rushed off in such a hurry that he left his freshly poured cup of coffee sitting on the dash, steaming.

Andrius sat in the truck for several minutes, feeling like a wussy, then, in a huff of frustration, he climbed into his raincoat, grabbed his flashlight, and joined Blake. The two stood on the river bank in the pouring rain, face toward the wind and driving rain, waving their red lights. The raw weather had Blake worried sick about the girls. He guessed that the temperature was about fifty degrees. Add in the wind and the rain, and it was a hypothermia factory for anyone exposed. He began to pray earnestly.

At 2:26 they heard the girls' voices calling out. Blake shouted, *Thank you, Lord!* At 2:28 they saw them paddling toward them, trying to quarter the wind. At 2:30 the exhausted girls missed the north edge of the boat landing. The guys waded out into the waist-deep water, grabbed the kayak, and pulled it back to the landing where the water was much shallower.

When Blake dragged the nose of the kayak onto the landing, Sam tried to step onto the shore but fell over the side, landing in the water. Andrius ran to her aid, helped her struggle to her feet, and walked her up onto the beach. Her legs were wobbly, her skin was cool to the touch, and she was disoriented. Andrius looked back at the kayak. Kit was too weak to stand. Blake lifted the exhausted female out of the kayak, cradled her in his arms, turned in the knee-deep water, and headed for the camper. When Blake walked by him, Andrius handed Sam off to the cowboy. The shivering woman clutched the gallant gentleman's arm and leaned on him for support.

While Blake ensured that the girls made it to the camper, Andrius dragged the kayak out of the water and deflated it with the super-fast method his partner had suggested— slicing every compartment with a Buck knife. Then he unscrewed the paddles, tucked the halves under one arm, and dragged the trashed kayak to the camper. He arrived as Blake and Ariele were helping Sam step up into the camper on her shaky legs. As soon as she was safely inside, the two guys shoved the paddles and the kayak unceremoniously in the back door, slammed it shut, and raced for the cab. When they were back on the road, Blake dictated a status report for Andrius to text to Woody. "Both packages safe and sound. Evidence of exodus in possession. ETA 12:30 p.m."

Ariele had been prepared. She had brought along dry clothes for both of the ladies in approximately the right sizes—based on Woody's guesstimations. And while the guys were standing out in the rain, she had cranked the heater in the camper up to 90 degrees—as high as it would go—and put two tea kettles of water on the stove to boil. When the gals were brought to the camper, they were so cold and stiff that they could barely stand and couldn't take their wet clothes off. Ariele figured that they were hypothermic or nearly so. She took out her shears, cut their wet clothes off, dried them off, and helped them climb into sweatpants, sweatshirts, and warm socks. Then she made them drink hot, spiced apple cider and tucked them into sleeping bags with hot-water bottles. *Glad I put my foot down and Blake took up my cause. These gals definitely needed my help. Sometimes you just need a woman's touch on a mission.*

***

At 12:40 p.m., after a ten-hour drive, a weary Blake—who had been awake for thirty-two hours straight—nosed his truck up to the lodge at the Compound. Before he could even shut the ignition off, pandemonium broke out. Folks came running out of the lodge to welcome the rescuers and the rescued. Kit, who had largely recovered by now, jumped out of the camper and raced for her father's arms. Tearfully, Woody embraced his daughter. As she basked in his hug, she sighed, "Daddy, I hope I never set foot in a kayak again. I'm done with water. I'm sticking with land. I'm just a dirt girl." Sam rolled her eyes as she indulged a side hug from her old friend. "Yeah, right. We'll see how long that lasts."

27

"Awright, braw!" a Scottish brogue intoned.

Joby looked up and found himself falling into the brilliant green eyes of the attractive redhead who had ordered a latte a half hour earlier, then sauntered over to a table, opened her laptop, and began working on something.

She handed him a business card, melted him with an alluring smile, flipped her luxurious hair, turned about, and walked out of the store.

The dazzled male flipped the card over. *Huh?* In elegant female handwriting was a note. "Give me a call for a lesson on tying a Lillian knot." Was it a come-on? The note was followed by a phone number, then another cryptic note. "Call me on a burner." He stared at it for a moment, slipped it into his wallet, then turned to focus on the next customer.

The gal working with Joby, who had peered over his shoulder to read the card, pinched him on the side and said, "I think that babe is crushing on you. Better give her a call."

Joby replied in his typical nonchalant manner, "I'll think

about it, but yeah, she's definitely hot."

He had trouble concentrating on his job the rest of the day. His mind kept wandering from customers and their coffee orders to the redhead and her mysterious card. He had a feeling that there was more to her note than met the eye. What was he missing? The fact that she had handed him her card in a flirtatious manner was not unusual. That happened from time to time. It was the message that was bothering him. What did she mean by tying a Lillian knot? That was slang he was unfamiliar with. Unless it wasn't slang. What was a Lillian knot?

His mind drifted to Woody, the only person he knew that was into knots: camping knots, mountaineering knots, nautical knots, and fishing knots. He stopped dead in his mental tracks. *That's it!* He remembered Woody telling him once how to set up a tenkara rod. The Lillian is the knot on the tip of the rod for attaching your line. His heart began to race. Was Woody trying to contact him? If so, then he must have made his way to safety. *But why would he be trying to contact me?*

The thought of contact with Woody terrified him. His old friend was wanted on federal charges. Connecting with him could get him in trouble with the authorities. Yet he felt a revulsion for the current government policies, and he did trust Woody. It dawned on him that the tension was simply the common fight or flight response. Fear was overwhelming his courage. After an intense inner struggle, his sense of honor overcame his fear of involvement. He determined to call the number that evening after work and get to the bottom of this. But first, he had to answer another question. *What in the world is a burner?*

When he got off work at 3 p.m., Joby went to the library, sat down at an open computer as far away from another person as he could find, and googled "burner + phone." He discovered that it was a prepaid cell phone used for a specific purpose for a short period of time, then tossed. It was a good way to maintain privacy and security. He cleared the history on the terminal, returned to his truck, and drove to Wal-Mart, where he purchased two prepaid cell phones. Then he made his way to the Sam Merrill Trail.

An hour later, he was a couple miles up the trail, sitting on a rock a few hundred feet off the path with a great view of the surrounding mountains and the valley below. He pulled out one of his new phones, set it up with a bogus name and address, retrieved the business card with the mysterious number, and dialed.

"Tenkara here."

"This is Bandana."

"Good to hear your voice. Are you secure?"

"Yeah. Things are going well."

"No, I mean, are you calling from a burner phone? Are you calling from a safe place where no one can overhear you? Are you certain that you weren't followed?"

"Sorry. Yes. I bought a burner like you said and set it up with bogus info. I'm on the Sam Merrill Trail about a hundred yards off the actual trail. I don't think anyone followed me." He hesitated, then continued. "I am nervous, though, about getting in trouble with the authorities. Not real interested in spending time in a FEMA camp. I've seen pictures on the internet. They look like POW camps."

"There's no need to worry. If you dispose of a burner properly when you're done using it, there is nothing to fear. The only time you need to worry is if federal agents are tailing you, park their electronic wizardry near you, and point their tools at you. Then they can intercept your burner call. But otherwise, you are pretty much a needle in a haystack, a big haystack."

"So where are you? Glad to hear that you managed to evade the manhunt. How'd you pull that off."

"I can't answer your questions right now. But you'll eventually get all the answers you want if you help us out with some important business."

"Sounds risky. What do you got in mind?"

"How would you like to move to a rustic place in the Rockies, far from the city, with more rainfall than you get in the San Gabriels, cooler weather in the summer, year-round springs and streams, a large plot of organic raspberries, and a grow-hole greenhouse?"

"Sounds awesome. But I'm guessing there's a catch."

"There is. Good things always come with a price."

"So what do I have to do?"

"Rescue a valuable asset."

"Where is it, and what is it?"

"It's not an *it*. It's a woman. And we don't know where she is. That's part of your job. Find her. Then rescue her."

"I think you need to give James Bond a call or maybe Ethan Hunt. I'm just a peacenik trying to stay out of trouble."

"Listen, Granola. We need your help. This woman needs your help."

"I don't know. The whole thing sounds dangerous—far out of my league. I don't have any experience in stuff like private investigation or special operations."

"It is dangerous. And we are fully aware of your inexperience. But you won't be alone. We'll provide help, as much as we can, along the way. You'll get the training you need to pull the mission off."

Joby was silent.

Woody pressed him. "Where is your compassionate, liberal heart? People here in America are being arrested and detained for knowing and disseminating the truth."

"But aren't they all troublemaking right-wingers? You know—deucers, patriots, and Soviet lackeys?"

"The media has tried to portray it that way. But their narrative is complete rubbish. More than half of the troublemakers have come from the left side of the aisle—62 percent according to several independent think tanks. So the issue is not political. The unifying factor is that they all knew about the comet."

"Is that what this is all about? The late-night radio hoax about a comet bigger than Mercury that's going to smash its way through the asteroid belt and play bumper cars with Mars?" His conscience bothered him a little bit as he spoke because he had already begun to believe deep inside that the story might actually be true or at least contain a core of truth.

"Joby. The comet is real. It's not a fairy tale. You remember the Sundown River message I got shortly before I disappeared?"

"How could I forget? Once the FBI found out about the email, they grilled me over it."

"Yeah. Sorry about that. The sender was my cousin, who had been head of IT security at NASA. He stumbled across intelligence on the comet and relayed the news to me. The government knows about the comet and has instituted a massive cover-up. They don't want the public to know."

"So Sundown means that the sun is going to set on planet Earth?"

"That's right. Massive disaster is on the horizon just like you worrywart liberals have been preaching since the 70s. Only the end isn't coming through man-caused problems like pollution or reputed man-caused problems like global warming. It is coming through an act of nature—a massive comet. And when this comet unleashes whatever it's going to unleash, you will probably be a lot safer with us in the West than down there in the Los Angeles area."

"To be honest, I do have my misgivings about being down here if society melted down, or the right-wing hawks got us embroiled in World War III, or a 9.0 earthquake flattened the Los Angeles area, so your offer is tempting. How long do I have to think about it?"

"Less than two minutes. It's either *yes* or *no*." Woody stopped talking for a moment, then he impulsively added, "One of your garden partners would be a strawberry brunette with green eyes. She's single, of Jewish extraction, loves old *Mother Earth News* magazines, and goes in for the organic thing."

Joby complained, "Not fair. Now you're playing my

emotions instead of appealing to reason."

"I think that's a lot of good reason. Ten seconds … nine seconds … eight seconds—"

"Okay. I'll do it. The fact that the government is covering up the comet and detaining folks who know about it makes my blood boil."

"I knew you'd step up. Left and right find a lot of common ground when extremism raises its ugly head. Here are your instructions. Tomorrow, the gal who gave you her card will call you back on this burner after 3:30 p.m. Be waiting for the call at a convenient location. You two will make arrangements to meet. At your meeting, she will give you your instructions. Follow them carefully and completely. Good luck."

"What about the Lillian knot?"

"Don't worry about it. When you show up at the Compound, I'll teach you how to tie a Lillian knot and use a tenkara rod."

28

The next day after work, at 3:40 p.m., Joby was sitting in his car in the parking lot of the Los Angeles Zoo when his phone rang.

"Hi, Bandana. This is Scarlet. We met yesterday, and I gave you my card."

"I remember. Tenkara told me that you would call."

"Let's do something where we can be alone and talk, like go for a walk."

"How about the Sam Merrill trail? It's one of my favorites. The trailhead is on the east end of East Loma Alta Drive in Altadena, which is just north of Pasadena. Shall we meet at 4:30?"

"Sounds like a plan. I love going on walks. But the meet there part won't work. Not gonna take a cab that far. Come pick me up at the Hampton Inn near the intersection of Colorado and South Brand Boulevard. I'll be waiting in the lobby. And, just to let you know, you'll be buying me supper. I'm famished."

About an hour up the trail, they found a place to sit down that offered them a little shade. Joby dug their sub sandwiches and bottled water out of his daypack, and Scarlet began to talk about the mission.

"There's a bit of a story behind this rescue attempt. About eight months ago a young lady named Ariele received a package from a former classmate at Caltech which warned her of a huge comet that was headed for Mars. The letter was accompanied by a DVD that contained numerous files and images. Ariele used the Hooker at Mt. Wilson—"

"The Hooker at Mt. Wilson?"

"The Hooker is a famous 100-inch telescope at the observatory on Mount Wilson."

"Astronomy was never a strong point for me."

"No worries. The only thing you need to know for now about astronomy is that a planet-sized comet will likely disrupt the solar system."

"It really is that big?"

"Yes. Its size has been confirmed by both NASA and the ESA. Anyway, to continue with my story, Ariele shot images twice a week on the Hooker for six months and discovered two further occulted stars which helped confirm that the comet was headed for Mars. She gave her findings to her boss, who reported her to the FBI."

"Reported to the FBI over the comet?"

"The US government is fostering a huge cover-up. They don't want the public to find out because they fear that the whole country would descend into chaos and anarchy."

"So I'm supposed to rescue this Ariele?"

"Nope. You are going to locate and rescue her friend Irina, the gal who sent her the package. Ariele managed to evade the FBI and make her way to a hideout in the Rockies. Once you rescue Irina, you'll escort her to the hideout."

"Do we have any idea where she is?"

"We suspect that she is in a FEMA camp somewhere."

"What was her last known location?"

"Cornell University where she was working as an astronomer."

"So what's the next step?"

"Travel to Wyoming, find a motel in a small town, and—"

He interrupted. "Can I give my boss a two-week notice?"

"No. We don't want anyone to be aware that you're leaving. We can't afford to tip off the FBI that you're up to something. Just load your truck with your belongings tonight and hit the road. Call Woody after you arrive in Wyoming. We'll expect to hear from you within four or five days."

"But what about my boss, my mom, or my friends? If they don't hear something from me, they'll put in a missing person's report. That couldn't be good for your rescue mission."

She looked at him silently for a moment, then replied, "You're right. Email your family, your boss, and your closest friends. Give them a story, something plausible that will keep them off our backs for months to come. But wait until you reach Wyoming."

She handed Joby a business card with info on the back. "Email Woody on Monday for further instructions. The top address is his. The bottom one is yours. Below your address is the username and password for your Buster account which we set up. Memorize the information on this card, then burn it. From this day forth, don't use any phone that isn't secure, and after you send your heads-up emails, quit using your email account.

"On top of that, leave all of your computers, laptops, tablets, and phones behind, and buy a new laptop—a robust, high-powered one. Don't set it up until you are in Wyoming. Then set it up with a false ID, only use Tor for your browser, and only use the email account associated with your Buster account.

"One more thing. You can use your cards and checkbook for now, but be advised that when you leave town, you will be cutting them up and going dark, eventually with a false identity." She looked him square in the eyes. "Do you understand?"

Her green eyes no longer looked inviting. They were glowering, green orbs of death. The attractive female could be very intimidating. "Yes."

"Here is an anonymous debit card with twenty-five thousand dollars on it. It should be enough to cover your expenses for a little while."

His eyes widened. "I could live off of that for six months, if not a year."

She shook her head at the naive young man. "You aren't going on a budget vacation. You're going on a high-risk mission that involves high-expense detective work. And there is only enough on this card to get you started. If you need to reload the card, contact Woody. He'll take care of your financial needs."

He looked at her, shaken, feeling like he was committing himself to do something foolish, like pursuing a dragon in its lair. *Hope I don't regret this. Most heroes die young.*

"One more thing. When you get home tonight, pull the battery and the SIM card from your burner and toss all three into a hot fire. Make sure they burn up entirely. Don't leave any breadcrumbs."

He nodded okay with a sullen heart.

After a couple minutes of awkward silence, Scarlet stood up and dusted off her skirt. "Well, we're done. Guess we should be heading back."

Joby said nothing. He simply threw his daypack over his shoulder, got on his feet, and started down the trail toward the parking lot. What could he say? His carefree life was over. Unwanted adventure and danger were his future. He felt like the unwilling hero in a movie.

After he had dropped Scarlet off at her hotel, Joby headed for home. By the time he drove into his yard, he was a maelstrom of emotions: sadness, fear, and purpose. Not saying goodbye to his friends at Sierra Coffee Company and making his last drive home to his farmstead in the mountains overwhelmed him with melancholy. Not saying goodbye to his mom brought worse heart pain than his father's funeral. And the mixture of purpose and fear that he felt about his cloak-and-dagger mission was sailing into uncharted waters. It far surpassed the fear he had felt when arrested for pot while in high school or the sense of purpose he felt when working on his homestead.

He sighed deeply. His life was going in a direction he had never anticipated: private detective work, risking arrest as a security threat or terrorist, and breaking someone out of a FEMA camp. He recalled a question a rabbi had once asked in a message. "Which character in the Tanakh do you most identify with?" At the time he was stumped. Now the question was easy. He identified with Balaam's donkey because the poor beast had balked at an ill-advised path that he had been forced to take.

He dragged his topper over to his Toyota Hilux, manhandled it into place with several grunts and a blood blister, and pinned it down with a sense of triumph. Then he loaded the back of his truck with boxes, duffel bags, suitcases, backpacks, toolboxes, a cooler, and his guitar. He would buy a new laptop when he passed through Las Vegas. With a wave of nostalgia, he took one last look at the interior of his cabin, grabbed his thermos of coffee and his canvas duffel bag which sat on the passenger seat, then walked out and locked the door. In his bag was an item he didn't usually carry, a copy of the Tanakh in Hebrew and English that his mother had given him. If the situation really was Bible prophecy like Woody suspected, that would come in handy.

At 8:45 p.m. he drove out of his yard, his not-so-optimistic hopes fighting a losing battle with his discouragement. *Goodbye living the dream. Hello reluctant hero. Not feeling like much of a hero, though. I wonder if heroes ever feel like heroes?*

***

On Sunday evening shortly after 6 p.m., Joby checked in to the Roadway Inn in Buffalo, Wyoming. After waffling between an economy room and a luxury room, he chose the latter. A king bed and a kitchenette didn't sound too over the top since he was going to stay for a while.

After he had dragged the last of his luggage and boxes into the room, he pulled his new laptop out of his duffel bag, set it on the desk, turned it on, and decided to hold off. The hero stuff was going to have to wait. His first order of business was dinner. He glanced at the take-out brochure and ordered a pepperoni pizza. While he felt guilty that this would be the fifth time in two days that he had indulged fast food, he justified his departure from his healthy eating habits with the fact that he was too tired and too busy to go grocery shopping. Maybe once things settled down, he would return to his organic ways.

While waiting for his pizza to arrive, he set up his laptop with a false name, downloaded Tor, logged in to the Buster account that the crew at the Compound had set up for him, and began to orient himself.

After dinner, he wrote a brief email to his mom, then sent copies to his boss and his closest friends.

Hi. This is kind of awkward, but I'm writing to inform you that I have recently undergone a radical transformation in my views on morality and politics. I no longer identify as a left-leaning pacifist. I have become convinced that there is evil in the world that cannot be defeated with pacifism and that I have an obligation to help stop it. I have responded to a call to serve my country in a secretive job that I cannot talk about, at least not now. You will not hear from me for a while, maybe a year or more. Please don't worry about me. Love, Joby.

29

"Frenchie?" Jack enquired as the burly cook slapped a pile of mashed potatoes on his plate and ladled a scoop of gravy over them.

"Swabbie?" he replied. "What are you doing here?"

Jack smiled. The Army cook he had met during the First Gulf War at Camp Eagle II loved to tease the SEALs and call them swabbies. Jack didn't mind. Frenchie had paid his dues. He had tossed a lot of lead before he started tossing salads. As a young man, he had enlisted as a Ranger, climbed the ranks to E-6, and earned a Purple Heart in Somalia when he took a bullet in his hip. But the shattered hip had ended his special-ops career and nearly ended his military career— the Army wanted to give him a medical discharge. But instead of leaving the Army, he chose to stay in and became a cook. Jack replied, "Same as everybody else. I got in trouble over the Rogue."

"What happened?"

Before Jack could answer, a redhead teasingly bumped

227

Frenchie out of the way—"If you're gonna gab instead of serve, step aside"—and took over serving the potatoes and gravy.

Jack continued through the line, then met his old acquaintance at the service door and resumed their conversation. "About a month and a half ago, while working at NASA as the head of IT security, I went to the Administrator's office to implement a scheduled security update. He had left a top-secret memo open on his workstation. My heart sank. I knew I was screwed. I had seen a classified memo that was far above my clearance, and it was beside the point whether I had actually read it or not. The suspicion would be that I had read it. While contemplating my plight, my eyes fell upon the words *massive comet* and *national emergency*, piquing my interest. Against my better judgment—reasoning that I couldn't get into any more trouble than I already was—I read a paragraph while pretending to be tinkering with the mouse and the cursor. I was stunned. Not only was there a massive comet, but Earth was threatened, and a cover-up was being fostered by the highest levels of government.

"After less than a minute, I got nervous, closed the memo, closed the other open applications, and updated the workstation software. That evening, I conveyed a message to my cousin Woody warning him that trouble was on its way. Not long after, the mishap caught up to me, and the FBI came looking for me."

Frenchie shook his head empathetically. "You look like death warmed over."

"Feel like it too. I endured twenty-one days of questioning

with sleep deprivation, starvation rations, illegal interrogation techniques, and a beating from two interrogators who were frustrated because they couldn't get me to tell them what they wanted to hear. I talked plenty, but I insisted that the only thing I was guilty of was stumbling upon the comet. They finally gave up."

"Did you arrive this morning?"

"Yeah, around 10 a.m. Did my paperwork, got my issue from Supply, and took a slot in maintenance, specializing in computers and the digital control units for the boilers. But Mr. Drake didn't think that position would keep me busy enough, so he required me to make a second choice. I picked the back warehouse—sorting, organizing, and shelving dry goods and household stuff, whatever comes in."

30

Two days later, Jack was seated in the dining hall with several guys from maintenance, discussing the benefits of networking the computers that were scattered throughout various departments. But he was having a hard time concentrating on the conversation. He was distracted by the ladies sitting at the next table.

"Definitely some good-looking females sitting over there," one of the guys remarked, noting that Jack kept looking their way.

"No doubt about that," Jack replied. But he didn't pursue the thought. He wasn't concerned about their attractiveness. He was trying to follow their conversation. His ears had perked up because he thought that he had heard a name that he recognized.

"So tell me more about this Woody," the brunette probed, loud enough for Jack to hear clearly. He was all ears now.

"I first met Woody," the blonde answered, "when I

transferred from Arizona State University to Caltech in July 2014 to join their Astronomy Department and head up their NEO research program. He and I didn't see eye-to-eye at first. I think he resented the fact that I was department head. And I assumed that he had been passed over because he was unqualified. But before a year had passed, I realized that he was more qualified than I was. It turned out that he had offended the gatekeepers because he rejected the Standard Model of the universe—a finite expanding universe with gravity as the only significant force in orbital relationships—so they blacklisted him as unfit for promotion or publication. We eventually became friends, and he came to my aid over and over again with projects and research. Eventually, I realized that what I thought was coldness toward me was really just shyness."

"Wait. You were attracted to him?"

"Excuse me, ladies," interrupted Jack. "Are you talking about Woody Lundstrom?"

"Yes, we are," the attractive blonde replied. "Why do you ask?"

"He's my cousin. Did he get away safely?"

"He appears to have, but I can't tell you for certain. And who are you?"

"Jack Lundstrom. I'm the one who sent Woody a coded message telling him to flee to our rendezvous in the West because trouble from the heavens was headed our way. Until a few weeks ago, I was the head of IT security at NASA."

"That explains why Woody was acting a little unusual for three weeks prior to his disappearance. How did you get a heads up on the Rogue?"

"While working in the NASA director's office on his computer, I stumbled upon a highly classified memo, and when my eyes fell upon a sentence referring to a comet called the Rogue, well, I read what I wasn't supposed to read."

She smiled. "That's one of the most common reasons for folks winding up in here."

They continued talking animatedly for the next ten minutes as lunch hour was winding down. Jack learned that the blonde was Sally Evans and the brunette was Irina Kirilenko. More importantly, he saw the fight in them. They were incensed about the cover-up that kept the public in the dark. And they were incapable of accepting their current circumstances as their lot in life. They wanted to do something about the comet and the cover-up. Bonds were formed in that conversation that led to them becoming inseparable friends—the three musketeers as they jokingly referred to themselves.

31

Buffalo, WY
Monday, July 22 … Friday, July 26, 2019

Joby slept in late and didn't roll out of bed until nearly eight. After a quick breakfast of pastry and coffee, he sent a message to Woody at 8:30 through secure chat. "Hi, Tenkara. I'm in Wyoming as directed, waiting for further instructions."

A few minutes later, Woody called Joby on his burner.

"Bandana here."

"Glad to hear you made it, Joby."

"So what's the plan from here?"

"The plan is to find Irina."

"I understand that. But what's the plan to find Irina?"

"You are the plan."

"Well, I don't have a plan."

"God gave you a good head on your shoulders. So use it."

"But—"

"There are no buts. Listen. If you can figure out how to survive in California on $11 an hour, you can do just about anything."

"So what am I supposed to do?"

"Approach it like you do a mountain. One step at a time."

"Where do you suggest I start?"

"Pretend you're a gopher and do a little digging. I suggest your old friend, the private detective." Woody waited for a response, but there was only silence on the other end. "Well, I have things I need to get busy with. I'll send you an email with all the mission-pertinent information that you'll need including a timeline of events and an outline of important persons involved. There will also be information on your Buster account and the Bitcoin account associated with it. Look for it shortly."

A cloud of demoralized helplessness fell upon Joby that reminded him of the time he had been caught on a ledge in the Sierras with night coming on, the wind picking up, and the temperature dropping. He fell on his bed and pounded it like a frustrated teenager, then lay there for a few minutes feeling sorry for himself. While he was trying to ignore the situation, a glimmer of hope flashed in his distraught mind. *Maybe I should take Woody's advice and call Toad. He might actually be able to help me, assuming I can figure out how to reconnect with him.*

Toad was Ted Benson, a friend Joby had made in his Rainbow Family days. The two had met at the Family Gathering in the Gifford Pinchot National Forest in Washington in 2011, and both had left early, disgruntled with the backwardness and the heavy pot usage. Toad had headed back east, and Joby had returned to California. For several years, they had maintained regular contact, during which time Joby had become a barista, and Toad had obtained a private investigator's license in Pennsylvania. But in late 2015, Toad had vanished without warning, changed his phone number and email, and left no forwarding address. Not once, in the nearly four years since then, had he contacted Joby with updated information.

So how was he going to find Toad? He desperately needed his friend. It wasn't merely that his private eye skills would come in handy. It was also the fact that Joby knew that he could trust him with this case. Toad disliked Big Brother government. He was apolitical. And he had taken shady cases before. On a venture, Joby searched the White Pages for Ted Benson and Theodore Benson in Pennsylvania. No luck. He tried several other people-search websites and struck out again. So he expanded his search to the entire United States, trying both the White Pages and three other search sites. Again he came up empty-handed. *Rats.* His friend must be flying under the radar. Perhaps he had offended someone powerful in the government or law enforcement or the mafia.

Joby took a different tack and searched for private investigators in Pennsylvania. To his exasperation, he discovered that there were hundreds of PI agencies in the state. Figuring that his friend would still be a loner, he began working through the Google hits, eliminating agencies that weren't solo operations and scanning those that were for clues that it might be Toad. A hundred and twenty-two websites and a large pizza later—somewhere past 1:30 a.m.—he crawled into bed so exhausted that his brain was shutting down. As he drifted off to sleep, he found himself stewing. *I hate private investigation work. It's worse than mom's dry meatloaf.*

The next morning, Joby was at his computer again by 7:30, working with an angry vengeance. There was no way he was going to let this stupid search humiliate him. As the morning wore on into the afternoon, however, his head of steam began to flag. His results were paltry. Six agencies merited a closer look, but none screamed Toad. He wolfed down half of a sub sandwich to quell his growling stomach and pressed on with his efforts, more out of determination than motivation. He felt like he was slogging through a waist-deep swamp with boot-sucking muck on the bottom.

That evening, a few minutes past seven, weary and frustrated, he stumbled upon a website that had a distinct Toad feel about it. His spirit perked up the moment he saw the title—Shamus Hawkshaw, Private Investigator. He suspected that the name was contrived and that it was really a subtle play of words, something his word-maven friend had been a master at. The website blurb also had a familiar ring to it. "Finding people and uncovering truth—for pain or pleasure." That kind of dry, twisted humor was one of Toad's calling cards. Things were looking promising.

Further down the page, underneath a paragraph-long mission statement, he found a quotation from Toad had often quoted this and had once claimed that it was his favorite quote. Another clue! In the footer he found an obscure Dick Tracy quote that Toad had almost obsessed over. "The nation that controls magnetism will control the universe." While at first glance that didn't seem to have anything to do with investigative work, his quirky friend had once informed him that he interpreted it to mean that the side that has an obvious technological edge will win the battle. Joby was now almost positive that he was on the right track. *Got a real good feeling about this.*

Twenty minutes later, on the very bottom of the "About Me" page, Joby found a disclaimer in tiny print which implied that Shamus Hawkshaw was an *operating as* name, not a real name. Below that was a Pennsylvania private investigator's license number which was broken up by several asterisks and the four suits from a deck of cards. *Nice work boss. Masking your legally required license number so your enemies can't google it and find you.*

With a whoop of joy, he returned to the "Contact Me" page and wrote down Toad's phone number and his address. He lived in Robinson Township, a bedroom community west of Pittsburgh. With anticipation, he dialed the number. It rang and rang. After the seventh ring, an answering machine, to his disappointment, responded. "Hi. This is Shamus. I am currently unavailable. Please be advised that I only take difficult cases. I don't do dirt, divorce, or Workman's Comp cases. Call someone else for that kind of petty stuff. But if you have something that is difficult or dangerous, please leave a *very* brief message. If I am interested, I will call you back when I am available, usually within a few days."

Joby left his message. "Hi, Toad. This is Joby. I'm calling because I need some private investigation help. It's a big project and definitely dangerous. Please give me a call at this number from a secure line."

***

Friday morning at 8:45 a.m., after two days of waiting, Joby's burner rang. His heart skipped a beat. "Hi, this is Joby."

"Hey, Hippie. Nice to hear from you. Sorry I didn't call you back sooner. I was out of state doing a little snooping for a case."

"No problem. Completely understand. But, before we get into the reason for my call, I'm curious. What happened? For years we had regular contact, then you just disappeared."

"Sorry, bro. Several years ago, I exposed some serious corruption in Philadelphia involving law enforcement and local officials. They had their hands in illegal gambling and cocaine. As a result, the local mafia placed a hit on me. Somehow, they missed twice. Thank God, the FBI was able to take down most of the mafioso, along with the crooked officials and cops who were cooperating with them. I spent a year hiding out of state. Then I returned to Pennsylvania and set up shop outside Pittsburgh under an assumed name. I am still lying low and haven't contacted my family or friends. My enemies in the underworld have threatened both, and I don't want to jeopardize them. But since you found me, I am going to leave you responsible for your own fate. So now I spilled my story. What's going on in your life?"

"Until recently, nothing exciting. Just the same old stuff. Working as a barista and improving my farmstead in the San Gabriels."

"And now?"

Joby hesitated, trying to calm his nerves. "I need help locating a young lady we believe is in a FEMA camp."

Toad was taken aback. "Dude, getting information on folks inside FEMA camps will be very dicey—the riskiest investigation I have ever undertaken. If this goes south, I don't merely have some mafia honcho putting a price on my head. I have the federal government on my trail—FBI, Homeland Security, the whole nine yards. It's much harder to hide from them. So there are three things you need to bear in mind. One, I won't take your case unless you can convince me that God and the average red-blooded American would be on your side if they heard both sides of the story. Two, if I take the case, my involvement is completely confidential. If necessary, I will deny that I know you. Three, if I take this case, not only will it be the diciest case I have taken, it will be the priciest."

"I understand. No problem." But Toad's response made him more nervous than ever about the operation. If a professional was that nervous, he was definitely in over his head.

"So, who is this young lady that you believe is in a FEMA camp?"

"Her name is Irina—Irina Kirilenko."

"And why is she in a FEMA camp?"

Joby turned to the outline of facts that Woody had sent him. He was unfamiliar with most of the details and didn't want to misspeak. "It started in 2017 when Irina discovered a massive comet out beyond Pluto which was headed for Mars. She reported the comet to the Minor Planet Center, who contacted CNEOS, who contacted the PDCO, who contacted the National Security Advisor. After an emergency meeting, the White House decided that this threat must be kept under wraps. To accomplish this, they broadened their powers with the Homeland Security Act and assumed control over the nation's observatories with the NASA CNEOS Bill, which authorized NASA to vet astronomical research projects under the guise of reducing redundancy in the hunt for NEOs, allowing them to make certain that no astronomers worked in the Taurus sector except those who were assigned to study the comet. They didn't want anyone stumbling upon the Rogue.

"When the MPC got back to Irina, they denied that she had discovered a comet and gave her a contrived story. The apparent occultation of stars she had observed was not actually a comet passing in front of stars but the diffraction of starlight caused by the shock horizon on a jet from a black hole passing in front of the star. But Irina wasn't convinced. When she argued with her boss about the black-hole jet interpretation, she was relieved of her research privileges and placed on the government's Orange One watchlist as a security threat. That opened her eyes to the coverup. She behaved herself for the next nine months and got her risk level reduced to Orange Two, which allowed her to go on vacation. During her Thanksgiving vacation, when she was supposed to be skiing in upstate New York, she drove to Kansas and mailed a package to Ariele Serrafe, a fellow astronomer. It contained a letter describing the situation and a DVD with pertinent pictures and files. She was arrested before she got back to the hotel. We don't know where they took her or where she is now. But we suspect that she is in a FEMA camp somewhere."

"Are you telling me that the tales on late-night radio and internet conspiracy sites about Planet X or a renegade comet headed for Earth are true after all?"

"Well ... kind of ... but not exactly. The comet is actually headed for Mars. The government is afraid that it is going to knock a number of asteroids out of the asteroid belt when it passes through and that some of them will pose a threat to Earth. But a few renegade scientists believe that it will dislodge Mars from its orbit when they tangle and send the Red Planet on a new orbit that could threaten Earth."

"So how do you know about this comet? How do I know that you aren't merely deluded by fake news from unscrupulous men who make a living deceiving the gullible with their conspiracy websites?"

Joby hesitated. He felt caught in a no-win situation. *How much can I ... should I ... tell him? If I give him sensitive information and he turns it over to the authorities, we're all in deep doo-doo. On the other hand, if I don't give him sensitive information, we're not going to get the information we need.* After wrestling for a few seconds, he decided that he was going to have to trust his friend and level with him. That seemed reasonably safe. Toad did, after all, detest Big Brother government nearly as much as organized crime. Joby broke his silence. "I got the information from an astronomer friend who got it from Ariele, the young lady that received the package in the mail from Irina."

241

Toad's mind quickly made the connections. "Let's see, you're from Glendale, and an astronomer friend gave you the information. By any chance, is your friend the astronomer from Caltech who is wanted by the feds for Homeland Security violations? I believe his name is Woodrow Lundstrom."

"Yes. Woody is the friend."

"Did anyone bother to verify this information?"

"Absolutely. Ariele, the young lady that received the package from Irina, observed the comet herself with the Hooker at Mount Wilson and calculated its orbit."

Toad hemmed and hawed, then he exclaimed, "Tell you what. Let me contact a friend in Anonymous. I want to verify the authenticity of the information you have given me on the comet and the coverup. If the story checks out, then we'll talk. I should know by Monday."

"Sounds like a plan."

"By the way, when is this collision with Mars supposed to occur?"

"Sometime in 2025."

"Holy Cow! Maybe my Christian friends are right after all that the end of the world is near."

"I've had the same kind of thoughts running through my head."

"Well, I'm too busy to think about spooky stuff like that right now. Talk to you later."

And with that, he was gone.

32

Buffalo, WY
Monday, July 29, 2019

On Monday morning, a few minutes shy of eleven, Joby's burner rang. Frustration sizzled in his veins. *About time, dude. It's been a long weekend. I read the TV Guide three times and the book of Daniel in the Tanakh twice.* But he clamped his tongue. "Joby here."

"Hey, bro! This is Toad. Your story checks out. Now you got me scared. The whole world is racing around the hamster wheel, pursuing their dreams as if the world will last forever. But it is coming to an end, and they are oblivious. It reminds me of Noah and the coming flood."

"That it does," Joby replied. "I just read the flood account a few days ago." He turned the conversation to the big question in his mind. "So, are you going to take the job?"

"Well, to be honest, though I'm convinced that your case is worth taking, I'm not convinced that you can afford to hire me. As I said before, this kind of PI work can be extremely expensive."

"Don't worry about the money. I have plenty."

"How much is plenty?"

"Twenty-five thousand dollars."

Toad stifled a laugh. "Hate to break it to you, bro, but that's chump change. It'll barely get us started."

"Okay, so what do you think we're looking at?"

"I'm guessing a quarter of a million. But it could go far north of that."

"Holy Guacamole! That seems a bit steep, don't ya think?"

"It's all a matter of perspective. You have to bear in mind that the kind of info you need is confidential and people won't cough it up unless you pay through the nose. Think about it. Those who divulge the information you want are risking serious consequences, so we have to make it worth their while. We are buying illegal information at black-market prices."

"Gotcha. I see your point. I'll touch bases with Woody and see what he says."

"Before you get on the phone with Woody, let me clarify that the $250,000 is for the information only. That doesn't cover my fees. My rate will be $5000 per week for this job, and I suspect it will take two weeks. So that's $10,000 if all goes according to plan. Plus, I want a $25,000 bonus if I'm successful in obtaining the info you seek."

"I didn't know PI rates were so high."

"They're not normally that high. But you gotta remember that I'm taking a risk here too—a big risk. I could permanently disappear in a FEMA hole somewhere."

"Understood. Let me call Woody. I'll get back to you

within fifteen minutes, one way or the other." He hung up, dialed Woody's burner, and waited, nervous as a cat in the middle of a busy freeway. *Maybe I'll get lucky. Maybe they'll call this whole thing off, and I can go back to being a normal person.*

"Tenkara here."

"Hi, Woody. I just got off the phone with Toad. I don't know how we can go forward. He says that twenty-five thousand dollars will barely get us started. He suspects that we'll need at least $250,000 to get the information we need. Plus, he's asking $35,000 for himself. How are we going to come up with that kind of cash?"

"Don't worry about the cost, Joby. Money is one thing we don't lack. Use the debit card for personal expenses. I'll put $250,000 in your Bitcoin account for case expenses. More is available if needed."

"Okay, Woody. Thanks." The distraught young man stewed. *Nuts. Feel like I'm trapped and can't escape.*

Joby called Toad back. "Woody says the money won't be an issue. We can send you whatever you need. He's putting $250,000 in my Bitcoin account right now."

"Sweet. Then I'll take the job. After we hang up, text me your secure email address. I'll send you my contact information and directions for payment to my Bitcoin account. Then send me the pages of information that Woody gave you so I can get started on the initial footwork—contacting a few spooks and savvy insiders. Sometime this morning, deposit $100,000 in my Bitcoin account. Once the funds are deposited, I'll pursue the case in earnest." He paused. "I don't know how to say this without sounding rude, so I'm just going to be blunt. Don't expect me to be babysitting the phone and calling you three times a day with updates. I don't do the handholding thing. Not even for friends. You'll just have to be patient. I suspect that I'll have some useful intelligence in three or four days, and when I do, I'll call you. In the meantime, go buy yourself a few good books and do some reading."

***

On Thursday afternoon, Joby's phone rang, startling him. He tucked a bookmark in his book, set it down, and answered.

"Joby."

"Hey, Bud. I got some interesting information."

"Well, spill it."

"Monday afternoon, I placed a call to the TNO Program with the Astronomy Department at Cornell University, pretending to be a freelance columnist for science magazines. I said I was interested in Irina's amazing TNO discoveries and asked if I could speak with her. The gal who answered told me that she was not available. I asked if she could take a message and have Irina call me back. She said no, that Irina had gone on an extended vacation and wouldn't be back for a while. I pressed her further and asked if she had any idea where Irina was. The lady was silent for a moment, then responded icily, 'I have no idea where Irina is. I'm done answering impertinent questions. And this conversation is over.' Her response made me feel uneasy. She was hiding something."

"Is there anything there to pursue?" Joby enquired.

"Probably not. The odds are, she doesn't know anything. Nor does anyone else in her department. But her response is nearly as helpful as if she had plainly told us that Irina had been taken into custody."

"How's that?"

"If anything other than a government conspiracy was behind Irina's absence from Cornell, the gal would have plainly told us what she knew. Since she didn't do that but gave us evasive answers, it's a safe assumption that the conspiracy theory is true.

"Later that day, I called Irina's parents and gave them a similar story—that I was a freelance reporter with an interest in Irina's TNO discoveries, that I had caught wind of her mysterious disappearance, and that I was interested in an interview. They graciously invited me over. I immediately booked a red-eye flight to Los Angeles, caught a few hours of sleep on the plane, rented a car upon arrival, and drove to their home in Yreka. They invited me to join them for a breakfast of fried eggs and potato pancakes, and somehow we got talking about the dangers of Russian nationalism. By the time breakfast was over, it was obvious that they had warmed up to me. Mr. Kirilenko noted that it was 7:30 Pacific time and that he had to leave for his first class in an hour, so he suggested that we move to the living room and get down to business.

"We settled in, and I broached the subject. I began by asking them if they had any idea where Irina was. Mrs. Kirilenko replied—she did most of the talking—that all they knew was what they had gleaned from two mysterious phone calls at the time of her disappearance and from a letter they had received from the Department of Justice about six weeks later. Their calls to the local police station and the Los Angeles Field Station looking for information had yielded absolutely nothing.

"I pursued the DOJ letter first. It turns out that it had come by courier rather than the US Postal Service. This seems significant to me, but I haven't had time to pursue it. The letter—I have a copy of it—stated that Irina was being held at an unspecified location on Homeland Security violations and that her assets were subject to forfeiture. There was no contact number for further information. The Kirilenkos weren't certain what the term *Homeland Security violation* meant, so they googled it. They were shocked to learn that this phrase implied that Irina was regarded by the government as a terrorist and that she could be held indefinitely without Miranda rights, formal charges, access to a lawyer, visitation rights, or communication with family.

"Over the next few days, they called the DOJ and the FBI field office several times apiece to no avail. Each time, they were informed that the department was not authorized to release any information. To add insult to injury, the next week a FEMA box truck arrived, accompanied by a Homeland Security escort, and confiscated Irina's grand piano. That same day, Irina's joint savings account that she shared with her grandfather was confiscated, emptied, and closed by the DOJ.

"I asked them if the government had contacted them in any way since Irina's disappearance, apart from the letter.

They replied in the negative. At that point Mr. Kirilenko went on a little tirade about the direction America was going. They had fled the threat of Russian hegemony, and now they faced the same totalitarianism in the land of the free.

"When they finished letting off some steam, I asked about the mysterious phone calls. The first was from one of Irina's friends from church—she wouldn't identify herself. She and a couple other girls had gone to upstate New York with Irina to do some skiing and shopping. Shortly after they arrived, Irina borrowed Olivia's Subaru and left for several days. At the time they suspected that her trip had something to do with a guy. The next day, however, the FBI showed up and questioned the girls about Irina's whereabouts, character, associations, and behavior changes. They told the agents that nothing had seemed out of place until that weekend. She had been a trustworthy friend and a model Christian. Everyone respected her. They were shocked to find out that Irina was some kind of terrorist threat.

"While two of the girls were convinced that Irina was a menace to society and that she had been playing them all along, the young lady who called wasn't able to believe that. She had been Irina's closest friend and had spent many hours with her in conversation and prayer. She told Irina's parents that she thought their daughter was a victim of a conspiracy that she had been reading about on the internet which involved a comet that threatened Earth. No other explanation made sense. Irina was an astronomer, not a political activist or an extremist. She had probably stumbled across information on the comet that the government was trying to cover up.

"The following Monday, her parents received another call, this one from a work associate who also refused to identify herself. She told them that the Astronomy department at Cornell had been summoned to a special meeting where they were informed that Irina was no longer with them, that she was guilty of violations of the Homeland Security Act, that the situation was sensitive, and that they were forbidden to talk about it. Things became a little clearer later that day when she overheard Dr. Goldblum informing his assistant department head that Irina had been picked up by the FBI for spreading apocalyptic-comet rumors."

Joby was glad for Toad's efforts, but he wasn't impressed with the results. "Sounds to me like we don't know any more now than when we started."

His friend countered, "Actually, we do. Don't underestimate the value of the information that we gained. We have demonstrated that her disappearance is probably not a matter of foul play or instability and that your theory of government conspiracy is likely correct. And we have garnered a few helpful clues. Don't worry. Things are going forward. You will get your money's worth."

250

33

Sally stood in line in the cafeteria laughing at herself. *Can't believe I called the cafeteria a chow hall. Jack's military terminology is starting to rub off on me.* When her turn came, she loaded up on pizza, then bounded down the hallway to the newsroom to join Jack and Irina. She enjoyed meeting them there for dinner though she was less fascinated by news and world events than they were.

Geoff Seaworthy's pleasant, masculine voice greeted her as she walked in. "Two space stories are in the news tonight. The first is a NASA report that Sunspot Cycle 25, now in its fourteenth month, continues to smash modern records with its dearth of sunspot activity. We have now gone 150 days straight without a sunspot. The current minimum began two and a half years ago and shows no sign of letting up. Typically solar minimums—the first part of a sunspot cycle—last one to two years, but can last five years or more. Extended minimums, which are known as grand minimums, can last for decades and cause temperatures on Earth to plunge, producing *little ice ages*. It was so cold during the last minimum, the Maunder Minimum, which lasted from 1645 to 1715, that the Thames River and portions of the Baltic Sea froze over. Normally, grand minimums recur every 100 to 200 years. The fact that we are overdue for one, coupled with the unusual severity of the current minimum, has led some scientists to speculate that we are entering a grand minimum. They suggest that we are headed for global cooling, not global warming, and that the warming of the past few years is merely a short-term trend.

"The second space story is the meteor shower which unexpectedly began in mid-June and is still going strong. This spectacular display—with green shooting stars, many large fireballs, and numerous minor impacts—has spawned a wave of claims on the internet that this shower has apocalyptic implications. To get a better handle on this situation, we have invited Dr. Franconi of the Smithsonian Institute to give us his perspective." Geoff turned to his guest. "Dr. Franconi, is there any truth to these apocalyptic claims?"

"Absolutely not, Geoff. The shower has a mundane cause. Earth is passing through the tail of a comet, specifically the Xingu comet, a large fragment of which landed in the Amazon basin last April. Over the past two thousand years, Earth has experienced a dozen extended meteor showers caused by the same circumstance. None of them presaged the end of the world. And neither does this one. This shower is just another run-of-the-mill comet-tail shower that is insignificant in the grand scheme of things."

"What about the numerous impacts?"

"The only thing that the hundreds of small impacts tell us is that the tail of the Xingu comet is fairly rocky. Somewhere on its journey, it picked up some stony hitchhikers. Again, this is no big deal. Many of the extended meteor showers in the past featured showers of stones, and some of them surpassed the showers of this comet."

"Well, there you have it. An expert's perspective on the story. Thank you for your time this evening, Dr. Franconi."

"You're welcome, Geoff. Thank you for having me."

The newscaster moved on to Middle East affairs. "A tragedy is unfolding in the Middle East. Turkey, Iran, Syria, and Iraq have launched a coordinated ground assault, involving dozens of brigades of infantry and armor, against their Kurdish regions. Extensive bombing raids led by the Turkish and Iranian air forces are raining devastation on vital cities and military positions, especially in the Iraqi Kurd's Autonomous Region. According to a joint statement released from Ankara, the coalition is determined to put an end to the Kurdish problem once and for all.

"The backdrop to the current situation began eight months ago when the American government agreed to stop supplying the Kurdish YPG, or People's Protection Units, in Syria with arms and intel—a step many regard as a tragic betrayal of an ally. Two months later, the Iraqi Kurds, formerly on good terms with Turkey, grew weary of watching their Turkish and Syrian brethren getting battered by the Turkish armed forces and came to their aid. The Iranian Kurds shortly followed. This step enraged Turkey and her coalition allies, and they began planning the operation that we see unfolding today. Now that the United States has backed away from the Kurds, it looks as if the hope for a Kurdish homeland—barring a miracle—has taken a fatal dagger to the breast."

Tears rolled down Sally's cheeks. "I really hoped that America and Europe would get behind the Kurds. Instead, they abandoned them. My poor grandma is going to take this hard. She was born and raised in the Zagros Mountains in a village northeast of Kirkuk." She managed a weak smile. "Got my green eyes from her."

Jack growled, "Stuff like this burns me up. Just one more example of nations sacrificing their smaller allies on the altar of geopolitical expediency. But money talks. We are more interested in trade dollars with Turkey than seeing the Kurds living free and unmolested in the homeland they have inhabited for thousands of years."

Geoff continued, "The top story in European news tonight is the collapse of Moldova. After weeks of unrest at home and political pressure from Moscow, the government capitulated to the demands of the pro-Russia party and surrendered its sovereignty. Once the formalities are completed, Moldova will no longer be a member of the CIS, the Commonwealth of Independent States, but an oblast of the Russian Federation.

"An inside source, who requested anonymity, claimed that the Moldovan government did not want the current unrest to turn into a drawn-out conflict like that which devastated Eastern Ukraine. They figured that it was far better to concede now with Moldova intact than wait until it was crushed."

Sally cringed when Jack slammed his fist down on his chair arm and groused, "The West had better watch out for the Russian Bear. I've been warning my friends about this day for years."

"But the Kremlin-instigated unrest," the newscaster proceeded, "isn't limited to Moldova. The pro-Russia uprisings that led to the annexation of Crimea, Moldova, and eastern Ukraine are now roiling western Ukraine and the Baltic states and introducing trouble in Romania, Bulgaria, and Hungary. Experts suspect that the Kremlin's plan is for the former to be melded into Russia itself and the latter to be coerced into leaving the EU and joining the CIS. Unless Western policy changes soon, this plan is likely to succeed. Lodging protests at the UN isn't enough to dissuade Russia from meddling in Eastern Europe. If the EU and NATO aren't willing to step up to the plate, the entire former Soviet bloc will be reabsorbed.

"Is Germany headed for the Russian fold too? That is a question many are asking in light of recent developments. Yesterday, Germany deployed the 1st Panzer Division and the Rapid Forces Division to Smolensk to train for three weeks with the Russian armed forces. Next week, Germany's finance, agriculture, energy, and trade ministers will be in Moscow to hammer out far-reaching agreements on trade, banking, and the development of natural resources.

"Why the turn to Russia now? The answer is economics. This was evident last October at the EU summit in

Luxembourg when the German delegates stormed out, berating policies that punished strong economies and rewarded weak ones. They warned that Germany was tired of carrying Europe on her back. Her allies regarded this outburst as a hiccup in European affairs. But they were mistaken. Since then, she has accepted an attractive package from Russia: no financial liability for her partner nations in the CIS, massive deals for coal and petroleum, and billions of dollars worth of technology and military contracts.

"The West is panic-stricken. Berlin strengthening her military and economic ties with Russia has ominous overtones for the EU. It is already reeling from the departure of the UK, the world's fifth largest economy. If Germany, the world's fourth-largest economy, follows suit, that would sound the death knell for the EU."

The newscaster turned the program over to the weather forecast, and Sally turned to Jack. "So where do you think this Russia stuff is headed?"

"The Russian-led invasion of Israel that we read about in Ezekiel in chapters 38 and 39. She will be accompanied by a formidable group of allies including Germany, Turkey, and Iran."

"Will the invasion be successful?"

"Nope. According to the Bible, the entire force will be destroyed by fire that falls from heaven."

"What happens then?"

"The revived Roman empire will take advantage of the fact that she is the only remaining superpower in the world. The head of the empire, known as the antichrist, will force the nations of the world to join his economic system and worship his image. And he will attempt to eradicate all who believe in Jesus and the Bible. This time is known as the tribulation."

Sally asked, "Is that antichrist and tribulation stuff really going to happen? I have always thought they were, I dunno, more like future myths than real things."

"They're as sure as the sunrise. The Bible's track record for the fulfillment of prophecy is one hundred percent. The prophecies about Jesus' first coming, the destruction of Jerusalem, the rebirth of Israel, and judgments falling on various nations in Old Testament times were all fulfilled exactly and literally. So it's a sure bet that the Bible's prophecies about the end of this age will also come to pass literally and exactly."

"But if the future is going to bring us the antichrist, the tribulation, and Armageddon, that's an ugly future to look forward to. Where is the hope in that?"

"You have to tear down the old before you can build the new. God is simply removing what's broken so he can bring in what's perfect. After the time of awful judgment comes the amazing blessing of the kingdom of God when Jesus reigns on Earth forever and brings in eternal utopia."

That night Sally tossed and turned restlessly, trying to wrap her mind around the things Jack had talked about: the Bible, prophecy, and Jesus. She tried to cling to the beliefs that she had been steeped in since childhood: evolution, man is good, man will make himself and the world better. But it was no use. She knew they weren't true. And though the immediate future looked ominous, for the first time in her life she sensed that there was real hope—for both the world and herself. Maybe Jesus really was the solution to the mess after all.

34

Buffalo, WY
Monday, August 5 ... Friday, August 16, 2019

First thing Monday morning, Toad called Joby with some exciting information. "My source in the FBI confirmed that Irina was detained, charged with security violations under the Homeland Security Act, and processed for detainment in the 200-series FEMA camps. But he didn't know which one."

"How many are there?"

"He wasn't sure, but based on a recent report that had come across his desk, there are four for sure and maybe a fifth."

"So where do we go from here?"

"Not far. I think we might be able to dig a little deeper in this vein. My FBI contact has a friend in another department who has access to the FEMA camp data. He figures his friend can probably find out exactly which camp Irina is in—for a fee."

"So how much are we looking at?"

"I dunno. I'll send you a text with the amount when I

know. But I should warn you, we've already burned through $50,000."

***

Two days later, Joby received a text while he was engrossed with the account of the day of the Lord in Joel in the Tanakh. "Send the remaining $150,000, we're going to need it. Got some good leads on good intel."

He agonized, unsure whether this was a wise investment or just throwing money down a hole. His penny-pinching side wrestled with the exorbitant expenditures. They were blowing through more money in a week than he had ever made in seven or eight years. But his humanitarian side wrestled back. Good causes always come with a price tag. After a few minutes of fretting, he decided to trust Woody's discernment in the matter and ignore his own emotionally charged uncertainty.

He logged in to his Bitcoin account and transferred the remaining funds to Toad's Bitcoin account. Then he sent a message to Woody. "You need to replenish the Bitcoin account. I just emptied it. Send $100,000." When he finished, he lay back down, emotionally drained. He wasn't cut out for this. Long stretches of anxious waiting mixed with short spurts of excitement. *I just want to be an organic farmer with a pretty hippie chic at my side.*

Two hours later, his phone buzzed on the tabletop and woke him from a restless nap. He picked it up, groggy and cranky. It was Toad. "Hope you got something worth mortgaging the ranch for."

"I do. I managed to verify that Irina is being held in a detention center near Syracuse, New York known as FEMA 286. The camp is located in an old factory building in the old industrial park on the southwest side of town."

"That's good as far as it goes. But what do we know about the place or Irina's schedule? Do we have any information that will help us come up with a rescue plan?"

"No, not yet. But I have a couple leads that will probably provide us with the kind of information you're seeking. They may take a few days to follow up on, however, so don't worry unless you don't hear from me by the end of next week."

"Next week? What am I going to do?"

"Go buy yourself a Bible in a literal translation and read the New Testament. My sister says it throws a lot of light on what is going on around us, both on Earth and in the heavens. She thinks we're on the verge of the last days. I picked up a copy myself after our first conversation and have started to read it."

"I just might do that. Got to do something."

***

A week later, on the evening of Friday, August 16, as Joby was getting ready for bed, his burner finally buzzed. He picked it up and snarked, "You weren't kidding about a week. I've been going crazy in this motel room. Do you have any idea how tired I am of pizza, subs, and takeout Chinese?"

Toad was humored at his friend's agitation, and it showed in his voice. "No need to lecture me on takeout food.

That's been my life story for years. As for the delay—sorry. We were using old-school intel techniques, so things moved slowly. But we got what we were looking for." He couldn't contain himself any longer and broke into a chuckle.

"What's so funny?"

"It's hilarious to hear my laid-back hippie friend talking like a frazzled salesman."

"Sorry. I'm really not cut out for this. I'm being stretched in ways I didn't know a man could be stretched." Joby paused. "Well, enough whining. What do you have for me?"

"I called a few connections who owed me favors, looking for someone with a link to the rumored Rogue Underground. One of them, an eccentric doctor in Mississippi who talks incessantly about prophecy and the end of the world, had a cowboy friend who he thought might be a member. The guy drifts into town twice a year and crashes at his place for a few days."

"What led him to suspect that this cowboy might belong to the Underground?"

"Two things. First of all, during his last few visits, he spoke about the Rogue and the government coverup with expertise and gravitas. Secondly, last April he asked Doc for help in procuring antiparasitic antibiotics for a friend suffering from amoebic dysentery. When Doc asked him why his friend didn't just go see a doctor, he shook his head and said, 'Sorry, can't go into the details. But coming out of seclusion is not an option. Either you help him and he recovers, or you don't and he suffers.'"

"Did he help him?"

"Yeah. Doc gave him a sample box of a new product similar to metronidazole."

"You trust this quirky doctor?"

"I do. Though he is a little unhinged when it comes to conspiracy theories and the end of the world, he is a shrewd judge of character. He reads people spooky good."

"So did this cowboy lead pay off?"

"It did. Doc contacted the cowboy, explained that some Rogue believers were hoping to break Irina out of FEMA 286, and asked if he had any connections that might be able to obtain the intel necessary for them to pull this endeavor off. The cowboy replied that he knew people that might have the right connections, but it would be a couple days before he could get back to him with an answer.

"Two days later, the cowboy called Doc back and told him that a contact in upstate New York had a contact in Syracuse who could smuggle messages into and out of 286. He wanted $10,000 for one message in and one out. Doc agreed to the terms and contacted me. I forwarded my request last Friday for info on Irina and intel on weak links in the security at 286. We had to wait a whole week for an answer as messages only go in and out once a week. The recipient inside the camp verified that Irina was there, reported that she worked in the kitchen from 4 a.m. to noon, Monday through Friday, and claimed we wouldn't have any trouble recognizing her—just look for a tall, stunning brunette with a slight Ukrainian accent who helps in the kitchen. He also said that a former Ranger in the camp assured him that food service was *the* weak link in camp security. They receive deliveries from Katahdin

Foods on Mondays and Thursdays, usually between 5:45 and 6:15 a.m."

"So how do we exploit the food-service truck?"

"That he didn't say. Guess you're gonna have to figure that out yourself."

"Great. Bring me to the evil lord's castle and leave me to find my way in on my own."

"That's right. You're on your own from here. I do have some free advice for you though. First of all, find a run-down motel in Syracuse that doesn't have video cameras installed. Once your mission goes down, whether successful or unsuccessful, the feds will be checking the video records of every hotel in the area.

"Secondly, you're going to need a false driver's license and a Visa debit card with your false name on it if you want to cover your tracks when you stay at the motel.

"Thirdly, you'll need to stop in New York City, find a chop shop, and trade your wheels in for a vehicle with clean plates and a cover story. This ensures that your butt is covered if you get stopped before the breakout and that the vehicle can't be traced back to you afterward.

"I don't have any leads for chop shops in New York, but I do know a cobbler in Pittsburgh that handles several grades of false IDs. He should be able to set you up with a fake driver's license and a Visa card with your false name. He'll probably help you craft a cover story too. His operational name is Phantom. If you're interested, I can text you his cell phone number and give him a heads-up that you'll be calling."

"Yes. Please do. So, how do you know this guy?"

"You don't want to know, and I don't want to tell." Toad was silent for a few seconds, then ended the conversation. "Hey, Bro, I have to run. It's been great doing business with you. Keep in touch."

"Will do. Thanks for the advice," Joby replied. But he was only half thankful. The counsel had aggravated his awareness of the dangers and difficulties that lay in front of him. The road just kept on getting worse and worse.

Shaking his head at his inescapable predicament, he sent a brief email to Woody outlining the information he had received from Toad on Irina, Camp 286, and the exploitable weakness in the food-service delivery. He also mentioned the PI's advice to stop in Philadelphia for a false ID and New York City for a clean car. After he hit the *send* button, he closed his laptop and shoved it away. Then he climbed into bed, grumpy and frustrated.

35

Buffalo, WY ... Minnesota
Saturday, August 17, 2019

Joby groggily answered the 6 a.m. wake-up call, then stumbled out of bed. He hadn't slept well. There was too much on his mind. He sat back down on the edge of the bed, paralyzed with dread. *I feel like a rookie stepping into a cage fight with a seasoned veteran.* With a sudden resolve that surprised himself, he picked up his laptop, opened Tor, and logged in to Buster. *Might as well get this over with.* He hoped that there wouldn't be a new message from Woody. He didn't want to continue with the operation. The investigation stage had pushed him beyond his psychological limits. The reconnaissance stage would be so far beyond his abilities that it seemed ludicrous for him to be involved. His heart sank when he saw a new message in the inbox.

Bandana,

Good work. Glad to hear that Irina is in FEMA 286. The food-service idea sounds promising. I have strong reservations against you going further in this operation on your own. At this point, all I want you to do is follow Toad's advice on getting a clean car, procuring a false ID, and finding an older motel without security cameras. Then hunker down. We have decided to wait for Jordy's boys before we go any further. They should show up in the next week or two, and we're hoping that they'll get on board with the mission and take over its planning and execution.

Tenkara

Joby breathed a sigh of relief. While it smarted a little bit that he was not trusted with the next phase of the mission, he knew Woody had made a wise decision. He didn't have the necessary skill set. Invigorated by his reprieve, he sprang up with a bounce in his step that had been missing for weeks, showered, loaded his car, checked out of the motel, and stopped at a gas station to grab a couple gut-bomb burritos for breakfast.

At 7:15, he headed out of town and began the long drive to New York City. The morning and early afternoon were uneventful, except for the natural beauty of the Black Hills and the Badlands. He had no idea that there was anything so grand in the Dakotas.

His tranquility came to a screeching halt that afternoon. After leaving Sioux Falls, South Dakota, he set his cruise control to eighty-three miles per hour. Sipping a fresh French Roast coffee, his mind drifted off into daydreams about the mission ahead. In the brighter ones, he pulled off a heroic rescue. In the darker ones, he got caught and went to a FEMA camp, or worse, got shot and bled to death.

Whaaat? You've got to be kidding!

Flashing lights were on his tail. With a groan he slowed, pulled over to the shoulder, rolled his window down, and grabbed his wallet. He waited tensely while the trooper called in his license plate. Several minutes later, the patrolman walked up to his car with his hand on his holster.

"Can I see your license, please?"

Joby handed it over.

"Do you know why I pulled you over?"

"No, sir."

"Do you know how fast you were going?"

"Eighty miles per hour, sir."

"You were actually doing eighty-four miles per hour. Do you know what the speed limit is here?"

"Eighty miles per hour."

"Nope. It's seventy. You were going fourteen over the limit. Right on the line for serious fines."

Joby looked at the patrolman like he could hardly believe what he was hearing.

The officer continued, "Do you know what state you are in?"

"South Dakota."

"Nope. You left South Dakota three miles ago. I picked you up two miles back, hit my lights a mile and a half back. Were you daydreaming?"

"Sorry."

"Sorry doesn't fix problems. *It won't happen again* is what fixes problems."

The officer peered into the cab of Joby's truck and eyed the gear bags on the floor and seat. He then walked around the truck, looking underneath and peering through the topper windows. When he reached the rear, he opened the topper and poked around. A couple minutes later, he reappeared at Joby's window.

"Where are you headed, son?"

"Out East."

"And what's the purpose of this trip?"

"Change of pace. I spent my whole life in California. I want to see the Appalachian Trail and visit New England."

"Are you carrying any firearms?"

"No, sir. Never owned a gun in my life. Never even fired one."

"Do you have any drugs with you?"

"No, sir. I got in trouble when I was seventeen and went to a Juvenile Justice work camp in the Klamath Mountains, sponsored by the California Department of Corrections. Never touched pot again after that."

"Well, an odor in the back smells suspicious. Wait right here. I'm going to make a call. We'll let the dogs decide."

Joby waited nervously. *What in the world did he smell? My herbal candles? Is he looking for an excuse to arrest me? Does he suspect that I'm connected with Woody?*

Forty minutes later, the dog team arrived from Fairmont. The officer asked Joby to get out of his truck and stand on the shoulder of the road about twenty feet away. His heart was in his throat as the dogs sniffed around, under, and in his truck. On the verge of panic, he looked upward in his heart. *God, please don't let them plant weed in my truck.* He felt ashamed. It seemed wrong to only pray when he needed help. After ten minutes of pawing and sniffing, the two canine officers loaded their dogs back up and departed. The patrolman walked back to his car, talked on his radio briefly, then returned to Joby.

"Sorry about the hassles, son. Nothing personal. But we've been seeing a lot of illegal drugs coming into the state in the past three months. So we search a lot of out-of-state vehicles." He handed Joby back his driver's license. "Here you go. Have a safe trip and stay out of trouble."

Joby walked back to his truck, relieved that the hair-raising situation was over and determined to pay closer attention to the speed limit signs along the highway. He didn't want to play Russian roulette with traffic stops.

36

the Compound
Saturday, August 17, 2019

Red and Woody were manning the grill on the outdoor patio, Red dropping the burgers and Woody basting the corn, when Red's motion sensor alarm went off on his phone. He tapped the security alert and checked the video feed. "It's Jordy and Beth at the gate and another truck with them. It looks like Tony and Andy."

Woody grinned. "That was a brilliant idea on Andrius' part to install a Wi-Fi camera at the gate and link it with a security app on your phone."

"It sure was. I hate to admit it, but I pegged the kid wrong. I was certain he was going to be more of a nuisance than a help. While he's a bit on the odd side, he's a whiz with electronics and welding."

"Yep. He's about as smart as God makes 'em. But he is getting a little country boy on him. I saw him getting a riding lesson with Blake and Ariele this morning."

"On a horse? That's a big step. I still chuckle when I think of his hysterical reaction to the grouse that flew up in front of us while we were out picking gooseberries."

Woody laughed. "And how about the time he knocked on Ariele's door and asked if he could sleep on her floor because the wolves howling outside his window were freaking him out? She told him that they were only coyotes, that they were probably a half mile away, and that their yipping is a lullaby from heaven."

The two pickups rolled up the road and parked by the patio. Andy and Tony hustled toward Woody with big grins. They appreciated the old-school special-ops vet. "Good to see you again, old timer," Tony said as he gave him a bear hug. When he finally released his grip, Andy took his turn. Woody worried that his ribs might break. But he preferred the crushing embraces to their crushing handshakes.

Woody motioned to the picnic table and the trio sat down. Ariele sidled over and flamboyantly introduced herself. "I'm Ariele, one of the scientists on staff here. But I wear a couple other hats, too, like chief hen-house keeper and associate garden weeder."

The boys grinned, amused and enchanted by the spunky female. Tony spoke up, "I'm Tony and this is Andy."

Woody interrupted and got right to business. "I would love to spend a few hours in small talk. But we're in the middle of a situation that requires immediate attention, and your expertise would come in handy."

Tony piped up, "Dad already briefed us on the Rogue. I'm not sure how much help we can be. Unless and until the comet actually brings trouble here on Earth, it seems more like a matter for scientists than for soldiers."

"Boys, the Rogue has already brought trouble to our doorstep."

The brothers looked at each other and smirked knowingly.

Woody ignored their scoffing. "The feds are dead serious about keeping this comet out of the public eye. Ariele and I both had to flee from the FBI when we became privy to sensitive information on the comet that made us security threats in the eyes of the government."

Andy looked at him quizzically. "Flee? Sorry, Woody. I'm having a hard time swallowing this. You're asking me to believe that the government is engaged in a massive conspiracy over a comet that won't even come close to Earth? The whole thing sounds more like internet nonsense than legitimate alternative news."

Ariele exploded. "I didn't flee because I watched a few videos by Billy Balderdash on quacknews.com. I fled because the FBI was going to arrest me and send me to a FEMA camp." She glared at them, making eye contact with both.

Andy soaked in her indignation with pleasure. *There's a little bit of red pepper in this girl.*

She continued, "My boss turned me in to the FBI for giving her a report on the Rogue, which I had put together from my own illegal research and that of others. I was questioned by the FBI and informed that I had an appointment that evening with Casper over potential Homeland Security Act violations. They trailed me home and staked out my apartment to make sure I didn't flee. But I managed to evade them. If they had wired me up to Casper, they would have discovered that I was guilty, and I would have been shipped to a FEMA camp."

"Okay," Tony countered. "Let's assume that you're correct that the government is covering up the comet. Why? What's the purpose?"

Woody replied, "Didn't your father explain to you that it was going to pass very closely to Mars, maybe even nail it head on?"

"Yes. But so what? If it misses Mars, nothing happens. It hits Mars, and the god of war gets a dent in it. Astronomers might find some significance in that, but it wouldn't mean much to me—about the same as a tea shortage in England."

Ariele piped up, "Do you remember Newton's third law from high school?"

"No," Andy butted in. "I was too busy chasing girls and deer."

"Newton's third law says, 'For every action, there is an equal but opposite reaction.'"

"Now I remember. You're talking about the little contraption in science class with the steel balls slapping against each other."

"Exactly."

"So Mars might move a little bit if the comet pastes it."

"It will be much worse than that. This isn't a little ball banging a big ball. This is a big ball banging a big ball. According to emails from NASA that I have in my possession, the comet has the same mass as Mars."

Tony stared at her dumbfounded, fumbling for words. "So dad was right after all. He told us that the Rogue was planet-sized, but we thought that was an exaggerated reference to a dwarf planet—a tiny dwarf planet. This changes everything." He sat silent for a moment, rubbing the stubble on his chin. "So what is going to happen when the two collide?"

"Well," Woody answered. "Our theory on what will happen when the two meet differs from NASA's, but we both agree that the results will pose a catastrophic threat to Earth."

"What does the government think will happen?"

"They believe that when the Rogue passes through the asteroid belt, it will smack a number of asteroids, fracturing them and sending the fragments on eccentric orbits. These fragments will bombard Earth with asteroids for many centuries to come—a disaster scenario far beyond Hollywood's imagination."

"How is your view different?"

"Imagine what would happen," Ariele proposed, "if the steel balls were all charged with electromagnetic energy."

Andy replied, "You mean, they were pushing each other without touching each other—like magnets?"

"That's right. According to the electric universe theory, the comet doesn't actually have to hit Mars for the bodies to be knocked into new orbits. It merely needs to come near enough that their magnetic fields collide."

"If that's the case, that greatly increases the odds of trouble in the solar system."

"Substantially."

Tony spoke up, "Guess dad's concern about the Rogue wasn't some hair-brained piece of sensationalizing journalism after all."

"That's right," the sassy gal chimed. "Why didn't you pick up on the clues earlier? Didn't you wonder what was up with the massive expansion of Homeland Security and FEMA, the two-hundred-and fifty-percent increase in FBI agents, and the tsunami of arrests for homeland security violations?"

"Yeah. We saw that stuff. But we just assumed that it was merely a matter of escalated terrorism and Russian intrigue. That was how the conservative news networks portrayed things."

"Didn't the comet rumors pique your interest?"

"To be honest, no. We don't trust the alternative news websites. Too much nonsense on stuff like UFOs, ancient civilizations on Mars, and Nibiru. We regarded the reports on the rogue comet as the same kind of malarkey."

"I understand your skepticism," Woody said, elbowing his way back in. "But you are in the know now, so let me get you up to speed." He proceeded to outline the chain of events: Irina's discovery of the comet ... the government coverup ... the black-hole-jet explanation ... the NASA CNEOS Bill ... the FEMA bill ... the Homeland Security Act ... Irina mailing the package to Ariele ... Ariele's research and flight ... Woody's flight ... Jack's apparent death ... and Irina's detention in a FEMA camp.

When he was done, the boys sat quietly, their skepticism deflated. Tony broke the silence. "So what kind of help do you need from us?"

Ariele burst out, "We need your help to get Irina out of FEMA 286."

The boys looked at her and Woody like they were crazy. Andy laughed. "Break someone out of a federal confinement center? Are you serious, or is this just wishful thinking?"

Woody replied, "No, this is a real-world mission. We already have a man on the ground. But he lacks the needed skill set. That's why we're asking for your help."

"Part of me wants to say *no*," Andy answered, "because I meant it when I swore to defend our country against all enemies foreign and domestic. I am a true-blue American. On the other hand, the cover-up is a game-changer. The federal agencies are the lackeys of a subtle totalitarianism that is looking out for the interests of the elite, not the interests of the nation as a whole. This inclines me to think that working against the cover-up is upholding my promise to defend America. After all, the rank and file are America." He turned to his brother. "I don't know, Tony. What do you think?"

"Well, I'm hesitant to regard those orchestrating the cover-up as domestic enemies. I would prefer to say that they are good men whose domestic policy threatens the welfare of their constituents. But either way, whether their actions are criminal or shortsighted, we still have an obligation to look out for America. And getting this astronomer out of a FEMA camp is as good a place as any to start. So I say, let's do it."

Tony turned to Woody. "How far are you in your planning?"

"Not far. Our man is on the way to Syracuse, NY, where FEMA 286 is located. And we have obtained intel that the twice-weekly food-service delivery is an exploitable weak link in camp security."

"So what kind of training does this guy have?"

"He doesn't."

"Any military, law enforcement, private investigation, security, or hacking experience?"

"Nope. He has no special skills. But he does have a PI friend with helpful connections in Anonymous, WikiLeaks, and the FBI itself."

"Sounds like you're sending a boy to do a man's job."

"Fully aware of that. That's why we're seeking your help. He has done pretty well up to this point—tracking down Irina and coming up with an idea to get her out. But reconning the situation, formulating a tactical plan, and executing that plan is way beyond his abilities."

"And you suspect that the camp's food-service delivery is our best bet for a strategy?"

"I do. A former Ranger on the inside assured us that the food-service delivery on Monday and Thursday was the most exploitable weak point in 286's security."

Tony admitted, "Sounds like a workable concept to me."

"Do you have a mole in the camp?" Andy asked.

"Not exactly, but we were able to communicate with two men on the inside."

Tony enquired, "When do you expect Joby to arrive in Syracuse?"

"I'm guessing Wednesday. He's supposed to call me after he checks into the motel." Woody eyed the two. "Are you boys in?"

They answered in unison, "I'm game."

"How much time do you need to get ready?"

"Not much," Andy said. "We have most of the equipment that we'll need. We can draw up an operation outline in a few hours. And we can hold a Compound meeting tomorrow evening to talk things over. Barring unforeseen circumstances, we should be on our way first thing Monday morning, and we should arrive in Syracuse by midnight on Wednesday, not far behind Joby."

Woody smiled. "Glad you're on board, boys." As they lifted glasses of spicy hot vegetable juice for a toast to mission success, Red decked the table with a platter of his famous elk burgers—brimming with Swiss cheese, mushrooms, and his secret pepper sauce.

37

the Compound
Sunday, August 18, 2019

At 7 p.m., the crew gathered for the special meeting that Jordy's boys had requested the prior afternoon. Jordy turned the floor over to Woody to give a brief update on the effort to rescue Irina.

"Operation Irina has progressed better than I had anticipated. Joby learned that Irina is imprisoned at FEMA 286 in Syracuse, New York and that Katahdin Foods' twice-weekly delivery is our best bet for a rescue attempt. He left his motel in Wyoming yesterday and is on the way to Syracuse. He plans on stopping in Philadelphia to obtain a false ID and in New York City to trade his truck for a vehicle with clean plates. Once he arrives in Syracuse, he'll rent a motel room and wait for Tony and Andy to show up.

"Last night I gave the boys our ideas and the information that we have gathered to this point and asked them to come up with a plan. They are going to share that with us now."

He nodded to them, and Tony spoke up. "This is only a rough draft of our rescue operation. In the upcoming weeks, it will be fleshed out, modified, and refined as necessary.

"Our plan is to confiscate a food-service truck and tie up the driver. Joby will then gain entrance to the camp by pretending to be a substitute driver. Once inside, he will make contact with Irina and send her to the loading dock where she will conceal herself in the load. After the delivery, Joby will drive to a prearranged rendezvous site where we will hide the truck and transfer to our escape vehicle.

"The first stage is general preparation. During this time, we will round up any equipment that we lack, craft our cover story, procure a vehicle in Pennsylvania that can't be traced back to us, and rent a room at the same motel that Joby is staying at.

"The second stage is reconnaissance. During this step, we will scope out the delivery route and the driver, choose the stop where we will confiscate the truck, recon the camp gate, locate a rendezvous point close to 286, choose our route from the rendezvous site to 286 and vice versa, scout these routes for cameras, and choose our route from the rendezvous point back to the highway.

"The third stage is technical preparation. During this stretch, we will focus on Joby's preparation: CDL training, a fake driver's license and medical card, a real uniform with a name tag, and a cover story as a substitute driver. We will also hire a hacker to neutralize the security cameras along our route from the rendezvous site to 286 and plant forged files in the Katahdin system to authenticate Joby's cover story. This stage will overlap with the second stage.

"The fourth stage is the mission itself. During this phase,

we will drive to the rendezvous site and leave the escape vehicle, walk to the truck-confiscation site, wait for the truck, and neutralize the driver when it arrives. One of us will return to the rendezvous point. The other will stay in the back of the truck to help Joby with loading the carts so his delivery pace will seem more natural. Joby will proceed with the route, drive to camp 286, rescue Irina, and return to the rendezvous site. Then we will hide the truck, drive to Pennsylvania, exchange the cover vehicle for our truck, and make an anonymous call to the authorities to let them know where the driver is hidden."

Woody heartily endorsed the boys' plan. Jordy called for a vote, and the entire crew gave it a thumbs up.

Jordy then asked, "Does anyone else have anything they would like to bring up that pertains to our attempt to rescue Irina from 286?"

Ariele bounced up and the Backstrom boys smiled. They had come to appreciate the little fireball, who was as smoking smart as she was smoking hot. She began, "I heard an interesting piece of information this week on a *Down the Rabbit Hole* podcast. There is strong evidence that many supposed soft-terrorist suicides were simulations staged by the feds and that the suspects are still alive in FEMA camps. Investigative teams have asked to see the death certificates and graves for dozens of radio personalities, alternative news webcasters, investigative journalists, astronomers, and NASA employees who reportedly perished when cornered by federal agents. The government balked at their requests. So the teams searched the records at every funeral home and cemetery that was even a remote possibility for the deceased individuals and found nothing. They followed this up by interviewing hundreds of family members and discovered that not one of them knew the whereabouts of their loved one's grave. The bottom line is, there are no graves. They are still alive.

"The reason I bring this up is that Jack may be alive at one of the 200-series camps. We need to make it part of our plan that when we rescue Irina, we also enquire whether Jack is there too. If he isn't there, then we have eliminated one of the four possibilities."

Woody agreed. "Ariele is right. We need to find out Jack's whereabouts. I have long felt that the official story was full of holes. There is no way under the sun that he would have blown himself up as a suicide bomber. He is probably biding his time in a FEMA camp somewhere, plotting his own escape."

Andy turned toward Ariele and assured her, "We will make sure that Joby enquires about Jack."

Sam spoke up, "We should do more than ask a few questions. We need to be proactive in case it turns out that he is alive and well at 286. I think we should make him a prison-break package and hide it in the delivery—like maybe a bucket of dry pancake mix. If he is there, he will appreciate the help. If he isn't, someone else will find a good use for it. And I might add, if he is there, this will be our only chance to connect with him. After the rescue attempt, the window will be closed."

Following a chorus of agreement, Blake ran with the

proposal. "That's an awesome idea. I suggest we include diamond grit hacksaw blades, two shorty hacksaw handles, needle-nose pliers, lineman's pliers, and a tiny screwdriver set that includes hex heads."

Tony added, "And I would suggest preloaded debit cards, some cash, a couple burner phones, a contact number for extraction, an LED flashlight with extra batteries, a hank of genuine parachute cord, water purification tabs, and some handwarmer packets."

"Don't worry about rounding this stuff up," Andy advised. "We have a supplier who carries these items in military grade—and nifty waterproof pouches too. We can stop there on our way to Syracuse."

Red enquired, "What about metal detectors? Aren't you boys worried that your escape package might be discovered at the gate, endangering the original mission?"

"I'm not too concerned," Andy replied. "The 200-series FEMA camps are moderate security institutions that are run on shoestring budgets. I doubt that they have metal detectors."

Woody turned the conversation to the extraction contact. "I agree with Tony that we should line up a contact in the area so that if Jack is alive and manages to escape, he can be hustled out of the area before the search gets underway in earnest."

"I have a good friend in Corning, NY," Jordy responded, "who is Rogue-aware and opposed to the government cover-up. Why don't you carry the meeting, Woody, while I try to contact him? Perhaps he will be able to help us out." He stood up, handed Woody his clipboard, hopped on his utility vehicle, and headed over to the lodge.

Twenty-seven minutes later, he returned to the group with a broad grin on his face. "I gave my friend a brief synopsis of our rescue operation and asked if we could use him for an extraction contact. He refused because he suspects that he is being watched. But he did give me a contact number for a Rogue ally in Pennsylvania whose code name is Bullseye.

"He also told me about a remodeled, dual-purpose barn in a rural area outside of Elmira, NY, ninety minutes south of 286 that would make a perfect hideout and pick-up site. It sits on eighty wooded acres and is accessed by a private road used by only two other homes, both seasonal. The owner ran a hobby farm on the location for years while working remotely for a hedge fund. Four years ago, he accepted an offer to manage a hedge fund in the Bahamas, and now the place sits empty. He hasn't been back since and has no plans to return. When my friend called a year ago and enquired about the property, he was informed that the property wasn't for sale.

"To access the property, Jack will need to cut the lock on the chain at the gate. After he drives through, he will need to replace it with a similar lock—a large, chrome-plated, key lock. He will also need to make his escape during a snowstorm so his tracks into the property will be quickly covered. Tracks in the mud or snow might cause the locals to suspect that something is amiss. The key for the barn is inside the outhouse, hanging on a cup hook over the door.

"If we want to use this barn for the hideout and

extraction point, I suggest that we add several things to the jail-break package: a New York highway map, a local topo map with the route to the hideout marked in red, a pair of compact bolt cutters, and a chrome-plated key padlock."

Woody approved. "I'm in favor of the barn and the additions to the package for Jack. And I suggest that we mark the bucket that the package is in so it can be easily found. I recommend a jack of clubs—Jack will recognize that immediately."

38

New York City, New York
Monday, August 19, 2019

Joby arrived in the Newark area Monday afternoon around 4:30 p.m. feeling frazzled. Seven hectic hours on Interstate 78 would have been bad enough by itself. But his day had started with a 7:30 a.m. visit with the Phantom—a seriously creepy guy—to get his spook tools. He had left Philadelphia two hours later with an Arizona driver's license and a Visa debit card that bore his false identity. Once he dumped his Toyota truck, which was registered in his real name, he would be Jeremiah Silverstone from Phoenix, Arizona. Though the driver's license would be exposed if a police officer ran his license number, it would work fine for things like hotels and the chop shop.

While the traffic had been bad coming into Newark, it was even worse heading north on Interstate 95. The snarl slowed to a crawl as Joby approached the George Washington Bridge. He jockeyed to get into the farthest right lanes of the Trans-Manhattan Expressway so he could make the exit for the Washington Bridge. Several times, he grimaced and jumped on his brakes when a driver cut him off. At the Edward L. Grant exit, he turned south with a stream of cars, shaking his head in disbelief. Los Angeles wasn't easy to drive in, but it was child's play compared to this. He began to relax a little. At least he was past the tangle of ramps and roads. Now all he had to worry about was the Bronx.

He was headed into Mount Eden to look up his cousin Shmuel Greenberg whom he hadn't seen since the Greenbergs had visited his family in California the summer of his fourteenth birthday. He wasn't sure what to expect. Shmuel was the black sheep in the family. Nobody had had any contact with the renegade for years except his sister Shifra. All Joby had was a cell phone number which she had given him when he had called her from his motel in Wyoming. "Can't guarantee that you will reach him," she had said. "Sometimes he responds to my texts and calls, and sometimes he ignores them. I'll try to give him a heads up that you might be calling."

He drove into the parking lot of a liquor store, parked, and sat there procrastinating. He wasn't looking forward to this. It felt awkward to call his cousin out of the blue—the cousin with a wild streak and criminal tendencies, who had introduced him to pot and booze, who was rumored to have connections with the mafia. But he needed to make the call. He knew no one else in the area that might be able to help. *Stop being a wuss. Just man up and do it.* He entered the number and placed the call. After four rings, he got an answering machine, "Hey, this is Slammer. If it's important, leave a *brief* message and I will get back to you. If it ain't important, don't waste my time." After the beep, Joby left his message. "This is your cousin Joseph from California. I'm in trouble, trying to outfox the feds, and I need your help." He added his burner number. That was one of the only times in his life that he had been glad to get an answering machine.

A sharp rap on his window startled him. Nervous, he rolled the window down. A brawny man barked at him, "Hey, dude. Are you coming into the store or not? This ain't a public parking lot. If you aren't here to buy something from my store, then get your truck off my property."

Joby nodded, started his truck, and drove off to find a place to park and get a bite to eat. *Need to keep track of where I am. Getting lost here would be a nightmare.* He continued down Edward L. Grant, which merged onto Jerome Avenue. A few blocks later, he spied a large park off to his left. He grabbed the first empty parking space he saw, stuffed his burner into his pocket, and hopped out. His first item of business was finding some chow.

"Excuse me," he said, accosting a middle-aged Hispanic man walking down the sidewalk. "Are there any restaurants nearby?"

"Are you looking for Mexican, Chinese, or something else?"

"Chinese."

The man pointed down an alley. "Go straight for two blocks. You'll see a Chinese restaurant on your left, next to a grocery store. They serve great egg rolls."

An hour later, shortly after six, while sitting on the grass in the park watching a soccer game, his burner chirped with the Mission Impossible ringtone that someone had loaded on it. Reluctantly, he answered. "Hi, this is Joseph."

"Joseph Rosenthal in trouble? That's a good one. Did you throw your yarmulke away?"

"You know that I don't—and never did—wear a yarmulke. I was raised Reformed, not Orthodox."

"You might as well wear a yarmulke. Shifra tells me that you're a goody two shoes now—no pot, no alcohol, even read the Tanakh from time to time."

"Well, if I'm such a goody two shoes, how come I'm involved in an operation that could put me behind bars?"

"Sure you are. A momma's boy like you?"

Joby was growing irritated. He didn't have time to listen to his cocky cousin mock his manhood. "Listen Slummy. I don't have time to listen to you talk smack. I have a dangerous job to do. And I need your help. I don't care if you help me because you feel pity for your sissified cousin or because you like being involved in criminal activity. So what is it? Are you in or not? Or maybe *you're* chicken?" *Whoa! Didn't know that was in me.*

"Relax, bro. What kind of help are you looking for?"

"I need to lose my car—trade it in for something that won't stand out, that has clean plates, that's not likely to get stopped, and won't be easily traced to me once I'm done here."

"No problem. I got connections. We can take your car to a chop shop, then get you a vehicle whose plates won't raise any eyebrows for a few weeks, maybe longer."

"How you gonna do that?"

"Trust me, you don't want to know. But I can guarantee that you will have clean plates, a rental agreement with a real number to call, and a good cover story if you get stopped."

"That's exactly what I'm looking for. How can I ever thank you?"

"You can start with five grand up front. One grand for me and four for the boys who will procure your car, do the paperwork, and return it when we are done with it. If any other expenses come up down the road, you will be expected to cover those too."

"A whole grand? A bit steep, don't you think, just for being the middleman? Doesn't family count for anything?"

"Chill, bro. That's a lot of nerve for someone who hasn't given me the time of day for years. This is a business deal— pure and simple. It ain't no family favor. I don't owe you any favors, and I sure ain't going to help you out for nothing. Not in this business. My risks are high. I'm always walking a tightrope. Look. I'm just trying to make good money for a few more years, then I'm out of here. I'm gonna buy a sandwich shop in the Bahamas."

"Sorry. I'm not used to the rules in your world. Your world is a little darker than mine."

"From the sounds of it, you're going down your own dark path."

"I prefer to look at it as a path of resisting darkness to rescue an innocent maiden."

"Now you're talking like a rabbi."

"To be honest, I have been thinking about becoming a rabbi. I started reading the Tanakh in earnest a few weeks ago, and I have been reading some in the New Testament too. I'm finding some pretty amazing stuff."

"So what are you finding?"

"The world is being strangled by dark powers that have stretched their tentacles into every realm of life. No matter where you turn in the world or what you turn to, you can't escape the darkness unless you turn to God. I want to find the blessings of truth and light that are promised in the Tanakh. The fact is, I'm beginning to wonder if Mashiach isn't the answer."

"Good luck with that," Shmuel snarked. An awkward silence followed.

Joby brushed the brusqueness off and cheerfully asked, "So what do I do from here?"

"Where are you calling from?"

"I'm calling from the huge park just north of Yankee Stadium, sitting on the grass by the southmost soccer field."

"Stay right there. I'll show up about seven. I'll have you follow me to the chop shop. They won't let you in unless I vouch for you."

"Okay. Sounds like a plan. See you."

Slammer didn't answer. He simply hung up.

A few minutes after seven, Joby was startled when his cousin blurted out, "Are you ready to go?" There was no hug or handshake, though Joby thought his eyes were moist. *Maybe he is glad to see me after all.* His cousin had grown at least six inches since he had seen him last and had beefed up quite a bit. They walked to Slammer's Crown Victoria, and he gave Joby instructions. "Pull up to the tail of my car in the inside lane and stop. Don't worry if people honk their horns or curse. I'll pull out in front of you. Stay on my tail— I mean tight. Things will get complicated in a hurry if we get separated. If I run a light, keep the pedal to the metal and stay right on my bumper all the way to the chop shop in West Bronx. Got it?"

"Yep. Got it." He hoped he wouldn't get T-boned. That would put a big dent in their plans.

At first things went fairly smoothly. Slammer ran several yellow lights but didn't run any reds. But Joby got edgy when their route took them deep into a rundown neighborhood that felt like a creepy set for a dystopian movie. When his cousin parked in front of a vacant house where toughs were sitting on the steps and milling around, he fought off a wave of panic. With his heart in his throat, he pulled in behind him. Slammer hopped out, locked his car, and didn't even glance toward the guys that were staring at them. Joby followed his lead. His cousin began sauntering up the street like they were walking in the park. That galled him. He wanted to walk fast. He hoped his cousin knew what he was doing. A block and a half up the street, they arrived at the gate for the chop shop.

Slammer talked to a gruff, tattooed fellow in a hoodie for a couple minutes about the Toyota truck his acquaintance wanted to sell. The guy mostly grunted. After a couple minutes of dickering, and a call to his boss, the tough gave the okay for the transaction. But he insisted that Slammer had to drive. Slammer simply nodded, then turned and headed back.

When they arrived back at their vehicles—Joby unnerved by the same intimidating glares— they crammed Joby's possessions into Slammer's trunk and back seat, then drove the truck to the gate. The attendant swung the gate open as they approached, and Slammer rolled into the ramshackle yard and angled toward his left. A battered garage door opened in front of them, and Slammer drove in without hesitation. Apparently, he had done this before. Maybe a few times.

Joby gawked in amazement. A half-dozen cars were in various stages of being dismantled, and another half dozen were parked along one of the walls, waiting for their turn. A massive guy wearing a huge gold chain walked up to Joby and introduced himself, "I'm Fat Max." He held out a wad of cash. "Here's five hundred bucks. I'm feeling generous today."

Joby didn't reach out his hand in return. "Five hundred bucks?" he snapped. "The truck is easily worth three grand. It's in pristine shape, and it has a recently rebuilt engine, a topper, and an expensive sound system."

The bruiser went off on him. "This isn't a used car lot, Dude. It's a chop shop. And the market for old Toyota trucks and parts in New York City is piss poor. And don't talk to me about your topper. Nobody uses them here. It's worthless. Two bucks worth of scrap aluminum. As for the sound system, it's a gift to a friend, so I won't make any money off of it."

Joby withered, not sure what to say.

The hulk glared at Joby. "Are you going to take the deal or back out? You won't get a better deal anywhere else. And if you renege on our deal, things could get ugly for your friend who stuck his neck out for you. You wouldn't want that to happen, would you?"

Joby felt like exploding on the thief, but he knew it wouldn't get him anywhere. "Alright. I'll take the offer." He reached out his hand, and Fat Max counted out five hundred dollars, mostly twenties with a couple fifties.

As soon as the money was counted, Slammer nodded to the big fellow, grabbed Joby by the arm, and started walking out at a brisk pace. After they had passed through the outer gate and walked a half block up the sidewalk, Slammer informed Joby, "Never overstay your welcome in a place like that. The only reason Fat Max even lets me in is that I bring him easy cash. He hates my guts. Don't know why. Don't care why. I hate him too."

They walked in silence the rest of the way to Slammer's car. As they climbed in, Slammer remarked, "Now we got to deal with the junk you stashed in my car. Do you got a place to crash?"

"Nope. I haven't even thought about that yet. The only thing on my mind has been getting rid of my truck and getting some wheels."

"Well, you can crash at my place for a night or two until we locate some wheels for you. But you can't leave anything in the car except for what's in the trunk. Things disappear around here. You'll have to carry your stuff up to my apartment. And just so you know, I live on the sixth floor, there is no elevator, and my parking spot is two blocks away."

"No problem." *This is gonna be miserable.*

It was beyond miserable. It took Joby eight trips to transfer all his gear to Slammer's apartment. By the time he was carrying that last load up the stairs, his legs felt like jelly, both his arms were cramped, and his back throbbed and stabbed with pain.

That night he laid down on his cousin's tattered couch, which reeked of stale beer and cigarettes, and tried to keep his eyes closed. When he opened them, it was a painful sight. The apartment looked like no one had ever cleaned the place. "Cheap rent," was his cousin's response when he expressed his displeasure at the smell and the filth. "I get paid to live here. The owner lets me have this room for free in return for collecting rent from the other tenants in the building. I rent out the spare bedroom to a guy who works as a bouncer at a local club. Plus, the owner and I get free parking at Wingnut's lot in return for Wingnut getting free rent. Works for me."

***

Tuesday evening, Joby was sitting on the slimy couch, eating take-out pizza, and suffering as his cousin regaled him with stories from his cage-fighting days. Slammer was walking him through the play-by-play of the fight in which he had received his nickname when the braggart's phone rang. He uh-huhhed a few times, said "Seven, got it, we'll be there," and hung up. He smiled at Joby. "Your wheels are ready.

And we gotta run like right now. These guys hate it if you make them wait."

They jogged to Wingnut's lot, leaving Joby a little winded. Then Slammer weaved and raced his Crown Victoria through the traffic. When they arrived at the chop shop, he parked next to the gate. The attendant recognized Slammer and let them walk through.

Before they went inside, Slammer handed his cousin a pair of thin leather gloves. "Trust me. Wear these at all times when driving or touching the car. Don't leave any prints on it. Fat Max's boys didn't leave any prints on it, but they are hoping that you will. When you are done with the car, make sure you don't leave your rental paperwork in it. And when you sign for the car, scrawl your signature. Don't use your normal handwriting. You don't want to give these boys the ability to throw you under the bus because they will do that without hesitation if they need to."

Joby nodded. "Gotcha. Don't trust the untrustable."

Slammer stared into Joby's eyes for a moment, giving him an *I'm-dead-serious* look. Inside the shady business, Joby cringed with the same aversion that he had felt the first time. The cacophony of music and shop noises rattled him—like mixing the blare of a raunchy concert with the nightmarish drilling and grinding noises heard in a dental office.

Fat Max met them near the entrance, ushered them into a small office, and closed the door. The sound from the floor was muffled, but still grated on Joby.

"Here. You need to sign this," the corpulent fellow huffed as he handed Joby a clipboard with a rental

297

agreement. The nervous young man scanned it and noticed that it was a polished document. *Must be downloaded from the internet. Doubt these guys are capable of writing this kind of English.* Joby grabbed a pen off the desk—

"Hey!" Fat Max barked. "Don't ever touch anything on my desk!"

"Sorry. I need a pen to sign this."

"You don't carry a pen! Every businessman who knows up from down carries a pen." He eyed Joby like he was a stupid novice and held up his pen, which appeared to be ebony with fourteen-carat gold inlay. "People who know how the world works carry pens like this." But Joby's eyes were glued to the massive watch dangling off the bruiser's wrist. "I see you're eyeing Rolex. Nice huh? Something folks like you will never be able to afford. The owner of this company gave me a huge discount, so I only paid a thousand dollars. But it's worth five thousand."

Joby played along. "That's definitely impressive." But inside he was smirking. *Probably a knockoff that's worth less than a hundred bucks. That's the kind of watch worn by people who don't know how the world works.*

Slammer nudged Joby—"Here you go, bro"—and handed him a pen. Joby signed the contract with his false identity, Jeremiah Silverstone, and handed the clipboard back to Fat Max. The big fella held up his massive arm and made the money sign—rubbing his forefinger and thumb together. Joby reached into his pocket and pulled out the wad of hundreds that he had picked up earlier that day from a Bitcoin ATM in Manhattan. He counted out forty

Franklins onto the bruiser's desk.

"No tip?" Fat Max asked, obviously irked.

Slammer nudged Joby again. The frustrated underworld novice counted out five more.

"That's what I'm talking about. I serve you. You serve me. Win. Win. Everybody's happy."

Joby stewed, *I'm about as happy as a cat in a bathtub.* But he bit his tongue.

Fat Max showed them the car, a white 2012 Volvo sedan with a slight ding in the front passenger door. Joby was nonplussed. He had asked for something generic like a Ford or a Honda. While it wasn't a BMW or Mercedes, the car still felt conspicuous. He was nervous that it was going to stand out far more than he wanted to. At least it was white.

Fat Max tossed him the keys—"Pleasure doing business with you"—and walked away, bouncing and jiving to the blaring music.

His assistant added, "Make sure that either you or Slammer return this vehicle here within a month, with no damage."

Joby nodded, "Got it, bro."

The man replied, "Ain't your bro," and walked away.

Joby shook his head. He didn't understand the underworld, and he didn't want to understand it. Relieved that the ordeal was coming to a close, he climbed into the car. One of the underlings hit the *Open* button for the door. When it neared the top, Joby started the Volvo, and slowly rolled out of the building. As soon as he saw his cousin approaching in his rearview mirror, Slammer sped away from the gate. Joby accelerated hard to keep up with him. He didn't want to lose sight of him. Not in this neighborhood.

On the drive back to Wingnut's parking lot, Joby's mind ran in dizzying circles. He fretted that he was getting himself involved in criminal activities that he had sworn years earlier to stay a mile away from. Yet, to have a good conscience in the current situation, he was forced to do things that went against his conscience. The moral dilemma was crushing him.

Hoping it might relieve the tension, he turned to prayer. *God, I know I haven't talked to you much in the past, but I'm in a jam and really need your help. Will you watch over me and bless this mission? If you help me to pull this off, I will become a rabbi.*

39

The next morning, Joby woke before 4 a.m., so anxious to get on the road that he knew he wouldn't be able to go back to sleep. He hopped up, grabbed his first load of bags, and hustled to his car. Seven trips later, at 5:37 a.m., he taped a note and a two-hundred-dollar tip to the door, picked up his last load, and headed out for good. Though his arms and back ached, he found himself humming *The Happy Nigun*. He was leaving the filthy rat hole and the underworld behind.

But the song didn't last. By the time he reached Denville an hour and a half later, he was stressing over the difficulties and dangers that lay before him in Syracuse. He felt like a Boy Scout assigned to a CIA mission. But he steeled himself to go forward despite his fears. One step at a time. If God could help Moshe deliver his people from Egypt, surely he could help in this endeavor.

He arrived in Syracuse about two o'clock, took the East Seneca Turnpike, and made his way to the Economy Motel.

A little research on the internet had revealed that it was an older-style motor inn with little in the way of amenities or security measures.

After checking in, the first thing he did was pull out his burner and call Woody. He was long overdue to touch bases with him.

"Hey, Woody. Sorry I've been out of contact for so long. I didn't dare call while I was in New York City because I was always with my cousin Shmuel. Anyways, I have a car with clean plates, and I am checked into the Economy Motel in Syracuse."

"Glad to hear that. No worries about the radio silence. That was a smart move considering the circumstances. You'll be glad to know that your reinforcements are coming sooner than we had anticipated. Jordy's boys showed up here on Saturday, and they are on their way there. So as soon as you hang up, go down to the desk and reserve a room for two for a month."

"So you think Jordy's boys will be able to handle the job?"

"Absolutely. They're pros. They spent four years in the Rangers and six years in Special Forces and Delta Force."

"That doesn't mean anything to me."

"That means that they are going to take charge of the mission, plan it, assign you your tasks, and make sure that you are properly trained and prepared to execute them."

"No complaints there," Joby exclaimed. "Makes me feel a whole lot more comfortable with the mission. I was pretty nervous about it."

"I was too. And I still am. It won't be a picnic. But if it can be pulled off, these boys can do it."

"When should I expect them?"

"Either late tonight or tomorrow morning. By the way, we have added a new responsibility to your part of the plan. You are going to hide a prison-break package for my cousin Jack in a bucket of pancake mix and mark the bucket with a jack of clubs on the lid. When you arrive on site to rescue Irina, you will notify the head cook that there is a special bucket for Jack."

"Sounds good to me. So, who are these boys?"

"Tony and Andy, the sons of Jordy Backstrom, the pastor of the Compound."

"So is the Compound a Christian place?"

"Not originally," Woody replied, "but it's headed in that direction. It started off as a group of friends prepping for hard times, disasters, and the end of the world as we know it. Now, most of the members are students of the Bible and its prophecies about the end times."

"Interesting! For years I gave no thought to the end of the world. But lately, I sense a growing attraction to it, like my destiny is somehow connected with it. This past week I read Daniel, Revelation, and several of the Prophets. I love the two-edged sword of prophecy. Some ugly judgments are coming upon the world. But they will be followed by the blessings of Mashiach's eternal kingdom."

"I can identify. For years I didn't pay much attention to the Bible's prophecies either. I thought there was zero chance that they were going to come true in my lifetime. Now the stage-setting prophecies are unfolding before our eyes. Looking back, my real problem was indifference. I didn't care enough about the Bible and its prophecies. But that is changing. I recently promised God that I will be a serious student from here on out."

"I made my own promise a few days ago. I promised God that if he helped me succeed in this mission, then I would become a rabbi."

"What kind of rabbi talks about the Messiah and has an interest in the book of Revelation?" Woody asked.

"One who sees that a large portion of the Tanakh is prophecy about Israel's future blessings, that these blessings revolve around Mashiach and the day he returns to Jerusalem, that the New Testament presents the same future blessings to Israel as the Tanakh, and"—he fumbled for words—"one who is grappling with the idea that perhaps Yeshua really is the promised Mashiach."

40

A few minutes before midnight, Joby heard a soft knock on his motel-room door which stirred him from his sleep. He sat up and listened intently. The rapping started again—five distinct raps. He hopped out of bed, heart pounding, and knocked three times on the door. The visitors on the other side responded with six raps. *That's the code. Must be Andy and Tony.* With a sigh of relief, Joby unlocked the door and swung it open. Two muscular guys over six feet tall strode through and tossed their duffel bags on the bed. The first one gave Joby his first directive. "Order two large, loaded pepperoni pizzas with double toppings. We're starving." The second enquired, "What do you got to drink?" Joby grabbed two kombuchas from the fridge and held them out. The two rolled their eyes. "Better order some Coke too." Then they sat down at the table in the corner while Joby dialed the pizza shop.

After he had placed the order, Joby joined the operators. The one who had requested the pizzas reached out his hand,

"I'm Andy." When Joby responded, it felt like he had stuck his hand in a vise. The other stuck his hand out. "And I'm Tony." Joby winced as he endured another dose of pain.

Andy eyed the kid from California. "So, we've been told that you're a complete greenhorn with no experience or training that might be useful for this mission."

"That's right. I'm a raw recruit. Thankfully, a private investigator friend helped me get a good cover and advised me on procuring a clean vehicle. So I got that much in order."

Andy nodded. "Glad to hear that. No worries about the rest. We'll get you up to speed."

"We already crossed clean wheels off our list, too" Tony added. "We stopped in Pennsylvania on our way here, dropped off our truck, and picked up a nondescript white utility van with clean Pennsylvania plates. The owner will be in South America for a few more months. When we finish our mission, we'll travel south through Pennsylvania, pick up our truck, take the van to a salvage yard, and sell it for scrap as a titleless car. When the owner returns from his trip, he'll discover that his van is missing from his rural property and report it as stolen. But it won't be found—not once it's crushed. The owner, however, will be reimbursed amply. Not only will he receive a check from the insurance company, he'll find an envelope in his mailbox stuffed with fifteen thousand dollars in cash."

"What are you driving?" Andy asked Joby.

"A white 2012 Volvo sedan with New York plates. I stopped in New York City and contacted my scuzzball cousin, who helped me sell my Toyota pickup to a chop shop and pick up the Volvo from the same place. The plates should be good for a few months."

"Nice. I saw that rig in the parking lot. It's definitely nondescript for this neck of the woods. Pretty savvy swap for a rookie who hasn't even been potty-trained yet."

Joby laughed. "Thanks to friends and family. Toad pointed me in the right direction, and Shmuel walked me through the transaction. I would have been at sea otherwise. I'm tickled to death that you guys are here to plan the mission and train me for my part, assuming I get a part. This stuff is out of my league."

"You absolutely get a part," Andy insisted. "The main part. You'll be driving the truck. Neither of us can be the driver. Our faces can't show up on video because we're needed for future missions."

"Sounds like you're saying that I'm expendable."

"You are expendable as an operator. The only reason that we're using you is because we have no other options. But don't let your lack of special-ops skills crush your sense of self-worth. If Woody's assessment of you is correct, you're going to be a valuable asset at the Compound."

"To be honest, I would rather be a gardener than a mercenary."

"Well, for now, you're gonna have to set your green thumb aside and find your inner warrior." Andy stopped talking for a moment, grabbed a duffel bag from the bed, and tossed it to the apprehensive young man. "Here. Familiarize yourself with the equipment in this bag. Learn it all, and learn it well."

Joby unzipped the bag, grabbed a hard case, opened it, and pulled out a pair of bizarre-looking goggles.

"Night-vision goggles," Andy informed him. "You need to learn how to use them. The same goes for the binoculars, the thermal scope, and the military radio. We'll use all of them during the reconnaissance phase of this operation. And you need to learn fast—like over the next few days. We don't want problems in the field."

They were interrupted by a rap on the door. Joby almost jumped out of his skin. Tony, swift as a cat, grabbed the night-vision goggles from Joby's hands, returned them to their case, placed the case back in the duffel bag, and zipped the bag shut. Andy motioned for Joby to go to the door. He looked through the peephole, saw that it was their pizza delivery, and relaxed. He gave the guy a fifty-dollar bill and told him to keep the change. It was time to feast.

***

Early the next morning, after a few brief hours of sleep, Joby found himself lying on a damp roof with Andy about 750 yards from the gate at Camp 286. He tried to focus on the mission but was worried sick about getting back down. What had he gotten himself into? The climb had been hair-raising—they had scaled a downspout—and the nervous young man figured the descent would be even scarier. Panic gripped him.

"Ease up, dude," Andy nudged him. "You're hyperventilating."

Joby calmed himself down, and they waited in silence as

morning slowly crept from the earliest signs of dawn towards civil twilight. Headlights appeared on the road. After what seemed like forever, the truck reached the approach for the camp and turned, giving them the side view that they needed. "Bingo," Andy whispered. "Katahdin Foods, the driver is alone, and the truck is a Sterling—an AT9500." Instantly he was stowing his gear and whispering directions to Joby. "Time to move. We want to be out of here before morning traffic picks up." He began to crawl back toward the downspout. "Just walk down with your hands behind the spout and your feet on the wall—easy-peasy."

Joby grumbled to himself. *If I keep hanging around these guys, I'm definitely not going to die of old age.*

That morning, after a fast-food breakfast, the three sat down for Joby's first briefing. Tony opened with an introduction to the mission. Andy then addressed their plan for the next few weeks. "Tony is going to focus on the truck's route and its stops prior to 286. Joby and I will focus on 286 itself. The main tasks at 286 will be to: verify that the truck stops on Monday and Thursday, ascertain the truck's arrival-time range, observe the driver's interaction with the gate guards, note what direction the truck turns when it leaves, and confirm the make and model of the tractor so Joby can get trained in the same kind. Tony's main tasks will be to: determine the truck's usual route before it arrives at 286, scout out the two prior stops, identify the stop most suitable for confiscating the truck, and find a good rendezvous point where we can start and finish the mission."

"What about my truck-driver training?" Joby enquired.

"I contacted an old friend," Andy replied, "a former Delta brother, who owns a trucking company in Poughkeepsie. Sig, as he prefers to be called, is going to supply the same kind of tractor that we saw at 286, along with a thirty-six-foot food-service van, and hang out here for three weeks to conduct your training. Starting Monday, you will train six days a week for three weeks. For all practical purposes, you will go through actual CDL training. Upon completion, you will be given a counterfeit CDL and a counterfeit medical card. They will be good enough to fool the security guards at the gate if they ask to see them. However, if you get stopped by a cop, and he runs your driver's license number, you are toast. So you are going to have to pay attention in your training and stay sharp when you are on the mission. You can't afford … we can't afford … Irina can't afford for you to make a boneheaded mistake while driving and get yourself stopped or involved in an accident."

Joby felt the pressure building inside. All his life he had run from pressure, whether stressful jobs, competition, or the good-looking type-A females that he was attracted to. But he couldn't run away this time. The only way out was forward. He swallowed hard, prayed to God, and steeled himself.

Andy continued, "Once the mission goes down, Sig will destroy his copies of your training and certification records, and you will destroy your CDL and med card. Copy that?"

Joby looked at him puzzled for a moment before he figured out what *copy that* meant. "Yep, got it. Destroy my license and medical card when the mission is done." His nerves on edge over learning to drive a truck, he asked, "What kind of stuff am I going to do in my CDL training?"

"The whole nine yards," Andy responded. "Computer logs, pre-trip inspections, driving, shifting, cornering, backing around a corner, backing into a dock, backing through a narrow gate, defensive driving, skid training— everything. Before we're done, you'll log sixty hours behind the wheel, including a couple trips on the actual roads and alleys that we're going to use in the operation."

Joby was crestfallen. Learning to drive a semi was not on his bucket list. Nothing about it sounded attractive or exciting.

Andy eyed the disheartened young man. "There's more."

Already feeling numb, Joby looked at him in a daze.

"You will also be trained on the use of the ramp, reading your route manifest and delivery paperwork, picking boxes, loading and running carts, handling carts on stairs, asking customers for directions to their coolers and freezers, basic terminology used in food service, and basic facts about Katahdin Foods. We can't have you sounding like an ignorant bimbo if someone engages you in small talk."

Joby smiled glumly and nodded.

"One last thing. You are gonna spend a lot of time watching film. We will film the route from start to finish the first day we drive it, and you will watch that film over and over again until you have it memorized. You will also watch a video of where and how the truck parks at each of the stops. And you will watch hours and hours of boring training videos on defensive driving, safety, food-service delivery, and DOT regulations. We need to get you up to speed in short order." He eyed Joby. "Any questions or comments?"

Joby complained, "Why do I need to spend three weeks learning to drive a truck and mastering equipment that I may never use again? And watching mountains of instructional videos? Seriously? Three weeks of training for a mission that will take an hour max? A little overkill, maybe?"

Andy glared at him. "There is zero overkill here. If anything, considering how green you are, we're facing an underkill problem." The experienced operator stared into Joby's eyes. It felt like a dentist was drilling into his brain. "Bear in mind, Granola, one small mistake, and the mission will fail. There is zero room for error. The only way to avoid mistakes is to practice until you're numb, and then practice some more. Practice makes perfect."

Tony added, "Consider yourself lucky. You're getting off easy. At least you don't have to endure months of selection program and special operations training before you begin training for a real-world mission."

The rest of the day went easier. They visited second-hand stores in the Syracuse area and found two Katahdin uniforms that were Joby's size and two work shirts with *Jerry* nametags in the right style. That evening, Joby learned to sew. After six false starts, he managed to sew the first one on with consistent tight stitches. When he laid his head on his pillow that night, he was pretty impressed with himself.

***

Friday morning, after a breakfast of granola bars and orange juice, Tony sat Joby down to a watchlist of sixty-two food-service training videos, many of them produced by Katahdin. "This is going to be a painfully boring binge-watching session, but you need to watch all of these videos by Sunday evening. First thing Monday morning, you will be behind the wheel in a real semi, and you need to be ready. Don't drone through these videos. Pay close attention. You will be tested orally on the material. You can break for food, coffee, and the restroom. Otherwise, keep your butt glued to this chair, your eyes fixed on the screen, and the playlist rolling. Got it?"

Joby groaned and dropped his head into his hands.

"Get cracking. You got thirty hours of video there. That's ten hours per day. Very doable."

***

Joby's driver training was a blur of hectic days and headaches. He spent six hours per day, Monday through Saturday, in the truck. He didn't mind driving forward. But cornering made him nervous, and he hated backing with a passion. It didn't help matters that Sig had a temper. On Joby's second day of training, the former Delta operator had hollered at him, "If Andy wasn't one of my best friends, I would toss you out of my truck and go back home. I don't have time for this. My little sister could back better than you. Can you just pay attention? Backing ain't hard if you listen to what I'm trying to teach you. You have to trust your mirrors. And you can't be afraid of the truck." Eventually,

Joby did get the hang of it—a huge relief to both Sig and Andy. Nonetheless, he still hated backing. *When this is done, I'll never set foot in a semi again.*

While Joby was training with Sig, Tony and Andy spent their time scouting the delivery route from three stops prior to Camp 286 to the first stop after—sometimes in street clothes, sometimes undercover as a faux security company, and sometimes at night in tactical wear. They settled on Monday for the mission because the truck arrived at Camp 286 a half hour earlier, giving them longer cover of darkness. And they determined that WorkPro Job Training Center, two stops prior to 286, was the best bet for confiscating the truck. Though the alley was cramped, it offered several positives: nobody was on site when the truck arrived, the lighting was poor, and there were only a few windows in the alley in the adjacent businesses.

They also found a nearly ideal rendezvous site that was only eight blocks from WorkPro JTC. It was an unused and dimly lit storage and dock facility, surrounded on four sides by buildings and sheds, with a single narrow, gated entrance. The one downside was that Joby would have to stick the tight corner just right. If he turned too early or too late or didn't hug the far side of the alley tight enough, the truck could get hung up on the gate.

Joby was nervous about the truck-confiscation part of the plan. "So how are we going to get the truck?"

"We're going to jump the driver," Tony replied, "tranquilize him, and tie him up."

"What if he resists?"

"There is no if. He is going to resist. Just not effectively."

"Is he going to get hurt?"

"Yeah. He'll get a little roughed up when we jump him. And the tranquilizer will leave him feeling like death warmed over when he wakes up. And it won't feel pleasant to have his hands and feet tied and his mouth taped shut."

Joby didn't like the plan. Though he was reconciled to the idea that it was morally right to resist government oppression, he felt sorry for the poor truck driver who was guilty of nothing except being in the wrong place at the wrong time. Tony just shook his head and said, "Collateral damage comes with the territory. You gotta learn to live with it." The answer frustrated Joby, but he couldn't think of a better way to do what had to be done.

***

The third week, Tony focused on critical details that needed to be taken care of for them to be mission ready. Early Monday morning, he watched the delivery at WorkPro JTC from a rooftop across the alley using low-light binoculars and caught the combination on the lockbox when the driver retrieved the key for the business. While their plan was to jump the driver after he opened the lockbox, they wanted to have the combination in case their plan went south.

Late Monday morning, he contacted Cyberwulf, a professional hacker with extensive experience in the NSA, the CIA, and the private sector, who was a strong believer in the Rogue. For a hefty sum, he was persuaded to hack into the Katahdin system, download copies of the company handbooks for supervisors and drivers, and set up a bogus driver file. For a further hefty sum, he was persuaded to hack the security cameras that manned their route from the rendezvous site to the camp and back.

Tuesday morning, Tony called Cyberwulf back with the security company names and the serial numbers from each of the cameras that they wanted to malfunction. All but a few were owned and operated by the same company.

Tuesday afternoon, Tony received a mission-critical package via courier, ordered from an associate who forged documents for the CIA—a package he had begun to sweat bullets over. He anxiously tore it open and examined the New York state commercial driver's license and medical card for Jeremiah Silverstone, first with the naked eye, then with a magnifying glass, then under ultraviolet light. With a sigh of relief, he handed them over to Joby, smiling broadly. "We're golden, Mr. Silverstone."

Thursday evening, Tony went over pictures of Irina with Joby so he would recognize her. He also made Joby memorize the names of his supervisor, the two drivers that the customers would know, and the saleswoman for the route. And he drilled him over and over again on his cover story. "If anyone asks, tell them that you received a call early this morning from your supervisor, that you're a substitute driver, that there was some kind of emergency, that this is your first time on this route, and that you have no idea whether you're filling in for one day or a longer time."

Sig kept Joby busy the entire week. He made him practice loading the cart with combinations of boxes and buckets, running the loaded carts down the ramp, and wheeling them up and down stairs. His driving lessons continued, with a third of his time focused on mock-ups of mission-critical tasks, including a turn from a narrow alley into a narrow gate that was similar to the gate at their rendezvous site.

When Sig noticed that Joby had a death grip on the steering wheel while approaching the gate for his second try, he counseled, "I know you're stressed out. But if you face these feelings head on now, you won't have to face them Monday morning." Joby smiled meekly. He knew himself. No matter how much emotional stress he faced today, he was still going to be an emotional wreck on Monday. He shook his head at his instructor and wondered if special operations soldiers were wired differently. *Do they even have emotions like fear and doubt?*

Friday morning, they returned the Volvo to Fat Max's shop in West Bronx. Tony rode with Joby, and Andy followed in the van. Though Joby was nervous about going back to the shop, he was confident that the Backstrom boys could handle anything that they might face.

When they pulled up to the gate, Tony tensed. "Something doesn't feel right," he warned. "Don't enter the yard. Just leave it right here."

Joby stopped short of the gate, the two jumped out, and Joby tossed the keys over the gate.

The guard cussed him out. "Supposed to drive it in here, bro." Joby just waved and climbed into the waiting van. As Andy drove away, he muttered, "I hate these kinds of places." Joby glanced at Tony. He forced a smile. "We had an interesting experience at a chop shop like this a few years back in Columbia while doing undercover work with a team from the CIA and the DEA. It didn't end well."

While the team was devouring burgers for lunch in Joby's room, Cyberwulf called Tony and informed him that he had successfully installed a bug that would affect all of the security cameras on their route to 286 and back except for two between the rendezvous site and the truck confiscation site. They belonged to a company he was unable to hack. The camera bug would mix the current date and time with film from 23 hours and 57 minutes earlier. On Monday morning, Cyberwulf would activate the bug. If it worked as planned, he would send a text informing them that the goose had laid a golden egg. There was nothing he could do about the video feed at 286. The security systems of the FEMA camps were hidden behind a high-grade firewall, beyond the reach of a one-man team with a short window of time.

That afternoon, the three operators did walk-throughs with Joby on the gate routine for Camp 286. Then they had him climb into the truck and go through the entire process three times. When he finished and stepped out of the truck, Andy slapped him on the back. "Outstanding, Granola! We might make an operator out of you yet."

Sig pumped his hand. "Congratulations. You did way better than I anticipated."

That night as he lay in bed, Joby wrestled with his fears. While he was encouraged with his training and the guys' appreciation for his hard work, he still felt emotionally unprepared. He was terrified of the driver's license part. Even though Tony had encouraged him not to panic if the guards asked him for his license, he couldn't stop worrying. He pictured himself being arrested and hauled off to a FEMA camp. When he found no peace, he turned to the heavens. *God, please watch over me at the gate. Help me to stay calm—relax.*

41

Syracuse, NY
Saturday, September 14, 2019

"Time to get up, rookie," Andy said good-naturedly as he shook him. "We let you sleep in until seven since your training is done. But it's time to get going. Today we MOB for the operation."

"MOB?" he replied groggily. "You guys and your military acronyms. Half the time I have no idea what you're talking about."

Andy laughed. "MOB is an abbreviation, not an acronym. It's short for mobilization. Now get your lazy buns out of bed."

"All right, already," Joby muttered as he crawled out from underneath his covers. Sitting on the edge of his bed, he stretched and yawned. "So what do we do when we MOB?"

"We'll set out all our gear, check it, organize it, and pack it. Then we'll review our operation order and our individual roles. Things will go at a lazy pace, but we will be dead serious. Tonight, we'll have a mobilization party with no liquor involved. Tomorrow, we'll relax, have a final review session where we'll go over the operation order and our roles one more time, then go to bed early."

"I like the party part."

"Oh yeah. I forgot to mention. We are officially on lockdown. No runs to the store or fast-food joints. We can't risk any accidents, traffic stops, or anything else that might hinder the mission."

"No fast food? What are we going to eat?"

Tony snickered and tossed him an MRE. "Happy spaghetti breakfast."

Later that morning, Joby laid out his gear for inspection: two Katahdin uniforms, a lunch box, his New York CDL, his med card, his wallet emptied of anything that might ID him, one pair of grippy gloves, steel-toed shoes, sunglasses, a cheat card for the electronic log, two ball-point pens, a clipboard, a gym bag for his mission kit, a gym bag with a change of civilian clothes and his real ID, and a tiny headset that fit in his shirt pocket. He would take the mission bag with him. The civilian bag and all the rest of his stuff would be packed in the van. He watched nervously while Andy surveyed his layout. When the experienced operator pronounced him ready, he breathed a sigh of relief and repacked his kit.

He glanced over at the other bed where Andy and Tony had laid out their gear. Tony was going over Andy's gear, and Andy was going over Tony's. Their kits were a little more impressive. Each had dark-colored civilian clothes, black trail shoes and socks, black facemasks, thin black leather gloves, a dart pistol with tranquilizer darts, a roll of duct tape, a flashlight taser in a belt pouch, a pistol taser in a quick-draw holster, nylon handcuffs, fake identification, and tiny wireless communication sets with earbud and throat microphone. Tony also had heavy-duty bolt cutters and a new lock for the gate. When the guys finished pawing through each other's gear, they looked at each other, nodded, and then repacked their gear.

That evening they held their MOB party. They gorged themselves on pizza, drank coke, swapped stories, and laughed. Since Joby was a rookie, the Backstrom boys made him do a skit. Thinking quickly, he turned a pair of his white socks into sock puppets with a permanent marker and performed Abbot and Costello's "Who's on First" routine. It bombed. Because they didn't think it was funny enough, they made him wear a string mop like a wig and sing a Britney Spears bubble-gum pop song. They even played the soundtrack on Tony's laptop so he could sing along. By the time the embarrassed barista finished, they were laughing their guts out. Joby actually loosened up, which was part of the purpose for the MOB party.

A few minutes before nine, Tony set his laptop up on the table, far enough back that everyone could see it, and navigated to the live broadcast on the CVN website. As they took their chairs, Joby found himself enjoying the moment. Though he didn't want to admit it, he was coming around to believe that the conservatives actually did have some worthwhile insight on issues like geopolitics and Islam.

"Good evening, I'm Geoff Seaworthy, and this is World

Report. Our correspondent in Minsk, Jane Greystoke, just informed us that Belarus, after months of pressure, has capitulated to the demands of the Pro-Russian insurgency. Just over an hour ago, at 1:45 a.m. Minsk time, President Kovalenko and Prime Minister Melnikov resigned, along with the entire Council of Ministers. For sixteen tense hours, the parliament building had been surrounded by the Russian "peacekeeping" force and Belarusian units that had capitulated. At 1 a.m. Belarusian KGB and Spetsnaz entered the building. A few minutes later, a large delegation followed which included Russian officials and members of Belarus' Militsya, the national police force. About 2 a.m. the resigned officials were ushered out of the building and hurried away in police cruisers.

"Andrei Kuznetsova, the leader of the pro-Russian organization Russky Dom, has been installed as the provisional president. His first act was to declare a state of emergency and introduce temporary martial law. His second was to sign an executive declaration of the dissolution of Belarus and its integration into the Russian Federation. An emergency session of the National Assembly has been convened, and it is expected that they will ratify the president's declaration in the next few hours. Prudence will prevail over patriotism.

"I have invited Dr. Andrew Johansson, an instructor of Eastern European affairs at the Harriman Institute at Columbia University, to give us some insight into how this situation unfolded." He turned to his guest and nodded.

"Thank you, Geoff. The backstory began over a decade

ago when Sergei Kovalenko began courting the West while trying to maintain a cordial relationship with Russia. Since that time, while ostensibly an ally of Russia, Belarus has at times manifested an independent streak that was determined to go her own way and forge her own identity and destiny. This was a fatal mistake for a former Soviet-bloc nation that borders the Motherland. As we have witnessed in the past twenty-four hours, Russia's stated desire to restore the glory of the Soviet Union and purge her immediate neighbors from Western meddling is not mere wishful thinking.

"The final chapter began in the fall of 2017 when Russia moved 25,000 troops into Belarus for the Zapad joint exercise, though the agreement with Belarus had only authorized 5000. After the exercise had concluded, Russia left at least 10,000 troops behind according to the estimates of NATO observers and foreign correspondents. When the Belarusian government formally requested their departure, the Kremlin refused on the grounds of regional security. These soldiers sponsored and promoted the pro-Russian insurgents. This is a classic Russian tactic, using a training maneuver to conceal the insertion of paramilitary operators who then engage in the subversion of the host nation."

"So, Dr. Johansson, what can we expect to see in the next few months in Belarus?"

"Two things. The first is that Andrei Kutznetsova won't remain in office for more than a few months. He is merely a political puppet. The second is that stability and normality will return to Belarus, and Russia will take credit for it."

The camera crew waved and indicated that they were

going to cut back to the correspondent. Geoff obliged. "Jane Greystoke is back with us live. Jane, what do you have for us?"

"Hi, Geoff. I've been interviewing Belarusians on the streets of Minsk for the past hour and the results are illuminating. While the majority—seventy-six percent—would prefer to retain independence as members of the CIS, the Commonwealth of Independent States, their outlook on the situation is a mixture of realism and pessimism. It will make little difference to them, economically and politically, whether Minsk or Moscow is in charge, so fighting for independence in the face of overwhelming odds seems foolish. They also point out that they have been downtrodden for centuries under the Lithuanians, the Poles, the Russian empire, and the Soviet Union. The present situation is merely a return to the status quo. Life will go on. They will still plant potatoes and drink vodka. And the dark clouds have a silver lining. They will no longer be caught in the middle of the cold-war tensions between the West and Russia." She paused. "Back to you, Geoff."

"Thank you, Jane. There are two more items in Eastern European news tonight. The first is the open-border transportation corridor that Russia has been seeking from Belarus and Lithuania so she can enjoy direct access to Kaliningrad via Minsk and Vilnius. Today, she obtained the Belarus part through the coup in Minsk. Lithuania must be sitting on pins and needles, wondering if she is next in Russia's crosshairs. While she quelched the pro-Russia uprisings that disturbed her last fall, the insurgency has continued to fester and spread through talk shows, social media, and town meetings. The message that is resonating with a growing number of Lithuanians is that America and the West let Taiwan sink, so why should they trust NATO? This fear has been bolstered by two recent developments: Germany recalled her NATO contingent back to Germany; and the rest of the NATO troops, including the small detachment of American troops, were redeployed to European hotspots like Kosovo and line-in-the-sand regions like Poland's border with Ukraine. In the wake of these developments, the Lithuanians have adopted a stoic outlook. They would rather resign themselves to the inevitable absorption into the Russian empire than cling to the empty hope that the West will come to their aid.

"The second is the unrest in Romania, Bulgaria, and Serbia. Over the past few weeks, the raucous marches with pro-Russia advocates shouting anti-American slogans have degenerated into open violence in several major cities, with shots being fired and cars set ablaze in Plovdiv, Sofia, and Belgrade. It's beginning to look like the Balkan peninsula is getting sucked down the same vortex that swallowed up Ukraine and Crimea."

Andy raised his eyebrows. "Holy cow. Things are really falling apart over there."

"No doubt about it," Tony replied. "Way faster than I anticipated. If the West keeps sitting on its hands, the writing is on the wall for the Baltic and the Balkan countries. The Russian juggernaut will continue to roll until she has all her former territory back."

"I gotta admit. I find it a little scary how dad's prognostications about Russia, Europe, and the Middle East keep coming true."

"Tell me about it. For years I thought that he kept getting things right because he was the most astute geopolitical commentator on the planet. Now I'm starting to wonder if he gets things right because he knows the Bible, and these geopolitical upheavals are Bible prophecy coming true."

Andy slammed his fist into the table, not so much in anger as mild frustration. "Either way, if this kind of turmoil keeps up, we're going to have a real hard time getting into Russia to pick up the mirror and the infrared sensors that Blake needs."

"Yep." Tony huffed. "Been thinking about that myself. Going after the telescope stuff in this environment will be more dangerous than the mission we did in Moscow." He met Andy's eyes and the two shared a knowing look. Joby shuddered. He couldn't even begin to imagine facing the dangers and tensions that they would be up against over there.

42

Andy and Tony rose at 2 a.m. after four hours of fitful sleep. They quickly packed what they didn't need for the mission and stowed it in their van. Then they walked to Joby's room, unlocked the door with his key, and entered stealthily. Tony gently shook the slumbering rookie, with a hand over his mouth in case he woke up in a panic. "Time to get up trooper," he whispered. "Today is the big day." Joby crawled out from under his covers, sat on the edge of his bed, and remembered where he was and what was going to do that day. He was overwhelmed with fear—more scared than he had ever been. And he was exhausted from the combination of fitful sleep and rising early.

Andy smiled at the trembling young man. "Are you nervous, Granola?"

"Shaking like a leaf."

"I see that. Remember not to drink anything this morning. If you need to take a leak, that will hinder your ability to concentrate. Once we are safe on the road, you can drink a little to rehydrate. After we pick up our truck in Pennsylvania, you can drink all you want."

"Are you guys scared?" Joby enquired.

"A little nervous—pre-operation jitters. But this is a fairly easy operation. Less chance of getting caught or hurt than most of the missions we did in the Rangers or Special Forces."

Tony motioned for Joby to step into the bathroom. He turned and plodded into the small room, not noticing that Andy was following him with a pair of scissors in his hands. When Joby turned around and saw the scissors, he objected indignantly. "What! You've got to be kidding!" He was almost neurotically protective when it came to his enviable mop of curly, sandy-blonde hair.

"Sorry, dude. I'm not kidding. The Telly Savalas look comes with the territory for this kind of operation. You are also going to scrub your whole body with exfoliation soap, focusing especially on your head and hands. We don't want to leave any skin flakes or hair at any of the three stages of this operation that might give law enforcement agents DNA to work with. Trust me, there's gonna be high-tech feds working this case. We have to bring our A-game if we don't want to rot in a FEMA camp. Fact is, for an effort like this, we could even wind up in solitary confinement at some Gitmo clone."

Two minutes later, Joby checked himself out in the mirror. He now sported an uneven, choppy-looking, military-style buzz cut. He felt like crawling under a rock and dying. That green-eyed redhead from Scotland that talked him into this mission would never give him a second look now.

"No time for gawking, California," Andy said as he handed him a razor and some shaving gel. "You aren't done yet. Everything must come off. No facial hair. Bald on top. Neck shaved. Use all the gel you please. You got ten minutes. If you nick yourself, we got a nick stick."

At 2:50 a.m. all three stood in tight, stretchy, microfiber long underwear and tops, examining each other for hair on the head, neck, and face. When all passed inspection, they finished dressing, doubled checked their equipment, and loaded everything in the van. Then they doubled checked Joby's room, left a "Do Not Disturb" sign on the door—as they had on their own—and departed for the mission. Joby, beginning to think like an operative, checked his watch. It was 3:10 a.m. They were right on schedule.

As they drove, the boys had one last conversation on strategy. "I have been rethinking a few things," Tony remarked. "Walking the eight blocks from the rendezvous site to the truck-confiscation site adds five minutes to the mission. I think we should drive the van to within a block of the confiscation site, make the call to Cyberwulf, confiscate the truck, then divide up. You and Granola would go after the mission while I would drive back with the van, open the gate, and wait for you."

Andy was steamed. "Five minutes of walking doesn't reduce the odds of mission success, it increases them. You can't forget the two cameras between the rendezvous site and the confiscation site that aren't hacked. We can avoid them if we walk in the shadows, but there is no avoiding them if we drive down the street in a white van. And we just can't risk someone seeing the white van anywhere near the scene of the crime."

Tony chuckled. "I know. Just jerking your chain."

"Buzzard," Andy scowled.

Both of them were trying to mask a Cheshire grin. The levity was good for them.

Twenty minutes later, they parked in a dark corner of an industrial neighborhood about a mile from the rendezvous site. Tony pulled out his burner and called his hacker. "Cyberwulf, this is Badger One. We are at commo point. Mission status requested."

"Badger One, mission status is a go. The goose has laid a golden egg—all hacks are completed. Hack one is a success. Adjustments to the security cameras were installed early this morning and activated ten minutes ago at 3:20. The cameras flickered, went to snow for a few seconds, then came back on. Any security guard watching the screen would just think it was a run-of-the-mill poltergeist.

"Hack two is a success. The fake driver file I installed on Katahdin's computer last night is still intact.

"Hack three is a success. A fax was sent a half hour ago to the guard shack informing them that the normal driver had experienced a medical emergency and that his route would be covered by a new driver, Jeremiah Silverstone. The note was accompanied by a fax of his driver's license and med card. I also enclosed an apology to Bart, the shift leader at the guard shack, for the short notice and promised that we would have Jeremiah swing by for fingerprinting after he finished the route. The guard shack replied that they had contacted their supervisor, and he was okay with the switch on short notice under the unfortunate circumstances.

"Hack four is a success. I set up a phone-answering bug that will redirect any phone call to Katahdin Foods from the guard shack or the Alpha Force office to a message which states that no one will be available until normal business hours, from 7 a.m.to 5 p.m. The program is time sensitive and will delete itself at 6:59 a.m."

"Copy that, Cyberwulf," Tony replied. "Mission is a go. Out."

Andy started the van, drove out of the shadows, and headed for the rendezvous site. Joby's guts were tying themselves in knots. Tony advised, with a twinkle in his eyes, "Just breathe. Amazing how much it helps."

The van pulled up to the gate. Tony jumped out with bolt cutters and made two quick snips on the chain. He picked up the link pieces and the lock that had fallen to the ground, shoved them in his pocket, unwrapped the chain, let it hang loose on the gate, and pushed the left side open. Andy raced past him. Tony jogged the gate back, looped the chain through so it appeared locked, and trotted toward the yard, bolt cutter in hand.

When he reached the end of the narrow entranceway, Andy turned right and parked near the back wall in a large, open-front shed. He and Joby were donning their gear when Tony jogged up. He tossed the bolt cutter in the sliding door of the van and grabbed his gear. After a quick buddy check to make sure everyone had their mission-critical gear, they walked to the gate, unlooped the chain, strode through, looped the chain again, and began their eight-block jaunt to the truck-confiscation site.

Andy led the way, hugging buildings and exploiting shadows as much as possible. Joby was in the middle. Tony brought up the rear, constantly scanning behind them. Barely two blocks into their journey, while still in the alley, headlights glimmered behind them. "Car," Tony whispered into his headset. Andy darted into a little bay on their left with a dumpster and two picnic tables. Tony grabbed Joby and pushed him into the bay, right on Andy's heels, just as the lights turned straight down the alley, only a block behind them. Andy opened the dumpster and jumped in. Tony boosted Joby over the lip and dove in himself. Andy pulled the lid down mere moments before the car stopped at the bay. They waited with bated breath. Was it the police? Security? Hoodlums? Whoever it was, had they been seen? They waited for the car door to open. Silence. Nothing.

Andy discovered that he could squint out the crack with his left eye if he tilted his head back and cocked it. He tweaked and turned until his eye was on the car—it took a concerted effort to maintain the awkward pose. He spied a lone patrolman talking on the radio. *Not good*, Andy thought, getting nervous. If they had been discovered, the mission was over, though they might be able to worm their way out of the current situation.

"Lone cop," Andy whispered into his headset.

Tony whispered back, "Roger."

Both of them readied their tasers. If the policeman opened the dumpster, things were going to get ugly. No matter which side he opened, he would receive the shock of his life. And once they tased him, they would be forced to cover his head, cuff him, tranquilize him, and get out of town. They would likely have twenty or thirty minutes max before the local police department would send another unit to find out why this one wasn't responding to communications.

As they waited in suspense, Joby mulled over the fact that their rescue mission might be compromised and felt a wave of melancholy sweep over him. The sadness was ironic. Hadn't he been wishing for weeks that he could somehow get out of the mission? Now he was grieved that it might have to be aborted. He turned to the only one he thought could help. *God, you got Israel out of Egypt. Can you get us out of this jam? Can you help us rescue Irina?* But no sooner had the words left his mouth than he found himself doubting. *How do I even know if He is listening to my prayers?* Quite the quandary for someone who was thinking about becoming a rabbi.

The car door opened. An overweight man stepped out and stood on the asphalt, his feet crunching on the grit and gravel that was strewn across its surface. The man, who looked to be about six feet tall, took a final puff of his cigarette, tossed it aside on the ground, where it lay smoldering, then wandered over by the picnic tables. He turned to the wall and took a whiz. Thirty seconds later, the uncouth officer turned around and walked back to his cruiser. Instead of climbing in, he opened the trunk, retrieved a roll of paper towels and Windex, and cleaned his side mirrors and windshield. The process took about five minutes. *When is this guy going to leave?* Joby fretted to himself. *This is ridiculous.* By now all three were miserable, their legs cramping and trembling. They had been crouching on their haunches for nine minutes. The officer returned his cleaning supplies to the trunk, climbed in his cruiser, and drove off, air drumming on his steering wheel. *About time*, Andy whispered, agitated.

They waited a minute, listening. Then Andy quietly opened the lid on his side of the dumpster, gingerly climbed out, crept over to the reeking wall, moved to the corner of the building, dropped to a low crawl position, and poked his head around the corner. After a few moments, he waved to Tony. The coast was clear.

They continued working their way down the street. When they were two businesses from the alley where they planned to appropriate the truck, they noticed headlights approaching them again from behind. "You've got to be kidding," grumbled Tony as they threw themselves on the ground. Hastily, they low crawled around a corner and tried to disappear in the darkness. They watched nervously as the same police cruiser drove by slowly. When the coast was clear, Andy jumped up, and they continued on their way. A few minutes later, they arrived at their destination and hunkered down in the shadows of a parking area across the alley from the industrial training center, about half a truck length beyond where the nose of the truck would stop. Crouching behind a dumpster, Andy glanced at his watch.

It was 4:16 a.m. *Sixteen minutes behind schedule. Cutting it close.* Now it was time to wait.

They didn't wait long. Four minutes later, the truck turned into the alley. Andy poked a fiber-optic camera around the corner at ground level and watched on a miniature monitor with the screen dimmed. The driver nosed up to the telephone pole that he used as his parking guide, did his electronic log work, hopped out of the cab, and walked to the back of the truck.

When the driver disappeared behind the back of the truck, Andy and Tony snuck up to its front and waited. They listened while he retrieved the key from the lockbox, unlocked the door, propped it open with the provided cinder block, and walked back to the trailer. They tensed when they heard him unlatch the trailer door. Andy made his move down the passenger side of the trailer after the driver latched the door against that side and turned around. When he neared the back, he peered under the trailer, looking for the driver's legs.

He was late. The driver was already swinging the driver-side door around the corner. Andy had missed the opportunity to catch him from behind and no longer enjoyed the advantage of complete surprise. He scooted across the back of the trailer to the driver's corner and readied himself. When the driver's footsteps reached the corner, he jumped out, and—at the same time that the driver started to yell, "Hey!"—slammed his fist into the poor fellow's solar plexus, doubling him up. Then he deftly moved behind him, clamped his left hand over the driver's mouth, and yanked his right arm into a submission bar. The man squirmed violently, with more fight and strength than Andy had anticipated, but he managed to keep him under control.

When Tony heard the commotion, he took off on a dead run for the fray. When he arrived, he stunned the driver with his taser, who stiffened for a second, then went limp. Tony then shot him with the tranquilizer gun, wrapped several turns of duct tape around his head to cover his mouth, put a stocking mask over his head backwards, zip-tied his hands behind his back, and duct-taped his legs together.

When Joby saw Tony make his move, he counted thirty seconds as he had been directed. Then he ran up to the boys, grabbed the invoices from the driver's pocket, hustled to the back of the trailer, pulled the ramp, climbed up into the trailer, and began loading the cart. The boys lugged the driver up the ramp and stared at the wall of boxes, shakings their heads.

"Sweet," groused Tony. "Only a few feet of room here at the back, and the boxes are piled sky high. This ought to be fun."

They stood the unfortunate fellow up, and Andy pinned him against the boxes. Tony clambered up on top of the load, grabbed the driver by the armpits, and dragged him up and back while Andy and Joby pushed. Once they had him on top of the load, Tony dragged the awkward bundle deeper into the load.

While Tony was struggling with his exhausting task, pulling the hapless man into a small depression, out of sight if anyone looked into the back of the trailer, Andy helped Joby. He grabbed the paperwork and began digging boxes out of the load. This made the delivery go faster because Joby only had to wheel the loaded carts into the building. At 4:31 a.m. stage one was completed. The truck was in their possession, the driver was secured, and the delivery was finished. The boys nodded to each other, then Tony took off for the rendezvous site, Andy took a seat on a box of potatoes, and Joby closed up the doors.

When Joby arrived at Grossman's Diner at 4:37 a.m., his heart sank. There were lights on in the building. *Rats.* The cook usually arrived between 5:15 and 5:30 a.m. *Now what do I do?* He decided that he had to go forward with the delivery. The cook had probably heard the truck pull up, and they didn't want him calling Katahdin and asking why the driver had stopped, then took off again without delivering. So he did his log work, grabbed his delivery sheets, and headed for the back of the trailer. When he swung the first door open, he whispered to Andy, "The cook is here."

Andy replied frustratedly, "Yea. As soon as you opened the door I noticed that the lights were on." He looked into Joby's eyes. "So you got a plan?"

"Yep," he replied. "We're going to make this delivery as if nothing was wrong. If the guy happens to notice you, we'll just tell him that you're my helper, and this is your second day on the job. You don't have uniforms yet."

Andy nodded. "I'll buy that."

Joby wheeled the first cart into the building and dropped the stack of refrigerator goods in the cooler. The owner came around the corner from the kitchen as Joby was backing out of the cooler and exploded. "Another new driver? For crying out! They better get their act together, or I'm going to drop them and go with their competition." He opened the cooler door, slammed it shut again, and laid into Joby. "Why did you drop that pile in the middle of my cooler? How am I supposed to put my order away if you're blocking the aisle? You did see how narrow it was in there, didn't you?"

"I did wonder about that," Joby started to apologize, "but—"

"Get your backside in my cooler, pick that stack up, and drop it outside the cooler to the right of the door, where my stuff has gone for the past ten years! Drop the dry goods and freezer items there too. When the entire order is inside, come and get me. I want to count everything."

"Yes, sir," Joby meekly replied. With a mixture of fear and indignation, he opened the door, wheeled back in, nosed under the pile, grabbed the top of the pile with his hand to steady it, tipped the cart back, walked the load back out, and dropped it next to the door. He looked around for the tyrant, didn't see him, and hurried back out to the truck. Six minutes later, with his fourth cartload, the entire order was inside. With a little trepidation, he went to look for the owner and found him in the kitchen working on one of his fryers.

"I've got everything inside, sir," Joby said politely, though inside he was ready to explode.

The grumpy old man blustered, "You're just gonna have to wait a minute or two," then continued with his project of cleaning and redoing the electrical connection behind the temperature dial. Joby glanced nervously at his watch. It was 5 a.m. *Not good.* They were supposed to be leaving this stop already according to the route manifest. Five minutes later, the grouch finished reassembling the dial, slammed his screwdriver and needle nose pliers down on the stainless steel table behind him, and strode toward the cooler. After three minutes of fussing and stewing over the piles, complaining about quality and dates, he signed off and walked away muttering. Relieved that this stop was finally over, Joby retrieved his paperwork from the pile of boxes and hastened back to the trailer.

He was surprised to discover that Andy had already stored the ramp and staged the order for Camp 286, so the delay hadn't been an entire loss. He had also prepared the prison break package for Jack, which left a pancake-mix mess next to the wall on the passenger side.

"I was starting to get nervous," Andy said as the frazzled barista handed his cart up.

"Me too," Joby replied. "I'll tell you about my crazy adventures later." As he swung the door around to shut it, he added, "Hide yourself good in the pile."

During the drive to 286, the light rain turned into a downpour. Joby smiled to himself. *At least one thing is going right this morning.* Andy had encouraged him that the forecasted heavy rain was a good thing because it would subtly change the psychology of the guards. They were merely security guards and didn't have the high level of professionalism that special-ops soldiers have, so they were likely to cut corners on their security measures, trying to avoid getting soaked by the downpour.

Joby's stomach churned as he headed down the drive to Camp 286. He was agonizing over the things that had already gone wrong and the predicament they would be in if anything went wrong here. He nosed up to the orange barrier arm and pulled his parking brake. A guard rushed out of the guard shack holding his clipboard over his head. Joby rolled his window down for him. The young man poked his head in the cab and said, "We got the message this morning. Sorry to hear about John." Almost apologetically, he continued, "I will need to see your driver's license."

"Of course," Joby responded. He fetched his wallet out of his lunch pail, retrieved the license, and handed it to him.

The young man hastily looked at the front, comparing the picture to Joby, glanced at the back, and handed it back to Joby. "Thanks," he said, "Now I need to check the cab, then the trailer."

"No worries."

The guard jumped down, opened the driver's door, took a quick peek, and ran around to the passenger side where he did the same. Then he jogged to the back. Before Joby had time to worry himself sick, the young man was climbing back up on his cab step. *Andy must have been right about the guards and the rain. He was barely gone long enough to crack the door.*

"You're clear. You can pass as soon as we raise the barrier arm and open the gate," the guard informed him. "You'll be using Dock 4." As the young man hustled back to the shack, giving his partner a thumbs up on the way, Joby breathed a sigh of relief.

When the arm raised, Joby passed through the gate and cautiously made his way across the crumbling asphalt, steering around the big potholes. When he found the loading docks on the East warehouse, he executed his set-up maneuver and found himself almost perfectly lined up with the dock. Glowing with a sense of satisfaction, he put the truck in reverse and backed up to the dock, nailing it perfectly. *Glad this is a dock delivery, so I won't get soaked.* He raced through his electronic log, grabbed his paperwork, and sprinted inside. When he raised the bay door, his heart sank. He had forgotten to open the trailer doors first. *Nuts.* He ran back to the truck, rolled it forward twenty feet, opened the doors, and backed up to the dock again. *So much for not getting soaked.*

When Joby exited the truck with his first cartload, he stood in the warehouse perplexed. *Now what?* He had assumed that it would be obvious where to go to make the delivery. That was not the case. There were no obvious cooler doors or dry storage rooms as he had seen at the prior two stops. Nor was there a sign or a person to point him in the right direction. Worse, the majority of the warehouse was filled with a massive pile of crates and boxes that blocked his view. In frustration he took off on a jog towards the left side of the room. When he skirted the left side of the pile, he noticed a doorway on the far end of the warehouse. *As good a choice as any*, he surmised. *Gotta start somewhere.*

The doorway opened into a dimly-lit corridor which he

followed. He passed a few dark openings on his right and came to an intersection that offered him three choices. Along the wall on his right were more dark openings. Straight ahead lay a pitch-black opening. The corridor on his left, however, was lit farther down. He chose left. He preferred light to darkness.

About seventy-five feet down, he passed a door on his right with a sign that said *Commissary*. Another forty feet down, he passed a door with a sign that said *Supply*. Neither seemed likely. The third door he came to was blocked open with a wedge and greeted him with kitchen odors. He wheeled his cart through the doorway and found himself in a small dry storage room. Voices and laughter echoed from somewhere ahead. *Thank you, God.*

He continued through the storage room and exited into a kitchen utility room where he spied the cooler and freezer.

"Hey! We got a new driver again," a petite blonde remarked, giving him the once over.

Joby blushed.

"You can drop your loads against that wall," she said, pointing to a short wall between the cooler and the freezer.

He dropped his load as directed and hustled back to the truck, fretting the entire way. *Gotta come up with a plan to make contact with Irina, or this mission is for nothing.* His brainstorming faltered once he was back in the trailer because he had to concentrate on his delivery checklist. But while he was wheeling his cart toward the corridor, a plan gelled. It did have a downside, though. Could he muster the courage to pull it off?

"Hey," Joby commented as he drew near the anonymous blonde. "I heard there's a really cute brunette here by the name of Irina who receives the delivery sometimes."

The gal laughed and hollered for Irina. When the brunette walked up, the blonde said to her, "You can finish the check-in. I'll take over with breakfast prep." Then she walked away.

When the blondie was around the corner, Joby moved close to Irina and whispered, "Ariele and her friends in Montana sent me to get you out of here. Listen carefully to everything I say and follow my instructions exactly."

Irina nervously agreed, "Okay."

Joby pulled out his picture of Jack and asked, "Is this man here?"

"Yes," she replied, "and so is Sally. They both work in the west warehouse in maintenance."

Sally wasn't part of Joby's mission, so he ignored the intel and followed his script. "I'm supposed to inform the head cook that I have a package for Jack."

"Francis Ferguson—he goes by Frenchie—is the head cook. He and Jack served together in the First Gulf War."

"Okay. Go tell Frenchie that there's a package for Jack hidden in a marked bucket of pancake mix. Then tell him that you don't feel good and want to go lay down. Walk out of here like you're headed for your room, but sneak away to the loading docks. Move as fast as you can. Once you get there, hide in the back of the truck. You'll have to climb up on top of the pile of boxes and crawl back until you find the low spot. Now go talk to Frenchie, then skedaddle to the truck."

Irina departed on her errand. Joby dropped his stack, then hustled back to the truck. As he rolled up the ramp into the back of the truck, his eyes surveyed the load. *That's not gonna work.* He rearranged boxes to make Irina a makeshift ladder for climbing the pile, then he loaded his cart with three buckets of pancake mix. He was barely out of the truck when Irina blew past him, panting heavily, and bounded into the back of the truck. A few seconds later, a woman's shrill, but muffled, shriek startled him. *Guess I should have warned her that there were already two guys hiding in the van.*

When Joby rolled into the receiving area with his third load, the original blonde was back.

"Where's the pretty brunette?" he enquired.

"She complained of not feeling well," she replied. "I was told to get back over here and take over."

Several minutes later, when he wheeled in his fourth and final load, Joby handed her the delivery paperwork and asked, "Are all of the deliveries this spartan?"

"Pretty much," she replied as she began counting the boxes. "We don't order much from Katahdin except for flour, pancake mix, biscuit mix, eggs, and some fresh vegetables like lettuce. The bulk of our food comes from government surplus, food pantries, dent-and-bent stores, and leftovers from farmers' markets." She signed the paperwork, pulled her copy, and handed the rest back to Joby.

Like a child reaching for candy, he snatched the papers from her hand, wheeled his cart around, and trotted off, shouting "Have a great day" over his shoulder. On the trip back, he struggled to maintain his pace. He was breathing hard and his pulse was racing.

The tension ratcheted up even further as he neared the gate a few minutes later. This was the moment of truth. He stopped the truck about six feet shy of the gate and waited for it to open. It didn't. As the seconds turned into minutes, he found himself on the verge of panic, trapped in the awful abyss of his fears. He tried to calm down, but he couldn't control his nervous fidgeting. Through the guard shack window, he could make out the two guards. One appeared to be on the phone and the other was flipping through a three-ring binder. *Long wait, phone conversation, regulation book—things aren't looking good.*

The guard on the phone hung up and gestured to the other, who grabbed his M-16 and ventured out into the rain. With a lurch the gate started to roll sideways, then stopped again, leaving a three-foot-wide opening. Joby's heart sank. The guard jogged through the opening, jumped up on his cab step, and poked his head in the window.

"I need to see your signed paperwork."

Joby handed him his clipboard with the 286 paperwork on top. The guard looked at it and handed it back.

"I also need to check the cab and the back again."

"No problem."

The guard raced through the cab check again, then turned his attention to the back. Joby heard the rear door get opened and locked to the side. Then he heard boots moving around inside. His pulse elevated. *Sounds like he's doing a real inspection.* His frantic mind began to consider scenarios. *Could I ram the gate? Could I escape a hail of machine gun fire? Maybe they would call the Sheriff instead of shooting me? Could I outrun law enforcement?* The sound of the doors getting locked back up interrupted his fearful imaginations. The guard walked past the cab door, talking on his radio. The gate started to move again, the barrier arm was raised, and the guard, standing on the covered porch out of the rain, waved him through. It was 6:03 a.m. Joby was only a few minutes behind schedule.

Feeling like a ton of bricks had just fallen off his shoulders, Joby disengaged his parking brake and rolled through. Once he was past the barrier, he accelerated, feeling the flush that comes when a man senses that victory might be within grasp after all. But his overloaded emotions began to break down as he negotiated the left turn onto the road. His eyes filled with hot, salty tears, blurring his vision. Blinking and wiping his eyes, he fought to stay focused on his route. At the appointed location near Harry's Body Shop, he stopped, snipped the coaxial cable to the electronic log, and put an aluminum hat on the satellite antenna. Then he continued on his way. Two blocks up the road, he turned off the Katahdin route and headed for the rendezvous site. He was on the home stretch.

As he bounced down the alley toward the yard, Tony swung the gate open for him, and the rookie driver prepared to make the tight corner. In his haste and nervousness, he failed to swing wide enough and ended up scraping the side of the truck and slightly bending the gate post. *No time to worry about that now.* He stopped when he had cleared the gate and waited for Tony to climb on his step. When they pulled into the yard, Tony banged on the cab door and pointed to an open door on the building to his left. Joby swung the truck hard to the right, pulled a button hook loop, and drove the truck into the open bay. With a rush of excitement, he pulled the air brake, turned the ignition key off, jumped out of the cab, and met Tony at the back of the trailer.

Tony spoke while he swung the door open and fastened it. "Parked in here, the truck won't be visible from the air. That'll buy us even more time. We just need to remember to leave a message with the local police department later on today so the authorities can find the poor guy before he dehydrates too much."

Joby was too numb to say much. "Good thinking."

"Did you remember to remove everything from the cab?"

Joby, embarrassed, shook his head *no*, ran back to the cab, grabbed his lunch box and driver's kit, and checked to make sure that nothing was accidentally left behind. When he returned, Andy and Irina were crawling down from the pile. He was amused when he noticed Tony giving her some serious side-eye.

Andy took charge of the moment. "Tony, go turn the refrigerator unit off, so the racket won't give away the truck's hiding place." He handed Irina a permanent marker. "Write a message on a box. Something like *Driver tied up on top of the load*. Then set the box on the deck of the trailer where it can be seen." Turning to Joby he said, "Go put your stuff in the van and wait for us." As Joby trotted off, Tony returned.

"Did you remember," Andy demanded, "to install the reflective covers over the license plates on the van?"

Tony grinned, "No camera is gonna catch us today, boss."

"Faaanntaaastik," Andy rasped in a horrible Terminator imitation. Jumping down, he continued giving instructions. "Slight change of plans. We need to leave the trailer doors open. The trailer might be too cold even with the reefer unit turned off. We don't want the driver to get hypothermic."

"Good idea," Tony said while helping Irina down. "I would hate to have a manslaughter charge added to our rap sheet. We're in deep enough already."

Tony hit the *down* button for the bay door, and the three of them bolted out of the garage bay, sprinted across the lot, and piled into the van. Andy fired it up, raced back to the exit, and braked hard at the gate. Tony jumped out and opened it. When the van had passed, he closed it again, wrapped the chain around twice, and clasped the new lock on the chain. When he climbed back into the van, his brother accelerated before he finished sitting down, throwing his brother back in his seat. They both laughed.

Fifteen minutes later, they were cruising down the highway on their way to Pennsylvania, and everyone was starting to relax—the adrenalin was subsiding.

Tony turned to Joby. "Well done, Granola. Not too shabby for a peacenik hippie. You are now officially a criminal. Twenty-four hours from now, your face will be in the national registry of the FBI, and you will have to avoid the surveillance cameras on the highways for the rest of your life. The new facial recognition software can recognize people at ninety miles per hour, even at night. You're going underground, bro."

Joby mumbled a feeble "Yeah, I know." Then he curled up on the floor in the back of the van. The lack of sleep and the emotional drain of the mission had taken their toll. But he did indulge a strong sense of satisfaction as he drifted off to sleep. The mission had been a success. Things had gone relatively smoothly. And he had performed better than he had expected. *I could get used to this adventure stuff.*

43

When Irina came to Frenchie with a feigned illness and a heads up about a marked bucket for Jack, alarm bells went off. This wasn't a normal Katahdin delivery. It was a Rogue Underground operation. He had been expecting something like this ever since the note that the supply angel had forwarded with questions about Irina and camp security. His gut instinct told him that the bucket was secondary and the primary objective was rescuing Irina. He didn't want to think about what would happen to his favorite kitchen helper if the effort failed. But there was nothing he could do. Hopefully, her rescuers had the skills to pull this effort off.

He turned his attention to the bucket. It had to be found and hidden fast. Once the camp director discovered that Irina was missing, the camp would be crawling with security guards and FBI agents. And if the authorities found the bucket, the repercussions would be grave.

He kept a watchful eye on the delivery from the kitchen, and as soon as Hazel, the morning blondie on his staff, had

351

signed off on it, he assigned her to the sweet-roll project in the kitchen. He wanted to put the delivery away himself. The fewer people that knew about the bucket, the better.

The marked bucket was on the bottom of the second pile of dry mixes. He smiled at the artwork, a crude sketch of a jack of clubs—*Jack's calling card*—then loaded the problematic bucket and three others on a pallet, covered them with boxes of paper napkins, and placed a slicer that needed repair on top of the pile. He towed the pallet to the workshop and parked it in Jack's wire-mesh maintenance cage. He added a note. *Swabbie, can you troubleshoot the digital electronics on the slicer and put the dry goods away? Thanks, Frenchie. P.S. Don't forget to look for the buried treasure.* Laughing at his own joke, he sauntered off.

Frenchie hustled back to the kitchen to check on his help, then made a beeline for Jack's dorm room. He woke his friend and told him that there was an urgent project in his cage that needed to be taken care of yesterday. Jack rolled out of bed without a word, dressed, made his bed, and was on his way within five minutes.

Next, Frenchie went to Jeremy Hendricks' room and woke the pastor. He whispered in his ear, "Hey preach.' We need to talk privately, ASAP."

"Okay. No problem," he drowsily replied. "Give me some time to wake up and get dressed. I'll meet you in the chapel in ten minutes."

When Jeremy arrived, he took a seat next to Frenchie on the edge of the platform. The cook shared the troubling news. "I think trouble's brewing, and it's likely related to the strange note we got through the supply angel a few weeks back. There was a different truck driver this morning. When he wheeled his second cart load in, he asked Hazel about Irina by name. How did he know her name? We aren't allowed to share our names with the drivers, and they aren't allowed to ask our names. Hazel, seeing his interest, traded work assignments with Irina. Several minutes later, Irina came and told me to be on the lookout for a marked pail of dry pancake mix that needed to get to Jack. She also told me that she felt sick and wanted to go lay down. The problem is, she didn't look sick. And when she left the kitchen, she turned left down the hallway instead of right. I suspect that she got on the truck and is now on her way to freedom."

"Hmm. Good for Irina, bad for us. Did you take care of the pail?"

"Yes. I buried it on a pallet, dropped the pallet in Jack's cage, then woke him up and sent him to take care of it."

"Good thinking. We need to find out immediately if Irina is still here or not. Fetch brunette Joyce and have her meet me in the kitchen in five minutes. I'll have her check Irina's bed, the bathroom, the showers, the laundry room, and her favorite haunts. If she is missing, Krake will have to dismantle his Wi-Fi stuff immediately."

At 6:45 a.m. brunette Joyce returned from her search and reported back to Frenchie and Jeremy, who were sitting at a table in the kitchen, strategizing on the situation. She apologized, "Sorry, guys. I looked everywhere you suggested and didn't find her."

Jeremy tugged on his chin, then replied, "We don't want

to report her missing right away. We need to delay—buy the rescue team a little time. Got any ideas?"

Frenchie nodded. "I can play along as if I assumed she was sick in bed. Sometime late into breakfast, I could send Hazel to check on her, maybe send up some dry crackers and 7 Up and see if she wants to eat. Obviously, she won't be there. When Hazel comes back and reports that Irina isn't in bed and that her bed is made, we'll have brunette Joyce arrange a search for her with six or eight girls. If they don't find her by 8:30 after searching the place with a fine tooth comb, then we'll report her missing to Bob Drake."

"Sounds good to me. But no matter how long we delay the storm, we can't stop it. I think we should warn Krake right away so he can be prepared for the tempest."

***

Jack spotted the pallet blocking the middle of his walkway as soon as he entered his cage. He snatched up the note, read it, and shrugged his shoulders. The electrical problem on the slicer made sense. But the napkins confused him. *I just brought these boxes to the kitchen two days ago. And buried treasure? What kind of joke is that?* He picked up the slicer and set it on his bench. Then he jacked the pallet up to tow it to dry storage in the back warehouse. He was a little cranky. *Urgent? Pfff. They have a backup slicer in the kitchen. And what kitchen situation is so urgent that they can't put the napkins and pancake mix away themselves?* In his frustration, he dragged the pallet jack too steeply out of the doorway and knocked a box off the back of the pallet. He stomped over, picked the box up, and slammed it on top of the pail. Then he picked the box back up and stared in amazement at a crude jack of clubs sketched on the lid of the bucket—the jack of clubs had been his calling card back in his SEAL days. *Maybe the buried treasure isn't a joke. Maybe there's a care package inside.*

He returned the box to the load, straightened the jack, and dragged the pallet to dry storage. Once there, he stored the napkins, then made his way to the back corner where he couldn't be seen by the camera. Using his pocket knife, he cut several tabs off—*hats off to whoever opened this without cutting the tabs*—then he pried the lid off, set it on the floor, and began scooping out pancake mix which he dropped on the lid. Three inches below the top, he uncovered a green military pouch that was nearly the diameter of the pail. He fished it out, dusted it off, and … had nowhere to hide it. A small box caught his eye. He opened it, set the cans on the shelf, placed the pouch inside the box, and folded the flaps shut.

After returning the pancake mix to the bucket, he snapped the lid back on and scraped the jack of hearts off the lid with his knife. Then he stowed the buckets on the shelf, swept up the pancake mix that had spilled on the floor, and tossed the pallet on the stack.

With the box under his arm, he returned to his cage, retreated to the bench in the back corner where he was hidden from the walkway in case one of his workmates showed up early, and opened his nylon pouch. On top was a folded slip of paper with a sketch of a setting sun over the mountains and a note "Don't be late for the rendezvous—Tenkara." He chuckled at his cousin Woody. *Just can't let that Japanese fishing stuff go.*

The package was a godsend: diamond-grit hacksaw blades, two nylon hacksaw handles, hardened lineman's pliers, a compact tool set, two anonymous debit cards, ten thousand dollars in cash, two burners with extra batteries and sim cards, two mini LED flashlights with red filters, twenty AA batteries, a hank of parachute cord, a Buck knife, a space blanket, a pair of Steiner military-grade mini binoculars, a New York state highway map, a topo map with the route to the extraction hideout marked in red, a pair of compact bolt cutters, and a chrome-plated key padlock. Apart from the padlock, it was all useful stuff.

An enclosed note gave him detailed directions to the extraction hideout—a remodeled barn near Elmira, the location of the spare key for the barn, Bitcoin account information, Woody's burner number, and a contact number to call for extraction, someone nicknamed Bullseye. It also informed him that he would need to cut the lock off the gate to access the property and replace it after he had passed through. Now the lock made sense. It further advised him to hide his escape vehicle in the hay pile in the barn. Finally, it asked him to lock the building and replace the key when he was done.

Jack lifted up his eyes to heaven and thanked God for the precious package and the friends that sent it. Then he stuffed the items back in the zipper pouch, shoved the pouch inside the box, and hid the box in the rear of a storage drawer. With a little extra bounce in his step, Jack headed for his room, whistling the *Titans* from the movie *Alexander*.

***

Frenchie's plan worked better than anticipated. When he and brunette Joyce reported Irina missing to Bob Drake at 8:29 a.m., the camp director's first response was to organize a search. He was skeptical that someone had actually escaped from his camp. Rather than immediately contact FEMA per protocol, he went forward on the assumption that she hadn't escaped but had merely wandered off. "Sometimes people do crazy stuff when they're sick," he informed them. "Did you check the roof?"

They shook their heads *no* and replied that they had not.

"Maybe she's despondent and needs medication. Probably didn't think of that, did you? Did you check the cooler and freezer in the north warehouse?"

Again, they confessed their failure.

"Maybe she was burning up with a fever and sought a place to cool off. She might even have wandered off in a fever-induced delirium. Then she could be anywhere. Fevers are dangerous. Did you contact the doctor when she said she was sick?"

"No, sir. Sorry. Didn't think it was more than a tummy ache."

"Did you check the closet where the hot-water heater for the kitchen is located?"

"Didn't think of it."

"Maybe she took a chill and decided to warm herself up

in the warmest place in the building." He glared at them, then chided them. "You two are pathetic. How did you ever make it this far in life? Get out of my office."

Angered, he got on the intercom and summoned the entire camp to an emergency meeting. "Whatever you are doing, drop it. I want everyone in the cafeteria in three minutes."

As they strolled in, Bob hollered, "Sit by dorm rooms at the tables. Men on my right and women on my left. Each dorm room leader is responsible for a head count." When all were accounted for, he began his rant, chiding the detainees for not watching out for each other. Then he divided them into ten search teams according to their dorm rooms and barked their instructions, "You *are* going to find Irina. You *will* search every nook and cranny of *every* section of *all* four buildings—every room, every closet, every possible hiding place. When you finish your assigned section, report back here to me. You have forty minutes. Everyone be back here by 9:20 a.m."

At 9:28 a.m. Bob reluctantly called FEMA with the news that one of his detainees, Irina Kirilenko, had mysteriously disappeared—possibly in connection with the morning's Katahdin delivery. After a brief internal investigation, FEMA contacted the FBI at 9:42 a.m. and passed on the news. At 9:58 a.m. the FBI issued a regional bulletin to be on the lookout for Irina and for a missing Katahdin truck with New York plates and the number 22 on the door. At 10:31 they issued a regional bulletin to be on the lookout for a white Ford utility van with two male passengers of unknown race that were at least six feet tall. They were way too late. By the time this bulletin went out, the rescue team was already at Klodhopper's Auto Sales and Salvage outside Sinnemahoning, Pennsylvania, selling the van for scrap and retrieving the Backstrom boys' pickup and camper. As the team rolled out of the yard, Claude Hopper was busy flattening the van with his bulldozer. He had already removed the plates and emptied the glove box. When he finished, he stacked the demolished van in the far corner of his salvage yard, under four other flattened vehicles—out of sight and out of mind.

44

After brunette Joyce had returned to the cafeteria at 6:45 a.m. and informed Frenchie and Jeremy that she couldn't find Irina anywhere, Jeremy knew that he had to talk to Krake. The discouraged preacher walked to Krake's room and found him studying in the cozy little office under his bed. "Got some bad news, Krake. Irina escaped this morning. We think she left on the Katahdin truck. I'm afraid that this probably spells the end of your secret Wi-Fi station and disseminating your studies. The feds will likely turn this place upside down before the day is out and incorporate stricter security measures over the next few months."

The wizened gentleman ran his fingers through his thinning gray hair, stared into space for half a minute, then replied. "You're right. I'm gonna have to dismantle the Wi-Fi stuff as fast as possible. Send me up a cup of coffee and a peanut butter sandwich. I'll be working through breakfast."

Jeremy set his hand affirmatively on Krake's shoulder,

then turned and headed for the kitchen to fulfill the request.

Krake stopped him. "You know, if I dismantle everything now, we would probably evade detection. Nobody would get caught or hurt. But if I do that, that would be a crushing blow to the *Down the Rabbit Hole* ministry. My research on various topics would be lost—no longer available for students of prophecy."

"So what are you suggesting?"

"I think I should safeguard the ministry. I need to upload all my research and tools to Buster so they're available for someone else to take over the ministry. Once that is done, I'll dismantle everything."

"How long will that take?"

"I don't know for sure, but I'm guessing a couple hours."

"Frenchie thinks that we probably have two hours max before they start turning this place upside down. If the Wi-Fi isn't disassembled by then, that puts folks in danger, not just yourself, but myself and those in maintenance who helped."

"Not worried about myself. I'm worried about the truth that I have uncovered. It needs to be disseminated. As for the others, I can't speak for them. What do you think I should do?"

"When this project started, I knew the risk. I was willing to pay the price then. And I'm still willing to pay it. Men need the truth found in the Bible, and they need to know about the comet. As for Bryce and Arnie, they both stated at the beginning that they believed in this project and were willing to be the fall guys for all of the maintenance department. I doubt that either of them has changed their minds since then. So it really comes down to you. What do you think you ought to do?"

"I think I should safeguard the ministry so someone else can take up the mantle."

"Then do so. I'll alert Bryce and Arnie to be ready at a moment's notice for the dismantling project. And I won't forget your sandwich and coffee." With that, the intrepid preacher ducked out.

Krake began immediately. He logged into Buster, quadrupled his storage size, and paid his account in advance for another decade including email, security suite, and other services. Then he began uploading everything vital: his current research, his extensive notes on a variety of subjects, e-Bibles, e-books and e-study tools, his open source e-reader, links to useful websites, info for his Bitcoin account, info for his secret Cayman Islands bank and investment account—the only assets the government didn't find—and all his usernames and passwords. It took him nearly two hours. When he finished, he composed two sticky notes on his homepage in Buster: one to Irina and one to his successor.

The notes posted, he threw up a quick prayer that Irina's escape attempt would be successful and that she would make connections with someone willing and able to maintain the ministry. Everything hinged on Irina. She was the only person outside Camp 286 who knew the username and password for the Buster account.

Seconds later, while he was logging out of Buster, Bob Drake's grating voice came on the intercom and announced that there would be an emergency assembly in the cafeteria at 8:35, only three minutes away. One-hundred-percent attendance was required—no exceptions. Krake closed the StartPage browser, glanced at his unfinished breakfast, and chuckled to himself. *Only took two bites out of my sandwich and left a half cup of cold coffee.* He threw back the coffee and dashed downstairs. *I may still get caught with the Wi-Fi stuff, but at least the ministry material is safe.*

At 8:55 Bob called Alpha Force, the security company that was subcontracted to FEMA for most of its camp security, and asked them to send four extra guards ASAP. They immediately dispatched two that had been on call and two that they freed up by downsizing a security team scheduled for a special event.

On the heels of a fruitless effort, the search teams returned to the cafeteria at 9:20, gave brief reports, and were dismissed after a torrid harangue by Bob Drake. Krake hurried to his room, accompanied by Arnie and Bryce, and they began to disassemble the Wi-Fi setup. They figured that it would take an hour to remove the components, hide the pieces in their utility cart, dismantle the secret compartment, redo the bed bookshelves, wheel the cart to maintenance, and hide the Wi-Fi components in the warehouse. As they worked, Krake felt a sad ache seeping into his heart. He pushed the melancholy feelings back out and refused to dwell on them. Yes, the best six months of his life were over. But he had known in his heart of hearts that his ministry from within 286 couldn't go on forever. This was real life, not *Hogan's Heroes*. Besides, as his German grandmother used to say, *Die Wahrheit ist untödlich*—the truth is unstoppable.

At 9:26 the four extra security guards showed up at Bob Drake's office. He directed them to make unannounced rounds of the entire complex, searching for anything that looked out of place. "I don't believe she got away without inside help," he insisted. "Someone in here had to have aided the attempt, maybe more than one. We will find them, and they will pay dearly." He sent two of them to search the men's dorms on the third floor and the other two to search the west warehouse. "Contact me if you find something suspicious." As soon as they left, Bob got on the phone and called Antonia Delavasquez, the director of the 200-series FEMA camps, to inform her of the situation.

At 9:37 two of the guards walked into Krake's room, which was E dorm, while he and Bryce were dismantling the secret cabinet. They raised their M-16s and shouted, "Halt!" Krake and his companions reluctantly dropped what they were doing and raised their hands. One of the guards kept his weapon trained on Bryce and Krake while the other motioned Arnie to walk away from the utility cart and join his friends. Then he opened the cabinet door on the cart, searched the boxes inside, and discovered the concealed Wi-Fi equipment. Hands trembling, he got on his radio and tried to raise the camp director. At first, he heard static on the other side, then the channel went dead.

Unbeknownst to him, Bob Drake was on the phone with FEMA getting his hind end chewed when his radio crackled. Frustrated, he had reached out and turned the knob off. Four minutes later, the guard reached him. "Mr. Drake. We found three men dismantling some kind of communication system in room E."

"Get their sorry backsides down here, immediately," he barked.

"Yes, sir," he replied.

The guards handcuffed their prisoners, marched them downstairs, and brought them to Bob's office. He was on the phone again—this time with the FBI—and angrily pointed the interrupters to the empty room next door. The guards deposited their charges on the beat-up chairs that lined one wall, then manned the door.

At 10:06 that morning, two FBI agents walked into the room where the miscreant detainees were being held just as Bob Drake was lighting into them. "It's over for you guys," he said, with acid in his voice. "You're in for a well-deserved vacation at the—"

One of the agents cut him off—"We'll take over from here, Mr. Drake. Thank you for your cooperation"—then pointed him to the door. The camp director strode out in a huff.

It may be over, Krake smiled to himself, *but it's not over. There are more chapters to this story, and it has a happy ending.*

Ten minutes later, Krake, Bryce, and Arnie were led away in handcuffs. Krake turned and smiled at brunette Joyce as they passed in the hallway, eyes locked. "Be faithful unto the end," he whispered.

"Silence," one of the FBI agents barked. "You aren't permitted to speak."

No one in 286 ever saw the three again. Rumors abounded

as to their fate: shot for treason, shipped to Guantanamo, solitary at the Supermax in Colorado, or serving as faux escapees for K-9 training. But the only rumor that gained lasting currency was that they had been recategorized and moved to one of the 300-series camps.

45

FEMA 286, Syracuse, NY
Monday, September 16, 2019

When the lunch rush was winding down, and only a few stragglers were left in line, the intercom crackled. "There will be a mandatory assembly in the east warehouse at fourteen-hundred hours, that is 2 p.m. civilian time. One-hundred-percent attendance is required. NO exceptions will be made. Men's dorm A is assigned to assembly duty. You will show up at 1:30 and set up the podium, the sound system, and sufficient chairs. Place eight chairs behind the podium, four on each side. After the assembly, return the chairs and equipment to storage. Again, this is a mandatory assembly. Do not be late. Roll will be taken. Anyone who misses this assembly will be reassigned within twenty-four hours to Camp 399."

Jack and Sally looked at each other nervously.

She made a pained face and whispered, "I'll bet it's about Irina."

He nodded. "Yep. I got a feeling this is gonna be a long day."

***

At 1:40 Sally scurried into Jack's cage, trembling with anxiety. He gave her a tender hug and reassured her. "Don't worry, Sally. They aren't going to find anything on us. We weren't accomplices. We were as surprised by her disappearance as they were. But no matter what happens, just remember that God is still in charge."

They walked in silence to the east warehouse a few minutes early and took their seats. The room quickly filled up, but a strange stillness hung in the air. There was none of the chattering and whispering that typically preceded an assembly. The eight chairs behind the podium were taken up by Bob Drake, the camp director; David St. Germain, the evening director; Sharon Baumgardner, the weekend director; Bradley Nelson, the evening director on weekends; Antonia Delavasquez, the director over all of the 200-series camps; and three men in suits they didn't recognize.

At two o'clock sharp, Bob took the podium and carried out a manual roll call, which took ten minutes. He then opened the meeting with a five-minute introduction, touching on the necessity of security, explaining how the detainees played a vital part, encouraging them to get a vision for their role, lamenting the recent breach, and warning that the camp would be clamping down on security. Nothing like that was going to happen again on his watch.

He was followed by John Perkins, an FBI representative with a PhD in criminal psychology. The dour agent lectured them for thirty minutes on the philosophy, necessity, and benefits of security rules and regulations. Jack had a hard time staying awake. Between his monotone delivery, the sheer boringness of the material, and a full stomach from his lunch, he found it almost impossible to keep his eyes open. Sally had to elbow him several times.

The boring agent was followed by one who was easier on the ears, Frank Johnson, introduced by Bob as the head of security over all of the FEMA camps. His talk was short and to the point. After a stinging indictment of the untrustworthiness of the detainees, who he insisted hadn't appreciated the freedoms they had been given, he lamented that he was obligated, against his preferences, to tighten up security. "Effective immediately, we will be upgrading the security in the 200-series camps. Extra cameras will be mounted on the fences and at the gate. Interior cameras will be installed, including units in the warehouses and dorm rooms, and they will be monitored 24/7. Thermal imaging will be installed at the gate. Never again will anyone escape from this camp or any other 200-series camp." He closed with a glowing tribute to the security community and a stinging tirade against those involved in soft terrorism.

When he was done, Bob returned to the podium and informed the assembly that he was going to read a list of names who needed to remain in their seats after the assembly was dismissed. A hush fell upon the audience. He read the list slowly, enunciating each name carefully. No surprise to themselves, Jack and Sally were among the names on his list—twelve in all. When he finished reading the list, those whose names weren't called got up and departed. After the crowd had left the warehouse, teams of FBI agents began streaming in through the same door, pushing equipment carts with polygraphs and Casper units. Jack was nervous, even though he knew he didn't need to be.

Bob approached Jack and Sally with one of the teams and addressed them sternly, "You two will follow these gentlemen to the office lobby. There you will be questioned, one at a time, in one of the offices. If you are concealing anything, we will find out in a hurry."

A few minutes later, Jack was sitting in the empty office to the left of Bob's, sweating bullets and trying to remain calm while two men wired him up for a polygraph and a visit with Casper. Then the questioning began.

The taller one asked him, "What part did you play in Irina's escape?"

"None."

"Did you help her escape?"

"Nope."

"Did you help her plan her escape?"

"No."

"Were you aware that she was going to escape?"

"Not at all. I had no idea that she was planning an escape until she was already gone."

"Did she ever talk about escaping?"

"Only the same way we all do, in a vague, daydreamy way."

"Can you elaborate?"

"On a few occasions, we talked about escaping someday, but only in a general manner, never anything that resembled making real plans. These conversations usually ended with tongue-in-cheek humor, like joking that we could have

Irina's rich Russian relatives send in a team of Spetsnaz on helicopter gunships and fast-rope us out of here. Truth be told, if she had an actual plan, she never breathed a word about it to me."

"Do you have any idea who in here may have helped her escape?"

"Absolutely none. While she was friendly to everyone, Sally and I were her closest confidants. She never breathed a word to us. And if she didn't tell us, she didn't tell anyone."

The questioning continued in this vein for another hour until every question had been asked from a half-dozen angles. When the agents finished their questioning, disappointed that they didn't get any positive readings, they unhooked Jack and let him go. *Sure glad they didn't ask me if the Katahdin truck brought me anything.* As he exited the office, he flashed a smile at Sally, who was waiting for her turn. She smiled back feebly. He wasn't half as worried about her as she was. *She's tougher than she looks and a whole lot tougher than she knows.*

46

Central Iowa
Tuesday, September 17, 2019

Irina lay awake on the cab-over bed in the camper, miffed. She hated the low headroom. She hated sleeping in her clothes. She hated the fact that she didn't have any clean clothes for tomorrow. She hated the fact that the bed smelled like guys that hadn't showered in a week. And she hated the fact that the bathroom was a cramped closet that smelled like a porta-potty—even had the nasty blue stuff in it. But as she stewed, she started feeling guilty for her lack of gratitude, which brought to mind the hymn "Count Your Blessings." She refocused and began to count. Less than twenty-four hours ago, she had been rescued from FEMA 286 by a Katahdin driver, who was really a barista, and two former Delta operators. She was alive. She was healthy. She knew Jesus. And there was hot cocoa on the counter. If she couldn't sleep, she was going to get up and indulge her love for chocolate.

"Hey Joby," she called. "Are you awake?"

"Halfways, but it's a quarter past midnight. Can't you let

a guy sleep? I haven't had a good night's rest for several days."

"Can't blame me. I've been lying here quiet as a church mouse for the past two hours, listening to you toss and turn. My advice, if we get up and do hot chocolate and pizza now, you'll sleep better later. Folks almost always sleep better on a full stomach. Learned that from my grandma."

Joby threw his blanket aside in frustration, knowing she was right. He got up from his pad on the floor, kicked his pad and blanket out of the way, placed a frozen pizza in the broiler, and turned the burner on for the tea kettle. Then he plopped himself down at the table and opened Tony's laptop.

Irina marveled at Joby. He was a sight for sore eyes. While the Backstrom boys were also good-looking and definitely more buff than the California kid, Joby could have been a model for surfboards or suntan lotion. He was exceptionally good-looking. When his hair grew back, he would be even better looking. On top of that, he was a real gentleman. But he was definitely not her type. She climbed out of the cab-over bed, sidled over to the counter, and dug out two coffee cups.

"It's so handy to have a satellite dish on the camper," Joby remarked. "I just pin-pointed our location with GPS. We're just west of Iowa City, Iowa, and maybe an hour from Des Moines. That puts us about halfway to the Compound in Montana."

"And halfway to cowboy country. Hey, head over to CVN.com. I want to catch the latest updates on the expansion of the triumvirate in the Middle East."

"The triumvirate?"

She joined him at the table. "The big three: Russia, Turkey, and Iran. Their activities in the Middle East have been tipping the balance of power away from Saudi Arabia and the West. I've been watching Russia especially close. She recently broke ground for her fifth base on Syrian soil, and the enlargement of her naval base at Tartus is moving along nearly twice as fast as Western analysts had projected."

"Been watching those three myself lately. I developed an interest through Andy and Tony. They checked conservative news sites every evening while we were planning the mission, trying to keep up on Russia, Israel, and the Middle East."

"Good for them. The way Russia, Turkey, and Iran have been flexing their muscles, it sure seems like things are shaping up for the Gog and Magog invasion of Israel prophesied in the book of Ezekiel."

"Funny you mention that. I've been reading in the Prophets lately and just finished the account of the Gog and Magog invasion a few days ago. Wouldn't it be cool if all the prophecies in the Tanakh about Israel and her Mashiach really did come true?"

While he was speaking, Irina quietly rose, made two cups of hot chocolate, set the mugs on the table, and touched her new friend on the shoulder. "Joby, they really are going to come true. Every passage, every line, every word."

"You really take this prophecy stuff seriously, don't you?"

"Absolutely. More than 100 messianic prophecies were fulfilled literally in Jesus, an occurrence that is statistically impossible. And dozens of other Old Testament prophecies against individuals, cities, and nations were fulfilled literally too. For instance, God's utterances against Tyre came to pass exactly as stated, some of them months after they were uttered and some of them centuries later. The bottom line is, the Bible has an impeccable record for accuracy, so there's no reason to doubt that the prophecies about the last days will be fulfilled too, whether they concern Israel, the church, or the nations."

"I sure hope you're right."

The introductory music for the broadcast started playing. Irina sat down and scooted close to Joby so she could see better.

"Good morning. It is 1:30 a.m. here in the Big Apple. I'm Howard Sutherland, and this is *World News Update* brought to you every half hour by CVN, the Conservative Viewpoint Network.

"Five minutes ago, we received a breaking story about a massive fireball that was spotted near the Solomon Islands. About twenty-two minutes ago, at 5:08 p.m. local time, a gigantic bolide streaked over the Pacific Ocean from the southeast, on a trajectory similar to that of the Mongolian comet last October. The glowing green orb, witnessed by more than 1000 sailors, was visible for seven seconds before it landed in the ocean approximately six miles north of the USS Ronald Reagan while she and her strike group were cruising approximately one hundred and fifty miles northeast of Santa Isabel Island.

"This oceanic impact is the second class-B comet this year. The first was the Xingu bolide which devastated sixty square kilometers of jungle in April in the Brazilian state of Pará and completely erased three small villages. We also had the class-C impact in Mongolia last October. That makes three major impacts within the span of one year. Some claim that this cluster must have apocalyptic implications because it is 100 times the normal impact rate—three impacts per century since the Middle Ages. We have asked Dr. Franconi from the Smithsonian Institute to reply to this claim. Dr. Franconi, what is your take on these impacts? Do they have apocalyptic implications?"

"Howard, the law of probabilities says that Earth will experience large impacts relatively close to each other from time to time. If we were able to look at a graph of every significant impact over the past billion years, we would find ourselves inclined to think that the recent impacts are just par for the course, not some apocalyptic event. From time to time, say every ten thousand years or so, there would be a cluster of impacts."

"For instance, let's step back a few thousand years and consider the last time mankind witnessed such meteoritic activity, which was at the end of the Bronze Age. The inhabitants of Earth feared that ..." The doctor paused emphatically.

"the end of the world was upon them," Howard replied, finishing his guest's statement. "And it wasn't."

"Exactly. The world is still here today. The bottom line is, we experienced three impacts close together. That's it. There is nothing apocalyptic about them."

While Dr. Franconi was pleading for men to temper

religion with science and reason, a brilliant green flash appeared through the curtain of the window over the sink. The two jumped out of their seats, ran over to the sink, pulled the curtain aside, and stared in amazement for several seconds as a green bolide streaked and exploded.

"Holy cow, that was awesome!" Joby exclaimed. That was the biggest, baddest shooting star I have ever seen. What made it green?"

"Most likely helium," Irina replied.

"Hopefully, that was an asteroid so they can find pieces of it."

"They'll find pieces whether it was a comet or an asteroid."

He looked at her dumbfounded.

She smiled wryly. "Comets are large chunks of rock with the same source and composition as the asteroids. Thousands of years ago, a planet used to orbit between Mars and Jupiter. But it exploded when Venus—in the era of her elliptical orbit— encroached on its Roche limit, and the numerous fragments became the asteroids, comets, Centaurs, Trojans, and TNOs, and even some of the moons."

A pensive expression sprawled across Joby's face. "If that's true, why does everyone teach that comets are dirty snowballs?"

"Because everyone believes the theory of evolution. And the evolutionary model of our solar system teaches that comets were formed in the Oort Cloud by the accretion of gas atoms and dust particles left over from the formation of our solar system."

"Well, you might be right. I just find it hard to disagree with science."

"But what kind of science? This really comes down to whether we are practicing real science where observation takes precedence over theory or hobby-horse science where pet theories are allowed to run roughshod over observation. The fact is, the theory of dirty-snowball comets faces two hurdles. First of all, the formation of large bodies through the accretion of gas and dust in an environment with an atmospheric pressure of zero and a temperature of four degrees Kelvin has never been observed in nature or demonstrated in a laboratory. Secondly, the probes that have landed on comets have uncovered information that makes scientists squirm. Not only do they look like rock, but when drilled, they are as hard as rock."

"Got no answer for that. If that's true, it definitely puts the kibosh on the dirty-snowball theory." Joby changed the subject slightly. "We sure have seen a lot of comets and shooting stars lately."

"We sure have," Irina agreed. "And they will continue to increase until the time of the end." She explained how the exploded planet caused the swarm of short-period comets and asteroids that hammered Earth during the Bronze and Iron Ages, and how it sent out a swarm of long-period comets that will buzz Earth in the future. Then she explained how the coming swarm dovetailed with Bible prophecy, especially the burning rocks and stars that slam into Earth under the trumpet judgments in the book of Revelation.

"That sounds both scary and exciting at the same time.

It reminds me of the day of the Lord in the Tanakh—fire and destruction."

"God has intentionally timed the swarm so that it will herald the day of the Lord. Nature keeps time with God's prophetic timetable."

Their conversation was interrupted by the ding of the timer on the toaster oven. Joby jumped up enthusiastically to retrieve their late-night repast, not sorry at all that he was doing pizza once again.

47

the Compound
Wednesday, Sept. 18, 2019

After two long days, the rescue team arrived at the Compound a few minutes after midnight. Originally, they had planned on arriving in time for dinner, but they had lost five and a half hours in Des Moines, Iowa when the water pump on their truck went out. Because it had been 2:30 in the morning when steam had started pouring out from underneath the hood, they had been forced to sit four and a half hours in the parking lot of the Flying J truck stop waiting for NAPA to open. They had also endured a stretch in Wyoming where they were pummeled with high winds gusting over eighty miles per hour, which had slowed them down considerably.

Andy nosed the black Ford Super Duty up to the lodge, and the road-weary travelers tumbled out and stumbled inside. They were greeted with a joyous reception in the great room, marked by a tearful hug between Ariele and Irina, a backslapping hug between Woody and Joby, and a flurry of hand-pumping congratulations offered to the guys on the rescue team. Woody teased Joby. "I liked the mop top better than the chrome dome."

Joby grinned. "Me too."

While most of the folks gathered around the boys to hear them recount the rescue effort, Woody edged his way over to Irina, who was visiting with Ariele, and enquired about his cousin and his boss. "How about Jack and Sally? Were they at 286?"

"Yes, they were," she replied. "Sally arrived at the end of June. And Jack arrived in late July. The three of us became close friends. Sally was deeply involved in the coverup, actually leading the Minoa Research team. Her frequent 'NEO' trips were actually trips to Washington, D.C. for meetings at the White House. Around the same time that I mailed my package to you—she looked at Ariele—Sally grew uneasy with the coverup and began to play the double agent so to speak. She looked the other way when you were misappropriating Hooker time to investigate the Rogue. And she played the dimwitted blonde when she allowed you—she looked at Woody—to go on your camping trip. To top it off, a week before her flight, when she sensed that her days were numbered, she hid a thumb drive in the mountains near Los Angeles that contains all the emails and documents that were in her possession. She risked a lot for the Rogue Underground. She is one amazing woman."

Woody soaked in the information like a thirsty sponge. But it left him feeling conflicted. He thanked Irina and retreated to the porch, where he gazed at the stars and nursed his misery. While he was happy to hear that Sally was okay, he felt responsible for her troubles. Once again he wrestled with the demons of guilt, but he came up with the same answer he always came up with—he had done what had to be done, and Sally had been complicit. She hadn't been oblivious to the dangers. She had taken a calculated risk. Irina was right. Sally was an amazing woman.

His introspection was interrupted by a shout from Red. "Can I have everybody's attention?" He held up a toasting glass and pointed to Betsy who was carrying a tray of them filled with sparkling grape juice. Woody walked back inside and grabbed a glass with everyone else. Red continued, "I offer a toast to Andy, Tony, and Joby for their successful mission and to Irina for her role in discovering the Rogue and exposing the cover-up." He clinked his glass with those nearest him. The crew followed suit. Then the ladies hurried into the kitchen and returned with platters of crackers, elk sausage, cheese, and jalapeno poppers.

***

The next morning, Irina found herself wide awake a few minutes before seven, too excited to stay in bed. She got up with the sunrise, showered, downed a glass of orange juice and a granola bar, and went exploring. Arrested by the silhouette of the gingerbread barn against the backdrop of the mountains, she headed up the road in its direction, drinking in the beauty of the region, especially the pockets of aspen which were beginning to show the first hints of their autumn glory.

The preoccupied woman hopped the wooden fence,

walked around the back corner of the barn to watch the horses, and stopped dead in her tracks—her eyes fastened on the gorgeous cowboy she had noticed the night before, savoring his crystal-blue eyes and his curly blonde hair half-hidden underneath a Stetson. When she dropped her eyes in embarrassment, she noticed that he was wearing real cowboy boots—he actually worked in them.

Blake stood smiling, reins in hand and horse in tow, wondering what was going through the mind of the pretty gal who appeared to be thoroughly flustered. "Interested in a ride?" he offered. "I'll show you the ridge and the telescope project."

Blushing, she nodded *yes*, and scampered up to him. *That looked way too enthusiastic*, she groaned to herself. *Show a little restraint.* He climbed up in the saddle, reached out his hand, and asked for her left. When she placed her hand in his, he instructed her to put her left foot in the stirrup. When she did, he pulled her up behind him. She nestled in, uncertain where to place her arms.

"Wrap your arms around me so you don't fall off," he advised. "And don't be afraid to hold tight. The trail does get steep in a couple places." Trembling with self-consciousness and excitement that bordered on bliss, she obliged.

"Giddy up," Blake commanded. The horse headed across the pasture at a trot. "The ridge ahead will take us to the same place as the road over to our right," he said, pointing. A few minutes later, they began working their way up the ridge trail. Irina savored the quaking aspens in their autumn glory, the chokecherry bushes emblazoned with red, the sporadic patches of late-blooming lupines and asters, the fragrance of pines and sagebrush, the chatter of red squirrels, and the sweet warblings of gray jays and mountain bluebirds. Best of all, Blake's rich baritone voice fell on her ears like nectar from heaven as he talked about the West and identified the plants and birds. The ride seemed surreal—like she had fallen down the magic rabbit hole and wound up in a romance novel.

The rest of the ride was a blur: touring the rustic cabin, seeing the telescope project, which was little more than a welded platform and piles of materials, and enjoying the return journey. When they arrived back at the barn, she didn't want the ride to be over but was relieved that it was. She hadn't been such an emotional wreck since the day of her arrest.

As she walked back to the lodge, she was overwhelmed with the blessings of the past few days, and tears of joy rolled down her cheeks. She had been unexpectedly snatched from 286 and carried to this magical setting in Montana. Here she would have access to an infrared telescope that would allow her to study the Rogue. And here she had met a cowboy—a real cowboy, who was a gentleman, a Christian, and an astronomer. The striking change of circumstances reminded her of the church's coming transfer from the uglies of this life to the glories of eternity.

Her happy thoughts were interrupted by the piercing clang of a chuckwagon bell. She quickened her pace, crossed the rough patch of grass in front of the lodge, bounded up the steps, and found herself greeted with the scent of fresh caramel rolls.

***

That evening, after a feast of grilled shrimp and asparagus, the members of the Compound gathered for their weekly meeting, which had been delayed until after the rescue team had returned.

Jordy opened. "We have a number of things on our plate over the next few months. The two most pressing, at least to my mind, are Jack and the telescope. At this point, there isn't much that we can do for Jack, apart from pray, until we hear from him. So I suggest we focus on procuring the parts that Blake needs to get his telescope up and running. Preliminary investigation indicates that we should send one team to Russia and another to Louisiana. The Russian mission will be dangerous, involving black market purchases from the mafia, illegal presence in a volatile nation where anti-American sentiment is high, and smuggling contraband items back into America. I think it goes without saying that Andy and Tony will be assigned to the Russian mission, so I would advise you two to press your Russian studies like workout fanatics."

Sam posed a mild objection to this focus. "Isn't there something we can do to speed up the process of bringing Jack back here safely? Would it be worthwhile to send Andy and Tony back to New York? Maybe there is another vulnerability that they can exploit? At the very least, they would be ready to pick him up at the extraction location as soon as he calls."

Woody nixed the idea. "A former Ranger at 286 gave us the only significant vulnerability that he was aware of that could be exploited from the outside. If there is another vulnerability, Jack will have to find it himself and exploit it himself from the inside. Moreover, we have no idea when Jack is going to attempt to escape. I hate to say it, but he may never escape. So if the boys went out there, they could be tied up for months, waiting around and doing nothing. That would be a misuse of our limited resources. Jack himself would veto such an effort as a profitless escapade. Besides, we already have a plan for Jack's extraction that can be implemented no matter when he escapes. All he needs to do is use one of the burners that we sent him and call the contact we gave him. An extraction team will pick him up at the hideout near Elmira, New York, and drive him to Meyersdale, Pennsylvania, where he will lay low with a biker club for a while until a safe travel option presents itself."

Ariele added a new dimension to the question. "Why are we only worrying about Jack? Now that we know that Sally is there, we have to do something. So what are we going to do about her?"

Jordy replied, "There isn't much that we can do."

"But we can't just leave her there," she remonstrated sassily.

Woody was feeling helpless himself and turned to Irina, hoping to uncover some tidbit of information that might offer them a ray of hope in the situation. "You were friends with both Jack and Sally. What can you tell us about their escape plans?"

"The three of us were close friends, and we hung out together. Knowing Jack, I suspect that if he does come up with an escape plan, he won't be leaving without Sally. They are pretty close."

Irina noticed Woody wince and realized that she had wounded him. *Sly dog. I think he's sweet on Sally.* Immediately she added, "If I was still there, I would likely be leaving with him too." But her recovery was too little and too late.

Woody was glad that Sally would likely escape with Jack if he escaped. But waves of jealousy troubled his heart. Were Jack and Sally more than friends? He tried to put the matter out of his mind, but it refused to budge. He clutched at the only thought that offered him solace. *Better the bittersweet pain of losing such an amazing woman than not to have known her at all. Besides, Jack is probably a better match for her.*

Irina changed the subject. "There is something else that demands attention and should probably be prioritized over the procurement of parts for the telescope."

All eyes were on her as she continued. "Sally told me that she hid a thumb drive on a trail near her home about a week before her arrest. It contains sixty times more emails than Ariele obtained and dozens of sensitive documents. The contents of this thumb drive would be extremely valuable not only for us here at the Compound but for the entire Rogue Underground. If we retrieved it, we could send a copy to Burrage Krakenhavn, and he could disseminate it through his *Down the Rabbit Hole* platform."

Woody chimed in, "I agree with Irina. We need to make this an immediate priority. The Backstrom boys could make a run down to California, retrieve it, and be back in less than a week. A one-week delay in our effort to procure the sensors, the mirror, and the stuff needed for making and storing liquid hydrogen, in the big picture, is a small loss for a huge gain. Not to mention, the boys could redeem the lost week by listening to Russian lessons down and back."

Jordy called for a vote on making the thumb drive an immediate priority, and the crew unanimously voted *yes*. After a few minutes of discussion, it was decided that the boys would take two or three days of rest, including a little fly fishing with Woody, then drive down to the Golden State for a mission that was almost a vacation. Irina wrote the directions on a page from her notepad and handed it to them.

> *Drive to Pasadena, then Altadena. Ride mountain bikes up the Mount Wilson Toll Road to the Idlehour Trail trailhead. Ride about one-third of a mile up the Idlehour Trail. At the hairpin corner, hike NNW through the trees and look for a big oak tree with a dark rock at its base that has roots growing around it. On the back side of the tree, look for a flat rock. Under the rock, you'll find an old ginger mint Altoids tin. Inside it, you'll find a small plastic bag with a silica-gel desiccant pack and a thumb drive.*

"Piece of cake," Andy replied after he read it aloud to his brother. "Gonna need a couple mountain bikes though. I guess we're driving to Billings tomorrow morning to go shopping and then get some bike riding practice in the afternoon."

Tony laughed. "I can't remember the last time I rode something that didn't have a motor."

"And don't forget," Ariele said, giggling, "that you'll

need full biker camo so you blend in with the biker environment—cute biker shorts and shirts, colorful shoes and socks, wild kneepads and gloves, and can't forget the stylish helmets."

Tony sniped, "I don't do cute."

"Are you volunteering," Andy enquired, trying to squelch a laugh, "to help us pick out what we need?"

She smiled sweetly. "Only if you promise to buy whatever I pick out."

Andy laughed. "That could be dangerous."

"Seriously," she replied. "You need to dress in such a way that you blend in with the locals and don't look like outsiders. Looking the part is not optional. And speaking of blending in with the locals, part of your plan should be that when you come to the hairpin corner, one rider will remain with the bikes on the trail so if you meet other riders, they will assume that your stop is a nature break. Also, you should determine right now that you are going to ride all the way to the top before you return. You want to act like real riders and not merely dress like them."

Jordy interrupted. "You three can hammer out the details later. We need to move on." He scanned the group for a few seconds, then continued. "We need to stay on top of the telescope project. We aren't the only ones in the market for infrared technology. There is a very limited supply of sensors. We don't want to come up empty-handed. We need some good leads, and we need them soon. Does anyone have anything new and promising?"

Ariele nudged Andrius, and he mentioned that he had

found two new markets on the darknet that looked promising. He was going to probe them deeper over the next couple weeks. Andy also spoke up and mentioned that he and Tony had a few contacts in Russia who might be able to help them make the right kind of connections. These observations, their first actionable leads, led to a lively discussion on the best way to pursue these leads until they either dead-ended, gave them new leads, or led them to the equipment that they sought.

48

the Compound
Tuesday, October 1, 2019

Because it was a nippy evening, the crew gathered for the Compound meeting in the great room at the lodge. On the docket were five main items: a report from Andy on the trip to California to recover Sally's thumb drive, an initial report from Irina and Ariele on the contents of the thumb drive, tentative planning for the telescope runs—as the Backstrom boys had started calling them, progress on Jordy's home, and Burrage Krakenhavn's two weeks of silence.

Andy got up smiling and gave his report. "The trip went smoothly. There were no unpleasant surprises or glitches. The directions we were given were spot on, and we found the thumb drive without difficulty. Kudos to Irina.

"The only difficulty we faced was really a deficiency in mission planning. Tony and I both got a bad case of monkey butt on our way to Muir Peak Road. We were chafed raw. Luckily, we met a young lady at the top who took pity on our misery. She gave us her Anti Monkey Butt powder. We were so saddle sore that we were forced to take a break and climb Muir Peak before we headed back down.

"So now I have a question for the cute little pixie who helped us buy our bikes and all the cool gear. Why didn't you tell us to buy Anti Monkey Butt powder?" Everyone laughed except Ariele. She blushed and shrugged her shoulders.

Irina followed Andy. "Our survey of the thumb drive indicates that it contains several dozen technical papers and several thousand emails. Most are from observatory teams that are involved in Minoa Research, but there are several hundred from NASA, JPL, the White House, the Pentagon, the FBI, Homeland Security, and the CIA. Ariele and I are currently in the process of combing through these emails, looking for anything useful that we don't already know. After we finish, we intend to delve into the technical papers.

"So far, we have found several items of interest. One, NASA reported in April 2019 that RN13, the official nomenclature for the Rogue, had passed Neptune and was now officially inside the solar system. While Ariele had already calculated that, it was nice to obtain confirmation from official sources.

"Two, NASA is sticking to its estimate that the Rogue is going to pass about 18,000 miles from Mars, despite the fact that independent calculations have suggested that the estimate should be narrowed to about 15,000 miles.

"Three, NASA officials are confident that the Rogue is not going to develop a coma because it is rock, not ice. In their belief system, comets develop comas through the sublimation of ice. And because it won't develop a coma, they are confident that it will pass through the solar system unnoticed by amateur astronomers.

"Lastly, a few NASA scientists suspect that the Rogue, due to its iron and heavy metal composition, might be the core of a former planet, but most believe that its origin lay outside our solar system."

Blake was brief. "Not much to report at this point on the telescope project. Andrius and I are making adjustments to the framework and experimenting with electric lift motors and drive motors. We are also drawing up designs for the cab and the telescope mounting assembly."

Woody followed with his report on the telescope runs. "The leadership team—Jordy, Red, and myself—have decided that Andy and Tony will compose the Russian team while Andrius and Blake will compose the Louisiana team. Departure dates are still up in the air as both missions are still in the information gathering stage." He halted. Ariele was fuming and Sam was nudging her. With a grin, he gave the floor to them. "Do you ladies have something you would like to add?"

Ariele piped up, "We do as a matter of fact! We have been talking this over. We think it's a waste of resources to send Blake and Andrius on the Louisiana mission. The guys should stay here and continue their work on the telescope project. Let Sam, Kit, and I go find this Lobo dude and track down the elusive Mr. Snedeker in his secret swamp hideout."

Woody tried to interrupt, "But—"

Ariele cut him off. "There is no but. Sam has more experience in this kind of adventure than Blake and Andrius put together. And Kit and I can take care of ourselves. It's not like we're the delicate and dainty type. Besides, if Andrius and Blake got seriously injured, killed, or arrested the telescope project would come to a grinding halt. But if we ran into serious problems, the project would merely be delayed." When she finished her tirade, she swiveled her head slowly and made eye contact with all of the guys at the table. Jordy's boys were grinning. Woody was smiling in apparent agreement. Red and Jordy exchanged looks with each other, then with Woody. Joby's deep-blue eyes were fixed on her in obvious admiration. Blake and Andrius both looked slightly embarrassed.

After a moment, Jordy spoke up. "Blake, do either you or Andrius have any problems with Ariele's suggested course?"

"Nope," Blake replied. "While it would be fun to take a break and go on an adventure, I agree that the girls could handle the task as well as we could. Maybe better. On top of that, freeing us up would expedite the telescope project."

"How about you, men?" Jordy added, looking to Red and Woody. "What do you think?"

"Woody knows the gals far better than I do," Red responded. "So, if he's in favor, then I'll trust his judgment."

Woody didn't hesitate. "I'm in favor. I wasn't going to ask them to do the mission, but if they want to volunteer, I'll back them."

Jordy turned to Ariele. "Well, that settles it. Plans are changed. You three ladies are now the Louisiana team." For a moment, the girls sat in amazed shock, then they exploded into a whirlwind of hugs with each other and fist bumps with several of the guys.

But Woody noticed something during the celebration that made him ill at ease. Irina was going through the motions of offering the girls her congratulations, but her response was restrained. He didn't know her that well, but something was eating her. That wasn't good. He knew only too well from his Special Forces days that you can't have team members down. When he caught her eye, she looked away.

Jordy waited for a moment for the din to quiet down, then he turned the meeting over to Red for a progress report on Beth and Jordy's home.

Mr. Reddington stood up. "Joby is helping on the construction crew, which speeds the project. The second-floor deck is finished, and we're busy erecting the second-floor post-and-beam framework. Our goal is to finish the roof and cover the framework with wrap before hunting season starts. Then we can work at our leisure this winter: filling the openings between the posts, framing interior walls, and installing windows, doors, wiring, and plumbing."

Jordy moved on to the subject of Burrage Krakenhavn's recent silence. "It's been two weeks since we received an internet message with a video link from *Down the Rabbit Hole*. Normally, there are new posts every Wednesday and Saturday. I learned from Irina that Burrage had been operating out of Camp 286 via a clandestine Wi-Fi link, which he used to convey his posts via secure email to an associate, who then posted them on the internet. While it could be a coincidence that his silence began at the same time as Irina's escape, she and I fear that he was discovered in the aftermath of her departure.

LEE W. BRAINARD

"I don't need to tell you that Burrage's disappearance is a huge loss for prophecy students and those interested in the Rogue. He was a brilliant teacher and a clearinghouse for information. But most of what he had to say never saw the light of day. He lamented in one of his last posts that only a fraction of his research had been published. Now it appears to be lost forever. And while the Rogue Underground bulletin board and chat room will continue, they will not be the same without him at the helm."

After the meeting, Irina pulled Jordy aside. "I need to talk to you in private. Woody and Red, too."

"About what?"

"Krake and his ministry. It may not be over."

He turned and motioned to the other two. They broke off their conversations and hustled over. Red brought them up to speed. "Irina thinks that Krake's ministry may not be over." The three looked at her with a bit of skepticism.

"His participation in his ministry is certainly over," she replied. "But the ministry itself isn't over, or at least it doesn't need to be. His Buster account was my Buster account. I helped him transform it for his prophecy ministry and disseminating information on the Rogue. Unless he changed the username and password, I can still access the account. That means his research is available for someone else to capitalize on."

Jordy eyed Irina, then the other guys.

Red nodded his head toward the basement stairwell next to the kitchen. "Let's go. This is too important to not look into it ASAP."

The group hustled down to the comm room in the basement. Red pointed Irina to his main terminal. Irina took a seat, opened Tor, and navigated to Buster. The three looked over her shoulder in restless anticipation as she entered Pandemonium Press to access the faux business login page for the Rogue Underground website. Her heart raced as she entered Krake's username, Krake2024RVM, and password, Ezekiel3839RoshMagog. She drew a deep breath and hit ENTER. The goofy cartoon of six frustrated hackers, one with smoke coming out of his ears, swirled like a lazy kaleidoscope. She was in!

Two sticky notes greeted them on the home page.

> Dear Irina:
> My days at the helm of this ministry have come to a close. Please ensure that this labor of love gets into the hands of someone you trust who is both wise and deep. The note to my successor includes a link to a document that will tell them everything they need to know to be able to take this ministry forward without exposing themselves to undue risk.
> In the Messiah,
> Burrage Krakenhavn.

> To whoever takes over this ministry:
> Please carry on my efforts to open the prophecies of the Bible to the followers of the Messiah and keep the world apprised of the fast-approaching Rogue.

The link below will provide you with directions on how to use my notes, tools, and resources and how to implement proper security measures. You will find, for example, instructions on how to use my untraceable VPNs on a server in Russia on the deep net—a combination virtually impossible to trace, even for the NSA. DownTheRabbitHole.odt

In the Messiah,

Burrage Krakenhavn.

Red turned to Jordy. "Looks to me like God is putting this ministry in your lap. What do you think?"

The preacher shrugged his shoulders. "I don't know. It seems way bigger than me."

"It is way bigger than you," Red granted. "But it isn't bigger than the God you serve." He watched Jordy for a minute, trying to read his reaction, then persisted in his point. "Listen, brother. It's absolutely vital that this work keeps on going. If it doesn't, it will be a huge loss for those who follow the *Down the Rabbit Hole* program for Krake's insight on Bible prophecy and geopolitical events."

Irina added, "It would also be a blow to the Rogue Underground. Just a week before my flight, Krake told me that this Buster account is one of the few remaining repositories for Rogue intel that the FBI has not cracked. The federal government has an army of agents and sub-contractors taking down websites and videos that mention the Rogue or any other heaven-sent apocalyptic scenario. Every week, Krake placed information and links on the

Rogue Runner bulletin board so that members of the Underground could replace stuff that had been removed by the government.

"If we don't continue his efforts, then his collection of Rogue data and videos is lost and unavailable to the Rogue community. We need to be there for them. Their resource options are dwindling. The FBI has stepped hard on Anonymous and similar groups, and they are running scared."

"I concur with Irina entirely," Red said as he placed his hand on Jordy's shoulder. "And you are the right man for the job—studious and fearless."

"Amen to that," Woody agreed.

"Okay guys," Jordy relented. "I submit. But only on a temporary trial basis. Let's see how it goes before we go making any permanent commitments."

"If you'll excuse me, gentlemen," Irina said as she stood up and handed Red a slip of paper with the login credentials, "I'll let you guys make your *Down the Rabbit Hole* plans. I have other business I need to attend to." Then she hustled out of the room.

Ariele, who was standing by the crackling fire talking to Joby, noticed Irina scurry across the far side of the great room, grab her jacket, and slip out the door. That puzzled her. The perky brunette loved to socialize. She excused herself and poked her head out the door. Irina was trudging down the road toward the barn with her head hanging low. She grabbed her coat and bolted out the door after her friend.

The two of them sat on the corral fence near the barn,

gazing at the starry skies over the pasture and reminiscing about their days at Caltech—before the Rogue, the Minoa cover-up, and their flights from the feds. After chattering for fifteen minutes, Ariele jabbed Irina in the ribs. "Speak up girl. I know you didn't come out here just to stare at the heavens and relive the past. Something has you down."

Irina looked at the ground, exhaled, then looked back at her friend. "It's just that … well … you, Sam, and Kit get to go on the Louisiana mission. How come I don't get to go on the Russia mission? Am I lacking something?"

Ariele placed her hand on her friend's shoulder. "Irina. You did notice that I fought for our inclusion, right?"

"Yeah. But that's your personality. You're on the aggressive side for a woman."

"This isn't about being aggressive. This is about being assertive and standing up for what is right. There is a big difference."

"But I'm not assertive."

"Being assertive is not a matter of your DNA. It's a matter of purpose and determination—choosing worthy goals and determining to pay whatever price is necessary to reach those goals."

Irina said nothing.

"I know you can be assertive. You defended your dissertation on rocky comets even though you knew full well that you would face objections."

"I was miserable the whole time. I died a thousand deaths between the preparation and the delivery of my dissertation."

"But you did survive, right? And you got what you aimed at, right?"

"Yeah," Irina admitted.

"Listen, girl. Standing up for what you believe is hard. It's costly. But anything worth having or doing comes with a cost. And that cost often requires men to step out of their comfort zone."

"But sometimes I feel like I am trampling on propriety."

"So what? Whose sense of propriety are you talking about? God's or man's? Cultural and social propriety are relative. God's estimate of what is right is absolute. If there is any conflict between the pursuit of something right and man's sense of propriety, the fault is with man. In such cases, we can safely jettison cultural and social propriety to the degree that it stands in the way of right."

Irina smiled feebly, biting her lip. She knew Ariele was right. "That makes sense." She sat in silence for a moment. "I'm also having doubts about whether or not it is God's will for me to go."

Ariele put her arm around her. "I'm no expert in religion, but it's hard to imagine that it wouldn't be God's will to aid a good cause when you would be an asset and you have no conflicting commitments to another worthy cause."

"Do you really think I would be a help?"

"No doubt in my mind, girl. You're super smart, you speak Russian like a native, and there is far more toughness to you than meets the eye. You remind me of one of those female spies in the action movies that are as lethal as they are hot."

Irina blushed. "So, what do you think I should do?"

"Go talk to Andy and Tony. If you win them over, you're

golden. They'll convince Woody and Jordy that you should be included on the team. Listen. I know Woody really well. He will go to bat for you if the boys do."

Irina threw her arms around Ariele. "Thank you," she whispered.

After a few moments, Ariele pulled back, screwed up her mouth the way she did when in deep thought or indecision, and looked Irina in the eyes. "You're not the only one who needs advice. I'm really starting to like Joby, and not merely because of his sparkly blue eyes or the fact that he'll be one-hundred-percent California babe once his hair grows back. It's something deeper. I'm attracted to his passion—his passion for his Jewish heritage, his passion for living by truth and principle, and his passion for a simple back-to-the-land lifestyle."

"So what's the question?"

"I don't know how to go forward. I've dated for fun, but I've never been seriously interested in a man or regarded any of my guy friends as marriage material. On top of that, his brand of Jewishness is new territory for me. He's really devoted to God and follows Yeshua as the Mashiach. I was raised practically irreligious. My family casually observed Passover, Hannukah, and Bar and Bath Mitzvah. And we occasionally went to a synagogue—but only liberal ones. Attendance was more about dad making business connections than responding to any felt religious needs."

Irina teased her. "Sometimes you have to step out of your comfort zone and be aggressive if you want something."

Ariele grimaced sheepishly. "I think I've heard that

advice before, somewhere." She blew her bangs off her face. "So, what should I do?"

"Ask him if you can study the Bible with him. That's more subtle and more effective than just telling him that you're interested in him. If men are attracted to you, they really get revved when you ask them for help or show an interest in things that they're interested in."

Ariele nodded approvingly and smiled. Irina rubbed her back tenderly, then excused herself and headed for the barn loft. As she walked down the main concourse in the barn she talked herself up. *I can do this. I faced adversity when I defended my dissertation. I stood my ground with Dr. Goldblum on the Rogue. I resisted the cover-up of the Rogue and sent Ariele my warning and research. I endured the FBI grillings and 286. The Russia mission can't throw anything at me that I can't handle.*

Jordy's boys were playing pinball in the Hallelujah Tavern. She leaned against the adjacent machine, crossed her arms, and watched the game. Andy, uncomfortable with her silent presence, caught the careening ball with his left flipper and looked over at her.

"We need to talk."

He nodded, then took aim at the right ramp. The ball skittered up the narrow alley in a deluge of lights and dings. "Okay. We can talk as soon as I finish this game."

"I think my need is a bit more pressing than a pinball game," she said bluntly.

The boys looked at each other startled, then looked back at her. Andy grinned and let his ball drain. "We're all ears," he replied. She pulled up a chair at a nearby table and the boys followed suit.

"I want to be part of the Russia team. I want to help procure the mirror and sensors and bring them back."

The boys stared at her, uncertain how to answer without hurting her feelings.

"This isn't a complicated question," she insisted. "It's not integral calculus. It's a simple *yes* or *no* question."

Andy replied, "It isn't that simple—"

"It is simple!" Irina exclaimed, raising her voice, jealousy getting the best of her. "Why can't I go? The other gals get to go on the Louisiana mission."

"The Russia mission is far more dangerous than the Louisiana mission," he explained. "You wouldn't merely be risking a return to a FEMA camp. You would be dealing with the mafia and trying to avoid the FSB and GRU. You could get severely beaten or shot. And if you don't die, you could end up in one of the Siberian labor camps. They make FEMA camps look like summer camp."

"I know the hazards. I wasn't born yesterday. My grandfather had several costly run-ins with the Federal Security Service and the Main Intelligence Directorate. And I am willing to run the risk."

"Irina," Tony interjected. "We didn't ignore you or overlook you. We actually talked this over with Woody, Red, and Jordy. There was a concern that you might be a hindrance to the mission."

"A hindrance? I would be an asset. I speak Russian fluently. I know the culture and the slang. I think like a Russian."

"In those areas, yes, you would definitely be an asset. But the concern wasn't about mental shortcomings. It was that you wouldn't be tough enough—physically and emotionally. You don't project toughness. And projecting toughness is critical for this mission. We will be dealing with the Russian mafia, and we could potentially have run-ins with the FSB or the GRU."

"Then I'll do whatever I must to gain and project toughness! I'm not taking *no* for an answer! This isn't beyond my reach. I risked my career over my dissertation. I forsook my career over the Rogue. I endured hours of grilling by the FBI interspersed with sleep deprivation and cold showers. I won't be intimidated by Russian agents, whether civilian or military."

The boys looked at each other and back at her, uncertain what to say or do. Andy eased the tension. "Tell you what. We'll give you a shot at making the team. But you are going to have to train hard. Harder than you ever trained for ballet. We will only go to bat for you if you satisfy us that you are fit for the mission."

"What kind of training?"

"Physical and conversational. You'll spend six hours every day on strength training and martial arts—Krav Maga and Systema Spetsnaz. And you'll spend four hours every day mastering the terminology and slang of the Spetsnaz, the intelligence community, and the Bratva."

"Ten hours is a lot of training."

"We have a lot of ground to make in a short window of time. When we make contact with the underworld, you will need to project the confidence and toughness of a female with

405

experience in the FSB and the Bratva. And if you get challenged somewhere along the line, you need to respond with fearless calm, like a woman with three aces up her sleeve."

"When do we start?"

"Tomorrow morning at 5:00."

"See you then, boys," she replied saucily, tossing her hair, and headed for the exit. But by the time she reached the road, fear and doubts were haunting her. *Lord, help me to face my fears … not be stopped by them.*

The next morning Irina sweated and groaned through two grueling hours of PT: sit-ups, pushups, burpees, flutter kicks, pullups, squats, and a dozen other body-abusing exercises. Every muscle in her body ached long before they were done. After a light breakfast, she endured four hours of introductory Krav Maga training, covering the theory and the basic blocks and punches. After lunch, Tony gave her a stack of books, two sets of DVDs, and a dark website that offered language training materials that had been pilfered from the CIA. She spent the afternoon studying military, intelligence, and Bratva slang. When her head hit her pillow that night, her body and brain weary, she thanked God for the opportunity and prayed that he would grant her the strength not only to endure but shine.

***

That night Jordy logged in to the Rogue Underground and made his first post. He gave a brief notice on the feared demise of Burrage Krakenhavn, then he posted Krake's testimonial letter that he had left on the Buster site.

Greetings Undergrounders, seekers, and believers:

Until recently I was a typical American, too busy chasing my dreams to give God or the Bible the time that I knew in my heart they deserved. I wanted, however, to keep them within arm's reach in case I needed them, so I went to church occasionally. But my life changed drastically when everything I had worked for was stripped out of my hands irrecoverably. In early November 2018, after I published a story on the comet known as the Rogue, I was detained by the FBI and Homeland Security without formal charges or trial. After two weeks of questioning at the Oklahoma City Field Office and the Dallas Field Office by the Joint Terrorism Task Force, I was charged with being a terrorist who was working with Russian agents to undermine the United States of America. The following week I was transported to FEMA 286.

While there, discouraged and broken, I began attending the chapel services led by Jeremy Hendricks, a former Army chaplain who had become a serious Bible student while working for the CIA. During the time that I sat under his ministry, I heard five things that changed my life.

One, there is an Intelligent Designer who created the insanely complex, almost magical universe that we live in.

Two, man is the first fruits of God's creation,

and it is God's intention to bless him with eternal life in an eternal, infinite utopia.

Three, man has gone his own way and substituted things like evolution and man-made religion for the eternal, infinite Creator. This has resulted in man being under judgment instead of blessing.

Four, God has provided man with a way to escape judgment, namely faith in Jesus, the eternal Son of God who died for the sin of the world.

Five, God has appointed a time of judgment at the end of this age, a time that is fast approaching, as evidenced by the signs that he has given us in the Bible.

Bearing these things in mind, it behooves man to be a serious follower of the Bible of the Messiah and the Messiah of the Bible. Give up going your own way. Turn to him in repentance and faith, and live for him. He will make it worth your while.

Do right though the stars fall,
Burrage Krakenhavn

49

Late in the evening, Sally walked into the east half of the
north warehouse, intending to use the treadmill. Noticing
movement out of the corner of her eye, she looked up and
observed someone that looked like Jack bounding up the
stairs near the center of the east wall, carrying a tool bag.
When he reached the second-floor landing, he turned left,
briskly walked to the farthest room, and shut the door
behind him. *What is the former SEAL stud up to? We don't use
those old offices for anything.* Determined to find out, she
crept up the stairs silently and snuck down the catwalk.
Gingerly, she turned the doorknob and cracked the door
open, cringing when it creaked. *Rats! No element of surprise
now.*

With a burst of adrenalin, she flung the door open and
charged into the room. It was empty. A pair of binoculars
and a yellow legal pad sat on a desk next to the window. A
chair was turned toward the window but pushed back from
the table.

A strong hand clamped around her mouth so she couldn't scream, and another gripped her arm like a vise. Her whole body tensed in terror.

Jack whispered into the ear of the trembling female. "Relax, Sally. It's just me." He removed his hand from her mouth and relaxed his grip on her arm. "What are you doing sneaking up on me like that?"

"I wasn't sneaking up on you," she snapped as she wheeled around.

"Oh yes, you were," he replied gently. "I could hear you trying to be quiet. That kind of stuff makes me nervous."

Her anger subsided into a chuckle. "You're right. I was sneaking up on you. Curiosity got the best of me. There was a little prankster in the mix too. I thought about saying *boo!* But the real question is, what are *you* doing? Lights off. Curtains barely cracked. Binoculars. Notebook. Looks like a spy operation to me."

"It is a spy operation. I'm scoping out the surrounding area and gathering critical information."

"Where did you get the binoculars?"

"The day that Irina escaped, the Katahdin driver told Frenchie to keep his eyes peeled for a marked pail of pancake mix that was intended for me. Frenchie located the pail and made sure that it got into my hands. Inside the pail, I found a jail-break package from my friends at the Compound. It included many useful items including this pair of military-grade binoculars—Steiner no less."

"You didn't tell me about the package!"

"I didn't dare say a word until the uproar over Irina's

escape blew over. I might be able to bite my tongue under extreme duress, but I wasn't sure if you could."

Sally felt a little disrespected but ignored the slight. "So, you're planning on escaping?"

"No real plans yet. Just gathering information."

"Jack without a plan. Bit of an oxymoron, ya think?"

He smiled sheepishly. "Guess I do have a plan in the works, but it's far from complete."

"So what kind of information are you gathering?"

"When Jiffy LTL Delivery is open, and when it is closed."

"What have you found?" she asked, looking at him expectantly.

"Jiffy is closed on Sundays. Nobody is ever there. And the latest I have seen one of their trucks return to the yard on Saturday evening is 6:42. If anyone is going to exploit Jiffy as part of their escape plan, then Saturday night is the best time to escape. They could steal a truck, hotwire it, make their getaway, and have at least twenty-eight hours—from Saturday night to Monday morning—before the company would discover that one of their trucks was missing."

"But where would you drive to?"

"Not just me. We. You are coming along. As for where, the folks at the Compound included a note in the jail-break package with the location of a hideout and a phone number to call for an extraction. If we break out, all we have to do is drive to the hideout, call the number, and make arrangements for a pick-up."

"Sounds like you have a plan for outside the fence. Now

we just need to find a way to get on the other side of the fence."

"Actually, I'm still working on two vital details of the outside part. I need to figure out how to avoid the security cameras at Jiffy while I'm trying to get on the roof to disable them. And I need to finish tracking which trucks go out on routes every day and which trucks are operable spares. There is at least one working spare truck in the yard—truck 21. On two different occasions, I have observed it going out on route when one of the regular trucks stayed in the yard."

Sally gave Jack a confused look. "Why does it matter which trucks are regulars and which ones are spares?"

He grinned. "Taking a spare buys us time. If we took a regular truck, the driver would notice right away Monday morning that his truck was missing. But if we took a spare, we might gain a couple extra hours before someone noticed that it was gone. Furthermore, we need to know which vehicles are working spares and which aren't. I don't want to waste precious time trying to hotwire an inoperable truck, thinking that it was a working spare."

Sally smiled back and nodded. "Gotcha. Is this why you've missed breakfast and dinner a few times in the past few weeks?"

"Yeah. I've spent a lot of time watching the yard to observe when the trucks leave, and when they return."

"What were you doing up here tonight?"

"Mostly trying to get a feel for what Jiffy looks like at night. But I can't see much from here. The glare from the lights is a bit of a problem."

"Maybe we should go down to your cage, make some popcorn, and do a little brainstorming?"

Jack agreed. "Sounds like a plan." He grabbed his binoculars, pad, and tool bag, and they headed for the maintenance area.

As she took a seat in his battered office chair, Sally smiled—a deeply contented smile. His cage was her happy place in 286. She enjoyed the peace and quiet. People rarely visited the west warehouse after work hours. For the most part, they lounged in the television rooms, played games in the cafeteria, attended meetings or Bible studies at the chapel in the east warehouse, or went to the north warehouse to use the laundry, the showers, and the gym. She enjoyed the ambience of Jack's man cave. It reminded her of Jupiter Jones' hideout in the *Three Investigators* books she had read as a child—stuffed with gadgets, tools, parts, and books. But amidst the chaos, there was order. His workbench, though busy, was organized. The crates, bins, and shelves of parts were meticulously sorted. The books on the two shelves were arranged by subject. She wished some of his knack for bringing order to disorderly situations would rub off on her.

She rose and walked over to the Canteen—the large crate to the left of Jack's desk which served as his kitchenette—and started a batch of popcorn in the popper. Then she set a tea kettle on his hot plate and dug out two cups and the powdered apple cider mix.

While she waited for the water to boil, Jack got up from his seat, a small crate with a cushion, walked over to his workbench area in the back corner, and rummaged in his cabinets. He returned with an OD green pouch which he held out for her to see. "This is the prison-break package which Woody and the gang sent me." He unzipped the bag and showed her the contents.

She pawed through it, impressed. "I have a stash of prison-break stuff myself," she offered. Started gathering things a few months back. Wanted to be prepared in case I was part of an escape attempt."

"What have you gathered so far?"

"Shirts and pants, a sweater, a jacket, insulated coveralls, stocking hat, gloves, socks, boots, garbage bags to keep stuff dry, Clif bars, protein bars, three tins of Spam, bottled water, a knife, a flashlight with spare batteries, and a small daypack. I keep the stuff hidden in several places in the west side of the north warehouse."

"Good for you. How much of your clothing items are cotton?"

"None. Woody taught me all about the advantages of wool and synthetics."

"Good. We have a decent start on equipment and a nearly finished plan for outside the camp. Too bad I don't have a feasible plan for sneaking out of here. The odds of escaping through the gate are about zero since Homeland Security upgraded the gate with cameras—thermal imaging and optical—that view the underside and the topside of vehicles. And trying to escape over the fence is a no-go. While climbing the fence is possibly doable for myself and might actually work under the right conditions, like a howling blizzard with fifty-foot visibility, I don't think you could make it, Sally.

"Another issue we're facing is time constraint. Brunette Joyce heard Bob cussing up a storm a few days ago because Homeland Security wasn't scheduling perimeter and interior camera upgrades until after January first, the beginning of the new fiscal quarter. This means we have three months to plan and execute our escape. Once those extra cameras are installed, the odds of us escaping will drop significantly."

He mulled the situation silently for a minute, stroking his chin. "What we really need is a tunnel or a sewer drain, like the Allied POWs used in the movie *Victory*."

Sally was jolted by the idea. "I don't know if this is a possibility or not, but I found a manhole while I was working yesterday in the western portion of the north warehouse. I was using a pallet jack to move crates of boiler parts and pipe, trying to clear out a room that I want to turn into a studio for refurbishing furniture. Anyway, under one of the piles of crates, I discovered the manhole." She looked at him hopefully. "What do you think?"

"It's definitely worth investigating. Did you remove the cover and take a look?"

"No. I didn't even try. It looked way too heavy to move."

"They're definitely heavy. Depending on the size and thickness, they can weigh between 100 and 200 pounds. Does anyone else know about the manhole?"

"No. I haven't told anyone but you."

"Good. Let's keep it that way." He sat in silence for a moment, calculating the next move. "This sounds promising, especially since there are no cameras in that part of the warehouse. I want to take a look for myself tonight.

But we need a cover so it'll look like we have a legitimate purpose to go back there. Let's grab one of the utility carts, pile a few chairs on it, add some paint, brushes, and tools, and make it look like we're taking stuff back there for your studio. That should fool anyone who might see us on the video cams or pass us in the hallway. When we return, we'll be pushing an empty cart."

Fifteen minutes later, Jack removed the crate that was covering the manhole and knelt beside the massive slab of iron. "It's twenty-six inches in diameter and over an inch thick—pushing a hundred and fifty pounds. I suspect that they used a heavy-duty cover here because of fork-lift traffic with heavy loads."

"Do you think this manhole might be a way out?"

"There's no way to tell until I get the cover off and take a look. And there's no way to remove it without a manhole hook, which I'll have to fabricate. In the meantime, we need to keep the manhole hidden so no one accidentally finds it."

"Can't we just put this crate back on top of it?"

"That's fine for tonight. But what we need to do is camouflage the manhole with your studio. Here's my idea. We'll sort the crates, stack those with lids to our left, and move those without lids to the next room. Then we'll use those with lids to make a U-shaped counter that surrounds your studio area on three sides. The right side will run along the east wall, the end will run along the north wall, and the left side will end with a crate that sits directly over the manhole. Not only will this give you lots of workspace and storage, it will hide the manhole in plain sight."

"I love it! What a wonderful idea. Too bad," she laughed, "that I might only get to enjoy it for a few months."

He laughed. "Yeah. That's a lot of work for something that's little more than a stage prop."

While Jack moved and sorted crates, they continued talking about the manhole and her studio. Sally pointed out a weak spot in their plan. "We don't want the cameras to see you coming back here night after night, especially staying two or three hours at a time. Somebody might get suspicious if they happen to notice and come take a look."

"You're right. Do you have any ideas?"

"I think so. If you climbed inside a cabinet cart in maintenance where there are no cameras, and there was a project or two on top of the cart, then I could wheel the cart back here, and no one would suspect that anything was out of place. I would work on my projects while you finish setting up the room. I was thinking we could come back here two or three nights a week, say from 7 to 9:30. We would quit early enough that we wouldn't risk breaking the curfew."

"That ought to do the trick."

Sally continued, "I was also thinking that maybe, after you finished the U-shaped workspace, you could stack a wall of pallets on the outside edge of the left side. That would make the studio feel a little cozier, and it would give you a little privacy if you needed to wash up and change into dry clothes after you emerge from the sewer."

"That's a fantastic idea."

"How long do you think it will take to set this up?"

"I'm going to guess two weeks if I work three evenings a

week. That's okay, though. It won't hurt to let things cool down a little more here before we get too serious about our own escape efforts. We also need to round up sewer clothes and supplies for me. I'll need two pairs of knee pads, several pairs of heavy-duty rubber gloves, a hard hat, a headlamp with low light and red light capabilities, and warm clothes that can take a bit of abuse. I'll also need dry clothes, like sweatpants and a sweatshirt, to change into when I come out soaking wet. And I'll need clean clothes to change into after I take a long hot shower to drive the chill out of my bones and wash the stink off. The clothes that I wear in the sewer and the sweat suit I change into when I come out will have to be washed—with hot water, double soap, heavy-duty setting, and an extra rinse cycle. Maybe we can start the load at night, then toss them in the dryer first thing in the morning. I will also need a lot of lotion. Wearing rubber gloves for extended periods of time is going to play havoc with my hands."

"How long do you estimate it will be before we get out of here?"

"I won't be able to make an estimate until I make a survey trip in the sewer. But even if things go well in the sewer— let's say I find a serviceable exit and prep it—we can't rush our escape date. We need to wait for the first good blizzard after our exit route is ready, even if we have to wait until January. We need snow to cover our footprints and tire tracks, both locally and at the hideout."

Sally sighed. "So close, and yet so far."

50

After dinner, Jack and Sally walked two miles of warehouse laps, then lounged in his cage, drinking coffee from a battered percolator, eating outdated fig bars, and watching CVN's *World Report* on a large screen monitor that was perched on a wooden crate.

Geoff Seaworthy turned to Middle East affairs in his newscast. "Today, Ankara took two further steps away from NATO. She signed a mutual defense pact with Russia and Iran, and she joined the Shanghai Cooperation Organization. The former was accompanied by an agreement that permits Russia to build an expansion at Mersin capable of berthing next-generation Russian carriers.

"This comes on the heels of the geopolitical earthquake two weeks ago when Turkey announced her departure from NATO and gave the US and NATO one month to pack up and leave—a decision which caught the White House and Brussels by surprise. They had regarded their differences with Turkey as bumps in the road, but Ankara had viewed them as insurmountable hurdles. Since then, the Pentagon and NATO have been scrambling to get their aircraft and equipment—primarily housed at Incirlik Air Base—out of the country before the deadline.

"The new alliance between Turkey and Iran signals a dramatic shift in the balance of power in the Middle East. For decades there has been tension between the Shia and the Sunni, particularly between the Russian-backed Iranians and the American-backed Saudis and Turks. But the traditional strife has given way to a more nuanced struggle between anti-Saudi nations like Turkey and Iran and pro-Saudi nations that are backed by America. The anti-Saudi camp is demanding that Saudi Arabia and its Wahhabi-led government cede control of Mecca. They regard Wahhabism as a false form of Islam that is guilty of defiling Mecca, and they count it an abomination for the Saudis to be under the patronage of America, the Great Satan."

Jack turned the volume down and remarked, "It's both exciting and nerve-wracking to see these changes take place. Pastor Jordy has been telling me for years that we could expect to see Turkey break from the West and side with Iran and Russia in the last days."

"Seriously? How could he know that?" Sally asked.

"From a well-known prophecy in the Bible, in the thirty-eighth and thirty-ninth chapters of Ezekiel, that foretells the rise of Russia in the last days as a superpower, her attempt to invade Israel with a massive gathering of allies including Turkey and Iran, and the destruction of the invasion coalition by fire that falls from heaven."

"You've talked about that prophecy a few times before. Does it actually mention Russia, Turkey, and Iran?"

"Yes. It specifically mentions Iran by its ancient name Persia. And Russia is represented by the four Scythian nations mentioned: Rosh, Magog, Meshech, and Tubal. The Scythian homeland stretched from the Black Sea northwestward to the Baltic Sea and eastward deep into Siberia—so deep, in fact, that one of the names which the Great Wall of China bore in ancient times was the Wall of Magog. Over the centuries these nations, with an influx of Scandinavian bloodlines, mingled together to become the Russian people. Both the people and the nation derive their name from the tribe of Rosh. The tribe of Meshech is commemorated in the name of Moscow, anciently called Muscovy and Moscovia. And the cities of Tobolsk in Russia and Tbilisi in Georgia preserve the memory of the tribe of Tubal.

"Similarly, Turkey is represented by the mention of Togarmah, Gomer, Magog, Meshech, and Tubal. These were among the many Scythian and Northern European nations that migrated into the region of modern Turkey. Each of them founded colonies and had regions named after them. Over the centuries Middle Eastern and Arabian peoples were also added to the melting pot.

"Modern Turkey is traced to the Turks, descendants of Togarmah who invaded from the steppes in waves starting in the eleventh century AD, forcing their customs and language upon the land and forging the Ottoman Empire, which dominated the Black Sea, the Balkans, and much of the Middle East for centuries. Following its defeat in World

War I, the empire collapsed, and out of its ashes, the modern nation of Turkey arose. Both the people and the nation derive their name from the root of Togarmah, spelled both T-G-R and T-R-G in the Indo-European languages, some replacing the G with a K. Thus we find such varied forms as Torgom, Thorgama, Togarmah, Tegarama, and Takaram."

Sally was wide-eyed. "That's pretty amazing. A lot of research there."

"Yeah. Jordy is a serious prophecy student."

"I'm surprised that you can just rattle that stuff off."

"There is no fuel like fascination."

Sally stared wide-eyed for a moment, then blurted out. "Can we really trust Bible prophecy? What if the similarities between current events and this passage in Ezekiel are just a lucky coincidence?"

"The Bible's track record for already fulfilled prophecies gives me complete confidence in its prophecies concerning the last days."

"Track record?"

"The Old Testament books, for example, made over one hundred prophecies about the Messiah that were fulfilled in Jesus' birth, life, and death. Some of them had been written over a thousand years prior. No other religious book on Earth offers anything that even remotely compares to this kind of prediction and fulfillment."

"A lot of people think Nostradamus was pretty savvy."

"Yeah, but people are gullible. The problem with Nostradamus is that his prophecies are so generic that it is almost impossible to deny or prove their fulfillment." Jack launched into a hokey crystal-ball voice. "There will be an earthquake in the Middle East in the next few decades. It will hit 7.0 or higher on the Richter scale. Buildings will collapse. Homes will be destroyed. Many hapless souls will be injured or killed."

Sally laughed. "I see what you mean. But how do we know that a prophecy has been fulfilled? Aren't all prophecies kind of mysterious or mystical?"

"Prophecy is only mysterious in the movies, thriller fiction, and religious unbelief which scorns taking prophecy literally. In the Bible, prophecies are straightforward predictions of definite things that affect definite parties in a definite location at a definite time in the definite future."

"So why is there so much confusion?"

"Ignorance and prejudice. Religious ignorance prevails in many circles because men are taught that prophecy isn't important, so they don't study it. Religious prejudice dominates in many other circles, misleading men with spiritualized interpretations of the prophecies that rob them of their real meaning. The worst of this confusion would evaporate in short order if men would recognize two things: prophecy composes nearly one-third of the Bible, and prophecy is just history foretold."

Sally mused, "A God who communicates definite things to man is a bold concept. That puts the Bible in much different light than the agnosticism I was raised with." She was silent for a few seconds. "So what do you think is most likely to happen as a result of these new alignments in the Middle East?"

"Jordy thinks that the tension between the Saudis and the Turkey-Iran coalition probably won't lead to war between themselves, but will suck the Saudis into the vortex of the campaign against Israel."

"How would that work out?"

"Iran has long been waging a propaganda war that portrays themselves as the leaders in the struggle against Israel and portrays Saudi Arabia as a hypocritical nation that sleeps with America and secretly supports Israel. This has damaged the Saudis in the eyes of the Muslim world. Turkey is now piping a similar tune. Saudi Arabia will be shamed into taking a risky step to maintain its prestige and leadership in the Muslim world. She will join Syria at the helm of the attack against Israel by her neighbors that we read about in Psalm 83—a war which the invaders will lose."

"How do we know that that war wasn't fulfilled in one of Israel's earlier wars with her neighbors?"

"It can't be the Six Day War or the Yom Kippur War. First of all, Saudi Arabia's involvement in them was negligible and Lebanon's almost nonexistent. Secondly, in the Psalm 83 War, the instigators are obliterated—never to bother Israel again. According to Jordy, there are only two options for the Psalm 83 War. Either it precedes the Gog and Magog invasion in Ezekiel 38-39, or it occurs at the same time. He used to lean toward the former. Now he leans toward the latter. Two coalitions with different motives cooperating in one massive invasion."

Jack continued for a half hour, talking about Israel, the seven years of tribulation at the end of the age, and the return of the Messiah to set up his kingdom. Sally listened intently. She was impressed by the knowledge that flowed from the tongue of her crazy-smart friend. But she found the Messiah even more impressive. The man returning to rule over the entire planet from David's throne in Jerusalem was a humble Jewish carpenter who had died for mankind. And his reign would provide man with all the deepest desires of his heart: peace, prosperity, justice, and unending life.

***

That night Sally lay awake in bed, pondering the things Jack had talked about. She wanted to believe in God and Bible prophecy. But the change seemed a little awkward. She had never been religious, hadn't been raised in the church, and had no idea where to start. On the other hand, the change had an easiness and naturalness about it. A God who makes and keeps promises sounded attractive. And the idea of a Messiah dying for the world was better than anything that any other religion or philosophy offered. She found herself wishing that she had paid closer attention when her cousin Evelyn had talked to her about Jesus during their high school and college years.

For the first time in her life, she approached God with more than a token prayer. *God. I don't know how to pray, and I don't know the first thing about you or the Bible, but I want to know you better. Help Jack and me get out of here. Bring us safe to Montana. And watch over ...* she couldn't pray his name. She halted and tears began to well in her eyes. *Please. Wherever he is, keep him safe.*

51

Sally and Jack were skittish as they headed toward her studio, she wheeling the cabinet cart, he cramped inside it. They had made the same trip six times in the previous two weeks, but today was different. Today was the day they had been waiting for, the day Jack was going to explore what lay underneath the manhole.

When she stopped in her studio and opened the cabinet doors, Jack shoved out the three bags that had been stuffed in on top of him—one with clothes and supplies for the trip, one with dry sweatpants and sweatshirt for when he came back up, and one holding clean clothes for after his shower—and then he came boiling out of the confined space himself.

He stretched for a minute, trying to get the kinks out. "Is the trail cam activated?" he asked while touching his toes.

"Yep. I'm watching the entryway into the west warehouse right now on my laptop."

"Fantastic." Jack inspected the customized manhole lifter that was sitting on top of the cart. It was his own unique design that allowed him to lift the manhole cover with a pallet jack rather than a metal hook, putting far less strain on his back and shoulders. He had taken one of the 36 X 36 crates that they were using for counters in the studio, screwed a piece of three-quarter-inch plywood to the runners on the bottom, and cut out holes for the pallet-jack wheels. Then he had routered out twenty shallow holes and inlaid them with neodymium hard-drive magnets which he glued in place with epoxy cement. Finally, he had shortened the crate three-quarters of an inch so it would be flush with the others.

This is gonna be a bear. With a grunt he manhandled his manhole lifter a few inches off the cart, swiveled around, lowered it as far as he could, then dropped it with a clatter. Grimacing from a sharp pain in his left shoulder, he retrieved the pallet jack, ran it under the crate that was covering the manhole, jacked it up, and moved it out of the way. Then he raised his invention with the pallet jack and maneuvered it over the manhole.

Looking over to Sally, Jack pursed his lips, and exhaled, a sign that he was either nervous or frustrated. "We gotta line this up right the first time. If I miss, there's no second chance. I won't be able to pry the magnets off the cover." Carefully, he pushed his contraption into place, checking to ensure he was lined up with the row of crates, then lowered the jack. When the magnets came within an inch of the cover, the crate lunged and thwunked into place. He examined his placement. "Only a quarter inch off," he announced. "Not bad at all."

He stepped over to the crate that had been over the manhole, pried its cover off, and began moving the steam fittings to his manhole-lifter crate. When finished, he transferred the lid to the new crate and hammered it down. "Time for the big test," he announced, grinning at Sally. Vigorously he pumped the handle on the pallet jack, lifting the cover a couple inches off the floor, then wheeled his manhole lifter backward about two and a half feet. "Easy as pie," he quipped, pumping his fist. "Now remember, if the motion detector ever goes off while I'm down in the hole, don't be afraid to push the crate forward and drop the lid on me. Just raise it again when the coast is clear." Sally nodded and shuddered. She hated the thought of locking Jack in the dungeon, even if it was only temporary.

The two of them peered down the hole, illuminated by a mini-mag flashlight. It was about ten feet down to the main line. They looked at each other and shrugged. Jack grabbed his bag of sewer clothes and donned a wool sweater, an ultralight jacket, knee pads, elbow-length gloves, goggles, a hard hat with an LED light, and his waist pouch with extra supplies, granola bars, and water.

Sally smiled impishly. "Good luck. Watch out for the crocodiles, dragons, and trolls."

"To be honest," he replied, "I actually am a little nervous about rats and snakes."

Sally shuddered.

"Here goes nothing," he muttered as he climbed down the ladder. Sally watched in admiration and trepidation. He reached the bottom, stood for a moment with only his arms and head showing, ducked down, tried to turn, man grumbled, and managed to get turned around. She could see his light flickering and twitching. More man grumbling followed. Then his head appeared again.

"The main appears to be a four-foot concrete line," he informed her. "The water is about six inches deep and smells awful—human waste, oil and gas, chemicals, blood and crud from the packing plant up the road. And the echo is annoying."

"Did you see anything?"

"Not much. Can't tell if I can see a hundred yards or five hundred yards down the line. The light seems to stop. Nothing but inky black beyond that."

"How long till I should expect you back?"

"Two to two and a half hours. I'm guessing that the exit is somewhere between a half mile and three-quarters of a mile away, assuming that the patch of woods northwest of here is actually where the outlet is. If I'm right, this line should eventually turn and feed into that line. No matter what, however, I'll turn back after one hour and ten minutes. We have to maintain our timetable."

"Sounds good to me. I'll have hot coffee, instant chicken soup, and a bucket of hot water with soap ready for the hero when he returns from his dungeon adventure."

Jack rolled his eyes and smiled. She liked that look. It reminded her of the man she daydreamed about. She gathered herself and refocused on Jack and the task at hand. Like the military veteran he was, Jack double-checked his pouch and equipment. Then he gave Sally a thumbs-up.

"Good luck," she replied with a thumbs-up of her own.

He ducked back down, turned around, and began his crawl into the darkness. For the first few minutes, Sally could hear the faint echo of his crawling and see the dim reflection of his light. Then there was nothing but blackness and silence.

She tried to putter in her shop while she waited for his return, but her nerves were too shot to make even a half-hearted effort at her current sanding project. She gave up, sat in a chair, cradled a cup of coffee, and let her mind wander. Would the truth about the comet be revealed to the public at large before it was too late? Likely not, but she resolved to give it her best shot. Had Irina made it safe to the compound? She suspected that she probably had since Woody had participated in the planning. Would she and Jack make it out? Would the sewer be their ticket out or a dead end? Would she ever see Ariele and Woody again? Time would tell. At least she had hope. And she could indulge the joy she felt knowing that her friends were safe.